FIELD OF VALOR

ALSO BY MATTHEW BETLEY

Overwatch

Oath of Honor

FIELD OF VALOR

A THRILLER

MATTHEW BETLEY

EMILY BESTLER BOOKS
—
ATRIA
NEW YORK LONDON TORONTO SYDNEY NEW DELHI

EMILY
BESTLER
BOOKS

ATRIA

An Imprint of Simon & Schuster, Inc.
1230 Avenue of the Americas
New York, NY 10020

First Emily Bestler Books/Atria Books hardcover edition May 2018

EMILY BESTLER BOOKS / ATRIA BOOKS and colophon are trademarks of Simon & Schuster, Inc.

For information about special discounts for bulk purchases, please contact Simon & Schuster Special Sales at 1-866-506-1949 or business@simonandschuster.com.

The Simon & Schuster Speakers Bureau can bring authors to your live event. For more information or to book an event contact the Simon & Schuster Speakers Bureau at 1-866-248-3049 or visit our website at www.simonspeakers.com.

Manufactured in the United States of America

10 9 8 7 6 5 4 3 2 1

Library of Congress Cataloging-in-Publication Data is available.

ISBN 978-1-5011-6198-8
ISBN 978-1-5011-6201-5 (ebook)

For my wife, without whom there would be no Logan West.

She keeps the family ship on course so I can wage this fictional fight. Without her, the ship sinks . . . the way Logan and John seem to sink every floating vessel they encounter.

May the ship continue to sail ever onward through calm or troubled waters.

One man's terrorist is another man's freedom fighter.
                                    —*original source unknown*

In times of war, the law falls silent.
                                    —*Marcus Tullius Cicero*

PROLOGUE

Crack-crack-crack!

The rear windshield of the Ford F-150 shattered onto the back-seat as glass was blown inward behind Logan West and John Quick.

The raspy and harmonious voice of the Stone Temple Pilot's lead singer filled the cab from the pickup's surround sound stereo system. Once Logan West—former Marine Force Recon platoon commander, recovering alcoholic, and the head of the president's Task Force Ares—had turned on the ignition, shifted gears, and floored the pickup away from the smoking headquarters building, the alternative rock band's music had provided an audio backdrop to the unfolding battle. He hadn't bothered turning it down as he'd fled the carnage, intent on only one thing—survival.

More bullets tore through the cab and punched holes in the front windshield, the *cracks* of the rounds audible inside the truck.

"Jesus Christ," Logan said, as he reached out and hit the power button on the stereo, interrupting Scott Weiland midvocal. "I always figured you for more of a country guy. STP? Seriously?"

"Hey, it depends on my mood," John Quick—Logan's second-in-command and former Force Recon platoon sergeant—said, and coughed, a sound that sounded tinny and hollow, concerning Logan. "I even like Eminem from time to time."

"Get the hell out of here," Logan replied. "Will wonders never cease?"

"You better hope not, or we might be screwed," John said, suddenly serious.

"Hey, I'm blaming you if this gets *really* bad," Logan said. "You could've at least had bulletproof glass." He slammed the accelerator to the floor as more bullets peppered the bed of the truck.

"It's my personal vehicle, not my work one," John said through gritted teeth. The pain from the gunshot was intense. "But if we survive this, I'll upgrade it just for you."

Logan glanced in the rearview mirror and pulled his Kimber Tactical II .45-caliber pistol from his outside-the-waistband holster on his hip and handed the weapon to John. He glanced down and saw blood soaking through John's shirt on the left side of his torso.

Motherfuckers, Logan thought. "How bad is it?"

"It's not good, I can tell you that," John replied, beads of sweat glistening on his forehead. "But I don't think I'm going to die in the immediate future." He laughed as more gunshots roared behind them. "But what the hell do I know? I'm not a doctor."

"Good. Then do us a favor and shoot back at these bastards," Logan said. "And if you do think you're going to leave this mortal coil, let me know first. Just try to send a few of them ahead of you."

"Sure thing, brother." John grimaced and turned in the passenger seat, resting his right arm over the backrest. The scene behind him was frightening. *Amira. Please God, let her have escaped.* They'd heard a gunfight in a different part of the building once they'd been separated, but after that—nothing.

The black Suburban rumbled down the dirt road behind them,

closing the distance to fifty yards. Beyond the Suburban, smoke billowed out of the two-story, rectangular red brick building that served as Task Force Ares headquarters.

Having been created by the president to counter the global forces that had been waging a shadow war against the republic of the United States for the past two years, Task Force Ares was now under direct attack.

John let loose with three shots, the roar of the .45-caliber pistol thunderous inside the vehicle. Spiderwebs appeared on the Suburban's bulletproof windshield, and the Secret Service agent who'd been firing at them from the passenger side ducked back into the SUV. *Probably reloading. Stick your head out again, asshole. Come on,* John thought, and lined up the sights on the Kimber with the Suburban's passenger mirror.

Moments later, the black shape of an FN P90 personal defense weapon emerged from the vehicle's window, followed by the head of the Secret Service agent wielding it. *Gotcha,* John thought, and pulled the Kimber's trigger.

Bam! Bam! Bam!

Two of the shots struck the agent in the face, shattering his black Oakley wire sunglasses and tunneling a hole into his brain, killing him instantly. The P90 fell from his fingers and on to the dirt road, cartwheeling into a resting place in the thick Quantico underbrush. The agent's head bounced off the top of the door as the Suburban hit a patch of rough road. A pair of hands pulled the dead agent back inside the vehicle.

"Nice shooting," Logan growled, glancing into the rearview window.

"I just killed a Secret Service agent. I'm pretty sure that's a crime, and this is now officially a really bad day," John said sarcastically, keeping the Kimber trained on the pursuing Suburban.

"Fuck him," Logan snarled, the anger threatening to take control of him. "In fact, fuck all of them. Before this is over, they're all going to die, and then I'm going to personally kill their *puppet master* myself."

"I'm pretty sure that's high treason," John said, but he didn't doubt the sincerity in his friend's tone—he knew better. Logan had sent many men to their graves. *And they all deserved it. But this one? This might be a problem.* "That might be frowned upon by pretty much the entire federal government."

"It doesn't matter," Logan said. The betrayal had been complete. "We never saw it coming. *I* never saw it coming, not until it was too late. Thank God for Jake."

"This one's not on you, brother. It's all on him," John said, his thoughts suddenly turning again to Amira Cerone, a fellow Task Force Ares teammate and his . . . *What exactly is she to me? I know I'm head over heels for her.* Since they'd returned from Sudan six months ago, their relationship had rapidly developed, but they hadn't defined it. *If anything happened to her . . . Lock it down. Now!* He couldn't risk his emotions, not with a bullet wound and a team of deadly Secret Service agents dispatched to kill them. "Did you see her get out?"

"I couldn't tell. I'm sorry," Logan said in a low voice. "The smoke and flames—she was on the other side of them, before we got out of the SCIF," he said, referring to the headquarters' Sensitive Compartmented Information Facility. "I'm assuming she and Cole escaped based on the gunfire we heard. No way they lose in a straight-up fight to these guys, no matter how good the bastards are."

"No doubt," John said, knowing what his friend said was true.

The entrance to the compound was now a quarter mile away, secured by a heavy iron, automated gate and security camera. The dirt road emptied out onto a two-lane road known as MCB-1, referencing the Marine Corps Base on which their clandestine compound was located.

Nestled in the heavily wooded northern training areas of Quantico, it was an ideal location, only three miles from the FBI Academy, the HRT compound, and other resources that resided there. The site had been selected six months earlier after their first meeting with the president. With potential catastrophic results for the United States, their nameless enemy had nearly started a war in the Middle East and then attempted to pit the US against China by attacking a Chinese oil exploration site in Sudan with a hijacked US space-based weapon. Had it not been for Logan and his team, the state of the world—as precarious as it was—might have been a lot worse.

"She'll be fine," John said, more to himself than to Logan.

"She will be. I have no doubt about it," Logan said as the tall gate grew closer. He maneuvered the pickup along the dirt road as the tires gripped the surface and kept the vehicle aimed toward the entrance. The Suburban had now dropped back to a safe distance. *Probably didn't want to risk another guy. Too bad.* "But if we don't lose these assholes, we may not be." *Twenty more seconds and we're clear,* Logan thought.

"Did you have any idea they were with him?" John asked, the Kimber still trained on the trailing Suburban.

"Not really. Not until Jake texted me back, but by then, it was too late. They were standing right there." The flat tone of Logan's voice expressed it all: it had been a masterful ambush inside their own headquarters, a magic trick of horrific proportions. It had happened too *fast.*

"Can you call Lance?" Logan asked, knowing the head of the FBI's HRT Red Team and his assembled team of shooters were only minutes away.

"No bars," John said, glancing at the encrypted iPhone he now held in his left hand.

"They came prepared," Logan said. "Check the antennas on the roof. See if the Kimber will do anything to them, although I doubt it."

Logan had wondered why the detail had brought the electronic countermeasures Suburban. Now he knew. *Fuckers are going to pay.*

"Goddamn boy scouts. Always prepared," John replied, and opened up again with carefully aimed fire.

The bullets ricocheted off the Suburban's dome-shaped antennas, leaving small dents but causing no significant damage. *Of course not, why would that work? Nothing else has gone right today,* Logan mused to himself. While they'd managed to escape after the confrontation, Logan couldn't be sure about the rest of the team since all of their communications equipment had been jammed.

The weapon emptied, and John turned around in the passenger seat to eject the magazine, only to see Logan's outstretched right hand holding a second magazine loaded with hollow-point ammunition. He dropped the spent magazine to the floor of the pickup, inserted the fresh one, and pushed the slide release, slamming it forward and chambering the first round. He aimed the weapon once again out the rear windshield, looked at Logan, and asked, "What now?"

"We're in keep-it-simple territory. Once we hit the road, we haul ass down to the Academy and get the FBI police in on the fun," he said, referring to the uniformed division that protected all FBI facilities. "But my guess is these guys will break contact rather than risk exposure. The hard part is getting there. So be ready for anything," Logan said. He reached up to the visor and pressed a button on a sleek, slim device that resembled a space-age garage door opener.

The black steel, reinforced crash gate slowly began to slide to the right fifty yards in front of the speeding white pickup. *Almost there,* Logan thought, his muscles tight with the tension from the confrontation at the compound and the escalation of violence over the last two days.

Thirty yards . . . twenty yards . . .

The sliding gate had exposed nearly half the road, almost enough to allow the pickup to clear the opening.

We've got this, Logan thought, a glimmer of hope materializing through the battle fatigue he wore like a heavy cloak.

But just as suddenly, the glimmer was eclipsed by a second black Suburban that pulled in front of the entrance, perpendicularly blocking their escape.

"You've got to be kidding me," John said, disbelief and despair in his voice.

"Hold on," Logan ordered, and slammed down the brakes of the pickup. The vehicle slid to a halt in the middle of the dirt road, stopping ten yards short of the open crash gate. A cloud of dust kicked up behind the truck, but Logan spotted the chasing Suburban come to a halt twenty yards behind them. *Driver doesn't want to get too close. Coward.*

"This isn't good," John said.

He's right. There's nowhere to go. The woods are too thick on each side to drive through. No way forward or backward—we're boxed in. No, we're screwed, Logan concluded.

Logan's encrypted iPhone began chirping from the cup holder, and "Unknown" flashed across the screen.

"Bet you three pints of blood that's our friends. They turned off the jammer to call us. What do you think? Should I answer it?" Logan asked.

"The last time you answered a call like this, it triggered the hunt for that cursed flag," John said. "That was not a good time, even with our vacation in the Sand Box," he finished, referring to the chase for a tactical nuclear weapon that had been acquired in order to attack Iran and start a new conflict in the Middle East.

"True, but we're already in it now, brother." Logan laughed, his predatory bright-green eyes blazing as they watched the Suburban that blocked the gate. "What more could go wrong?"

Without another moment of hesitation, he grabbed the iPhone and answered. "What do you want?"

"What do you think we want?" said a cool, calm voice that reminded Logan that even though these were lethal adversaries, they were still elite warriors and professionals. *Special Agent Motherfucker, of course.* He knew they wouldn't be dissuaded. "The list, pure and simple."

Logan didn't hesitate. "It burned up in the fire."

"I don't think so," the head of the detail said from the Suburban behind them. "There's no way you would have left your headquarters without it. You know what's on it, and so do we. You grabbed the thumb drive. I *saw* you do it, through the flames. This isn't a negotiation. I'm not going to beg you to give it to me, but what I will do is tell you what's going to happen: You have thirty seconds to open your door, get out of the vehicle, and walk toward us. If not, we're going to light you up with RPGs. It's that simple—give me what I need or die. You have thirty seconds to comply." The line went dead.

"I told you not to take that call," John said in mock exasperation.

"I know, but I didn't—" was all Logan had time to say. His phone rang again, this time in the harmonious tune of chiming bells—*Sarah. Bad timing, babe.*

But he answered, knowing it might be the last time he talked to his wife, and he needed to ensure her safety.

"Sarah, I need you to listen to me," he started, speaking quickly and firmly. "I need you to execute the E & E plan," he said, referring to their personal plan to go off the grid in the case of an emergency and link up at a predetermined location later. While he was not overly paranoid, the events of the last few years had taught him to be prepared. "Do you understand? And I need you to do it right now. John and I have some trouble at work, and I don't know if we're going to make it." He thought he heard a slight intake of air on the other end. *Way to stay calm, babe. It's one of the many reasons why I love you.*

Fifteen seconds to go . . .

Logan and John watched as the side panel of the Suburban at the gate opened, revealing a crack of the dark interior, which was illuminated as the opposite-side door slid open. *To vent the back blast. These guys are serious,* Logan thought.

"Logan . . ." John said with growing concern.

"Sarah, I love you, and I'm sorry if I can't meet you there. But no matter what—know that I tried. I really did, babe."

Ten seconds . . .

"Logan," Sarah said through a voice thick with emotion, "I'm pregnant."

Silence. The countdown stopped momentarily in Logan's head. He felt—literally, physically—a momentary disembodiment, as if his reality were no longer his but someone else's. *How can this be, God? Why now, of all times? To find out I'm going to be a father moments from my death. You're a cruel taskmaster, you sonofabitch.* A swirl of emotions consumed him in a flush of feeling.

Five seconds . . .

Before Logan could lose himself inside his own head, John shouted, "We're almost out of time! Do something, goddamnit!"

Logan's mind crashed back to reality at his best friend and brother-in-arm's beckoning. He instantly realized the only option he had left. *It's suicide,* the rational part of his mind screamed. *Shut the fuck up. We're doing this my way, the Wild West way. No more talking.*

"I love you, Sarah. You'll be an amazing mother. I have to go," Logan said, and did the hardest thing he'd ever done in his life—disconnected the call as he heard the only woman he'd really loved say, "I love you, too. Fight hard."

No other way, babe. I'm not going out with a whimper.

Zero . . .

The Suburban's side doors were now wide open, and another Secret Service agent held an American version of an RPG, aimed directly at them.

His iPhone rang again, and "Unknown" once more appeared on the small screen. *Giving us another chance? Fuck you.*

"Are you ready, brother?" Logan said, his voice steady, his hands tightening his grip on the steering wheel, the roiling rage he'd been fighting for six months ready to be fully unleashed.

"Fucking A," John replied. "And congratulations on becoming a dad. I love you, brother."

"Ditto." There was no time left to talk. The two warriors had reached the end of the proverbial and literal road.

Logan reached forward and pushed the power button on the stereo, twisting the dial to the right. *Fuck it. Might as well go out with a little music just for the occasion.*

"Here we go," Logan said, and gripped the steering wheel tighter. "Buckle up and enjoy the ride. It's going to be a rough one."

PART I

BLOOD RUNS RED ON THE HIGHWAY

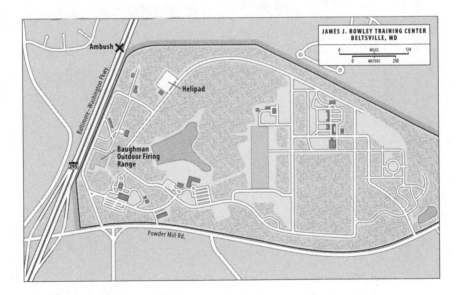

Ambush ✕

Helipad

Baltimore–Washington Pkwy.

295

Baughman Outdoor Firing Range

Powder Mill Rd.

JAMES J. ROWLEY TRAINING CENTER
BELTSVILLE, MD

0   MILES   1/4
0   METERS   250

CHAPTER 1

Smack!

The right hook glanced off John Quick's left jaw as he slipped the punch to the right, barely avoiding the full force behind it. *Gotta move faster.* He pushed his opponent's arm with his left hand, hoping to expose the attacker's right side. He stepped in to deliver a right hook to the body and was rewarded with . . . empty space.

The figure had spun around him in a whirl of motion, stopping adjacent to his right shoulder. John immediately knew he'd lost. *This is going to hurt.*

He felt a warm breath on the side of his neck, followed by, "Too slow. You keep exposing yourself."

"Stop talking and—" he started to say in frustration, but his words were cut off as his attacker stepped fully behind him, back to back, and hooked his left arm, securing it. The attacker dropped to a knee and gained momentum, twisting and yanking John off his feet.

He found himself briefly staring at the fluorescent lighting, and then he crashed to the ground, landing on his back. Before he could react, his attacker straddled him and pinned his arms to his sides with two lean, muscular legs.

John stared at the face of his attacker as he managed to yank his right arm from under the crushing force. Before he could do anything with his free hand, though, his opponent leaned in and pinned his right arm to the floor above his head.

Merciless blue eyes studied him from inches away. There was no quarter to be given. He thrust his hips upward, trying to buck the figure off, but his efforts only elicited a small smirk.

"Not so fast, tough guy," a low voice said. "I'm not done with you yet." The face was closer, looming large in his field of view, and he felt himself being scrutinized. *Not again—this is getting old.*

Mercifully, an instrumental version of the Marine Corps hymn started playing from John's encrypted iPhone, and he reflexively glanced toward the sound. Realizing his mistake, he turned back . . . as warm lips suddenly closed on his, and he felt a rush of exhilaration course through his body like electricity as Amira Cerone kissed him hard.

John felt himself getting lost in the intense physical connection they shared, but just as quickly, Amira pulled away, and said, "Playtime's over, babe. Time to work. It's Logan."

She rolled off of him and toward the phone, reaching it with such fluid grace that John couldn't help but stare. A moment later, he found himself snatching the phone out of midair, even as he kept his eyes on Amira.

She smiled, and said, "You might want to take it."

"You're beautiful, you know," John said, even as he pushed the accept button on the screen.

"You're not too bad yourself," Amira said as John put the phone to his ear.

Logan started talking, and John's eyes followed Amira as she walked across the rubber combatives floor she'd installed in her large penthouse, open-floor-plan apartment.

"I'll be in the shower. Join me if you have time," she added without looking back, as she pulled her black tank top off and moved toward the master bedroom.

John was captivated by her slender, muscular physique, and thought, *There's no hope for me.*

His attention was brought back to the phone as Logan said, "We have a hit on the Recruiter."

John's mind effortlessly shifted gears at the mention of the name of one of Task Force Ares' most sought-after high-value targets—the man who had recruited a contemptible human being named Jonathan Sommers into the world of treason and espionage. In addition to being the president's former national security advisor, Sommers was also one of the most despicable traitors the country had been subjected to, even if the general population wasn't aware of it.

Fortunately for the US, Jonathan Sommers had been betrayed by one of his own victims, Colin Davies, who'd set in place precautionary measures—out of habit, of all things—but who had no idea that the national security advisor was in fact an insider threat. As a result, he'd outlined the meetings he'd had with Sommers and placed the information in the Google Cloud. Those meetings had started the pursuit for the hijacked DARPA project ONERING, ultimately leading to Colin Davies' violent death at the hands of a clandestine Russian special ops team. But in the end, Colin Davies had achieved his vengeance from beyond the grave.

Once the task force had returned from Sudan with the ONER-ING, the first order of business had been to kidnap Jonathan Sommers from his Georgetown home. Logan, John, Cole Matthews, and Amira Cerone—the core members of Task Force Ares—had executed the operation and then faked Sommers' death with assistance from DC's chief medical examiner, whose brother coincidentally was a special agent and executive assistant to Jake Benson, the director of the FBI. More importantly, Jake Benson had been uncle to Deputy Director Mike Benson—longtime friend and brother-in-arms of Logan West—who'd been killed by the Chinese.

The faked death had been intended to send a message to the shadowy organization that was Jonathan Sommers' real employer, hoping to draw them out into the light. While Sommers had languished away in a specially designed cell in the basement of Ares headquarters on Marine Corps Base Quantico—in violation of multiple major laws and statutes, although they all had presidential pardons protecting them—subject to nearly daily interrogation, the task force had waited . . . and waited.

While they gleaned a treasure trove of information and intelligence from the enthusiastic Sommers—names, contact information, and operational details for other members of his organization, which, as it turned out, was in fact called the Organization—nothing he provided was actionable, and they all knew it, including Sommers. It was tradecraft 101: the Organization had to assume he was either dead or compromised, which also meant everything he knew could be compromised. As a result, all those identities had likely changed within a day or two after Sommers had been removed from the playing field.

But something's changed, or Logan wouldn't be calling me.

"How?" John asked.

"Through the contact Sommers told us about at the Venezuelan embassy," Logan said. "After Sommers gave us his list, we put all of them on tasking at every law enforcement agency and member of the Intelligence Community we could."

"I remember how busy the FISA court was. The judges and government attorneys finally earned their keep," John said, referring to the notorious Foreign Intelligence Surveillance Act court responsible for issuing warrants against foreign agents inside all US borders. "We assumed all the intelligence he had would be dead ends. I can't believe any member of their organization would *keep* the same mobile devices or computers."

"Well, one Luis Silva, a member of the SEBIN, did," Logan said, referring to the Bolivian National Intelligence Service. "NSA told Jake that Luis received a phone call yesterday morning on one of the mobile numbers, one he hadn't utilized since we discovered it. The call originated from a landline in a Firehouse Subs shop in Fredericksburg. Jake sent two senior FBI agents with the Counterterrorism Division to talk to the owners of the restaurant. It turns out the phone was located near the front of the store next to the register. No one recalls anyone using it, and the store didn't have any surveillance cameras."

"So then how exactly did we find out about it?" John asked.

"Dumb luck. Turns out there's a new bank under construction across the parking lot, and the construction company had installed cameras the *day before* in order to prevent vandalism. The agents said there was no way anyone walking in or out of the sub shop would've known about them, the way they were hidden and how far they were located from the shop. They talked to the foreman at the construction site and were able to review the camera's footage."

"Really?" John asked.

"Uh-huh," Logan responded. "And guess which sonofabitch showed up on candid camera?"

"The Recruiter," John said.

"Bingo. Based on the description we have from Sommers, there's no doubt about it. Once they had the date-time stamp from the video, they provided it to Jake, who then asked NSA to search their databases for the call to Luis' cell phone. Once they found it, they listened to the content, which turned out to be a twenty-second encoded message. Fortunately, NSA has some brilliant cryptographers, and someone who used to work in South America in the eighties figured out that it was a Cuban cipher code used during the sixties in the Cold War," Logan said.

"And I thought the only good thing to come out of Cuba was cigars," John retorted.

"Funny—as in you're not," Logan said, and continued. "More importantly, the message was a time and location for a meet. And guess where and when it's happening?"

"Logan, Amira just kicked my ass for the third time this week. I'm really not in the mood for guessing games, especially from you," John said drily.

"Hey, I can't help it if you can't handle your woman," Logan said good-naturedly.

"I'm going to tell her you said that."

"You better not—I don't want to be on her hit list," Logan said, remembering how she'd aggressively interrogated—with a stiletto—a Chinese operative after Logan and Cole Matthews had been temporarily captured in Sudan six months ago.

"Fine. Just get to the point. Amira and I are supposed to be having lunch with her dad today, remember?"

"Damnit. That's right," Logan said. "I'm sorry, brother, but lunch is going to have to wait. The meet is set for thirteen hundred at the Udvar-Hazy Air and Space Museum near Dulles Airport. The Recruiter specified 'Discovery,' which could only be the space shuttle display."

"That's less than five hours from now," John said.

"I know, and here's the kicker: it's a Tuesday afternoon, and schools are out for the summer. The head of security told us that it would be bustling with activity. So it's straight-up civilian attire and concealed weapons."

"Got it. I better let Amira know," John said.

"And John, after what happened with Mike, don't forget your

vest. Put it in your pack and bring it. You can put it on there. We shouldn't need them, but there's no fucking around with these guys, you understand me?"

"Absolutely—no taking chances. I got it. By the way, where do you want to meet? You know he could already have someone inside casing the place, right?" John stated.

"I know. It's why Cole will be in as soon as the doors open at ten hundred. He's as good as it gets when it comes to counter-surveillance, and I'm sure he'll enjoy showing off that stupid beard of his," Logan added.

"Don't be jealous of our Delta Force of one," John said, mentioning Cole Matthews' background as a Delta operator only to irritate Logan. "You can't help it that you're a pretty boy with those dashing looks and dreamy bright-green eyes of yours."

"Jackass," Logan said dismissively. "I'll be in the security center on the lower floor, down the steps once you get through the initial security checkpoint. Be there by eleven thirty. When you and Amira get to screening, tell the guards who you are, and they'll send you my way. Remember, these guys know who we are, but we don't think they were able to identify Cole or Amira before we took Sommers out of play."

"Understood. Now if you don't mind, I'm going to go let Amira know our plans have changed, and I'm *totally blaming you* for it. See you soon," John said, and hung up on his closest friend and ally.

Moments later, he knocked on the door to the bathroom loudly enough to be overheard above the sound of running water.

"What's wrong with you?" he heard Amira say as he opened the door. "I told you to join me, didn't I?" she added in mock exasperation.

John stared at her through the glass door, the steam from the shower concealing the details of her gorgeous physique yet somehow accentuating her beauty.

"We've got a problem, but not in a bad way. We're going to have to cancel on your dad, though," John said, delivering the bad news as quickly as possible.

"How is that not a bad thing?" Amira asked, staring at him intently. "You know how he is. He's been expecting us since we had to cancel last week." Her father, a retired DC homicide detective and widower, cherished the infrequent occasions he spent with his daughter. He knew who her real employer was, and he'd accepted the fact that her country unfortunately took top billing in these troubled times.

"I know, but it's the Recruiter—he popped up, and he's going to be at the Udvar-Hazy Air and Space Museum at thirteen hundred."

At the mention of the target, Amira changed—a subtle hardening of her taut figure—and John could sense the tension increase across her frame. He smiled at her, waiting for a response.

Even though he was in his midforties, he epitomized rugged handsomeness, with short brown hair, defined features, and brown eyes that studied her. Suddenly he gave her his best puppy-dog impersonation and said, "But I could still join you. It's the least I can get for getting knocked on my ass again."

Amira didn't immediately answer.

Finally, she said, "So you want to be rewarded for losing, is that it?"

"Whoa!" John said, and raised his hands. "I'm just doing my best millennial impersonation. Don't hold it against me."

"Cute," Amira said, and then, "just get your ass in here. We don't have much time."

God knows I'll take any time I can get, John thought as he took off his shirt and stepped toward the shower.

CHAPTER 2

Logan hung up the phone and looked at Sarah, who'd walked into his personal office on the main floor of their new home in rural northern Virginia. It was located a few miles west of the small community of Hoadly, in close proximity to Quantico.

While Sarah didn't know the specific details behind the task force her husband now led, she knew enough and could surmise the rest. And after killing two intruders who had attacked her in their former home in Maryland, she was practically an honorary member, a title earned in blood.

In addition to the location, there was an added benefit, one Sarah had insisted on—actual neighbors. After several years of virtual isolation from the outside world as a result of Logan's downward spiral into alcoholism and then the events of the past two and a half years, both had agreed it was time to assimilate—albeit slightly—into society. Logan joked that Dr. Phil would be proud of their unified self-realization, but each knew that it was important. They couldn't be outliers and self-imposed societal pariahs, no matter how horrific the things they'd seen and done. Less than two weeks after Mike Benson's death, they'd started looking for a new home, discovering the blossoming community of Reilly's Bluff, built upon the hills overlooking the Occoquan Reservoir.

Each home was located on a little more than two acres of land, which afforded plenty of privacy but also a sense of community. Unlike in the West Friendship suburban countryside setting, here they actually knew their neighbors, many of whom worked for either the federal government or the military. Logan and Sarah fit right in with Logan's cover as a private security consultant for the FBI.

Logan had joked, "It would probably be the worst neighborhood in the *world* for the bad guys to take a run at. I'm pretty sure ninety percent of the neighbors have guns and know how to use them. Hell, if I had time, I'd organize a community tactical squad and call it Reilly's Raiders in homage to the Marine Raiders from World War Two."

"Sure, babe, and I'll start the local Jane Wayne Club, complete with cupcake and demolition competitions," Sarah had shot back.

"That's a hot combo. I'd pay to see it," Logan had wistfully retorted.

Joking aside, he'd been right—the neighborhood provided a sense of security neither of them had felt before but now appreciated greatly. It helped that the house had been built in the name of an LLC and that Logan had a small arsenal scattered throughout the rooms. But the presence of neighbors was still comforting, nonetheless.

"I take it the day off is no longer the day off," Sarah said as Logan hung up the phone.

"Sorry, hon. Something came up, and I've got to meet the gang in three hours for some sightseeing," Logan said. His green eyes flashed at her, and even though she knew he was playing, she felt the attraction toward him that had never left, even when they'd been separated. Even the faint scar that slowly tracked down his left cheek somehow accentuated his attractiveness. *If only all the women admirers knew how deadly you are,* Sarah thought, deeply satisfied by the knowledge.

"If you say so. That's okay. I need to get my annual physical, anyhow. I'll call and see if Dr. Sykes has any cancellations."

"Is everything okay?" Logan asked with concern.

"Just a routine checkup. I'm not thirty anymore, in case you haven't noticed," Sarah added.

"I would've said 'sixteen,' but I didn't want to push it," Logan replied.

"Which also would've made you a pedophile," she wisecracked back at him.

"Fine," he said. "Eighteen."

"Why not just play it safe and call it twenty-one?" she asked as she walked over to his desk and leaned in to kiss him. "Do your thing. I'm going to head to *my* office and call the doctor. Keep me posted, and I'll see you after work. We can go out to dinner, unless you're exhausted."

"Never for you, babe," Logan said.

"Good answer. You know, sometimes you really are a smart man," Sarah said as she walked out of his office.

Actually, a lucky man is what I am, Logan thought as he dialed the number of Cole Matthews. He looked at his watch. It was already zero eight fifteen, and he needed to get Cole in place. *Time flies when you're having fun.*

CHAPTER 3

A voice originated from the wall-mounted television over the fireplace in the enormous study, one side of which was constructed entirely of bulletproof glass. "The expected solar storm could be as large as the infamous Carrington Event of 1859, which is believed to be the largest in recorded history," the stocky Weather Channel anchor, known for his dramatic penchant for weather-related phenomena, said. "I wouldn't be surprised if we have major communication outages, power disruptions, and even serious damage to any satellites caught in the plasma cloud. This is going to be a big one, folks."

Indeed, the Founder thought, and stared out at the choppy waters breaking against the small island outcropping of rocks thirty yards offshore. Intended to keep boaters from the shallow beach area forty feet below his five-acre sprawl built on a small cliff, the outcropping also provided a landmark from which the Founder spent many a day casting for the bay's prized possession—striped bass, locally referred to as rockfish. He'd had a small wooden bridge built to it from shore. Thirty yards to the right was the main pier, where he kept his small fleet of boats, including his prized Sunseeker 131-foot, four-deck yacht, which he used throughout the Caribbean and along the East Coast.

————

It's a long way from the killing chambers in Pawiak, the tall, thin man in his eighties thought, the horrors still fresh in his mind, as vivid as if he were still that eight-year-old boy in the Warsaw Ghetto who had witnessed his mother shot in the head by a young, prideful SS officer. Her only crimes had been being a Jew and trying to shield her oldest son from a random patrol. His father, a Jewish tailor, had been forced to watch his wife's execution as another sadistic SS officer laughed and pinned his head to the ground under a black leather boot. *I can still see the leather glistening, even in the blood and muck.*

His father and brother had then been ripped from his life and sent as inmates to Pawiak Prison, which the Gestapo had incorporated into their Nazi death camp system. He'd never seen either of them again.

The Founder had been left in the middle of the street, screaming in horror at the emotional and literal destruction of his family. Fortunately for him, a close friend of his mother's had picked him up and taken him away to the decrepit apartment she'd shared with three other families. She'd tried to care for him, but he'd been ruined, a shell of a boy who survived on a day-to-day basis in the most deplorable conditions imaginable. Even to this day, the first year after the traumatic massacre of his family was a blur of extreme hunger, cold, and despair.

Yet somehow, he'd survived, and after ten brutal months, he'd been successfully smuggled out of the ghetto and into Hungary through Slovakia. Landing in Budapest with other Jewish children who had escaped Poland, the Founder ended up in a Jewish Polish orphanage run by several Hungarian Jewish women who dedicated themselves not only to rescuing refugees, but also to bringing back their damaged psyches from the brink of madness and ruin.

It was in Budapest that the broken boy had slowly transformed into a wounded but healing teenager, working for one of Budapest's blossoming shipping companies after the war was over. It was there he discovered while still an adolescent that he possessed a shrewd business acumen, which a visiting Greek shipping tycoon had identified when the boy resolved a logistics problem between the Greek company, a fledgling Hungarian company, and the Hungarian government. It had helped that the boy had learned Hungarian and English, in addition to his native Polish and Yiddish tongues.

As a result, the Greek tycoon had made the teenager—then seventeen—an offer: *Come work in my Mediterranean logistics division. You have a rare gift and the potential to be more than just a boy who survived the Holocaust. I can see it in you, even if you can't.*

Still recovering from the horrors of the war, the boy had felt no real emotional ties to Hungary, and he'd leapt at the opportunity to move even farther away from Germany. In Greece, he'd quickly risen through the ranks of the company until he achieved the position of chief of global operations at the young age of thirty-eight, which coincided perfectly with the European boom in manufacturing and the production of oil in the Middle East. The fates had smiled upon him for once, and he'd built a multibillion-dollar industry, reaching heights not even his Greek benefactor had envisioned.

When the tycoon had passed away in 1972, he'd bequeathed the entire business to the Founder, who'd done more for the Greek's family name than any blood relative. It was after that funeral that the Founder realized that even greater opportunity lay west, and he'd personally established a new base of operations in New York City.

But building an empire, especially in the United States, required money and influence. He had plenty of the former and only a little of the latter. A political novice, he thoroughly researched the backgrounds of the most influential politicians in Washington DC, and discovered that no matter how diverse their backgrounds, they all had one thing in common—a thirst for power, even if shrouded in some self-delusional belief that they served their constituents. It was during that time that he developed a deep distrust and intense dislike of politicians, whom he viewed as morally deficient. In his mind, they were no better than the German SS officers who had slaughtered his family and permanently scarred him—just *different*. As a result, he did what any ambitious billionaire would do: he identified those most susceptible to the lure of unlimited wealth, and he bought them.

His wealth and influence grew, and with it, new relationships with other billionaires and politicians around the world. As the world changed, he insulated himself and maintained as low a profile as possible, content to quietly amass a fortune worthy of a Second World nation.

But September 6, 1986, drew the Founder out of the shadows, with an event that completed the transformation of the broken boy into a burning, lethal global force with which to be reckoned. Two gunmen opened fire on the Neve Shalom Synagogue in Istanbul, Turkey, slaughtering twenty-two worshippers before blowing themselves up. They were later confirmed to be tied to the infamous terrorist Abu Nidal, the founder of Fatah, the Revolutionary Council, which had split from Yassir Arafat's PLO in 1974.

The attack, while horrific, wasn't spectacular in scope and scale. But it was the name of the victims that triggered the Founder to relive his boyhood trauma. One of the worshippers was the grown son of the Hungarian Jewish woman at the orphanage who had cared for him in the immediate months after his escape from the Warsaw Ghetto.

Throughout his adult life, the void that he felt deep within his soul had remained. He'd tried to fill it with success and fortune, but he knew there was no physical remedy for what ailed him. His soul was beyond repair. The one thing that had brought value to his life had been the fact that after he'd become successful in Greece, he'd become the benefactor to every staff member from his orphanage, as well as their offspring. While he couldn't buy happiness—or even a remote sense of peace—for himself, he'd tried to buy it for others, helping financially in every way possible.

But it was never enough. The cruelty in the world could not be contained, and forty-one years after the end of World War II, anti-Israeli sentiment and terrorist operations were on the rise. And out of all the death and horror from numerous attacks, it was the death of one middle-aged man, the son of a woman he hadn't seen in decades, that shattered the psychological house of lies he'd built, crumbling the false sense of security with which he'd shielded himself. After her son's death, the elderly Hungarian Jewish woman had lost all desire to live. She died of natural causes—a broken heart and destroyed soul.

Two days after he'd been notified of her death, he'd made a decision. He would counter the new wave of evil with all his available resources. He immediately realized how expansive the undertaking would be, but he would not be deterred. Over the next ten years, he built the leviathan organization the world didn't know existed.

Comprising wealthy industry tycoons, politicians, world leaders, and senior global intelligence professionals, the Organization had one purpose—to prevent the spread of global instability. It was an ambitious, endless pursuit, measured in small successes and shrouded in secrecy. The Founder—as he'd become known to the senior members of the Organization, who knew his true identity—had decentralized the Organization, authorizing and encouraging his agents around the world to pursue and execute independent operations, with only one constraint: there must be a positive outcome.

While the purpose was specific, the name was deliberately ambiguous, a nebulous term that could refer to anything. No one would think twice overhearing a conversation about some generic "organization." For him, the banality was a strength.

The Founder was no longer a naïve, broken boy; he was now an aging man of conviction unbound by societal norms or common morality. He understood the developing world, the exponential trend of increasing technology and global growth. But he also saw the potential pitfalls, the underbelly of human nature that somehow insinuated itself into all ventures in life, no matter how noble the intent. And that underbelly needed to be managed.

The methods of the Organization were necessary but often against the law—both local and international—though as long as the instability was managed, the Founder considered them acceptable. Enemy terrorist attacks were limited to one-time occurrences or small-scale events, and the groups responsible were held accountable in human capital. The Founder was particularly proud of the assassination of Abu Nidal in Baghdad in 2002, orchestrated to look like a questionable suicide to place blame on the Iraqi government.

The Organization had served its purpose for decades, but since 9/11 and the US war in Iraq, the balance of power had shifted, throwing the Middle East into complete disarray. The Founder's Council of senior global leaders had watched quietly as American servicemen and -women were sacrificed by what the Founder considered a flawed and petulant president, hell-bent on eliminating a thorn in his family's side. It was the civilian death toll in collateral damage to both sides—the Americans and the insurgents—that truly outraged the Founder, reminding him that the aggressor in a conflict was often the one committing the most atrocities. But the

Organization had taken no action on that front, patiently waiting as the drawdown inevitably concluded and Iraq regained tenuous control of its own destiny.

But then a traitorous man named Cain Frost had betrayed the Council, seizing the opportunity to wage his own personal war against Iran. Cain's thirst for vengeance for his brother's torture and mutilation-murder had overruled his reason, and his bloodlust had temporarily placed the entire region on the brink of disaster. Fortunately, the US had prevented that eventuality with the assistance of a small group of skilled and determined individuals. The Organization had been forced to deal with Cain Frost directly though, as his trial threatened to expose them. Even though he'd been a loyal member and faithful to the mission, in the end, the Founder had been given no choice. Cain Frost had to die. The bomb placed inside a food truck outside the DC courthouse had accomplished that objective, but innocent civilians had also perished, a moral burden the Founder felt each day and which caused him to question his own mission.

If I've become no better than the men I vowed to destroy, am I now as evil as those same men? He hadn't been able to answer that question definitively, a fact that greatly disturbed him.

As a result, he'd ordered a freeze on global operations, but someone inside his organization—a Council member, he was certain—had violated that ban and orchestrated multiple attacks, this time *against* the US, with the express intent of *creating instability* between the US and China. The operation had been thwarted once again by the actions of a task force of FBI consultants and CIA operatives, and even worse, the Founder had not been able to identify who the traitor or traitors were. But the events had pushed the Founder toward a decision and a course of action he'd always kept in the back of his mind but never realistically expected to execute.

No matter what he'd personally become, he'd always been able to justify the actions of his Organization, but suddenly that scale had teetered to the wrong side, and he knew it was time to act. There was no way he was going to let his life's work be hijacked by forces acting against him. And that was why the barrel-chested, middle-aged man with short gray hair stood behind him, watching and waiting for his instructions.

"I never thought it would come to this," the Founder said. "No matter what happens, I know that we've done more good than bad." He turned to look at his audience.

"I know, sir," the Founder's chief of all US security operations said. A retired military officer, the advisor was also the Founder's right hand when it came to sensitive and clandestine Organization operations. "But it has to happen. When you approached me four years ago, it was the ideal of what you were doing that captured my attention. I knew from my decades of service that the world no longer functioned like it should, that politicians and political correctness were threatening our very existence. Our leaders refused to make the hard right choices. But you assured me we could make a difference, even if our methods were questionable or morally repugnant." He paused for a moment, the overcast clouds seeming to capture his attention. "You know what the best definition of integrity is?"

The Founder turned to him, momentarily intrigued by the question. "I have an idea."

His advisor nodded. "In the military, there are a few definitions, but a version of this one stuck with me from Officer Candidate School and guided my career—'doing the hard right thing at the right time for the right reasons, especially when no one is watching.' And that's what we're about to do, sir—a *very hard right thing*."

"I know, but once we open this Pandora's box, there's no closing it. The other Council members will realize I'm responsible, and whoever the traitor is, he'll come for me."

"Let him," his advisor stated resolutely. "If what I'm about to do draws the bastard out, even better. I can deal with him as well."

The Founder nodded. "You've become a loyal friend, Jack, and I trust your judgment on these matters, even though I wish we didn't have to do this."

"It really is the only way. You and I know he'll have the list on him," Jack said. "I've known him for years, and I once considered him a friend. He may not be the ringleader orchestrating all of this, but he's gone rogue and has to be put down. The amount of damage he can do in his position is unthinkable, not just to us, but to the entire nation *and the world.*"

A moment of silence stretched out between them, and Jack wondered if the Founder had changed his mind. He pressed forward. "Sir, he's set to testify at the Senate Intelligence Committee in two and a half hours. My men are in place, but I need you to confirm it."

The Founder sighed. There was nothing more to say. "Do it, and Godspeed, Jack."

"Consider it done, sir. I'll update you when it's over." Jack turned and walked out of the glass-walled library, leaving the Founder to stare at the white-capped waves.

How did it come to this? God help us all.

CHAPTER 4

Special Agent Frank Beckmann kept a watchful eye on the road ahead of the black Suburban, scanning for threats as the two-vehicle government convoy traveled south on I-295 from Fort Meade. The road was notorious for lengthy traffic delays at all hours and random accidents caused by reckless Maryland drivers, and he was pleasantly surprised as he maneuvered the second Suburban in the convoy in the right lane down the parkway. *Must be our lucky day.*

A fifteen-year veteran of the Baltimore Police Department, Frank was a Baltimoreon, born and raised in the inner-ring suburb and tough, working-class neighborhood of Dundalk. An athletic and street-savvy young man with jet-black hair who'd driven a gas-operated forklift at the Dundalk Marine Terminal through high school, he'd had ambitions beyond the blue-collar jobs many of his friends had landed upon graduation. Frank had kept his job at the terminal, but he'd also earned a two-year associate's degree in law enforcement at Baltimore Community College, applying to the Baltimore Police Department during his final semester. Not overly optimistic about his chances—a young white kid from

Dundalk in a town like Baltimore—he was surprised when he'd been accepted.

Frank had spent the better part of his fifteen years in a patrol car, never overly ambitious but enjoying the satisfaction of each day that he felt he could make a difference *and still go home alive.*

But the city had changed, and so had Frank, with political correctness running rampant through the mayor's office and a sense that City Hall no longer had the backs of the police officers who protected it. His goal had been to do his twenty years and then retire to something else, *anything else.*

Fortune had shone upon him when a close friend from the National Security Agency Police had called, and he'd been offered a position in the operations center. He'd taken it, excelling at coordinating internal on-site daily operations—inside the relative safety of multiple perimeters—and before he knew it, he'd found himself on the director's personal security detail, or PSD.

How time flies, Frank mused to himself as a voice from the backseat suddenly interrupted his automatic scanning of the environment and his own internal thoughts.

"How we doing on time, Frank?" the four-star Marine general asked. "I don't want to keep those arrogant jackasses waiting too long, even if some of them could use a lesson in patience."

Marine General Thomas Taylor—call sign "Major Tom" from his F-18 fighter pilot days and his penchant for David Bowie music—was the first Marine director of America's largest intelligence agency, which focused on information assurance and signals intelligence, commonly referred to as SIGINT.

General Taylor had risen swiftly through the ranks as first a squadron commander and then Marine aircraft group commander at Cherry Point, North Carolina. While all his peers had assumed he'd be the next commander of the Second Marine Air Wing, he'd been promoted to brigadier general and slated to a different billet—director of intelligence, or DIRINT, as the commandant of the Marine Corps' chief intelligence officer. Two impressively successful tours and two promotions later—to lead the relatively new Marine Forces Cyber and then to Cyber Command deputy commander— it was no surprise that he'd been promoted to four-star and appointed commander of the United States Cyber Command and director of the NSA.

"We're still on track for eleven thirty, sir. Shouldn't be a problem," Frank replied, quickly glancing at the fifty-five-year-old director with a Marine crew cut and forty-year-old physique. *Some men just age well,* Frank thought, reminded of the small love handles he carried around his waist. *Must be a Marine thing.*

"Good to go, Frank." The general looked down at his classified personal iPad and then spoke to his aide, a young army major, who sat in the right passenger seat next to him. "You're sure this is correct, Mike?"

"That's what the SID DIR said," Major Mike Winston replied, referring to the signals intelligence director responsible for the production of all SIGINT. "It looks like the North Koreans are getting ready to do another launch, and it could be as early as tomorrow."

"Christ," General Taylor said. "When will that guy learn? All he's going to do is piss off South Korea more—and maybe even China, if he goes too far—and get more sanctions placed on him."

"I know, sir, but that's not how he thinks," Major Winston said, referring to the Democratic Republic of Korea's infamous leader. "He thinks that provocation will bring us, the south, and other members to the table."

"He's fucking crazy, is what he is, by playing with fire like this," General Taylor responded as he looked at the cars they passed on the parkway. "And I'll make sure the senators understand that. I can't believe any of them would *even consider* opening negotiations with this lunatic, at least not until he starts acting like a responsible adult."

"Agreed, sir, but you know how squirrelly they get, especially around election time. It's all about the optics," Major Winston stated with resignation.

"Fucking optics are what's going to ruin this country," the general replied with disgust. "But all hope is not lost," he added almost absentmindedly.

"What do you mean, sir?" Major Winston asked.

"I mean there are people in Washington—both in Congress and out—who believe strength is the only way to handle bullies like this one and that we can't ever let our guard down," General Taylor said.

The black Suburban suddenly slowed, and General Taylor looked forward through the windshield. He saw two rows of brake lights, brightening and moving toward them like an airport runway lighting up for the first time. "What is it, Frank?"

"Can't tell, sir, but it looks like some kind of construction," Special Agent Beckmann replied. "Can you see anything, Matt?" Frank asked Special Agent Matt Browning in the front passenger seat.

"Negative, but I don't think it's traffic. I see flashing lights up ahead. Probably another accident. Let me see if I can find out on the scanner, sir," Special Agent Browning said, turning the volume up on the police scanner on the dashboard of the Suburban. The steady sound of static emanated throughout the SUV's interior, even as he changed channels.

"That's odd," Frank said.

"It could be that super solar storm they were talking about on the news. It's supposed to be one of the biggest ones we've ever seen, and I thought I heard them say it could disrupt both radio and cellular communications," Major Winston said from the backseat.

Fan-fucking-tastic, Frank thought. *Just what I need—a solar storm.*

The traffic slowed to a crawl in the late-morning commute to DC, and vehicles in the right lane began to merge into the left one.

"Looks like we'll be through it in a few minutes, sir," Frank said.

"Good to go. Just don't let anyone get between us and the lead vehicle. You never know," General Taylor said in mock suspicion.

"Never, sir," Frank said, and kept his attention on the lead Suburban in front of them before finally spotting the source of the delay.

An eighteen-wheel flatbed truck with a large commercial, bright-orange Hitachi excavator on the back blocked the right lane, and several Maryland State Highway Administration vehicles were parked at odd angles in front of it. The excavator's powerful articulated boom hung off to the side, above the left lane of the parkway. The two lanes of southbound traffic merged into the left lane as a flagger in a yellow hat methodically waved traffic past the chaotic scene.

I feel for you, buddy, Frank thought, remembering his long days of manual labor at the port.

The lead Suburban moved over, and Frank nosed the director's vehicle close behind to avoid some aggressive Maryland driver from separating them.

This won't be much of a delay, after all. The lead Suburban had just entered the choke point in the left lane when Frank had a realization—the flagger was gone. *That's odd. Where the hell did that guy go?* It was the last thing he'd remember before his quiet morning turned into a chaotic nightmare.

A small Selectable Lightweight Attack Munition, known in the military as the M2 SLAM, that had been buried in a preexisting pothole and covered over with a thin layer of gravel, detonated, triggering the ambush.

B-BOOM!

The enormous explosion thundered across the quiet parkway as the antitank mine sent a copper EFP—or explosively formed penetrator—upward and directly into the engine block of the lead Suburban, immediately destroying the engine and disabling the vehicle. Small chunks of pavement tore into the Suburban's tires, but the run-flat tires functioned as designed, and the vehicle lazily rolled forward, nearing the cab of the truck as smoke filled the vehicle.

Frank's senses were momentarily overwhelmed from the proximity of the explosion. His head rang with a loud buzzing-ringing, but his tactical training and muscle memory took control of his actions, even before he could fully process the situation. *Have to get the director out of the kill zone.*

He'd heard the stories about Iraq from his military veteran peers at the NSA Police. When an ambush occurred, there was often only one option—move forward and through the kill zone and beyond to safety. The thought of leaving his brothers-in-arms on the PSD to fend for themselves pained him, but the director's safety was paramount, and he knew they'd understand.

He heard shouting from the backseat, but he ignored it as he slammed the accelerator down . . . and went nowhere.

The left rear window of the Suburban imploded, and the rending shriek of metal on metal filled the inside of the SUV.

Frank turned around to his left and saw enormous black tines from the excavator's bucket protruding into the backseat. The director and his aide were crouched down on the floor space, although neither appeared to be injured. *That's one small mercy,* he thought, his positive nature somehow looking for a silver cloud in the black reality of their situation.

The bucket suddenly angled up and pierced the roof of the vehicle, securing a grip on the armored SUV.

"We've got to get out of here!" Special Agent Matt Browning screamed from the passenger seat, but suddenly they were in motion.

We're out of options, Frank thought as the excavator suddenly tilted the Suburban on its side, pinning it against the wheels and undercarriage of the flatbed truck at a forty-five-degree angle. *We're fucked.*

He heard a small *pop* and watched in horror as a black-gloved hand dropped a small, cylindrical canister through the opening the excavator's bucket had created. *Oh no.*

Thick, gray, acrid smoke quickly filled the backseat of the Suburban, and Frank looked forward, catching a glimpse of the scene playing out near the other Suburban.

The four doors of the disabled SUV were open, as the trapped members of the PSD had realized their only option had been to stand and fight. Unfortunately for them, it hadn't been much of a fight. Four attackers—two on each side—clad in all-black tactical gear and neoprene balaclavas, fired shotguns at point-blank range into the Suburban. A third shooter on each side stepped in behind the shotgun-wielding attackers and fired a type of pistol Frank didn't recognize. The gun didn't matter, but the fact that there was no return fire from the Suburban sent a fresh rush of adrenaline-fueled panic through him as the smoke filled the front of the SUV and obscured his view.

"Get out *now*!" Frank screamed, reaching for the handle of the Suburban with his left hand and drawing his Smith & Wesson .40-caliber M&P pistol from its holster on his right hip.

He heard scrambling movement from the backseat as the driver's door swung upward and slammed back down on its hinges, open. Frank switched the gun to his left hand, pointing it through the opening at the sky beyond, and released his seat belt with his right hand.

He looked down and saw Special Agent Matt Browning doing the same thing. "We have to get out of here or we're dead!"

Frank knew he needed to get out of the vehicle as soon as possible and help the director in the backseat. He stepped on the side of the cushioned seat, trying to gain leverage to get up and out of the vehicle.

As he grabbed the doorframe, the Smith & Wesson was firmly yanked from his hand, and he was pulled out of the Suburban and sent crashing to the pavement below.

Special Agent Frank Beckmann looked up into the bright morning sun, coughing as the dark outlines of multiple figures appeared over him. Smoke billowed out of the Suburban above him, shrouding him from the sun in dancing shadows of darkness, and he heard additional attackers pulling the other members of the PSD and the director onto the pavement next to him.

"Who the fuck are you guys?" Frank asked, his eyes watering and lungs burning, knowing all hope had been lost. He didn't really expect a response, but he at least hoped for a quick death. *They executed this flawlessly. No chance we walk away.*

Special Agent Frank Beckmann was right—one of the attackers stepped close to him, pointed a black tactical shotgun at his chest, and fired point-blank. He felt a punch to his chest that knocked all the breath out of him and immediately immobilized him. *That hurts a lot more than I thought it would,* he thought. He'd heard enough stories from men who'd been shot, and it was always, "Man, I didn't even know I'd been hit." Not this time. It hurt like hell.

A second gunman pointed the odd-looking weapon he'd spotted earlier and fired, and Frank felt a sudden sting on the right side of his upper chest. He looked down and saw a small white dart with a black feather on the back sticking out of his shirt. *What the hell?*

His stunned mind suddenly remembered a call to the Baltimore Zoo he'd responded to in his early days on patrol. One of the large cats—he couldn't remember what kind—had somehow escaped its enclosure, and the zookeeper had shot it with a tranquilizer dart.

The tranquilizer had taken less than a minute to work, sedating the animal into nonthreatening unconsciousness.

In Frank Beckmann's case, it was a much stronger dose of a newly developed and quick-acting agent, and he drifted off into oblivion within seconds.

CHAPTER 5

"Sir, we've got to be out of here in four minutes if we're going to make the rendezvous. There's no doubt more than one of these civilians has already called this in," one of the operators said. "The chaos might buy us some extra time, but we need to do this now."

The Baltimore–Washington Parkway had become a parking lot. Several people had exited their vehicles and were fleeing northward, away from the scene. Traffic had come to a standstill, and abandoned vehicles now formed a permanent blockade that would take hours to clear. The two northbound lanes were forty yards away, separated by a median with intermittent clusters of trees. The vehicles were slowing down, their drivers instinctively aware that something had happened on the southbound side, but unsure as to what, they kept moving northward to their destinations.

Six members of the ambush team fanned out in order to provide perimeter security around the flatbed truck and the two disabled Suburbans. Fortunately, no civilians had decided to be impromptu heroes, delusions of *Die Hard* glory playing out in their heads. The assault team and the four-star Marine general were the only living souls within two hundred yards.

The leader of the assault team stood over the director of the

National Security Agency, whose olive-green service alphas were torn in several places after the rough extraction from the Suburban. The director was obviously distressed at the sudden and violent ambush, but there was an underlying current of anger and resistance that shone forth above everything else.

"Who the hell are you?" General Taylor asked with restrained contempt, the combative Marine ever present. "You're obviously not some ragtag bunch of assholes."

The leader of the assault team nodded to another member, who jumped into the Suburban. The interior was now clear, the smoke having dissipated.

"No, Tom, we're not," the leader responded. General Taylor cocked his head slightly, recognizing the tone of the voice. The leader lifted the bottom of the balaclava, momentarily revealing the face beneath. "It's good to see you, brother, even under these circumstances."

A look of resignation washed away the anger on the general's hardened face, and his posture softened slightly in acquiescence. "Hey, Jack," General Taylor said to the chief of security of the Organization. "I guess if it had to be anyone, I'm glad it's you."

"I'm not," Jack said, and lowered the balaclava back down. "We were friends once. Hell—more than friends. That bond forged in combat never dies, Tom. You know that." Jack's voice was thick with emotion. "But you betrayed the Organization, and you brought this on yourself. You and the other traitors on the Council. Why?"

"It's the world, pure and simple. The Founder's approach was too passive. A few of the Council members believed a proactive strategy was necessary, and I agreed. I won't apologize for it," General Taylor replied.

"I didn't expect you to," Jack said. "No man of honor would, and no matter what the world will or won't find out once this is all over, you are a man of honor."

A black-clad figure emerged from the Suburban with a black shoulder bag. "Sir, I've got the iPad, an agency BlackBerry, and what looks like the general's personal iPhone."

"Is that where the list is?" Jack asked.

"I know you have to go, but how did you figure out it was me? Come on. You can tell me. It's not like I'm walking away from this one."

"Tom, you might be the director of one of the most powerful spy agencies in the world, but you're not the only one with CNE capabilities," Jack said, referring to NSA's infamous cyber network exploitation. "Remember, the Organization is global, and we've been working with a private Russian firm. After Cain Frost went rogue and last year's events with China, we knew Council members had gone off the reservation. The Russian firm deployed a software suite onto the mobile devices of all Council members. More importantly, they also hardened the Founder's personal servers with additional sensors, sensors that not even your agency could detect. Bottom line—when you had the agency hack the Founder four days ago, we knew about it. And when we discovered the operation had been personally ordered by you, we had you."

"Fucking Russians. Go figure," General Taylor said. "We've been telling Congress and the president what a cyberthreat they are, but no one wants to listen or do anything about it."

"The list, Tom. Is it on your phone?" Jack pressed.

The distant sound of a helicopter broke the silence of the ambush's aftermath.

"Smart evac plan," General Taylor said.

"*Tom*, the list? Please don't make this worse than it already is."

"How can it be any worse?" General Taylor said, as if scolding a child.

"The passcode, please," Jack asked.

"One, one, one, zero, seven, five," General Taylor replied.

"Seriously, Tom?" Jack asked. "The Marine Corps birthday?"

"No matter what you might think of what I've done, I'm still a Marine through and through. It's legitimate."

"Thank you," Jack said, and nodded. "Are you ready? Do you want to say a prayer?"

General Taylor scoffed, "Will it help?"

"I honestly don't know," Jack said.

"I resigned myself to this life a long time ago. Just do it. If you can somehow, let my wife and son know I died with my head held high," General Taylor said.

"I will if I can," Jack said, and raised the Colt M1911 .45-caliber pistol he'd held at his side throughout the entire conversation.

"See you on the other side, Jack," General Taylor said, then raised his head and closed his eyes.

"Semper Fi, brother," Jack responded quietly, and shot the director of the National Security Agency point-blank in the forehead.

"Godspeed," Jack said, as the general's body fell forward to the pavement.

CHAPTER 6

Special Agent Austin Chang fired the remaining .357-caliber rounds from his SIG SAUER P229 at the US Secret Service hostile threat target he'd hung twenty-five yards away in lane four—his lucky number—of the Baughman Outdoor Firing Range at the Secret Service James J. Rowley Training Center—JJRTC, for short—in Beltsville, Maryland.

The sprawling training complex covered five hundred acres north of the DC Beltway, directly adjacent to the Baltimore–Washington Parkway. Usually a bustling campus of advance marksmanship training, control tactics, water survival skills, and physical fitness, the multiple facilities were currently deserted due to the break between eighteen-week special agent training courses.

It was Special Agent Chang's favorite time, when he was alone with the abundant supply of deer that ran rampant through the campus woods and training areas. He still remembered his first visit to the facility in the fall of 2000—before the world had changed—as a new cadet, where the class was scheduled to run a vehicle demonstration at the Protective Operations Driving Course, only to discover more than forty deer lounging around on the paved surfaces, as if to say, *We're here for the show, too.* It had been eye opening, but in the years he'd visited the campus, he'd come to appreciate the symbiotic relationship between the deer, the cadets, the special agents, and the instructors. It was a shared habitat where the wildlife respected the humans—armed with enough firepower to make Bambi's mother run for cover—and the humans allowed the wildlife to exist.

Bam! Bam! Bam!

The last three rounds struck the target in the ten area at the top of the head. *He wouldn't walk away from that one,* Austin thought to himself, and smirked.

A former leader of a crisis action team—known as a CAT team, even though the acronym had "Team" in it—on the president's detail, Special Agent Chang was playfully referred to by his peers by the politically incorrect moniker Wokker, Texas Ranger, because of his marksmanship skills and Chinese heritage. He was one of the agency's senior marksman instructors. Physically nonthreatening at only five feet eight inches and 170 pounds, he was nonetheless one of the most lethal and blazingly fast shots the agency had in service.

Austin removed his battery-powered hearing protection as he walked toward the target to further inspect his accuracy.

Had he finished shooting minutes earlier, he might have heard the initial explosion and follow-on gunshots. But Special Agent Chang was focused on his marksmanship. There was no such thing as perfection in shooting, but repetition bred consistency and accuracy.

The growing sound of rotors pierced the relative tranquility of the training campus. Austin assumed it was either a news helicopter or one of the Anne Arundel County police birds, although he knew the latter didn't start their rotary overwatch until later in the day.

What the hell? It sounds like it's landing.

Leaving his dead target to dangle on its clips, Austin jogged from under cover of the range's roof and looked northward.

Through the trees, he spotted what looked like a news helicopter descending rapidly in the vicinity of the enormous concrete heli-pad. *Is that the Fox News 45 bird out of Baltimore?* He couldn't be sure, but he thought so.

He drew his cell phone out of his back pocket and dialed the security gatehouse at the main access control point at the south central entrance on Powder Mill Road.

"Security," a monotone voice answered.

"This is Special Agent Chang out here at the range. I spotted what looks like a news helicopter descending near our helo pad. You guys got anything going on today?"

"Negative, sir. You want us to— hold on a second." There was a momentary pause, and Austin heard increased chatter in the background from the command post's radios. "Sir, there's something happening on the parkway. Anne Arundel Police are reporting a possible shooting on the highway and are responding to the scene."

"Roger," Austin said. "I'll let them handle it," he added, knowing that the county or state troopers had primary jurisdiction. "But I'm still going to go see what's up with the bird. I hope the pilot didn't put down on our helo pad in order to let some idiot reporter out."

"Do you need any support?" the uniformed officer on the other end asked.

"Negative. I'll call you guys if I need you." And then he added, "Come running, though, if you hear gunfire."

"Sir, this is a training facility. We *always* hear gunfire," the officer responded drily.

"Exactly," Austin said, and laughed. "I should be good. Out here."

"Call us if you need us," the officer replied, and disconnected the call.

Chang put away his cell phone, loaded a fresh magazine into

the SIG, holstered the weapon on his hip, and began a quick jog to the helicopter pad more than a third of a mile away.

At least I can get some extra PT in, if nothing else.

––––––

Jack led the seven-man unit across the grassy no-man's-land that divided the parkway. As he paused at the shoulder of the northbound lanes, he looked up to see the Bell 412 helicopter painted with the Fox 45 Baltimore News logo hovering just above the tree line. It was similar in body style to the Eurocopter AS365 Dauphin that the local news crews actually utilized, and there was no doubt in his mind that no one—trained or not—would think that the helicopter was anything other than a news crew arriving on scene to film the aftermath of the ambush. In fact, he was counting on it.

He turned to the operator to his right, and said, "Set the screen."

"Roger, sir," the black-clad team member said, and turned to another team member. "Smoke on the left side. I've got the right."

Traffic slowed slightly as the morning commuters gawked at the heavily armed gunmen that had appeared on the left side of their road.

Both men pulled British-manufactured EG18X green military smoke grenades from their Kevlar vests, yanked the wire loops, and hurled the grenades in unison into oncoming traffic. The grenades ignited, sending a brief shower of sparks across the highway as they tumbled end over end before coming to a rest and erupting into thick plumes of smoke.

There was little wind, and as panicked drivers slammed on their brakes at the sudden appearance of smoke, the two darkening plumes merged to form one thick green wall that blocked both lanes of the parkway.

Not too shabby, Jack thought. *So far, so good.* "Let's go," he said, and all seven men dashed across the pavement, ignoring the blaring horns and curses they heard from the other side of the improvised smoke barrier.

Within seconds, they were down the embankment on the other side of the road, where they disappeared into the thick Maryland woods.

"This way, sir," the operator on point said to Jack, who was right behind him in the single-column formation known throughout the military as the ranger file.

"Roger. Lead the way," Jack said, and maintained his pace.

Thirty yards later, the column halted in front of a corner intersection of an eighteen-foot-tall aluminum reinforced fence that ran south, parallel to the parkway to their right but cut at an angle to the northeast away from them.

The helicopter was much closer but still hovering above the trees.

The lead team member felt along the intersection, and moments later, he pushed inward, revealing a three-foot-by-three-foot opening in the fence.

"I still can't believe they didn't detect Boone cutting it last night," Jack said.

"Like I said, sir, this is a dead space between their motion sensors. They placed them too far down each wall, and this corner isn't covered, at least this eight-foot section of it," the point man said.

"And we cut after the last patrol went by on an ATV at zero four this morning. With shift change of the uniformed police, we knew there was no way they'd detect this breach so soon," Boone said from behind them.

"Nice work. Too bad for them," Jack said. "Let's go. We're almost at the end of this rodeo."

Jack looked at his watch. *1050. Only five minutes since initiating the ambush. Right on track.*

As if synchronized to his thoughts, the Bell 412 helicopter finally began to descend below the tree line.

The men scampered through the fence opening one at a time, completing their insertion into one of the most heavily trafficked training facilities in federal law enforcement. The irony wasn't lost on Jack as he went through the fence. *They're going to be talking about this one for years, once they figure out what happened.*

"Two hundred yards, and we're in the clear. No stopping for anything until we hit the bird," Jack said. "Let's finish strong." This time, Jack took point, running through the woods at full speed, leading his team of veteran warriors. *This is what it's all about,* he thought, as he focused on his breath and pushed forward.

———

Special Agent Chang jogged down the main road that ran through the entire training campus in a big, misshapen oval. The helicopter had descended more than a minute ago, dropping out of sight. He knew there was only one facility suitable on the Rowley grounds for a helicopter—the enormous concrete landing pad 300 feet wide by 260 feet deep.

In addition to containing a mock-up of the HMX-1 presidential helicopter and the front of Air Force One, it also served as a real-world landing pad for various elite military and law enforcement units to conduct realistic training on the campus.

Austin ran a little harder, his curiosity piqued more than anything else. *I just hope the pilot and the bird are okay.*

He was only thirty yards from the landing zone when he saw through the trees that the news helicopter had landed on the pad, as he'd suspected. The edge of the woods that ran along the road and the small, single-story, square maintenance building adjacent to the left side of the pad obstructed his view, but he'd have a clear line of sight in a few more seconds. *I can't wait to hear this one,* he thought, and then his phone suddenly rang.

He momentarily considered ignoring it, but personal discipline earned the hard way in his second year on the job forced him to stop in his tracks. He remembered a story a fellow Secret Service agent had told him. He didn't even remember the man's name now, but the story had stayed with him: a phone call from the Cleveland Field Office while he was serving a warrant on a counterfeit case had saved the agent's life. The young agent had frozen in the middle of his approach to the front of the objective house when his phone had rung. The field office had called to inform him that the suspect had recently been reported to be heavily armed and had robbed a drug dealer, leaping from counterfeiting to violent crime in the span of hours. The young agent and his partner had stopped midstride and moved off the sidewalk and out of sight from the front of the house. The agent told Austin it was then that he'd learned how fast life could end with one wrong decision. Gunfire had erupted from a first-floor window, strafing where the two agents had been seconds before. A standoff had ensued, ultimately ending with a SWAT team's sniper 168-grain match hollow point projectile. But the agent had learned a valuable lesson that day— always answer the phone. As a junior and malleable agent at the time, Austin had taken it to heart.

He pulled out his phone and hit the accept button, recognizing the number of the security gatehouse.

"What's up?" Austin said, his eyes focused on the part of the landing pad he could now clearly see.

"Sir, there's been some kind of ambush and shooting on the parkway," the uniformed Secret Service police officer stated, his voice authoritative and devoid of all humor. "NSA Police and Anne Arundel County are responding immediately. We just heard the Anne Arundel County headquarters radio room sending the call out to the patrol cars. Initial civilian reports are several armed gun-men dressed in black and multiple casualties. That's all we know at this time."

What the hell is going on out here? Austin thought, his senses now heightened as he kept moving forward, his SIG SAUER P229 al-ready in his right hand at the ready position.

"What the hell are the NSA Police—" was all he had the chance to say as Special Agent Austin Chang's normal training routine turned into actual combat.

The last part of the woods fell away, and Austin was afforded a clear view of the entire training area . . . just in time to see a single column of black-clad *operators*—which was how his mind identi-fied them immediately from their movement—materialize from the back of the woods in between the mock-ups of Air Force One and HMX-1. Their objective was clear—the news helicopter that now sat idling on the landing pad, its rear doors open in antici-pation of its passengers. A millisecond later, it hit him—*it's a fake news helicopter.*

Austin's mind kicked into overdrive thanks to years of special-ized training. He let the cell phone drop from his left hand and brought up the SIG SAUER in a thumbs-forward combat grip. He transitioned from his jog into a steady combat walk, keeping his upper body relatively stable to avoid bobbing up and down.

I need cover, or I'm dead, his tactical brain screamed. The oper-ators were more than 250 feet away, and he was overwhelmingly outgunned and outmanned. *I've got a better chance of winning Powerball than winning this gunfight, but I might be able to slow them down or stop them from escaping,* he thought, ignoring the loud shouts emanating from his fallen cell phone. *These bastards are using our facility as an HLZ to get away with whatever crime they just committed.* His mind momentarily reeled at the brazenness of the scheme—infiltrating one of the most elite federal training facilities in the US as part of an escape plan—but then he cleared his mind, focused on the front sights, and exhaled. *Not today, assholes.*

He pulled the trigger, knowing his aim was true.

———

We're almost clear, Jack thought, acutely aware of the ensuing chaos and law enforcement manhunt that would soon be under way. *You passed the point of no return, Big Dog.*

The helicopter was now less than fifty feet away, the doors open, his former JSOC Special Operations Aviation Regiment pilot looking in their direction from behind the Oakley sunglasses he wore over a black balaclava.

Movement in his peripheral vision made Jack turn his head, and he saw a lone individual in khaki cargo pants and a black polo combat-walking toward the maintenance building, a pistol aimed at the helicopter. Jack realized the Secret Service agent's intentions—he assumed he was an agent; they were on their campus, after all—even as the lone gunman pulled the trigger.

Bang-bang-bang!

Spiderwebs appeared on the pilot's acrylic windshield, even as Jack screamed, "Shooter, two o'clock! Hit him low and drop him!" The thought of collateral damage repulsed him, but the mission was more important than one man, even an innocent Secret Service agent who thought he was doing the right thing.

Two operators behind Jack opened fire with Colt M4 Commando assault rifles. Even at two hundred feet, the gunfire was accurate, and at least two shots struck the Secret Service agent in the legs. He toppled forward, his head bouncing off the ground, and lay still.

Jack looked back to the helicopter and saw that their pilot was pressing his right hand against his left shoulder. *Oh no.*

The column of men covered the remaining distance to the helicopter, several of the operators keeping their weapons trained on the fallen Secret Service agent.

Jack stepped into the front passenger seat of the Bell helicopter and shouted above the din of the whirring blades, "How bad is it?"

"I'll live, sir, but my left arm is fucked. No way I can fly with only one arm. Help me out of this seat and get Simpson in here per the backup plan," the pilot said.

Jack nodded and turned to the men as they filed into the passenger compartment of the helicopter.

"Simpson, it's up to you to get us out of here," Jack shouted.

"Got it, sir," one of the men acknowledged, and stepped forward to help release the pilot from the harness. Within seconds, he had pulled the wounded man out of the pilot's seat and passed him to the team medic, who was waiting for him in the back.

"I got you, Jones. Let's see how bad that wound is," the medic said.

The rest of the team was onboard, and as Jack secured himself into the copilot's seat, he said, "Can we please get the hell out of here?"

"On it, sir," Simpson said, twisting the throttle-grip on the end of the collective pitch control and pulling the lever up at the same time.

The Bell helicopter slowly lifted into the air, a lumbering beast eager to free itself from gravity's grasp.

Finally, Jack thought. *Another successful mission that might just be the capstone of all I've accomplished.*

———

Austin opened his eyes, the roaring rotors propelling him out of unconsciousness. He remembered trying to run for cover but being knocked down, as if by an invisible hand.

His head throbbed, and he realized he must have slammed it

against the ground as he'd fallen. Sharp, stabbing pain in his upper right leg jolted him awake, followed by a second, nearly excruciating pain in his lower left one. He looked down, saw his cargo pants soaked in blood, and knew immediately that he'd been shot, at least twice.

This fucking blows, he thought. He started to feel faint at the blood loss. He looked up and saw the helicopter lifting into the air. *Must have had a second pilot. I know I hit the first one at least once. Guess it wasn't enough.*

The sound of sirens from the approaching uniformed police SUVs reached his ears. *Thank God. At least I won't bleed to death out here.*

He glared at the fleeing helicopter as it lifted higher and then suddenly stopped, momentarily hovering. The bird turned on its vertical axis, facing east, and Austin was temporarily provided with a broadside view of the flying machine, adding insult to his very real injuries.

The passenger compartment door was still open, and one black-clad operator leaned out, looking at Austin one hundred feet below. And then he did the unthinkable—he waved to Austin, as if saying, *Sayonora, motherfucker. Better luck next time.*

Austin was suddenly filled with a battle rage that squashed all sensation of pain, a physical compulsion to forcibly reply. *No way you get away with that. No . . . fucking . . . way.*

He looked down and saw his SIG lying a foot away from his right hand. *Jackpot.*

With blinding speed fueled by fury, he snatched the weapon from the ground, rolled backward onto his left shoulder, and obtained a nearly upside-down clear sight picture on the arrogant, faceless operator.

Wave at this, he thought, and pulled the trigger as the operator realized a moment too late what was happening.

A singular *crack* echoed across the concrete slab.

Austin suddenly felt exhausted, the momentary adrenaline rush subsiding, and he wasn't sure if he'd hit his mark.

The operator lowered his arm . . . and then pitched headfirst out of the side of the helicopter.

Austin watched with grim satisfaction as the man plummeted to the ground headfirst. He hit the concrete with a sickening *crunch,* his skull shattering beneath the balaclava and his back and neck breaking in multiple places.

I hope you were dead before the fall, but too bad if you weren't. Austin was too tired for sympathy, especially for someone who had just shot him.

The sirens grew louder, and he knew help had almost arrived. His eyes felt heavy, and he put his head down on the ground, looking at the dead operator seventy-five feet away from him, blood from his ruined head leaking through the black mask and darkening the concrete.

So much for an easy training day, he thought, and passed out.

PART II

SPACE
COWBOYS

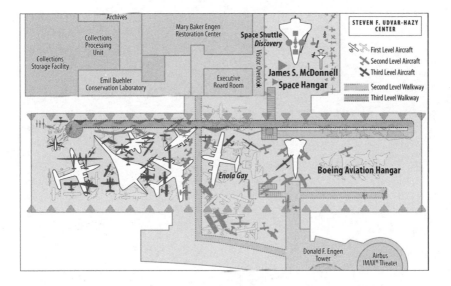

CHAPTER 7

Steven F. Udvar-Hazy Center
Chantilly, Virginia
1130 EST

Although connected to Dulles International Airport by a mile-long concrete road composed of the same material as the runways, the Udvar-Hazy Center was isolated, surrounded by woods, fences, and fields. In addition to Dulles to the north, the Fairfax County Police Department Driver Course and a business park—complete with a private school—were directly to the west on the back side, less than 175 yards away. The only public access road to the museum was the Air and Space Museum Parkway, connecting Route 28 to the east and Route 50 to the west. More important than its location, however, was the facility itself—a living and breathing monument to every little boy's dream of flight, space exploration, and adventure.

A massive structure that was awe-inspiring upon approach, the facility was composed of several buildings of shiny steel, glass, and concrete. From the parking lot, a visitor first spotted the huge cylindrical IMAX museum on the right, connected by a single-story glass building to one of the hallmarks of the museum—the 164-

foot Donald D. Engen observation tower. From there, visitors could watch airplanes land and take off from Dulles Airport next door, complete with a resplendent background of the Blue Ridge Mountains. The multistory, black-glass main entrance was left of the tower, and farther past the entrance was the museum store and the sole restaurant—a McDonald's. As impressive as the facade was, it was the enormous hangar behind the front buildings that was the centerpiece of the museum.

The Boeing Aviation Hangar was one thousand feet long, approximately one hundred feet wide, and one hundred feet high. The walls and ceiling of the structure were white with enormous HVAC tubes hung on each side halfway up the full length of the hangar. A series of interconnected walkways linked one side to the other, bisecting the cavernous space and passing, suspended, by one of the main attractions—the Boeing B-29 Superfortress *Enola Gay*, famous for dropping the first atomic bomb on Hiroshima on 6 August 1945. In addition to the *Enola Gay*, nearly two hundred aircraft from all periods of aviation were on display, hanging dramatically from the ceiling, resting on the floor, or mounted on various pieces of machinery that raised the aircraft. It was a dizzying display of technological marvels that was a testament to mankind's ingenuity and quest for glory by defying gravity.

Even though the pièce de résistance was the main hangar, beyond the hangar was an additional space—the James S. McDonnell Space Hangar, which contained the space shuttle *Discovery* and other dazzling exhibits. To the left of the exhibit, a second-floor walkway led through a door and overlooked the huge glass-enclosed restoration hangar. Other areas that served various functions—processing, storage, archives—were beyond the restoration hangar but inaccessible to the public.

The first thing that John Quick noticed when he walked through the main entrance was the constant thrum of humanity, like a live wire that crackled through the atmosphere. He saw through the atrium into the main hangar beyond, the glimpse only hinting at the size of the gargantuan space. *Oh my God. This is going to be a nightmare.*

A late-fiftyish African-American federal police officer in a white short-sleeve shirt and black pants waved him over to the security desk as John heard Amira say "Wow" behind him. *That about sums it up.*

As they neared the desk, John opened his mouth to speak, but the guard held up a hand as the radio on his belt crackled. John reached into his pants for his FBI badge when the guard looked at him and waved it away dismissively, revealing a tattoo on his right upper arm that was partially hidden by the sleeve.

"Roger, sir. I'll walk them down myself," the guard said into the push-button handset attached to his left shoulder. "Be down in less than a minute." The guard focused his attention on John and Amira, momentarily pausing at the strikingly beautiful woman dressed in black yoga pants and light-purple Under Armour zipped hoodie.

"No need for that, Mr. Quick. Your friend is already downstairs in the security operations center. They spotted you from the over-head cameras the second you walked through the door. Let's get you down there so you can join the party," the guard said.

"Where'd you serve? Saw our beloved Eagle, Globe, and Anchor on your arm," John said, as the man stepped from behind the desk and motioned to a staircase on the right side of the atrium.

"I did twenty-six years with the Marine Corps and retired in 2007 after two tours in Iraq and one in Afghanistan." The guard eyed John cautiously, as if assessing the fit, rugged newcomer. "What about you? I can see it on you. When did you get out?"

John smiled. "It always shows, no matter how hard we try to hide it. I got out in 2004 after twenty years. Last tour was in Fallujah," he added, but left it at that. *No need to reopen the horrors of that operation, especially since the ones responsible are all dead.*

The guard nodded as they walked down the stairs, as if contemplating the answer to a complicated math problem. "The name's Anthony. I help run this show. Nice to meet you, Mr. Quick."

"Call me John, and this is Amira, and she was *not* in the Marine Corps," John added.

"I could've told you that," Anthony replied.

"How so?" John asked as they reached the bottom of the stairs.

The guard stopped, looked at Amira, and said in a friendly and flattering way, "No offense, ma'am, but you're too damned beautiful. Let's go." Anthony motioned to a set of glass doors to the left of the stairs. "That's your stop."

As they walked side by side, John leaned in and said, "You know he's talking about me, right?"

"Moron," Amira said in a hushed tone.

"All day long," John said, and smiled. "All day long."

CHAPTER 8

Lau Han sat at a table closest to the tinted glass of the McDonald's, which afforded a full view of the front entrance. A Chinese man in his late fifties, black hair falling casually across his forehead and a new Nikon DLSR camera hanging around his neck, he blended in with the endless supply of tourists at the museum.

Dressed in a tan polo and white shorts, he slowly sipped the McCafé latte he'd purchased after his unhealthy lunch of a Quarter Pounder—no cheese—and french fries. *How could Americans eat this filth?* Years of living in Europe and the Mediterranean had spoiled him, and he'd become accustomed to the fine cuisine in Greece, including fresh calamari snatched from the coast of the Aegean Sea.

I loathe this country, he thought, the anger that had been a smoldering ember for the last six months suddenly burning brightly at the sight of John Quick and a beautiful light-skinned woman of African—*I think it's African*—descent walking up the steps to the front entrance. The casual observer might have noticed a subtle change on Lau Han's face, a flash of rage in the eyes that glowed with hatred, but it was gone just as quickly. Not the actual rage. That was never gone, not since Lau Han's son, Lau Gang, had been killed in Sudan six months ago while conducting a covert operation—one for which Han had recommended him—for both the Organization and China.

It was guilt that consumed him, knowing that he'd sent his only son to die, brutally killed, either at the hands of the man he saw walk in the front door or someone else. They'd prevented Lau Gang from successfully completing his mission, but Han didn't care about that, not anymore. The only thing that mattered now was *revenge*.

He'd known that his son was impulsive, and he'd counseled him to make his decisions as calculatedly and dispassionately as possible. Han had seen in his son the potential to be a master spy for China's Ministry of State Security, even though it wasn't the MSS that was Han's true benefactor—it was the Organization. He'd recruited Gang into the real shadow world, a world in which very few clandestine operatives dwelled but also where the real power was wielded. Unfortunately, that world and the secret rebellion occurring in it had killed him.

Han had sided with the members of the Council who sought to exercise the power the Founder so rarely utilized. He understood a key fact of human existence—conflict was continuous. There was no end to it, *ever*. The Founder naïvely believed he could manage it through small operations, but Han understood—real change required major *actions*. And that was what Gang was attempting to do when he'd been killed—bring about major change, a change that the members of the Council could manage once the tipping point was reached.

In fact, bringing the world to the brink had been the *real* objective, but his son had fallen short, paying with his life. The rebelling members on the Council had planned for the possibility of failure, but while they planned strategically, Lau Han planned emotionally. After months of calculations fueled by revenge, he'd contacted the

Recruiter, and he'd devised a plan that could serve both the purposes of the rebels on the Council and his own.

It was why Lau Han sat in a McDonald's restaurant, knowing that all the players—his and theirs—were now in the arena. John Quick and his partner had been the last to arrive to the battlefield of his choosing, and only one word reverberated in his lizard brain—*revenge*. The day had finally come, and Lau Han was eager to get started.

Udvar-Hazy Security Operations Center

Unbeknownst to Lau Han, Logan West was focused on the same thing, although he called it something slightly different—vengeance for the death of Mike Benson. But unlike Lau Han, Logan knew that the physical compulsion for vengeance—*it's revenge, Logan,* his subconscious told him, *pure and simple*—was dangerous and self-destructive. He was self-aware enough to recognize how serious the compulsion had become when he'd had the nearly uncontrollable desire to pummel a driver who'd cut him off and nearly caused an accident on I-95. He was used to careless drivers—he had to be, navigating the treacherous concrete death traps of the DC Beltway—but it'd taken him more than the normal ten or twenty seconds to calm down. He'd actually *considered* following the reckless offender, until he recognized how irrational that behavior would be, especially for a man leading one of the most clandestine units in the US government.

As a recovering alcoholic more than two and a half years sober, he knew that obsessing over Mike's death was both dangerous and an insidious and destructive form of resentment with no tangible object for his frustration. Instead, he internalized the anger and outrage, doing his best to conceal it from his wife and closest friends. Yet it was always there, just under the surface, as if taunting him from his Freudian id, *daring* him to deny it what it wanted— *payback in blood.* And in light of the first substantive lead they'd had in the last six months, the monster was itching to be let out of the cellar.

Not yet, Logan thought, and exhaled, staring at the bank of camera monitors that filled the entire back wall of the security operations center.

"We have cameras on every support beam in both the main and space shuttle hangars. We pretty much have line of sight over ninety-nine percent of the square footage in the museum. You can actually see them, if you look up and know what you're looking for," Lieutenant Ricardo Christenson said.

A former Army Ranger who'd separated after ten years as an officer with multiple deployments to Afghanistan, he'd had enough of war. Having lost several friends in combat, he'd taken what he considered the easy alternative—stability and a federal law enforcement position. Working his way through the bureaucratic quagmire—which was often especially burdensome for federal police—he'd spent his entire career at the Udvar-Hazy Center, until one day, after promotion after promotion, he found himself the officer in charge of security for the entire facility. He'd been grateful, and he hadn't looked back for one second, especially with a seven-year-old daughter and a wife who cherished the fact that he came home every night.

"They look like wireless routers, but the antennas actually transmit the video signal, as there was no way to run wiring a hundred feet up to the center of the ceiling, not in a massive place like this," Lieutenant Christenson continued.

"It's impressive," Logan replied as he continued to study the wall of monitors. "But I don't know how the hell we're going to spot the man we're looking for. There are *so many people*," he said, almost in disbelief.

Logan looked from monitor to monitor, until he stopped on one that was centered on the Lockheed SR-71A Blackbird spy plane just past the main entrance into the massive hangar. A man with a short beard, dark-blue jeans, light-blue polo, and a black Oakley backpack studied the world's fastest jet-propelled aircraft, snapping an occasional picture.

"Check this out, John," Logan said, as John walked over to the screen. "Fits right in, doesn't he?"

John scoffed and leaned in for a better look. Cole Matthews "fit in" as a tourist about as much as John Quick did as a seminarian.

"You really think the Recruiter is going to show up today?" John asked.

"Honestly, I have no idea, but it's the first real break we've had. We have no choice; we have to see it through." Logan turned to Amira. "Interested in getting in on the action? Since they know who John and I are, you and Cole are the next best things. I'd even rank you above him, but don't tell him that, it will hurt his fragile ego."

"You know, sometimes you're almost as bad as your boyfriend here," Amira responded.

"Not in this lifetime. He's got me beat six ways to Wednesday . . . or whatever that stupid day of the week is," Logan added with a grin.

Amira looked at the monitors once again, deciding on a location. "I'm going to roam the suspended walkways and try to stay on the top level. It's got a view of the entire floor and walkways below."

She inserted a miniature wireless earbud that would be invisible under her hair, which was pulled back in a ponytail but covered her ears.

"I'll start the app on the phones and dial in John and Cole once you walk out of here," Logan said, referring to the software program they'd purchased to protect their internal communications, especially in a public venue like the museum. The software utilized the wireless Internet service at the museum, sending 256-bit, unbreakable, encrypted voice and text messages between the phones.

"Keep me posted if you spot him. Otherwise, I'm going to go do my best to pretend I'm interested in the scenery," Amira said, and headed for the door.

"Whoa!" John said. "How can you not be into this place? It's every kid's dream!"

"No," Amira said. "It's every *boy's* dream. I'm a *grown-up*. I'll stick to gun ranges and obstacle courses. That's what gets my adrenaline going," she said, winked, and walked out the door.

"That's why I love her," John said, and looked at Logan. "And why I'm totally doomed."

"I have zero sympathy for you. It must be so hard to have such a beautiful and formidable woman at your side," Logan quipped. "Now pull up a chair, try not to talk, and let's see if we can spot this sonofabitch. Otherwise, it's going to be—"

Logan's phone rang before he had a chance to complete the sentence or initiate the encrypted application. He looked down and saw "Jake" flashing across his screen.

"It's Jake. I told him we'd update him if something breaks," Logan said as he answered the call.

"Hi, Jake. What's up? We're just getting everyone into position here, but I don't have anything for you yet," Logan said to the director of the FBI and a man he considered family.

"It's not that. I know you have that under control. There's been an incident, an attack—actually, more like a ruthless execution," Jake Benson said.

This isn't good. His voice has an edge to it, Logan thought. "What happened?"

"A highly trained team ambushed the director of the NSA's two-vehicle convoy on the BW Parkway. They incapacitated his entire security detail—leaving them alive—but then they shot the director point-blank in the middle of the road."

"Jesus Christ," Logan muttered, knowing the director was a Marine general, one of the good ones, from what he'd read about the man. The suppressed anger was suddenly at full throttle. For Logan, an attack on one Marine was an attack on all. *Stay calm*, he told himself, and breathed deeply.

"It gets worse. These guys were so brazen, they did this right next to the Rowley Secret Service training facility. They used the helipad the Secret Service has as an LZ, landed a helicopter that was apparently painted like a local Fox News bird, and then took off, after they shot an agent who'd been training on one of the ranges."

"How's the agent?" Logan asked, dreading the likely answer.

"He's going to make it, but he didn't go down without a fight. He shot and killed one of them as the bird was lifting off. Even though it's a Secret Service training center and we've got multiple agencies and jurisdictions, we're sending an FBI forensics team to see if we can get a quick ID on the body," Jake said.

"Good for him, taking one out," Logan said, his blood pressure slowly decreasing with the knowledge that at least one of the murderers had been stopped, cold. "Any idea where they went?"

"Negative. The smart bastards knew what would happen and planned for it. By the time Anne Arundel County PD got their police helicopter in the air, the team was long gone, but the *real* Fox News helicopter had arrived on scene."

Logan closed his eyes, imagining the confusion and chaos.

"And because of the solar storm, the helicopter's radio wasn't working properly," Jake continued. "The local police couldn't get the news bird's attention, and the copilot actually fired his M4 to get them to comply."

"I'll bet that was one hell of a shock for the news crew," Logan said, almost feeling sorry for the journalist sky jockeys.

"It did the trick, but what matters is that by the time both birds landed, the bad guys were long gone, and no one seems to know where," Jake finished.

"Sounds like you have your hands full. I'll keep you posted if anything breaks here. Thanks for the update," Logan said.

"I just wanted you to know, in case you hadn't seen it on the news yet. The day just got busy for both of us. Happy hunting," Jake said, and then added, "but even though this Recruiter bastard is responsible for Mike's death, try to take him alive, Logan."

"Understood, and I will," Logan answered.

But as he hung up the phone and turned to John to tell him about the attack, the ugly iron door in his mind that kept the monster at bay rattled a little louder, as if sensing it was going to get some outside time very soon. *At least I hope I will,* Logan thought, and mentally kicked the monster into submission. The door quieted for the moment.

CHAPTER 9

By one thirty, Logan knew something was wrong. Between Cole, Amira, the security guards performing "normal" foot patrols, and the cameras, both entrances into the James S. McDonnell Space Hangar were covered by at least two dozen sets of eyes.

"Maybe the attack on the BW Parkway forced the Recruiter to call it off?" John said in an uncertain tone.

"It's possible, but I don't know," Logan said. "I feel like we're missing something. This guy doesn't go underground for six months, suddenly reappear, and then cancel at the last minute. I don't buy it. Something else is going on."

"Why do you say that?" John asked.

"Because we still haven't seen Luis Silva, who the Recruiter is supposed to meet," Logan answered.

Logan stared at the screens, as if the answer might magically materialize on one of the closed circuit monitors. *I'm tired of sitting around on my ass. Enough.*

"That's it," Logan said, and stood up from the chair. "I'm going out there."

"Are you kidding me?" John said. "These guys know who you are. Hell, they know who we *both* are."

"I don't care. Maybe my sudden appearance will spook them. Maybe it will even cause these bastards to make a mistake," Logan added.

"And maybe it will get you shot in the head, in which case I'm going to have to explain to your much better half how you got yourself killed because you were bored and stupid."

"What's that mean?" Logan asked.

"It means I know how you're feeling. I know you're still struggling with Mike's death. I've known you a long time, brother; it's not like we just teamed up yesterday. I'm concerned, and more importantly, I think this is a really bad idea."

Logan knew better than to try and deny it. He could no more lie to John than he could to Sarah, not after all they'd been through. Instead, he said, "Noted, but I'm doing it anyhow. Keep me posted on the phones."

"If you say so, boss," John replied sarcastically. "Just remember to duck when the bullets start flying."

———

I knew one of them would come out into the open, Lau Han thought as he followed Logan West from the main floor up to the elevated walkway on the south side of the main hangar. *Where is he going?* No matter—he would make the kill as quietly as possible. He felt the weight of the small SOG Flash II tanto knife still folded in his pocket. He'd picked it up at a Dick's Sporting Goods in Springfield, VA, buying several other items for a "camping trip" just to provide a basic cover for the knife. He doubted the sixteen-year-old boy who'd sold him the gear would remember a middle-aged Asian man. He'd paid for all of it with cash just to make sure.

Han had two three-man teams that had been roaming the museum since it had opened, and he was certain that they hadn't been spotted. They were too skilled at countersurveillance to be detected by museum security guards. Each team had specific, unique instructions, but one order he'd given to both was the same—remain undetected unless they were needed.

He'd picked teams with two different nationalities—one French, one Spanish. He figured foreigners blended in better at a place like the museum. The teams had flown into the country with one set of passports and would be leaving with another. *Benefits of the Organization,* Han thought.

The man responsible for the death of his son reached the elevated walkway that bisected the middle of the museum and started a slow trek across the nearly three-hundred-foot-long overlook. Han counted at least twenty-five other visitors on the walkway. *Perfect—more cover.*

Han maintained a casual pace, looking right and left, as if searching for a new exhibit to snap pictures of with the Nikon camera still hanging around his neck. He increased his pace, slowly gaining ground on his target, who suddenly stopped halfway across the walkway.

Han paused for a fraction of a second . . . and then kept going, knowing better than to hesitate. He slipped his right hand into his pocket and unfolded the blade with a flick of his thumb. He removed his hand to avoid suspicion, letting the blade hang in his pocket. He remained calm, his body relaxed and prepared for the violent action he was about to take, but more importantly, for what it meant—*reclamation of my son's honor.*

Thirty more feet, and it would be over before Logan West knew it had begun.

Han didn't know why his enemy had stopped, but he didn't care. Only one thing mattered—*this man's death.*

Twenty feet . . .

Han reached back into his pocket and gripped the handle of the blade, preparing to strike. In front of him, Logan West suddenly looked down at his cell phone, his eyes squinting as if confused by something he saw. He pressed a button on the phone in his left hand and looked down at the floor of the museum, as if searching for someone or something.

Something's wrong, Han realized, but it was too late. He was committed to his course of action.

———

Logan stood on the bridge, momentarily studying the most controversial exhibit in the museum—the *Enola Gay*. He'd overheard one of the docents leading a small group of visitors mention that years back someone had thrown a vial of blood on the plane in protest.

He wondered what the men who'd piloted the aircraft had thought and felt, knowing that while the intent of their actions was to end the most violent global conflict the world had seen, the lives of tens of thousands of noncombatants—*innocents*—would be snuffed out in the blink of an eye. *It had to have been horrific, the weight of it*, Logan thought, himself a man who'd made life-and-death decisions, although not on that scale. *And I pray I never have to.*

His eyes scanned past the plane to the space beyond, glancing over the sea of humanity like a predatory bird skimming across the treetops, searching for its next meal.

Bzzz-bzzz-bzzz. The phone in his left hand buzzed, and he saw "Unknown" flash across the high-definition miniature screen. His senses immediately kicked into overdrive at the realization that Task Force Ares' security had somehow been compromised. *No one other than the team members, the president, Jake Benson, and the director of the CIA have this number. God help me. Here we go again with another anonymous phone call,* he thought, momentarily flashing back to the phone call that had started the chase for a nuclear weapon two and a half years ago, and pressed the accept button.

"It's a trap. You need to abort, and you need to abort *right the fuck now, Marine,*" said a voice that shook loose cobwebs of memory in Logan's head.

"Who is this? More importantly, how the *hell* did you get this number?" Logan asked urgently.

"It doesn't matter, what does is that you live to fight another day. This is the only warning you're going to get," the voice added. "If you don't get out of there now, you die, plain and simple. Unlike Atlas, you can't hold up the heavens. Your enemies will rain down hate upon you."

Atlas . . . the heavens . . . The gears turned quickly in Logan's head. He'd heard that specific phrasing before. It was a common misconception that the mythological Titan was holding up the earth, but it was actually the celestial spheres, the cosmos. Even Logan had held that erroneous belief, until he'd been corrected—once. The realization hit him like a proverbial punch to the gut. *No. It can't be.*

He opened his mouth to ask the question that was burning through his psyche, but the encrypted channel started flashing on his phone. *Amira.*

Logan knew better than to hesitate. Like the man who had called him, he knew hesitation was how men died. He disconnected the call to hear Amira speaking urgently over the channel as events overlapped and escalated.

———

Amira was near the staircase of the three-story observation tower at one end of the elevated walkway. The Rolex emblem on top still amused her. *Who the hell sponsors a staircase in a museum? Would corporate shamelessness ever cease?* Although she had to admit, it was excellent marketing. *And they make a damn fine timepiece, even if it is outrageously expensive.*

The tedious nature of her work, especially the art of surveillance, suited her patient disposition. Unlike most others in her profession, she relished the tactical planning that went into each operation. Due to the extremely sensitive nature of her work, she was a firm believer in obtaining every possible advantage over her enemy, whoever and whatever it was. She was as methodical, deliberate, and painstakingly thorough as she was physically fierce and skilled. But in her line of work, she had no choice: it was be better than your opponent or be dead. She preferred the former.

She smiled inwardly and looked down from the highest point in the middle of the hangar. Knowing herself, she was also amused that she was seriously falling for a man like John Quick—sarcastic, irreverent, self-deprecating, and aggressive to the point of near lunacy. *Maybe there really was something to the "Opposites attract" adage.*

Amira hadn't had a serious relationship in a long time. The last had been in college, before she'd been recruited by the agency directly from the University of Maryland, where her father had managed to finagle in-state tuition, even though they'd lived inside the District of Columbia.

What was that?

Logan was halfway across the walkway when he'd stopped in front of the *Enola Gay*. A tourist—*what appeared to be a tourist,* she reminded herself, remembering people were often more than what they seemed—had stopped midstride for a fraction of a second. Amira doubted anyone else on the bridge noticed it. *Hell, I might not have if I didn't have this angle.*

She lifted to her eyes a Canon camera with a compact zoom lens she'd zeroed in at the walkway's distance to provide a full-body close-up when she looked through the viewfinder. What she saw chilled her instantly—a middle-aged Chinese male, dressed like a tourist in white shorts and a tan polo, the outfit complete with a camera dangling around his neck. He looked familiar, even though she was certain she'd never seen this man before.

What's he doing with his right hand? Inside his right front pocket, she saw the wrinkle of fabric as if he were manipulating an object. *Something's not right.*

Amira's senses screamed at her to act, and she hit the "talk" button and spoke quickly into her earbud, "To your right, twenty feet away. Chinese middle-aged male."

No answer. *What the hell?* She scanned the lens to the left and saw Logan speaking, but it wasn't to her or the team. *Had he taken another call from the FBI director?*

She flashed back to the target, the lens focusing on the man's face, which was now turned toward Logan. Recognition struck her like a bolt of lightning—*Lau Gang's father. His son had the same angular jaw and nose. Oh my God.*

Lau Gang had been the head of the team sent to Sudan to attack a Chinese oil exploration site in order to frame the US. She recognized his father because she'd been the one to kill his son inside a building under construction. She'd been up close and personal with his features as she'd plunged one of her stilettos into the back of his head. But before she'd killed him, he'd made a reference to his father, *something about him being less merciful than he was.*

"Logan? Logan? Where the hell are you?"

A moment of fear gripped her at the recognition, but rather than freeze, her training kicked in, and she drew her SIG SAUER P250 compact 9mm pistol from her inside-the-waistband holster under her top.

Logan's voice suddenly filled her ear. "What is it?"

Amira lined up the sights of the pistol on the approaching man.

She didn't want to take a shot in this environment: there were too many civilians on the walkway and the floor below. *Well, this is one way to get the party started.*

She held her finger straight and off the trigger. "Look to your right, *now*. It's Lau Gang's father. Move!"

———

Lau Han watched Logan West's mouth move quickly and quietly, as if talking to an invisible friend, and Han realized he had to be speaking into an earpiece with a built-in microphone he couldn't see.

It's finally time, Han thought, and gripped the blade tighter, at which point the object of his rage turned directly to face Lau Han, bright-green eyes blazing with an intensity and a fury Han himself felt.

The two men glared at each other, the din of the museum falling away outside the intense battlefield cocoon they'd just created.

No talking, Han thought, and attacked.

CHAPTER 10

As Logan stepped backward, the knife flashed forward and up in an arc, streaking by his face, reminding him of how he'd received the scar across his left cheek. He stepped inside the arc and grabbed Lau Han's right wrist with his left hand, delivering a solid punch with his right to the man's midsection.

He was rewarded with a grunt, but Lau held on to the knife and spun to his right toward Logan. The move broke Logan's grasp on his wrist, and as he completed the turn, he brought the blade down, this time trying to slice diagonally across Logan's chest. Logan was too fast, and he blocked the attack with his right forearm and punched the right side of Lau's face at his jawline with two fast blows from his left hand.

A woman let out a scream somewhere on the bridge, and Logan felt, rather than heard, the pause, the moment before real panic raced through the museum like an invisible tidal wave.

Lau staggered, and Logan grabbed the man's wrist with both hands and yanked down hard, slamming the hand with the knife into the glass barrier that prevented visitors from touching the cockpit of the *Enola Gay*.

The impact caused the black blade to fall to the walkway, and

Logan adjusted the position of his hands, putting Lau in a wrist-lock and applying leverage. Logan then lashed out with a short front kick that struck the older man in the left knee, knocking him off balance. Logan raised his hands, lifting and pressing harder as Lau dropped to one knee.

The door in Logan's mind had swung wide open, and the beast that was his fury had been set free.

He stared at the trained operative with a predatory intensity. "You thought you could take me with a *knife?*" Logan growled, his voice low and deliberate.

Lau Gang's father wore a mask of defiance, meeting Logan's gaze, refusing to speak.

"You know, I didn't kill your son," Logan said quietly, even as civilians scattered away from the two combatants on the bridge. He leaned forward within inches of Lau's face, his grip a vise, and growled, "*But I wish I had.* You sent a boy to do a man's work, and that boy died violently."

Lau uttered a guttural cry, the words piercing his soul like the stiletto that had killed his son.

"And the world is a better place for it," Logan said, the last words uttered almost as a whisper.

The steady background of conversational noise had now been replaced by running footsteps echoing across the multitude of surfaces in the enormous hangar.

"And now your failure is complete, because I'm taking you, and my government will hopefully throw you in a dark, dark place for the rest of your days. Now get the fuck off the floor . . . unless you want to resist some more?" Logan asked, the question hopeful in its malicious sarcasm.

"It will never come to pass," Lau said. "No matter what you think, I'll never see a trial."

Logan twisted his hands quickly, and Lau found himself with

his right arm held upward at a forty-five-degree angle in an escort wristlock position. Logan's left arm looped around Lau's right, and both hands pressed down on the bent hand. If Lau struggled, Logan could apply pressure to end any resistance.

"We'll see about that—"

The glass barrier exploded at the same time as the first shot reverberated across the cavernous space, and the screaming began in earnest.

Lau Han seized the moment and twisted his arm free, as if he'd been expecting the opportunity to present itself. Before Logan could react, Lau Han coiled and leapt over the railing, his body soaring toward his objective—the suspended cockpit of the *Enola Gay.*

You've got to be kidding me, Logan thought as he leapt up to the railing to pursue his prey.

The Steven F. Udvar-Hazy Center that was every boy's daydream had just become every parent's worst nightmare.

———

Who the hell is shooting? Amira thought, and realized the shot had come from her right. She'd held off on pulling the trigger at the last moment once she'd seen Logan disarm Lau, but then the glass had shattered, turning the museum into a shooting gallery.

Amira saw a white male in his early thirties wearing a white polo, khakis, and a small black sling bag across his back more than one hundred feet to her right on the walkway. He held a black semiautomatic pistol she couldn't identify from this distance, and he was still focused on the perpendicular walkway below, appearing to line up another shot.

Too many civilians. No clean shot. Have to get closer.

People scattered away from her, spotting the pistol she held in a combat grip, ready for action. Knowing she had no choice and hoping to divert the shooter's attention, she did the only thing she could—pointed the pistol toward the ceiling and fired three quick shots in succession.

Crack-crack-crack!

The shooter's attention turned toward her, but she'd already lowered the pistol, blending in with the fleeing figures moving toward the staircase. She fought her way through the bodies, her eyes focused on the shooter.

She glanced back to the *Enola Gay* just in time to see Logan West leap toward the bomber as Lau scrambled to his feet. *So much for not touching the exhibits.*

She looked back to the shooter, but he was no longer at the railing. *That's not good.* And then she spotted him moving away from her toward the far end of the walkway and a sloping, circular, three-story ramp that led to the main floor below.

And so much for stealth, she thought as she started sprinting toward the escaping shooter.

———

Cole Matthews had spent most of the morning on a guided tour of the James S. McDonnell Space Hangar. His docent was a gentleman in his late sixties who had retired as an electrical engineer from NASA and wanted to stay useful, having a love for space exploration.

By the time Larry Freeman was into his explanation of satellite telemetry and orbits, Cole realized that while he himself might at one point have been the head of the CIA's clandestine paramilitary action arm, he was grossly underqualified to be a tour guide. There were nine groups of subject-matter experts who went through at least twelve periods of instruction and knowledge tests before being certified and assigned to a senior docent, which Larry was.

Larry was midsentence discussing the new generation of anti-satellite missiles, commenting on how the Russians seemed to be ahead of the rest of the world in developing new weapons—at least according to the press—when the first shot was fired into the hangar.

Cole observed the look of confusion on Larry's face, as if the docent's mind was in denial that a gunshot had just broken the early-afternoon silence. Cole, on the other hand, had already unholstered his SIG SAUER P229 Enhanced Elite 9mm pistol.

"Don't worry about the gun, Larry. I'm one of the good guys." Cole smiled, the predator he was finally surfacing. "I'm with the FBI, and you might want to get these people out that exit door in the far corner. And by the way, great tour," he said, turned, and ran into the fray, leaving a stunned-looking Larry standing next to the disabled missile. A few seconds later, three more shots rang out, and Larry was spurred into action, urging people to stay calm and move to the nearest exit.

Good man, Cole thought as he passed the nose of the space shuttle *Discovery,* which occupied the center of the space hangar.

He spoke rapidly into his earbud as he ran. "I'm in the space hangar. Be there in twenty seconds."

But that was before the man near the photo exhibit with a pale European complexion and brown hair pulled a Glock 22 .40-caliber pistol from a camera bag, his intent clear and malevolent.

The man was only fifteen feet away with his back turned to Cole, who immediately adjusted his trajectory midstride and thought, *Welcome to the museum, asshole.*

———

Logan landed on the cockpit of the *Enola Gay,* his tactical tan Oakley boots searching for a grip on the smooth surface of the silver fuselage and rectangular glass panels of the cockpit. His boots found none, and he sprawled forward, landing with a *thwump* as his body hit the bomber.

Lau had somehow maintained his footing and was already moving away toward the right wing of the plane. *Where the hell is he going?* And then he realized Lau's intent—to use the wing to drop to the Thunderbolt airplane suspended on hydraulic lifts underneath the *Enola Gay* and then scamper to the ground below like some kind of middle-aged Jackie Chan.

Even as Logan pursued him, he was impressed. The Chinese operative had to be in his late fifties, and yet he had the agility of a thirty-year-old. *Maybe it's all that ginseng they eat,* Logan thought drily. *Concentrate, jackass,* his mind yelled at him, and all thoughts of holistic healing were wiped from his mind.

Lau reached the wing of the bomber as Logan finally stood. *Fucker's fast. Why do I always have to chase the fast ones?* he thought.

Lau stepped onto the enormous propeller engine, the four blades forming a perfect vertical and horizontal cross.

Logan realized he only had one option. *This is going to hurt like hell.*

As Lau reached down and grasped the right side of the propeller, Logan took two steps and launched himself into the air, praying he had enough momentum. He soared across the huge gap between the fuselage and the engine, which was too big a leap. But the engine wasn't his target.

Oh Christ, I'm not going to make it, he thought, but his left foot landed on the long edge of the left propeller blade. He used his momentum to spring off the blade like a suicidal gymnast and landed on top of the engine, just in time to see Lau leaning on the top of the right propeller blade, preparing to drop into a hanging position.

As Logan balanced himself on top of the engine, he calculated his options once again, and his tactical mind returned only one answer, an answer that was driven by one imperative—*prevent Lau from escaping.*

With complete, reckless abandon, Logan leapt from the engine and tucked both legs up as if performing the world's worst cannonball. As he reached the hanging man, he shot both legs down like pistons, violently driving them into the back of Lau, crushing him against the propeller on which he was suspended. He heard an expulsion of breath, and he thought he felt something crack—*a rib, hopefully*—but he didn't have time to contemplate it.

Exactly as he'd intended—and was crazy enough to try—whatever locking mechanism the museum utilized to keep the propeller in a fixed position gave way with a loud *snap,* and Logan prepared himself for the fall.

The propeller suddenly dropped, spilling the wounded Lau off the blade. Lau's body rotated as he fell, so that as he plummeted to the plane fifteen feet below, he stared up at Logan with fury and pain.

Logan ignored him as he himself concentrated on landing on top of the tail section of the Republic P-47 Thunderbolt fighter aircraft below.

Both men hit at the same time, but with different results.

Lau's back slammed onto the horizontal stabilizer, which bent with the force of the impact but somehow supported him. He lay there, injured and immobile, staring up at the underbelly of the *Enola Gay,* his mouth moving but uttering no sound since he had yet to regain his oxygen supply.

Logan's feet hit the top of the tail section, and he bent his knees, knowing what was coming next. *Bad idea gets worse.* He was propelled into a forward shoulder roll, which carried him off the side of the plane. As he completed the roll, he regained awareness of his surroundings and shot his arms up, hoping he'd judged correctly.

Slam!

His hands grabbed the rear edge of the right wing, and his arms went taut as his momentum was stopped. His legs continued momentarily, swinging up under the wing, and he thought, *Here it comes.*

Knowing it was inevitable, he let go and fell several feet through thin air, curling his head and neck forward and placing his hands behind his head.

Thud!

Logan's body crashed to the floor, and he felt a sharp pain in the back of both hands as they made contact with the unforgiving surface, all the while protecting his skull from serious damage. He lay still, the sounds of chaos in the museum reaching his ears as if for the first time. *Need to move and make sure Lau stays down.*

He rolled onto his side, only to be greeted by the sight of a teenage boy dressed in a Washington Nationals hat, blue shorts, and a white tee shirt staring at him in amazement.

"Didn't you hear the gunshots, kid?" Logan asked, bewildered that the boy was still standing there.

"Not the first time, and I was moving to the exit, but then I saw you and the other guy on the plane," the boy responded. "That was awesome!" he said, suddenly grinning like a lunatic.

Logan didn't feel awesome. In fact, he felt like hell. *Kids nowadays.*

"Yeah. Well. It wasn't my best dismount," Logan said, standing up beneath the wing, a dull throb of pain spreading across his lower back. "Now get the hell out of here before something else happens. I don't need you getting caught in the crossfire."

At the use of the word *crossfire*, reality hit the boy, who suddenly seemed less relaxed. "Thanks for the show, mister," he said, smiled, and joined the rest of the throng running for the exits.

Logan stumbled over to Lau, who was still laid out on the stabilizer. He finally started to sit up, and Logan heard a moan escape his lips. Without hesitation, Logan reached up, grabbed Lau by an arm and his torso and yanked him forward, pulling him off the stabilizer to plummet several more feet to the floor.

A shout of pain rose from the operative, and he rolled over, glaring at Logan with indignation. *It's not your day, old man. Too bad for you.*

Logan leaned down and grabbed the wounded Lau under his left arm. "Get up. And if you try to run, I swear to God I'm going to break your fucking knee, and AARP won't be able to do jackshit for you. You got me?"

Lau hung his head, the thought of speaking to his captor too demoralizing. He knew there was no way out, which also meant his time was almost over. *I'll see you soon, son,* he thought, and exhaled, steadying himself.

"I just have one question," Logan asked. "Why this place?"

Lau straightened up and faced Logan, and Logan sensed the man's demeanor change subtly, growing . . . *more confident? That can't be,* Logan thought.

"Because it was my son's favorite place, but not for the reasons you might think."

"No?" Logan said.

"No. He came here when he was a teen, before he followed me into my line of work," Lau said. "And he recognized it for what it was—is: a display of arrogance, regardless of the technological marvels, by one of the most corrupt countries on this planet. So I thought, 'What better place to seek my vengeance than here?' And now I have it," Lau said, and sighed, emitting a sense of calm.

"How's that? You're about to be in the custody of the US government, subject to special laws for interrogation I'm not even sure you're aware of," Logan said. "It's over for you."

Lau smiled, a genuine smile, not of anger, but of relief. "Maybe for me. But not for *you*. And in the end, you will *lose*. What you're fighting is too big, even for the size of *your* ego."

The conviction was evident, which unsettled Logan. *What the hell is up with this guy?*

There was no time for answers as three shots rang out, and two bullets struck Lau in the back and the head, sending a red mist into the air and across Logan's neck and chest.

Even as Lau's body collapsed to the smooth floor, Logan dove to the ground and rolled behind the large yellow apparatus that held up the right wing of the *Enola Gay*, wondering when his day at the museum would finally end. *If Ben Stiller shows up, I'm really going to lose it.*

CHAPTER 11

As soon as the encounter with Lau had begun, John Quick had asked the retired Marine—specifically, retired Marine Corps Master Sergeant Anthony Raven, now Lieutenant Raven, who was constantly amused at the irony of becoming an officer after all the years of enlisted service—to order his men to post themselves at the exits and assist with the evacuation.

John had known immediately that the fight had been part of an ambush, the entire thing one big setup. He'd also known it was just the beginning.

He'd asked Lieutenant Raven to follow him, even as he'd withdrawn his Colt M1911 .45-caliber pistol—the same one he'd carried in Force Recon and in Iraq—and bolted for the door. *If I have to have backup, at least it's a Marine, even a retired one,* he'd thought, grateful for the Corps once again.

The two men heard the first shot shatter the glass barrier as they'd sprinted out the door and toward the main floor of the hangar, which was on the same level as the security operations center. More shots rang out as they'd made a straight line for the main area, weaving in and out through civilians. The shots had been followed by screams and chaos.

They found themselves just inside the hangar, their view of the *Enola Gay* partially obstructed by other aircraft and exhibits. John scanned for Logan, hoping he had Lau under control. *I told you this was a bad fucking idea, Logan. Goddamnit!*

"Where are you guys? We just came out on the floor, but it's pandemonium. I can't see anything," John said.

No answer, which was when three more shots—the ones that killed Lau Han—came from a shooter no more than thirty yards in front of them.

Bang-bang-bang!

John searched for the man's target and spotted Logan and his captive, even as his captive fell to the floor, apparently struck from the shooter's bullets. *Why the hell did he take him out instead of Logan?*

It didn't matter. He didn't have time to consider it, as the shooter turned and started walking quickly *and directly toward* John and Lieutenant Raven.

Both men simultaneously raised their weapons—John, the Colt M1911; Lieutenant Raven, his Smith & Wesson National Security Model 686, chambered in .38 Special.

"Drop the weapon!" John screamed as the shooter, a pale-skinned man who looked European, finally noticed them. He held a black semiautomatic down low at his side. It was obvious he'd hoped to slip away with the crowd, but John and his new friend had ruined that plan.

Whoever he was, there was no hesitation—the shooter raised his arms with trained proficiency, and all three men opened fire.

As John pulled the trigger, his only thought was for collateral damage. *Please, God, don't let any rounds go wide.*

Boom-boom-boom! Crack-crack!

One of John's rounds struck the man in the chest, and he saw two more small holes appear near his well-placed shot.

The shooter staggered, wounded but not out of the fight. It was only in Hollywood or fiction that people who were shot instantly fell to the ground, a quick and merciful end. Reality was something different, which was why real shooters aimed for the head to permanently end the conversation.

The shooter lined up his sights, and John raised the M1911 slightly. Both men fired, even as two more *cracks* from Lieutenant Raven added to the fire.

Boom-boom!

John's round caught the shooter in the nose, tunneling through and turning the back of his head into a gory mess. But the now-dead man's final act caught John in the chest, and John let out a small groan as he took a knee.

"Holy shit. How bad is it?" Lieutenant Raven asked urgently, moving over to John and looking down at his chest, not seeing any blood.

"I'm . . . fine," John gasped, barely audible. "Vest."

"Thank God," Lieutenant Raven said.

"Go make sure he's down," John said quietly. "I'm going to sit here for a second. Hurts like hell."

"Sir, you shot him in the face with a forty-five. I'm pretty sure he's dead."

"Good point," John said. "Then help me up, and let's go see how my friend is."

———

The shouts, shots, and screams merged into one steady roar that masked Cole Matthews' footfalls as he sprinted the short distance and launched himself at the gunman who now pointed the Glock 22 .40-caliber toward the center of the hangar. His focus was on one thing—stopping him before he pulled the trigger.

He hurtled through the air and slammed into the small of the man's back and was rewarded with a *whewf* as the air was knocked from the shooter's lungs. The man crashed to the floor with Cole on top of him, the Glock still in his right hand.

Cole's immediate concern was the weapon. *I don't need innocent bystanders getting a bullet from this asshole.* He reached up with both hands and grabbed the man's wrist, raising it off the floor and slamming it down. Once. Twice. Three times. *Bingo.*

The shooter let out a string of curses but finally released his grip. *Is that French? Who the hell is this guy?*

Cole yanked the gun away and threw it forcefully to the side, sending the gun skidding and bouncing across the floor until it landed against the glass of a life-sized exhibit of a space suit from the 1960s.

Now disarmed, the man—who'd miraculously regained his breath and strength—focused his efforts on removing Cole from his back, and he delivered two quick elbows with his left arm to Cole's exposed side, his arms still over his head from having thrown the pistol away from the fight.

Rather than risk a cracked rib, Cole rolled to his left, away from his opponent. He sensed rather than saw the man scramble to his feet. *This guy's quick, but I'm quicker.*

He suddenly rolled back *toward* the man and lashed out with a front roundhouse kick with his left foot. The blow landed above the man's ankle, and he tumbled forward off-balance but regained enough control to turn his fall into a forward roll.

The two combatants had moved near a large green screen that served as the photo station where visitors and family members paid to have their images digitally transposed and memorialized in various space environments, including on the moon and inside the space shuttle *Discovery*. Several lights were mounted on individual stands, and a young Middle Eastern man stared frozen in shock at the two men who'd invaded his space. He held a remote for the expensive camera in his hand.

Cole got back on his feet, his eyes boring into the back of his opponent, who also stood up. *What the hell is he doing?* Cole thought as he lowered his right hand to his SIG SAUER P229 Enhanced Elite on his right hip. He didn't want to kill the shooter, but he wasn't about to risk getting shot if the man had another gun.

"He's got a knife!" the young photographer screamed, even as the man spun to face Cole, a black curved blade with a serrated edge in his right hand.

Cole reacted quickly, seizing the initiative before his opponent attacked. He snatched a light-stand tripod, spinning in a blur of speed, converting the stand into an awkward staff and swinging horizontally as the Frenchman lunged forward. His timing was flawless, and the heavy bulb shattered against the man's hand and knife.

Crash!

Glass embedded itself in the man's wrist and hand, and the Frenchman let out a true cry of pain and horror. Blood splattered the floor of the museum as several deep gashes opened. The knife fell to the ground and bounced away.

Cole reversed his hands and stepped forward, the tripod bottom now aimed at the man's chest. A series of flashes lit up the impromptu battleground as Cole drove the tripod into the man's chest and knocked him backward, propelling him directly into the giant green screen. His arms flailed and blood sprayed across the fabric as if he were some modern action painter, the French reincarnation of Jackson Pollock.

The bloody screen finally collapsed around the man, and it looked to Cole as if the man were being swallowed by a swirling green black hole, disappearing completely as he fell to the ground in a mixture of blood and cloth.

Cole never hesitated. He walked over to where the wounded Frenchman was struggling to free himself and launched a well-aimed kick.

Smack!

His boot landed on the side of the Frenchman's head, and the man finally went limp.

Hope he doesn't bleed out, but oh well if he does, Cole thought as blood poured out of the unconscious man's wrist. *Damnit. He's pulling a Gerry Cooney on me,* he thought, recalling the boxer's bloody loss to Larry Holmes.

He bent over, grabbed the man's dark polo, now darkened even more with blood, and tore several strips from it.

"Is he dead?" the young photographer asked.

"Not yet," Cole said. "And I'm trying to keep it that way."

Cole wrapped several swaths around the man's wounded wrist until he was satisfied with his impromptu battle dressing. *Should keep him alive, at least until a paramedic gets here.*

He looked up at the young man, who glanced around at what had once been his livelihood. "Hey, thanks for the heads up on the knife," Cole said. "I need this bastard alive, and that gave me the half second I needed to act."

"No problem, sir," the photographer said politely, though he was obviously still processing the events.

"And don't worry about this mess," Cole said. "Come find me before this day is over, and I'll make sure it's all replaced, brand-new."

The man nodded as Cole spotted an armed security guard moving in their direction from the main hangar. He waved him over hurriedly.

Good. He can keep an eye on this guy while I go see if anyone else needs help.

Cole stood up, stepped over to the photographer, and offered his hand, which the young man accepted. "Like I said, come find me, and I'll take care of you. You earned it. Now I gotta go."

He turned and ran to meet the security guard, leaving the young photographer to stare after him before sitting down, the surge of adrenaline finally dissipating in the aftermath of the fight.

———

Amira knew there was only one exit—the large, corkscrew ramp that wound its way to the first floor—at the far end of the suspended walkway. In the midst of the chaos, she'd sprinted, appearing to be just another panicked bystander, gaining ground on the shooter in the white polo.

By the time she was within forty feet of the corkscrew, she spotted her next obstacle—the bottleneck at the top of the ramp. It was now packed with a mass of civilians who'd also decided to use that way as their escape route.

Amira spotted the shooter, his black sling bag weaving in and out of the crowd until he disappeared down the ramp.

Damnit. Crowd's too thick. Think-think-think.

She looked around for options, even as she moved forward, closing in on the bottleneck of human flesh blocking the fifteen feet to the ramp.

She smiled inwardly. *Too bad John's not here to see this one; he'd think what I'm about to do is crazy-awesome.* And then her professional killer's mind added, *Focus, Amira. Tell him about it after the fact. Time to work.*

Amira sprinted to the edge of the walkway and leapt upward as if flinging herself over the side of the three-story drop. She landed gracefully, balancing on the two railings—the outer one higher than the inner by six inches—that ran the length of the walkway and allowed for various placards to be placed in front of the suspended exhibits. She concentrated on her next movement, and the sounds of chaos and fear fell away. *Here goes everything.*

She took two carefully placed steps and launched off the railing, soaring through the air three stories above the main floor like a trapeze artist with a death wish in a purple hoodie and black yoga pants. Her jump carried her forward, and she started to drop. *Please let this be right.*

Smack! Her hands caught the right front wheel of an enormous bi-wing glider suspended slightly above the walkway. The glider shifted and swung with the sudden weight of a new passenger, but the cables held, creaking loudly with the strain.

Amira reached forward and moved to the left wheel, swinging her legs front and back like a circus performer, keeping her eyes on the next obstacle, which she knew was the most dangerous part of her aerial course. *Now.*

Reaching maximum momentum, she kicked out with both legs and released her grip on the wheel, flinging herself forward, her body starting its new course parallel to the ground and providing her with a temporary view of the ceiling. But then her legs and gravity carried her forward, pulling her torso upward, allowing her to see her final destination, and she knew she'd calculated her leap of faith correctly. *Thank God.*

Amira Cerone crashed onto the plastic cover of the *Double Eagle II* suspended gondola located directly adjacent to the second level of the corkscrew. Grabbing one of the wires with her left hand to control her landing, she bent her knees to absorb the shock and, just as quickly, sprang forward, appearing to the onlookers who'd spotted her to bounce off the gondola.

She cocked her right arm up in front of her midflight, soaring over the railing of the corkscrew just in time to see her target turn and look at her. *Too late for you, sweetie.* His bright-blue eyes went wide—which was all she had time to see—as she crashed into his upper body, striking him on the side of his head with her forearm. Their momentum carried them into several civilians, who were knocked down like human bowling pins and sent tumbling down the ramp into other bystanders.

Amira was a former member of the CIA's LEGION program, which deployed trained assassins to various stations across the globe. That had been her profession until she'd met John Quick and Logan West in Sudan six months ago. She'd been good, *extremely good, as in one of the best in the world,* at that profession, with blinding hand-to-hand skills that were second to none, as she'd proven time and time again. *And now is one more of those times.*

Amira was already on her feet as the shooter began to stand, and she delivered a fast, low roundhouse kick that connected with his jaw, knocking him back down to his knees. She moved in and brought both hands up, her fingers interlocked, intent on ending the confrontation quickly. She started to drop her weight and bring her arms down, but she was jostled to the side by a panicked man trying to escape the new threat.

The shooter took advantage of the brief respite, reached under his polo, and withdrew the compact CZ 75 pistol he'd used earlier.

Damnit, Amira thought, and changed tactics instantly, refusing to allow the shooter to risk the lives of the civilians around them. In an effortless motion, a black stiletto appeared in her right hand from under her purple hoodie.

Even as the man—who moved quickly—brought the pistol up toward her, Amira stepped inside the arc of the gun, grabbed his arm with her left hand, and plunged the stiletto into his side repeatedly with violent precision.

The man's blue eyes—now locked with Amira's own pale-blue gunslinger gaze—widened, this time as brilliant, hot pain lanced through his body. *Should have dropped the gun. Bad call.*

Rather than wait for him to bleed out, Amira withdrew the stiletto and switched grips in a blur of speed. She slid her left hand to the pistol as with her right she pierced his wrist at the base of his hand.

He screamed at the new pain, but his fingers opened reflexively, and she pulled the gun away from his bloody grip. He stumbled forward two steps but somehow remained standing, and Amira stepped aside, morbidly curious as to how soon he'd collapse and die. Unfortunately for him, it was too long.

A young man with long hair ran down the ramp from above them and crashed into the dying shooter. The impact drove the shooter forward *into and over the railing*, and Amira watched silently as he disappeared from sight.

A moment later, she heard the distinct *thud*—even above the noise—as he hit the museum floor two stories below. A new shriek—this time of horror—rose from the ground.

Someone always screams, Amira thought as she calmly wiped the blood off the stiletto, slid it back into its sheath under her hoodie, and joined the rest of the descending throng.

What none of them realized was that the second team that Lau Han had activated was continuing to follow its instructions: three Spanish killers and former Spanish Special Forces Command green berets blended in with the civilians and slipped out the numerous exits now secured by the federal police.

CHAPTER 12

It took several hours to sort through the chaos in the aftermath of the museum confrontation. The security guards attempted to corral the visitors—whose number measured in the high hundreds— outside the museum, but many fled to their vehicles as soon as they hit the parking lot, even before the local first responders arrived.

One of the security guards provided emergency medical treatment for the bleeding-but-alive Frenchman, cleaning the gash and staunching the heavy loss of blood. The sole survivor now rested on a cot in the medical section of the security operations center, waiting for a transfer to the Fairfax County Adult Detention Center, which held a contract to detain federal prisoners on an "as-needed" basis.

Logan had called Jake immediately and explained how the situation had been an ambush orchestrated out of revenge by Lau Gang's father. They'd managed to take one of the French team alive, but he refused to speak, requesting diplomatic immunity and a phone call to the French embassy, both requests that Logan initially shrugged off.

They'd had multiple conversations throughout the afternoon

after Jake Benson—in his director of the FBI hat—had dispatched Assistant Director William Burgess in charge of the Washington DC Field Office to personally oversee the investigation at the museum. Assistant Director Burgess had not been read in to Task Force Ares, but Jake had ordered him to provide "any and all assistance" to Logan and his team.

The assistant director was a career agent who'd seen all aspects of both covert and clandestine operations, and he was smart enough to know when not to ask questions, even at the current apex of his career. He was a true professional, and Logan and John both appreciated that immensely, going to great lengths to show that appreciation through the respect they showed him.

Logan looked down at his watch, which displayed 1601 in dark-gray digital numbers. Jake was still at the Rowley training center in the wake of the ambush of the director of the NSA and had no idea when he'd be leaving. The plan was to link up at Ares headquarters the next morning, and Jake hoped to have more information on the perpetrators of both ambushes, since multiple FBI forensic teams were processing the crime scenes.

Logan, John, Amira, and Cole—the last three who jokingly referred to themselves as Team West, a moniker they loved in direct proportion to how uncomfortable it made Logan—sat in the security operations center, combing through multiple videos from multiple camera angles, searching for additional shooters they might have missed.

"There's nothing on any of the surveillance feeds," Amira said. "I've looked."

"Then we've missed something," Logan said in exasperation, more at himself than at the situation.

"I know my trade, and I'm telling you—either this was Lau's only team, or the other one is so good at their job that we'll never be able to pick them out," Amira said.

"Goddamnit," Logan said. "There has to be something." He still hadn't had a chance to tell them about the phone call that had warned him of the impending ambush. They'd been surrounded by police officers, security guards, and paramedics since the last shot had been fired.

"If there is, you know the forensics guys will find it," Cole added.

"I know," Logan replied. *I have to tell them. John won't believe it.*

"Brother, we need to talk," John suddenly injected into the conversation. His tone indicated to all four of them that this talk needed to be private.

Logan nodded. "I know, but not about what you think." Logan turned to Assistant Director Burgess and Lieutenant Christenson, who were huddled around a conference room table near the monitors and control panels. They were discussing when and on what to brief the press, who'd been herded into the main foyer near the ticket booths and were harassing the FBI for a statement.

"Gentlemen, excuse me," Logan said, and the conversation stopped. Both men looked up, waiting for Logan to continue. "Can we get the room for a few minutes? I need to discuss a sensitive matter with my team. I apologize for the inconvenience, and I hate kicking you out of your own operations center, Lieutenant, but there's something that can't wait, and trust me when I tell you it's something you don't want to know about," Logan finished.

"You got it," Assistant Director Burgess said, and turned to the head of the museum's security. "Come on, Lieutenant. I need some coffee, and my wife keeps telling me to try one of those McLattes or whatever the hell they're called. I'm buying."

"You know, as a former Ranger, I can't drink anything other than black coffee, sir. It's forbidden," Lieutenant Christenson said, and then grinned. "But since you're buying, I may just try one and have them put four or five extra shots of espresso in it."

"Jesus Christ. You trying to give yourself a heart attack?" Assistant Director Burgess said as they walked out the door.

"After today's excitement, sir, that's the least of my concerns. If a bullet didn't get me, sure as shit a McDonald's latte won't either." And then the door closed, leaving Team West alone for the first time that day.

"I like that guy," John said. "He's one of us in every sense of the word," he added, and grinned.

"I'm glad you've got your sense of humor back, because you're going to need it after I tell you who called right before the fighting began." Logan said seriously. "Everyone grab a seat at the table."

"You're such a killjoy," Cole said. "Thanks to your impatience, this turned into a great field trip. Look. I even got a souvenir!" he said in mock excitement, holding up for the umpteenth time the picture the young photographer had delivered to the security operations center more than an hour ago in an attempt to assist the investigation.

The ten-by-twelve-inch glossy photo showed a background on the surface of the moon, complete with the command module from the Apollo 11 mission. Digitally imposed were the two figures of Cole Matthews and the French shooter, locked in battle and appearing to defy gravity. "No matter what, I'll always have this. In fact, it's going on the wall back at our little clubhouse."

"Are you done?" Logan asked.

"For now. Feel free to carry on, Mr. West," Cole said, and proudly put the photograph back on the table.

"Thanks. But before I get to it, I need to say something," Logan said.

"Here it comes," John whispered to Amira, even though the other three could hear him. "It's the 'You-were-right-John-I-should-have-listened-to-you' part of the presentation."

"Would you shut it for just one second?" Amira said, chastising him.

"No. He's right," Logan said as sincerely as he could. "I let my emotions get the better of me. As a recovering alcoholic, I'm more self-aware than I used to be. I know you've all seen it, the way I've been suppressing my anger at Mike's death. It's like I'm living in a perpetual state of outrage, and I'm trying to manage it. But it's hard, *really hard*."

There was a moment of silence, and then John broke it. "We know, brother. You'd have to be an idiot—which you're *not*, most of the time—to not know that we've been watching you closely. We've got your back, but we also don't want you making rash decisions that could get you killed." He paused to let the weight of his words sink in, and then continued. "Christ, Logan, could you imagine what Sarah would do to me if I let you die?" John said, and grinned.

"She is fierce," Logan acknowledged, smiling.

"You just need to figure out how to deal with it, *and* you need to let us know how we can help," Amira said. "We're all in this together."

There it is, Logan thought, feeling the gravity of his responsibility and the terror at letting them down. They were more than a team. For better or worse, they were now family, brothers—and one sister—in arms.

"Thank you," Logan said quietly, and took a deep breath to regain his composure. "Okay. I've said my piece *and* exceeded my daily quota for admitting I made a mistake. Bottom line—I won't do something that stupid again, and I'm sorry for putting all of you at risk. Don't hesitate to put me back in the box if I start to wander."

"Consider it done," Cole said. "Now get to the good stuff. Who the hell called you right before the fun started?"

When Logan answered, John's only response was simple. "No fucking way."

"Way," Logan retorted. "And it means this thing just got a lot bigger, and we have a new player on the board."

"Are you absolutely sure, as in cross-your-heart-and-hope-to-die sure?" John asked quietly, all humor gone from his voice, regardless of the words.

"Absolutely, brother," and then Logan told them a story that he and John knew well.

PART III

BEFORE THE SANDBOX

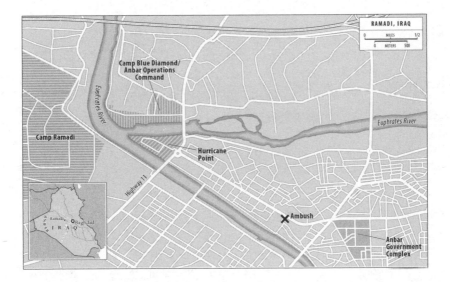

CHAPTER 13

March 2004
Ramadi, Iraq

Captain Logan West studied the passing scenery as the three-vehicle convoy turned west and away from the Al Anbar Provincial Government Center situated squarely in the middle of the city along the main Amman–Baghdad road, which the US military renamed Highway 11 when the occupation began in 2003.

The capital of Al Anbar Province, Ramadi lay seventy miles west of Baghdad along the Euphrates River, which, running west to east, served as its northern boundary. Just west of the city, a large canal branched off to the southeast and eventually emptied, ten miles away, into Lake Habbaniyah, making the city look like a giant pointed triangle. The irony wasn't lost on Captain West, as Ramadi itself served as the southwest corner of the infamous Sunni Triangle. The tip of the city was known as Hurricane Point, a small palace complex formerly belonging to Saddam Hussein and now a combat outpost for an infantry company and weapons company from 2nd Battalion 4th Marine Regiment, nicknamed the Magnificent Bastards by its commanding officer in the 1960s.

From Hurricane Point, the city of four hundred thousand mostly Sunni Iraqis sprawled out to the east and southeast. Orchards of Iraqi date palm trees—one of the main Iraqi exports—were strewn along the river, canal, and throughout the city. Even though it was in the middle of the Iraqi desert—which was the entire country—Ramadi was a habitable environment except for one thing, the nest of insurgent activity that the US army had kicked over.

Thanks to its Sunni population, Ramadi had been subsidized by oil income and blood money from the Hussein regime for years. The patronage system had slowly deteriorated the societal fabric of the city, as normal civic functions such as law, taxes, and the judicial system were used as leverage to control the population. The rich became richer; the poor become poorer—*an urban evolution that seemed to know no national or geographic boundary,* Captain West reflected as he thought about US cities like Detroit, Chicago, New Orleans, and Baltimore. *It's human nature,* he realized, marred by greed, power, and envy.

And now that Baghdad was under reconstruction by a mostly Shia ruling class, the main source of income for the citizens of Ramadi had been cut off. What remained was a city rife with instability and uncertainty, neither of which were good for the US forces charged with rebuilding it.

While the city had been run largely as a tribal society, it was now occupied by disorganized, former-regime military units, large criminal elements, and a blossoming insurgency.

First Marine Expeditionary Force—known as I MEF—was in the final stages of assuming operational control from the US army for all of Al Anbar Province, including the city of Ramadi. During that transition, the commanding general of I MEF had emphasized the need to work with the local tribal leaders in order to help create a stable and safe environment. Every Marine knew a brutal fight was coming, but if working with the local Sunni leaders provided the Marines with even the slightest tactical advantage, it was worth the effort. And Lieutenant General Jack Longstreet was known as a Marine and a man who put in the work required to get the job done. It was also why the general had been willing to personally meet with several tribal leaders at the Provincial Government Center in the middle of the city.

One of the senior sheikhs not only had intelligence on a local insurgent group that was in late-stage planning of a major attack against the Marines, but also reportedly knew of a different group tied to al-Qaeda in Iraq that was involved in an external plot, another 9/11-style, mass-casualty event intended to focus US attention inward and ultimately draw the US out of Iraq.

After 9/11, the US government had pulled out all the stops in investigating any and all threats to the homeland, including incorporating the FBI into overseas operations through Operations Order 1015. In addition to its primary purpose of collection and analysis of all information pertaining to any threats against the US, the order also integrated FBI assets into both deployed military and CIA units in Iraq.

Order 1015 was how Marine Captain Logan West found himself in the backseat of a Humvee not only with General Longstreet, but also with FBI Special Agent Mike Benson, a hulking, muscular African American whose size made the confined space of the all-terrain vehicle look like a clown car. It was his job to vet the veracity and accuracy of the intelligence before reporting it back to Baghdad and, ultimately, to FBI Headquarters in Washington DC.

The meeting had occurred, but the sheikh with the intelligence had failed to show. None of the other leaders had been able to reach him on his cell phone, a fact that had sent Captain West into a heightened state of alert. He didn't believe in coincidences, and as General Longstreet's personal security detail for the urban rendezvous, he'd quietly urged the general to shorten the meeting in order to return to the safety of Camp Blue Diamond, the new home of the Anbar Operations Center across the Euphrates River from Hurricane Point.

Unlike many general officers, General Longstreet understood and respected the advice of his subordinates, which was why he'd never questioned Captain West's judgment, had pretended to receive an urgent text message on his encrypted BlackBerry, and had ended the meeting with extraordinary deference and a display of respect for the tribal leaders. There was no doubt in Captain West's mind that they had believed the general was being called back to his operations center to handle a crisis. While they didn't relish the occupation of their city by US forces, they did respect the position of the man charged with overseeing the stabilization and transition.

"What do you think, Captain West?" General Longstreet said as he turned around in the front passenger seat to address the young officer sitting behind him.

"I'm sorry, sir. It doesn't make sense. No way they go through all this trouble to get a meeting with you and then have the main act not show up for the performance. I don't like it. The bad guys know we're here, and what better way to welcome the new kids on the block than to take out their leader?" Captain West replied.

"I agree with the captain's assessment, sir," Special Agent Benson said from the seat next to Logan's. "Although to be honest, I sure as hell hope he's wrong. I've only been in country for two months helping set up the FBI's Baghdad operations center. This is the first trip I've made out here, and I'd prefer it if it weren't my last."

Captain West nodded. There was something about the man that set him at ease. After ten years in the Marine Corps, Captain West could spot a professional warrior, whether he or she was military, law enforcement, or intelligence. The man also had a sincerity about him that was hard to fake, *and* he had volunteered to come to Iraq to the front lines and serve his country. For Captain West, *that* said everything about the man.

"Is this your first deployment?" Captain West asked the FBI special agent.

"To Iraq, yes. But overall? No. As I'm sure you have, I've been to a few places, some of them better, and some much worse than here. The bad guys are global, Captain West, and I go where the work takes me," Special Agent Benson said.

"Fair enough, sir. I reckon you can handle yourself, then, if this goes sideways," Captain West responded, and turned back to the passing scenery of the city.

So far, so good, Captain West thought as the convoy navigated a slight turn in the road to the right. *It's a two-kilometer straight shot to Hurricane Point from here, a right turn over the bridge, and home safe.*

"Sir, can you hand me the prick-117 handset, please?" Captain West asked, referring to the AN/PRC-117 radio the Humvees used for internal communications between vehicles.

The general didn't respond, raised his eyebrows at Captain West, and handed him the handset, extending the cord into the backseat.

"Thanks, sir," Captain West said, pressed the talk button, and spoke into the handset. "Gunny, you got anything back there? We're on the homestretch."

"Negative, sir. There's a little less civilian traffic, but it's not totally gone," Gunnery Sergeant John Quick, Captain West's Force Reconnaissance platoon sergeant, replied from the third vehicle, which Captain West had dubbed Tail-End Gunny in deference to a World War II British Royal Air Force bomber's tail. The US military had learned a harsh lesson early in the occupation: a sudden absence of any children, civilians, or other life was a threat indicator that meant there was a very high likelihood of an imminent attack in the immediate area. "It's just me and the lesser captain, chilling out, enjoying the ride," he added.

"Gunny, I told you how he doesn't like to be called that," Captain West replied. "And whatever you do, don't call him Captain America. He fucking hates that."

A new voice suddenly emitted from the encrypted radio. "You know I can hear you, right, Logan?" Captain Steve Rodgers—spelled differently than the Marvel superhero—said. Captain Rodgers was a joint terminal air controller—known as a JTAC—from First Air Naval Gunfire Liaison Company at Camp Pendleton, California. "And I was always partial to the Punisher. There's no give in that guy."

Logan heard Gunny Quick in the background say sarcastically, "Like most Marines. That's so cliché. You're going to have to come up with something better than that, Captain Other."

"Glad you two are getting along," Captain West said. "Now stay sharp. I'll see you back at base. Out."

"Are they always like that?" Special Agent Benson asked, amusement written all over his face.

"Gunny Quick is, sir. In fact, I don't know a more sarcastic soul on this planet," Captain West said. "But I also don't know a fiercer warrior when it comes to a fight," he added. "It all evens out in the end."

"Captain West is one thousand percent correct, Special Agent Benson," General Longstreet added. "It's also why I brought him and his sidekick."

Captain West leaned over the middle of the backseat and said loudly enough for the general to hear, "I'm pretty sure I'm the sidekick."

"You guys are definitely a rare breed, but at least I know I'm in good—" was all Special Agent Benson had time to say as the lead vehicle suddenly stopped in the middle of the road, the big wheels kicking up dirt and sand as the Humvee slid to a halt.

Sergeant Matthew Childress, the general's driver for the duration of the deployment, had been momentarily distracted by the banter in the backseat. As a result, when the first Humvee slammed on its brakes, Sergeant Childress reacted too slowly. Realizing his error, he'd managed to swerve to the right as he slammed on the brakes and missed the first Humvee by several feet before skidding to a halt.

"Good Christ, Childress," Captain West said from the backseat as he leaned forward. "Are you trying to get us killed?"

No answer. *What the hell?* Captain West thought. And then he saw what had transfixed both the young sergeant and the senior Marine officer in all of Iraq, and his blood turned cold. It was a sight that would haunt him for years to come, but he didn't know it at the moment. The dream would change, but the helplessness and horror would be constant.

Standing before them, less than ten yards away, was a teenaged boy with an old donkey hitched to a wheelbarrow with leather straps. The donkey looked as beaten as the wheelbarrow, which was covered by a burlap sack, a fact that chilled Logan's blood even more. But more unsettling was the way the boy eerily pointed directly at General Longstreet in an accusatory manner.

That can't be good. I hate it when I'm right, Captain West thought. And then what he'd feared the most happened: his day went sideways.

CHAPTER 14

B-BOOM!

The IED inside the covered wheelbarrow detonated, triggering the ambush and tearing apart the donkey and the boy. Chunks of gray, furry flesh were flung in all directions, and there was a loud *smack* as something heavy hit the windshield of the Humvee.

Captain West found himself staring into the blinking, lifeless eyes of the teenager, his head somehow momentarily suspended against the vehicle's ballistic glass. The head finally fell away, bounced off the Humvee's hood, and rolled off into the sand-swept street.

"Go! Go! Go!" West shouted at Sergeant Childress, knowing the worst was likely yet to come. He reached for the radio handset, but he never made it.

A tremendous roar suddenly engulfed the Humvee, and West felt the vehicle lift up and tilt to the right as the sun was blotted out by debris and flying earth. A deafening ringing and buzzing suddenly drowned out the roar, and he realized he'd likely ruptured an eardrum.

The angle of tilt on the Humvee increased, and West braced himself for the impact as he suddenly found himself perpendicular to the street. *Here we go,* he thought, but the vehicle somehow stopped on the passenger side, standing straight up. *That's one small mercy.*

West heard muffled voices through his diminished hearing, followed by a faint *pop-pop-pop. And now they're shooting at us,* he thought, a realization that spurred him into action. He reached forward into the front seat to pat General Longstreet on the shoulder to check on his status.

"Are you hurt, sir?" West shouted.

He heard an incomprehensible muffled response but at least saw a thumbs-up from the front seat.

Thank God. Step one—check. Step two—get the fuck out of here before we become target practice.

Special Agent Mike Benson had the same thought, and as Captain West checked on the general, Benson found a foothold on which to stand and opened the rear driver's side door by pushing upward. Momentum grabbed the heavy door, and it swung forward and away, remaining propped open. Sunlight, dirt, and sand poured into the vehicle all at once.

"Through here!" Benson screamed down into the vehicle. "It's our only choice!"

The sounds of battle grew louder as the ringing slowly subsided, and West heard the radio erupt with Gunny Quick's voice. "Get the hell out of the Humvees! We've got multiple enemy on both sides of the street. We've got to get away from the vehicles. There's a three-story building forty meters on the left, but you have to *get out now!*"

The urgency in Gunny Quick's voice sent all four men into furious action.

"Move! I'll help each of you up and come out last," Benson shouted as he reached down and pulled Captain West up and toward the opening.

The sound of small arms fire reached West's clearing head, and a new sound—a *much louder* one—joined the fight as the gunner on the Mk 19 40mm automatic grenade launcher mounted on Gunny Quick's vehicle opened fire.

Thwoop! Thwoop! Thwoop! Thwoop! Thwoop!

Rough hands gripped his torso and pushed upward as West managed to grab the frame and pull at the same time. His Kevlar helmet bounced off the doorframe, and then he found himself hanging out the opening. A terrifying thought occurred to him: *Please don't let one of these assholes get a lucky shot.*

Motivated by fear, he pulled his legs out of the Humvee and flattened himself on the side of the vehicle. Knowing time was running out, he leaned in and shouted, "My M4!"

Special Agent Benson was once again one step ahead of him and already had his modified M4 in hand, passing it to him through the opening.

This guy's great for an FBI agent, West thought. "Now the general! Hurry! It's turning into fucking *Blackhawk Down* up here!" he screamed, referring to the infamous ambush on the Army Rangers and Delta operators in Somalia in 1993.

Gunny Quick's Humvee had pulled close to the upturned vehicle and was now fully engaged in the fight. West didn't have time to look around. His only priority was getting the general out of the Humvee and to some semblance of safety.

Seconds later, General Longstreet, notoriously fit and a former Force Reconnaissance officer himself, was through the opening. West never hesitated. "On the ground, sir, and take this! Shoot anything that moves!" he shouted over the noise of the gunfire and grenade launcher. The initial haze had cleared, and the full warrior that was Captain Logan West was present and accounted for with one thing in mind—*pain for the enemy.*

He pushed his M4 into the general's hands. The commanding

officer accepted the weapon, grinned maliciously in acknowledgment, his own battle fury now fully engaged, and said, "Absolutely." He dropped off the side of the Humvee and into the fray.

Moments later, Sergeant Childress, the smallest of their fire team, scrambled up and out, leaping to the ground below, his M4 searching for targets.

"Your turn, Big Man!" West screamed into the Humvee.

Benson nodded. "Here. Take this," he said, and passed his Kevlar helmet—all four of the vehicle's occupants had been wearing both Kevlar helmets and flak vests—to Captain West.

West set it aside and concentrated on the new task—helping the enormous, muscular FBI special agent out of the ruins of the Humvee.

Benson struggled through the opening, managing to prop himself halfway out. Unfortunately, he wasn't able to get enough leverage to get his legs all the way out.

West leaned into the darkness of the vehicle and grabbed Special Agent Benson's tan cargo pants, pulling upward as he yelled, "Scoot forward! You may fall off the side, but it will get you out of this death trap!"

The sounds of the raging battle were slightly dampened inside, and Captain West had a vertiginous feeling as he hung upside down, accompanied by an irrational thought that he'd fall back inside the vehicle, unable to escape.

Special Agent Benson's legs went flying by his face, and West reverse-crunched his way up to the opening in time to see the big FBI man roll off the side of the vehicle to the ground below.

West didn't hesitate but followed him over the side, landing on his feet and getting a glimpse of the carnage for the first time.

While Captain West's Humvee lay on its right side, the first Humvee that had stopped short of the boy and the donkey had been blown up *onto its left side*. The vehicles' undercarriages faced each other, separated by an enormous crater at least twenty feet across. The driver of Gunny Quick's Humvee—Sergeant Edward Ramirez—had pulled the surviving vehicle in front and perpendicular to the two Humvees on their sides. As a result, the three vehicles formed an upside-down U-shaped wall of protection from enemy fire.

Miraculously, the four Marines of the first vehicle had escaped relatively unscathed and were searching for targets with their assault rifles. Insurgents from both sides of the street fired from rooftops and several windows. The Marines' marksmanship and training were already earning dividends, as West watched two men in black-clad clothing sustain multiple gunshots to the face and plummet to the sand thirty feet below the rooftop they'd been using as an ambush position. *Good. Two less of the bastards to deal with.*

But no matter how well trained the Marines were, West knew they had to move soon, before the insurgents gathered the courage and numbers to assault their position.

"Sir, we've got to get off this street," West said to General Longstreet, as West drew his personal sidearm, a Kimber Tactical II .45-caliber pistol for which he'd obtained special permission to bring to the desert.

"You want your M4 back?" Longstreet asked. "I still have my 1911 from my recon days."

As if in response, West leaned around the front of the Humvee, spotted an Iraqi male with an AK-47 creeping along the side of the street toward them, and fired two shots. The first round struck the insurgent in the throat; the second, in the head, finishing the job and sending him face-first into the street.

"I'm good," West replied. His marksmanship had made the point. "You'll need it more than I will, with what I have in mind."

"Which is?" Longstreet asked, not concerned but extremely

interested in how the Force Recon officer intended to get them out of the kill zone.

"Wait here, and get them ready to move on my mark, sir," West said, and sprinted around the crater to the rear driver's side door of Gunny Quick's Humvee. He glanced up to see the Mk 19 gunner rotate to the left side in the turret, searching for targets.

The rear door opened slightly, and West saw Gunny Quick open his mouth to speak when the gunner let loose with another quick volley of 40mm grenades.

Thwump! Thwump! Thwump!

West looked up to see the grenades strike a low wall on the second-story rooftop of a stone building. The two insurgents who had been using it for cover were blown backward and vanished in the explosion of shrapnel, smoke, and chunks of wall.

"Wow. That was awesome," Quick said, and looked back at his commanding officer. "You have a plan." The question was more of a statement, for after years of training with Captain Logan West, Quick had no doubt his platoon commander had an idea of how to get them out of the mess in which they found themselves. *It's probably going to be a little crazy, like he is, but that's why they call him Wild West,* Quick thought.

"First, we need to get off the streets. Our best bet is that three-story building to the right of the one the gunner just hit. It's got the highest viewpoint in this area. And we'll have at least two hundred feet of standoff from the fuckers on the other side of the street," West said.

The ambush had occurred in a stretch of highway that had four lanes—two in each direction—and a low, concrete median that separated them. While the homes and buildings to the right were near the road, there was an extra swath of dirt and grass between the highway and another street that ran parallel to it in front of the neighborhood on their left. It was this distance that was currently their best friend and worst enemy—the insurgents didn't have a high enough angle to shoot over the Humvees, but once the Marines broke cover, they'd all be exposed and in the open. *But we'll definitely die if we stay here,* West thought.

While the gunner had hit a two-story home, West hadn't seen any movement from the three-story one next to it. *That's our out. We just need to get there.*

"We'll have good fields of fire, and Captain Rodgers can start working his magic with his radio and call in rotary close air support out of TQ," West said.

"Already done. We should have two SuperCobras on station within six to seven minutes. The pilots were in the birds on the deck since the general was out here. They're scrambling a Pioneer drone, but that won't be here for at least twelve minutes," Rodgers said.

"Good on the flyboys for being prepared. You didn't call Hurricane Point and ask them to scramble the QRF by chance, did you?" West asked, referring to the quick reaction force on standby at Hurricane Point.

More rounds peppered the exposed passenger side of the vehicle, and Captain Rodgers winced. "As a matter of fact, I did," he responded, smiling. "They'll be here about the same time or a little bit after the Cobras."

West nodded, and said, "I may have to take back some of those bad things I said about you behind your back. Not all, just some." He grinned wildly, adding, "Close the door, and as soon as we line up next to you, start rolling toward the building. We're going to have to make two trips because the Humvee won't shield all of us at once. This is going to be exciting." West turned and ran back to the Humvees to assemble the Marines and lone FBI special agent.

"You know he's a little nuts, right?" Rodgers said to Gunny

Quick as he watched Captain West issue orders to the Marines engaged in the fight.

"Absolutely, sir," Quick said. "And it's one of the reasons why we love him. He'd do anything for us, and vice versa."

Rodgers absorbed the sentiment, nodded, and said, "Semper Fi, Gunny. Let's get some."

CHAPTER 15

The plan was simple . . . and extremely dangerous. Three Marines from the lead Humvee and General Longstreet would go on the first trip. Captain West, Special Agent Benson—who'd refused to go with the first stack—Sergeant Childress, and a remaining Marine from the first Humvee, Staff Sergeant Tommy Farrell, who carried an M249 SAW 5.56mm light machine gun with a bipod and ACOG scope, would provide cover from the front and rear end of both Humvees. If the two ruined Humvees and crater had to serve as their Alamo, Captain West wanted as much firepower as possible. *Four shooters, four fields of fire. It's as good as it's going to get,* West thought.

As soon as the four Marines were lined up, with General Longstreet third in the stack, the Humvee started rolling, and West silently said a prayer to the gods of war to keep them safe. The vehicle picked up speed and pulled away, and West turned back to his sector of fire, the safety off. *All right, motherfuckers. You started this. Come and try and finish it.*

Two Iraqi males in dark clothes appeared in West's sector from beside a house 150 feet away and started sprinting toward the fighting position. One of the men carried an AK-47 and fired wildly at them as he ran. The other enemy combatant held a heavier, longer weapon. *Great. Was wondering when they were going to break out the RPGs.*

"Two shooters at five o'clock! AK and an RPG!" West screamed. Twelve o'clock was where the blocking Humvee had been moments before and served as a point of reference for the defending Marines to use when communicating with each other. West had positioned himself near the rear of the Humvee in which he'd been riding, allowing him to cover the three to six o'clock sector.

The insurgent with the RPG suddenly stopped and dropped to one knee, even as West acquired him through the reflex scope of his M4, which he'd reclaimed from General Longstreet.

West began to squeeze the trigger.

Boom! Boom! Boom!

The two insurgents were blown apart and off their feet by three explosions, and West realized the Mk 19 gunner must have spotted them first. He'd been so focused he hadn't even heard the automatic grenade launcher.

The insurgent with the RPG must have pulled the trigger before being blown to bloody chunks because West watched as the rocket streaked upward and away at a forty-five-degree angle like a children's model kit, harmlessly streaming toward the heavens above.

"They're almost there!" Benson shouted, notifying the rest of the ad hoc fire team.

"I've got four at one o'clock!" Staff Sergeant Farrell said, before pulling the trigger on the M249 he'd positioned on top of a mound of dirt that had been pushed against the undercarriage of the Humvee by the IED. He went quiet and let the SAW do his talking, as 5.56mm rounds punched holes in the assaulting insurgents as he strafed the light machine gun from side to side. Moments later, four enemy combatants lay dead in the street, their attack having ended like a bad reenactment of the Charge of the Light Brigade.

"They're on the way back!" Benson announced.

Thank God, West thought. The intensity of the firefight had increased. More fire was being concentrated on their position from what seemed like all directions. *At some point, they're going to get brave again, and if we can't return fire, these guys will make an actual coordinated assault, in which case we're screwed.*

"Three at seven o'clock!" Sergeant Childress announced.

West kept his focus on his sector. He heard the Humvee near the position, and then Sergeant Childress fired a short, controlled burst.

"Got 'em," Childress said.

His sector clear, West looked at the rally point just as the Humvee completed its turn and stopped exactly where it had started. *Time to go.*

"Staff Sergeant Farrell, line up and take point with the SAW! Childress, get behind him. FBI, you're third," West ordered, even as the first two Marines lined up next to the Humvee. "Let's get the hell out of this death trap. Now run!"

The Humvee started rolling, and the warriors started running. The trickiest part was for the driver to match the speed of the four armed, battle-gear-rattling men sprinting for safety. *If he slows down or speeds up, we're dead*, West thought as enemy bullets kicked up puffs of sand and dirt.

West ran harder, keeping a safe distance between himself and the huge FBI agent in front of him. The Kevlar vest and helmet weighed him down, but his surging adrenaline allowed him to push through the pain and exertion. *At least it's only in the low seventies. This would've really sucked in the summertime*, he thought. *Halfway there—ten more seconds.*

The only good thing about what happened next was that it happened on the other side of the Humvee. The Mk 19 gunner was focused on the left side of the battlefield in order to preempt the insurgents from making a suicide charge at the Marines and the FBI special agent. As a result, he never saw the RPG-wielding insurgent who fired from the doorway of a concrete building two hundred feet away.

The RPG warhead streaked across the short distance and slammed into the front right corner of the Humvee, destroying the wheel and right half of the undercarriage in a tremendous explosion of shrapnel and debris.

The force of the explosion stunned West and his sprinting partners, who were either knocked down or dove to the street.

The Humvee suddenly ground to a halt, the nose burying itself into the loose soil of the patch of ground on which its short journey had ended.

So close, West thought as he looked up, righted his Kevlar helmet on his head, and screamed, "We have to keep going!"

All four doors of the Humvee opened simultaneously, and as if from a circus act clown car, Gunny Quick, Captain Rodgers, and the other Marines piled out at once.

West ran over to Gunny Quick and screamed, "You and I take the rear. Everyone else, keep *fucking going!*" There was no time for debate, no other options to consider. It came down to one hard truth—run or die.

"Fucking A, sir," Quick said, the intensity and battle focus worn like war paint.

The entrance to the three-story building's property was only forty feet away. The first Marines who'd reached its relative safety fired from behind its large gate at targets West couldn't see and didn't have precious seconds to find. He knew the Marines' aim was better than the enemy's, and he hoped the trained killers of his beloved Corps were inflicting serious casualties on the insurgent force.

The Marines and lone FBI special agent dashed across the open ground, with Captain West and Gunny Quick covering their movement as they back-pedaled in the rear of the disorganized formation, firing at anything that moved.

At least this will be over in a few more seconds, no matter what happens, West thought as he dropped an insurgent who thought it would be a good idea to run across the open highway. *Nice try, jackass.*

A sudden scream broke through the sounds of battle, and West whipped his head around to see Sergeant Childress on the ground, blood leaking from the back of his left leg and darkening the desert digital camouflage pattern. But just as quickly, two enormous hands gripped him by the carrying handle sewn into the top of the back of the Kevlar vest, and Special Agent Mike Benson hoisted him over his left shoulder like a life-sized rag doll. *Man, I love this guy,* West thought in amazement at the true courage on display under fire as the FBI special agent kept moving toward their objective.

Gunny Quick snatched up the M4 dropped by Sergeant Childress, who had unholstered his Beretta M9 9mm pistol and was firing across the street. As he hung across the enormous FBI special agent's shoulder, he screamed in rage, "Fuck you, you fucking cocksuckers! It's going to take more than that, motherfuckers! Come get some!"

West looked at Gunny Quick, and both men smiled for the briefest moment in unspoken recognition of the true warrior ethos of the Marine Corps on display and in full glory. *Live or die, I wouldn't want to be anywhere else at this moment,* West thought proudly.

And just as quickly as it had started, the mad dash ended as the group of Marines and warriors burst through the gate and didn't stop until they reached the building's front door, which was ajar.

West heard voices from deep inside the home—one screaming rather loudly—as he looked into the face of a small boy no older than seven or eight. *God, I hate to do this,* but he pushed the door open and stepped into a large foyer. *Now I can add home invasion to the list. Great résumé builder.*

CHAPTER 16

The large foyer had a white marble floor, which spilled into a much larger living area that was segmented with four columns. Beyond the living room was another room, through which West spotted a small courtyard in the back and a privacy wall that demarcated the rear of the property. A low wall on the right side of the living room with a large opening above it revealed a spacious kitchen. The front of the house and the side walls were constructed of some kind of concrete, *which should provide some decent cover*, West thought. But first, he had to get the chaotic scene inside under control before the coming battle ensued.

Ironically, the small, black-haired boy was the only family member that seemed calm, although how, West had no idea. *Kid's already seen too much*, he realized, and pushed it out of his mind. There was no time for sympathy, not with a massing enemy outside intent on killing them all.

A middle-aged Iraqi man in a white robe and dark-brown hair was shouting at a woman in a dark burka. West assumed she was his wife. There were several other civilians in the room of various ages and genders, but it was the man that was his focus.

"Who speaks Arabic?" West said loudly to his team as the gunfire and explosions outside quickly subsided. *They're preparing to make an assault. We don't have long.*

"I do," Captain Rodgers said. "I lat-moved from intel to infantry. I used to be an Arabic linguist."

"Good call for us," West replied. "Now please express to this gentleman that we're sorry for the intrusion, but unless he wants him and his entire family to die, he needs to stop arguing with his wife and show us how to get to the roof. We don't have much time. The quiet outside means they'll be coming soon. Also, tell him to get his family to the back of the house, if he wants to try and keep them safe. I have a feeling these bastards will come from the front. From their amateur-hour maneuvers on foot after the initial attack, I don't see a bunch of tactical geniuses."

"Understood," Rodgers said, and started speaking quickly and directly to the man they all assumed was the patriarch of the household. The rest of his family quieted down as the mother held her son to her, arms draped over his tiny shoulders, crossed protectively across his chest.

"Captain America is full of surprises, sir," Quick said quietly to Captain West.

"Thank God for small wonders," West replied.

"Agreed. But that silence is ominous. We need to get into position," Quick said.

"You're right," West said, and turned toward the door, which was cracked open and afforded a view of the gate and the no-man's-land beyond. The Marines were still at the gate, awaiting orders from inside. "Staff Sergeant Farrell, take that SAW outside and tell them to pull back from the gate to the front of the house. Find some cover from different angles so they can't shoot straight at you. Make it a choke point of death for these motherfuckers," West growled. "You understand?"

"Absolutely, sir," Staff Sergeant Farrell said.

"Good luck, and happy hunting. Now go," West said.

"Roger that," Staff Sergeant Farrell replied, and disappeared into the sun without another word.

Godspeed, Marine, West thought.

"We're all set. What's the plan?" Captain Rodgers said.

West turned around to see the Iraqi man—as well as the rest of the Marines and one FBI special agent—waiting for his final instructions. The man's family was already moving to the rear of the house, and West nodded, knowing that if things went really wrong, they'd all likely be dead, including the man's family for involuntarily helping them.

West felt a fleeting moment of gravity, the weight of his position threatening to put his mind in a paralyzing vise. *Oh no, you don't. Nice try.* And just as quickly, he compartmented the emotion and confidently issued his orders in the manner to which his Marines were accustomed. Wild West was back in charge, and he intended to ensure the enemy would rue this day.

CHAPTER 17

Like most homes in Ramadi, the upper floor had a middle stairwell that led to a door emptying out onto a mortar-constructed rooftop. The home's owner, Samir, had informed them that the door opened up toward the front and was flush with the sides of the walls of the stairwell in which they now stood. *Which means if there's someone out there, they could just light us up through the walls.*

West stopped at the door, listening for the slightest sound or movement. All he heard was gunfire and the occasional impact of rounds on the front of the concrete home. The enemy had intensified its fire within the last two minutes, which told West the assault was imminent. *Here goes nothing.*

West turned to Special Agent Mike Benson, who was stacked up right behind him, and reached for the old brass doorknob with his right hand. He held up his left hand and three fingers, dropping them one by one in the universal signal to go. He exhaled as he lowered his last finger and turned the knob.

Rays of sunlight invaded the dim stairwell, illuminating the swirling specks of sand and dirt that swarmed in through the opening on the right side of the door. He pushed harder, increasing the size of the gap . . .

. . . which allowed the insurgent on the roof who'd been patiently waiting to insert the barrel of an AK-47 into the stairwell.

"Gun!" Benson screamed instinctively, but Captain West was already reacting.

Boom! Boom! Boom!

The insurgent fired three deafening shots into the stairwell as the door was flung wide open. Chunks of concrete were torn from the left wall of the stairwell, stinging the left side of West's exposed face.

Ears ringing and furious at himself for not detecting the ambush, West grabbed the hot barrel of the AK-47 before the insurgent had a chance to pull the trigger again. Rather than expose himself to additional fire, he pulled the insurgent forward and into the stairwell entrance, pushing the barrel of the assault rifle to the ceiling.

While the insurgent might have momentarily held the advantage through the tactical element of surprise, that was all he had.

Captain Logan West, adrenaline pumping and fueled by anger, pressed the full weight of his body against the smaller enemy, leaning in from inches away with unmasked rage to glare at the bearded man.

For Special Agent Mike Benson, the next moment was the introduction to the real Logan West that he would come to know, respect, and love as a brother-in-arms against a multitude of enemies. It was the true essence of the gladiator inside the man and the Marine. He saw the blade that had appeared in Captain West's right hand plunge into the side of the man's neck, then blood gushing from the wound as the Marine officer rotated his wrist forward for maximum damage.

The man's eyes widened in pain, and a strangled cough escaped his lips. But it was Captain West's eyes that Benson would remember. *There is absolutely no mercy in them. Thank God he's on our side,* he thought as Captain West dropped the dying insurgent to the stairs, grabbed the AK-47, and handed it to Benson.

"Here. This will beat that Glock of yours," West said. "Now let's secure this rooftop and go to work."

West turned back to the open doorway and unslung his M4, stepping over the dead insurgent and exiting the stairwell in a crouched combat walk.

For some reason West would never understand, the front of the roof was clear, but he heard the sounds of movement behind and to the left of the rooftop entrance. Efficiently functioning on automatic pilot, he turned to the right, his M4 up and in the ready position, one eye looking through his reflex scope, the other open and looking past it. He reached the back of the structure and walked past the edge of cover, all hesitation gone—unfortunately for the two insurgents standing side by side, pointing their AK-47s at the front of the entrance on the other side of the structure. *Too bad for you two idiots.*

At such close range it was an execution, which suited West just fine. The first two shots struck the man closest to him in the side of the head, spraying blood over his partner. The second Iraqi blinked the blood away and tried to turn, but his momentum was stopped as two more bullets caught him in the face, ripping open his right cheek and tearing away a chunk of his nose before killing him.

What the hell? West thought as he stared at the shiny object that rested on top of the small concrete railing behind the two insurgents. *An aluminum ladder? You've got to be kidding me.* The insurgents had shimmied across it from the adjacent home. While the extra standoff distance from the highway had been his main concern, he'd failed to realize *how close* the neighbors' homes were. The enemy had tried to capitalize on that closeness. *Maybe these guys aren't as stupid as I thought they were.*

"Clear!" West shouted, and Special Agent Benson, Captain

Rodgers, Gunny Quick, and Sergeant Ramirez joined him on the rooftop. He'd asked General Longstreet to stay downstairs with the wounded Sergeant Childress, hoping the lowest, innermost room of the home would provide maximum protection. He didn't want to be the one responsible for getting a commanding general killed.

"Help me with this ladder, Gunny, on the off chance we have to use it to likely do something stupid," West said.

"Stupid is as stupid does, sir," Quick quipped, grinning maniacally as he helped pull the aluminum ladder onto the rooftop and place it at the bottom of one of the side walls.

"Seriously? Fucking Forrest Gump right now? I might make you run all the way to Baghdad, Forrest," West said, and shook his head. "I swear I might shoot you myself."

"Captain West, you may want to get up here," Benson shouted from the front of the rooftop. Special Agent Benson and Sergeant Ramirez—another SAW gunner—were providing overwatch from the front of the roof while Captain West and Gunny Quick dealt with the ladder. "I think we're out of time."

Captain West and Gunny Quick joined the rest of the group and stopped at the scene spread out before them. *This is going to be harder than I thought*, West realized.

"Sergeant Ramirez," West said calmly as he stared across the street, "you and I have the front two corners. Make 'em pay with that SAW. Gunny, you and Special Agent Benson take the two rear corners. Steve, you stay here near the door and stay as low as you can. I need you on that air support. Also, start prepping call-for-fire missions just in case things get really bad. Those army boys better be ready," West said, referring to the US army artillery battery charged with providing support to the Marines and army units operating inside Ramadi. If all else failed, he could call in a series of 155mm artillery strikes danger-close from the self-propelled Paladin howitzers. *That's a last resort, Logan. Don't get crazy*, the rational part of his mind told him. *Not unless I have to,* another part of his mind replied as he watched the impending storm assemble itself.

"Good Lord," Rodgers muttered.

"I hope he's here with us, because we're going to need all the help we can get," Quick said, moving into position in the back left corner of the roof.

On the other side of the highway three hundred feet away, a mass of at least forty fighters with an assortment of weapons—AK-47s, RPGs, and sniper rifles—moved like a living organism with malevolent intent. The horde suddenly divided itself into three equal-sized groups, each with its own avenue of approach that immediately became self-evident. *Great. A three-pronged assault. This is going to be interesting.*

"Fuck 'em," West said coldly. "There's only one way through the gate, and we only need to buy a few minutes. Let them come, *and let them die.*"

CHAPTER 18

The initial fusillade of fire was overwhelming, the *crack* of rifle rounds filling the air above and around the house like a swarm of angry mechanical birds. *This is worse than the butts at the rifle range,* West thought, remembering the first time an M16 5.56mm round passed merely feet overhead of the heavy berm that protected the Marines pulling targets up and down in the pit area of the range. *It's a long way from Camp Pendleton.*

Had it not been for the concrete construction of the home, West was certain they would have all been killed. *Wait for it . . . wait for it . . . wait for it.* He focused for a moment on his breathing. *There it is*—the brief lull in fire he'd expected as the assault force reloaded.

To proficiently shoot, move, and communicate was an acquired tactical skill honed through thousands of rounds expended and multiple ranges run. West was confident these insurgents weren't conducting live-fire exercises on a daily basis. Running across an open killing ground as some of them had done earlier wasn't the most tactically sound plan on earth, and he'd hoped that lack of discipline extended into all their military maneuvers. And he'd been right.

Our turn, West thought as he exhaled one last time, turned, and looked over the short wall on the rooftop.

The three groups, with approximately fifty feet of separation between them, had crossed both sides of the highway and reached the extra swath of land that West intended to exploit. He spotted several men standing and reloading, obviously incapable of reloading on the move, but those weren't his first concern. As he'd reminded his Marines, the first priority was the greatest threat—the RPG-wielding insurgents. His intent was to remove them from the battlefield before they could wreak havoc on the front of the house, punching holes in the walls and creating extra points of insertion for the attacking force.

Bingo. A man wearing tan-colored robes and combat boots knelt outside the gate opening and aiming a long, menacing tube at the house.

West screamed, "RPG two o'clock!" and opened fire, sending a short burst into the man's chest from more than 120 feet away. He couldn't see the impacts, but he knew his aim was true when the insurgent toppled over to his right, the RPG harmlessly falling to the ground.

"RPG ten o'clock!" Sergeant Ramirez yelled, dropping a target on the left.

Moments later, West heard two more weapons open fire as Special Agent Benson and Gunny Quick joined the firefight, firing from the rear of the roof and along the sides of the house at targets only they could see.

Within the first ten seconds of the real battle, at least six insurgents lay dead in the dirt, their rockets useless and no longer a threat.

"I don't see any more RPGs!" West screamed, which Sergeant Ramirez took as his cue to unleash a brutal salvo on the main assault force approaching the gate.

Staff Sergeant Farrell, who lay in cover twenty feet to the right of the front door behind a small group of rocks in what passed for a yard, picked up the SAW and braced the light machine gun with the bipod on the rocks.

Moments later, the two machine guns were "talking," firing in alternating bursts of devastating gunfire that tore into the insurgents.

The sound was deafening, as all members of Captain West's defending force were now engaged. *It's mass suicide,* he thought as he watched bodies drop to the ground from all three groups. *There's no way they can keep this up. It's going to be over soon. This is why you don't assault a fortified position across open ground.* He adjusted the M4 slightly, acquired a clear sight picture on an insurgent running with a pistol—*a pistol?*—and fired, striking him in the head and ending his suicide sprint.

Less than a minute later, most of the assault force lay dead or dying, and not one had breached the front yard. *This is better than I expected,* West thought, still scanning for moving targets among the carnage.

A low reverberation began to shake the roof, a mechanical tremor that increased in intensity. *Spoke too soon.*

"Sir, we've got a problem back here!" Gunny Quick yelled.

West dashed to the back of the roof and saw the new threat, and his blood turned to ice. Two hundred meters away, a Russian-made BMP-2 tracked infantry fighting vehicle was lumbering down the street that ran parallel to the back of the front row of homes. It wasn't the co-axial 7.62mm mounted machine gun that worried West—it was the 30mm autocannon, which could turn the entire home into rubble in minutes with its high-explosive and armor-piercing ordnance designed to take out enemy aircraft and armored vehicles.

"How the hell did they get their hands on a BMP?" Quick asked no one in particular.

"My guess is it's a throwaway from the Republican Guard, but it doesn't matter. If we don't get it away from here, we're all dead," West said.

"What do you have in mind?" Quick asked. "I assume it's going to be incredibly reckless. So I'm all-in."

"Me too," Benson said from beside them.

"You're not Atlas, Captain West," a voice spoke up from behind them.

The three men turned to see General Longstreet, who had joined them on the roof.

"Sir, you should be downstairs—I don't need my commanding general getting killed today—but regardless, I don't plan to hold the earth up by myself," West replied.

"It's the heavens—not the earth—that Atlas is holding up," Longstreet replied.

"Why did I think it was the earth?" West said almost absent-mindedly, acutely aware of the absurdity of the conversation in the middle of combat.

"Everyone does, but *they're all wrong*," the general said.

"No disrespect, sir, we can talk mythology later. Now who wants to help me with this ladder?" West said, and picked up one end of the forty-foot aluminum ladder.

CHAPTER 19

Farouq al-Khouri stared through the periscope, his dark eyes focused on the target building 150 meters away. The Americans would learn a hard lesson today—one he intended to deliver in explosive steel. While the military invasion might have gone as smoothly for them as any in recent history, he planned to ensure the follow-on occupation did not.

A former tank commander in Saddam Hussein's famed 2nd Al Medina Armored Division, he'd survived and escaped the bloody battle of Al Kut in 2003 at the hands of the 1st Marine Division. He'd returned to his home city of Ramadi once the Republican Guard had been disbanded, hoping for some semblance of a normal life. Unfortunately, the sudden poverty and lack of resources due to Baghdad's severing the lifeline to the former Saddam loyalists had prevented it. No normal life was to be his, and the American invaders had guaranteed it.

On a clear, sunny Wednesday afternoon, as he and his wife and five-year-old son walked back from a local mosque after the Duhr, the noon prayer, a local insurgent leader ambushed a small US army convoy. Unfortunately for Farouq and his family, the ambush happened fifty meters away from him and had turned into a running gun battle. He'd sought the safety of a nearby alleyway, dragging his wife behind him, but it hadn't been enough.

Stray fire had found his wife and child, cruelly sparing him. As he'd knelt next to their lifeless bodies, their blood pooling, hands still clutched together, he'd looked up and seen the singular image that would shape the rest of his life—a US army soldier standing next to a patrol vehicle, pointing a weapon in his direction, guilty knowledge written all over his pale face. The soldier had then stepped back into the vehicle and disappeared down the street as if casually dismissing the wreckage he'd left behind.

Farouq's soul had been broken that day, and an uncontrollable wrath had consumed him. He'd hunted down the local insurgent leader who'd initiated the ambush and shot and decapitated him in front of his closest advisors, who'd been paralyzed at the sudden violence he'd delivered to their leader. And then he did something unexpected: he assumed leadership of the fledgling insurgency, reaching out to his connections in the former Republican Guard in order to build his arsenal and army.

Once he'd acquired a significant number of men willing to die for his cause and the armament to support them, he'd waited, planning for a day that had finally arrived. *This day.*

He'd known just killing American soldiers wouldn't send the message he intended; the action would have to be bigger to get the attention of the politicians and puppet masters in the hell the Americans called their capital—Washington DC. And like a gift direct from Allah, he'd been provided intelligence on the meeting between the new American commander of all forces in the region and the local tribal leaders. It was an opportunity he could not pass up, and it was how he found himself in the commander seat of the BMP-2 one of his former commanding officers had provided as a personal gift for Farouq's saving his life in the initial American invasion.

The swift fury of Allah is at hand, Farouq thought, as the building loomed closer in his periscope. The mechanical beast of death rumbled closer. *Fifty more meters, and I'm razing it to the ground.*

His gunner kept the autocannon trained on the structure, now twenty-five meters away. *Almost time for vengeance for my family and to make the Americans truly pay in a way they'll understand.*

A figure in an American desert-pattern uniform suddenly emerged from behind the building and dashed across the front of the vehicle, disappearing behind a home to the right.

"Ahmed, you see him?" Farouq asked his gunner.

"No. He went behind that house," Ahmed responded.

"Very well. Leave him. Target the house, praise Allah," Farouq said.

"*Allahu akbar.* As you command," Ahmed replied, aiming the 30mm autocannon directly into the center of the first floor of the back of the house.

Clink. Clink. Clink.

"What is that?" Ahmed asked.

Fear and anger smashed into Farouq as he realized his mistake. It wasn't fear of death—he'd died long ago in that alley with his wife and son—it was fear of failure. *The American on foot was trying to flank them.* But before he could speak, the three grenades simultaneously detonated in front, on top, and on the left side of the BMP-2, dazing the occupants of the vehicle.

B-B-BOOM!

———

West only needed to buy another minute or two. The last thing Captain Rodgers had told him as he climbed down the ladder was that two AH-1W SuperCobra attack helicopters were inbound and would be on station within minutes. *If I live that long,* he thought as he prepared for the part of his plan that was truly dangerous, *not that running in front of an enemy armored personnel carrier wasn't crazy enough.*

He prayed the grenades that Captain Rodgers and Special Agent Benson had dropped on the war machine had created the desired effect inside the cramped compartment—confusion and disorientation. *Otherwise, this is going to be a very short gambit.*

He pulled the charging handle back on his M4 and ensured a round was still in the chamber, flipping the firing selector up to three-round-burst mode. He wasn't going to need precision fire. *No point in delaying the inevitable. Better ride like the wind, Christopher Cross–style.*

Captain Logan West—who years later would race another vehicle of destruction on foot across the top of the Haditha Dam—sprinted from behind cover, spraying the front of the BMP with 5.56mm rounds.

———

Farouq's head was buzzing with the loud, constant ringing in his ears, the voices of his driver and gunner drowned out by the constant siren of sound.

Plink-plink-plink-plink-plink-plink-plink.

Praise be to Allah. The same soldier who'd sprinted across the road moments before the grenades had been dropped was now firing at them from the middle of the road. *Was this American trying to martyr himself?* Farouq thought instinctively, aware of the cultural irony. It didn't matter. His instincts told him to remove this bothersome pawn from the battlefield.

"Kill him," Farouq said, not realizing he was yelling to be heard over both the noise inside his head and the BMP. "Once this American is dead, we'll level the building."

This is going to be satisfying, Farouq thought, knowing what the 30mm rounds would do to a human body.

———

The M4 magazine emptied, and the bolt locked into the rear position. There was no time to reload. West dashed down the middle of the narrow road, away from the home in which his brothers and friends were now sheltered. He risked a glance back and saw that the BMP's long autocannon was traversing toward him, a fact that both relieved and terrified him. *This might actually work. Just keep running,* he thought, a small grin appearing on his dirt- and sweat-stained face. *Some pop culture references never die, but you might if you don't run harder.*

He reached his destination, a wider alleyway two homes down from the one they occupied, and broke hard left—just as the BMP's gunner opened fire with the 30mm autocannon.

———

Farouq watched as the barrage of 30mm high-explosive and armor-piercing rounds *disintegrated* the corner of the building the American had disappeared behind a split second earlier. *There's no way you can survive that. I've seen less do much more damage.*

Farouq didn't realize it, but he was smiling the broad grin of a madman on the edge of accomplishing his goal. Even though he knew the first building was the main objective, his hunter's instinct had full control of his decision making, and he wanted the American's blood painted across the walls of the Ramadi neighborhood. For Farouq, the running American symbolized all that was wrong in the Middle East—American aggression, oppression, and a callous disregard for human life—and he intended to crush him into a thousand liquid pieces.

West was sprawled face-forward on the dirt-packed alleyway, which was filled with rubble and a thick cloud of swirling dust. He lifted his head, willing himself to move. *Almost bought it there. You're not going to get that lucky next time. Now get the fuck up and move, Marine!* A brief vision of his sergeant instructor from Officer Candidate School screaming at him inches from his face spurred him into action.

He scrambled to all fours, propelling himself forward and deeper into the alleyway. He reached his feet as he felt the ground shake harder from the approaching BMP. His goal was now in sight one hundred feet directly ahead between the two homes—the open space that had served as their killing field.

West ran hard, concentrating on his breath, running not just for his life as more 30mm rounds decimated the corner of the home, but more importantly, for the lives of those in his charge.

"Go down the alleyway. We'll fit. For all that is great, kill that man!" Farouq shouted.

The BMP reached the alleyway, and Farouq was disappointed to discover no dead American. *This rabbit runs fast.*

The vehicle turned into the alleyway—just wide enough to accommodate the machine—and moved forward. The BMP pushed through the cloud of debris, crushing the rubble underneath its heavy tracks.

I have you now, Farouq thought as he spotted the fleeing American at the end of the alleyway. The running figure looked over his shoulder, breached the opening past the front of the homes, and disappeared to the right.

"Catch him!" Farouq shouted, anticipation that the chase was nearing its end. *There is nowhere for the American to hide.*

The BMP accelerated, speeding recklessly down the alleyway, scraping chunks of concrete from the side of the home on the right as the driver course-corrected. Within seconds, the man-made predator emerged from the confines of the buildings and into the open space.

The BMP turned to the right as the gunner adjusted the autocannon. But Farouq already had his periscope aimed in the direction of his prey, and what he saw added mental alarm bells to the physical ringing inside his head.

Fifty feet in front of him was a small cluster of rocks. Crouching behind those rocks was the American, except his head was sticking up from behind cover. *What in Allah's name is he doing?*

Farouq zoomed in with the periscope, the face of the American filling the image and turning his blood cold. It was the face of a warrior—a fearsome one; Farouq knew the look of a fellow fighter—and he was smiling with a sense of righteousness Farouq knew well. *What have I done?*

The anticipation of victory instantly transformed into a suffocating panic as Farouq realized he'd been lured into a trap. *But from where?* The Republican Guard's training reasserted itself, and he sought to identify the threat.

He whirled in his seat and looked through the rear firing port, spotting what the American had known all along would be there. The chase *was over,* just not in the way Farouq had intended. Realizing he had precious moments to live, he closed his eyes and said a prayer to his wife and son. *I'll see you soon, my loves.*

———

Kneeling in the front of the yard near the entrance gate, Gunnery Sergeant John Quick lined up the reticle in the optical sight of the

RPG-7 on the rear of the BMP. The hammer on the trigger device had already been manually cocked by its deceased insurgent owner, and the weapon was armed and ready. Gunny Quick's index finger rested along the side of the trigger guard, straight and off the trigger until he was ready to fire.

"Wait until the first one impacts before you fire," Quick said.

"Roger, Gunny," Sergeant Ramirez responded, an RPG mounted on his right shoulder.

While Captain West had acted as bait in the urban maze, Gunny Quick and Sergeant Ramirez had a different task—shimmy down the ladder after Captain West, move to the front of the house, and find two RPGs to use to destroy the BMP. It was startlingly simple, which was often how the best plans were designed—the simpler the plan, the less could go wrong.

"Now, let's *really get some*," Quick said, and pulled the single-action trigger.

A tremendous *whoosh* exploded from the back of the launcher in a cloud of bluish-white smoke as the warhead was propelled out of the tube toward its target. Instantly, the propulsion system in the middle of the warhead ignited, rocketing the grenade into the rear of the BMP and punching a hole in the rear door that also contained diesel fuel tanks. The grenade exploded, sending a wave of overpressure and shrapnel that mortally wounded the crew inside. The fuel that was splashed throughout the interior ignited, creating a conflagration that instantly consumed the oxygen inside the BMP and suffocated the dying men.

"Now," Quick said, and Sergeant Ramirez followed suit, sending the final nail in the BMP's coffin hurtling toward its target.

Whoosh!

The second RPG tore through the opening the first grenade had created, detonating inside and triggering a series of secondary explosions that devastated the armored personnel carrier.

"Wow," Ramirez said quietly as the vehicle popped and groaned, smoke billowing from the multiple hatches in the roof and the hole in the back.

"I'll second that, Sergeant," Quick said.

A moment later, the jogging figure of Captain West appeared from the left side of the burning hulk and reached them. He had multiple small lacerations on his face, and blood trickled from each.

"It's about time you earned your keep, Gunny," West said wryly.

"Just hoping to get a good FITREP, sir. That's all," Quick said, referring to the Marine Corps' evaluation system.

"Suck-up. Noted," West said, adding in a serious tone, "Nice shooting. Thank God for reliable Russian weapons."

"I'll second that," General Longstreet said from behind them. He and Special Agent Benson had come down from the roof through the inside of the house to notify the Marines inside that the battle was over.

As if on cue, two SuperCobra helicopters appeared from the east, roaring toward them at low altitude.

Captain Rodgers spoke into the handset of his portable back-pack radio. "Negative, Warbird One. We have no targets in sight on the objective. I say again. We are clear."

"Just in the nick of time, huh?" West said.

"Hey, better late than never, especially if your plan hadn't worked. At least *we* would have made it," Rodgers replied with good-natured sarcasm.

"I think he's got you there, sir," Quick said.

"Thanks for the support, Gunny. That FITREP's getting lower by the minute."

A convoy of Humvees and two amphibious assault vehicle troop carriers appeared on the highway several hundred yards down the road from the direction of Camp Blue Diamond.

"And here comes the cavalry," Longstreet said. "Captain Rodgers, can you please express our sincere appreciation to the host and his family, apologize for the destruction, and tell him that if he comes to the camp, I will personally ensure that he is either reimbursed for the damage or we'll have his home repaired and rebuilt."

"Roger that, sir," Rodgers said, and disappeared into the front of the house.

"As for you, Captain West, that might have been one of the most reckless, brave acts of pure heroism I've witnessed. We're all in your debt, and it's an honor to serve by your side," Longstreet said. "And I might have been wrong. After that display, maybe you really *are* Atlas and *can* hold up the heavens."

The weight of his commanding general's compliments in the wake of the fight momentarily moved him, and Captain West exhaled quietly to subdue his emotions. "Thank you, sir. But I was just doing my job, just like each of the Marines here, as well as Special Agent Benson."

West stepped up to the giant FBI agent and extended his hand. "That was a brave thing you did back there, scooping Sergeant Childress up on the run."

"Like you said, Captain, just doing my job," Benson replied, gripping the hand firmly, solidifying the bond that had formed between them.

"I'm pretty sure that's not in the FBI field manual, but I could be wrong," West said. "I'm not a G-man, just a Marine."

"There's always time," Benson said, grinning.

"I don't think that's in the cards, but I'll take it under consideration if things don't pan out for me," West said.

"Fair enough," Benson said. "But I mean this: anytime you need anything, *ever*, you let me know, and I'll be there. No questions. No hesitation."

"Spoken like a Marine," Quick noted.

"Negative, Gunny. Spoken like a friend and fellow brother-in-arms," Benson said. "Oh. And I don't mean 'brother' as in I'm black, in case your sarcastic ass was wondering," he added, demonstrating the sense of humor they'd get to know well, even if it wasn't always on display like John Quick's.

Quick laughed out loud. "It never occurred to me, Special Agent Man. But thanks for opening that door."

"Now you really did it," West said. "Gunny's like a vampire with his humor: once you invite him in, you can never get him to leave."

"I guess I did, but there are worse fates," Benson said soberly, as if realizing for the first time they were surrounded by bodies and a burning armored personnel carrier.

"That there are," General Longstreet said. "But that fate is not for us. Not today. Now let's get the hell out of here and back to base. I have a feeling this is going to be a very long tour."

PART IV

TWENTY THOUSAND LEAGUES UNDER THE SEA

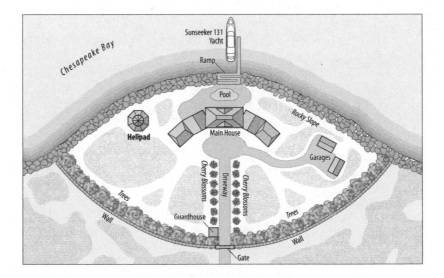

CHAPTER 20

Udvar-Hazy Security Operations Center
Present Day

"One week later, the real fighting and dying began, as the insurgency exponentially grew in strength, organization, and resources. But you already know how that story ends," Logan said to John, Amira, and Cole, who'd listened raptly.

"It still doesn't feel like Mike's gone," John said, referring to the fallen Mike Benson.

"I know, but he is, and we have a job to do, one that I *know* he would want us to see through to the end," Logan said.

"So what now?" John asked.

"You mean now that we know that retired general and former Marine Commandant Jack Longstreet is somehow involved in all of this? That a man that I once respected completely somehow *knew* about the plan to kill us here today?" Logan's voice grew stronger. "What does it say that a man, a Marine, *a legend* that I haven't seen since he visited my home in Maryland after I left the Marine Corps, suddenly reappears and saves my life?" Logan paused for effect. "Simple. He's neck-deep in all of this, and obviously knows more than we do. Bottom line—finding Jack Longstreet just became our main priority."

"How?" Cole said. "If he's involved in this shadow world, then he's off the grid."

"Oh. I know! I know!" John said, mimicking an eager student trying to please the teacher.

"If you raise your hand, I'm going to hit you," Amira said coldly. "Don't make me kick your ass more than once today."

"Ouch," Cole said. "I wouldn't test her."

"Funny," John said, ignoring Cole's jab. "You going to make the call, Logan?"

"Already on it," Logan said as he unlocked his cell phone and scanned through his list of contacts, finding the one that he wanted. He pressed the name, and the phone automatically dialed the number.

"You're calling Jake, aren't you?" Amira asked.

"None other," Logan said as he held the phone to his ear, the earbud no longer necessary. "Remember, we may be a motley crew, but we do have the full weight, authority, and power of the entire US government behind us. I'm pretty sure that Jake can find the general much easier and faster than we can."

Jake Benson, the director of the FBI, answered on the third ring. "Logan, what's up? It's kind of crazy here right now. We're about to hold a press conference. I'm pretty sure if you turn on a TV—any TV—you're going to see me give a very vague statement about this attack."

"Sorry to interrupt you, Jake, but we have a new player on the board. He called to warn me right before I was attacked. He knew this was a trap, but he also gave away his identity, I think intentionally. I think he wants something from me. And I need to know where he is," Logan finished.

"Where who is?" Jake asked.

"Get ready for this one—retired General Jack Longstreet," Logan said flatly.

"The one you, Mike, and John fought with and saved in Iraq?" Jake Benson's voice went quiet. "Jesus. How does this stuff keep haunting us?" he asked in a manner that made it seem like he didn't want the answer.

"I don't know, but it does, and unfortunately, we have to deal with it," Logan said. "I figure you can have the FBI assign some agents, go through some databases, and figure out where he is so that—"

"Got it," Cole Matthews suddenly interrupted.

"Jake, hold on a second, please," Logan said, looking at a grinning Cole Matthews doing his best cat-ate-the-canary impersonation. "Seriously?"

"Hey, I'm not just some good-looking operator. I *know* things," Cole said seriously.

"Like what?" Logan said, playing into the banter.

"Like Google," Cole replied, and held up his smartphone, showing a picture of Jack Longstreet in a suit facing Logan. "See?"

Logan didn't react. Instead, he said, "Jake, I'm going to have to call you back. Better yet, go do the press conference and hit me back when you're done. I think we're going to be at the museum a little bit longer."

"Will do," Jake responded. "Talk to you shortly."

"Have fun with the press," Logan added, his disdain for the media evident.

"They're not too bad, if you know how to handle them," Jake said. "*And* they can serve a purpose if nudged the right way. One of these days, you'll see that," Jake finished, and hung up, leaving Logan no time to reply.

"All the power in the world, and we don't even need it. All we need is fucking Google. Go figure," John said.

"What do you have?" Logan asked, his patience wearing thin.

"Everything," Cole said. "Looks like the general has had quite the retirement. It also looks like he can't stay out of the game."

"Why do you say that?" Amira asked. "Where is he?"

"He's chief of security for operations on the East Coast for Kallas Shipping," Cole said.

"The multibillion-dollar global shipping empire?" Logan asked.

"Yup," Cole said. "That's the one."

"Isn't the owner some Holocaust survivor? I remember reading something about him in *Forbes*," Amira said.

"Constantine Krawcyk-Kallas, although he just goes by Kallas," Cole said. "He took the original owner's name but kept his Polish one; thus, the two last names. But wait—there's more," Cole added, sounding like a Sham-Wow salesman.

"Just tell me before I lose my patience," Logan said.

"Chill out. It's all good," Cole said, and smiled. "It turns out Mr. Kallas has a home on the western shore of the Chesapeake Bay."

"You're kidding me," Logan said.

"Not one bit," Cole said. "I'm willing to bet our general is in the area and might be there."

"I'm willing to do you one better," Amira said, processing the information. "I'll bet *all the players* are in the area."

"I bet you're both right," Logan said. "Okay. Who's ready to do some research? John, can you grab Lieutenant Christenson? We need to log in to a few of these computers."

"Why?" John asked.

"So we can get as much information from the Internet as possible on Jack Longstreet and his current employment with Kallas Shipping before we talk to Jake. It's like you said." Logan paused, smiling. "Fucking Google."

CHAPTER 21

Shady Nook, Maryland
Thirty Miles South of Annapolis on
the Western Shore of the Chesapeake Bay
Wednesday, 0830 EST

Concealed behind a brick wall and a row of thirty-foot-tall Leyland cypress trees, the waterfront home of Constantine Kallas was invisible from the street. The five-acre property was shaped like an oval at the end of small peninsula, and the brick-tree barrier ran from one end of the property to the other, touching the Chesapeake Bay at both ends to create an impenetrable wall. The only entrance was a solid metal security gate, at which a mounted intercom on a post was cemented into the side of the beginning of the driveway.

Rain beat down on the windshield of the black Ford Explorer as Logan pushed the white circular button on the intercom. The oppressive heat from the previous day had been blown apart by a cold front that had swept in from the west, barreling across the mid-Atlantic and bringing pouring rain and wind, expected to last into the evening. Maryland weather was notoriously inconsistent, and it wouldn't have surprised Logan if it snowed by the end of the day.

"I still don't think he was out of town," John said.

"Neither do I, but his office in DC said he was, and we have no probable cause. Remember, we actually are law enforcement officers sworn in as FBI agents . . . technically," Logan said.

"If you say so," John muttered. "But I would've loved to have been here yesterday. My gut tells me this Kallas guy is our man, but I guess we'll know soon enough."

After the realization that the retired general was now in the employment of Constantine Kallas, the team had spent an hour on the museum's computers, researching whatever they could find, which was shockingly limited for a multibillion-dollar shipping empire. Other than a number of flattering articles about the profitability of Kallas Shipping, nothing remotely hinted at even the slightest link to a global clandestine organization of intelligence and operations.

It was why when they'd informed Jake Benson of what they'd uncovered, he'd had no choice but to have the FBI contact Kallas' DC headquarters, only to be told that Mr. Kallas was out of the area but would be available to meet Wednesday morning at his Chesapeake Bay home.

Logan had made the decision then for the team to get some rest, since there was nothing they could do. The surviving attacker had been transferred to the Fairfax County Adult Detention Center, and Amira and Cole planned to question Jonathan Sommers at Ares headquarters the next morning regarding retired General Longstreet's role in the global conspiracy. Logan and John would take the meeting with Constantine Kallas.

"May I help you, sir?" a polite and mechanical voice said from the intercom.

"Special Agents West and Quick here to see Mr. Kallas. He's expecting us," Logan said.

"Indeed he is," the voice replied, and within seconds, the large metal door vertically split in two, and the two halves retracted behind the brick wall on each side of the driveway, revealing a guardhouse just inside to the left of the entrance. More startling, though, was the secluded compound that Kallas had built overlooking the rough waters of the Chesapeake Bay.

"Wow," John said. "We're definitely in the wrong line of business, even with an unlimited black budget."

"No kidding," Logan said, and studied the layout in front of them as he pressed the accelerator, inching the Explorer slowly forward.

The driveway was composed of cobblestone—*likely imported,* Logan thought—whose stones fit so snugly the vehicle barely registered the terrain. On both sides, the drive was lined with cherry blossoms that had bloomed and still had petals on their branches. The trees danced in the gusting winds of the summer storm. *I'll bet it's breathtaking when it's not raining, like something out of* Home and Garden, Logan thought. The large driveway ran straight through the front half of the property, parting the sea of grass and ending in a giant oval that could accommodate several vehicles, including the four parked black Range Rovers. *Why do these guys always have black SUVs? So do you, jackass.* Off to the right, two four-car garages were set back from the main house.

"You see what I see?" John asked. "Christ, if this guy is involved in the hit on the NSA director, we're slightly outgunned for this confrontation."

Logan didn't respond but only looked to the left of the driveway in the back corner of the property where an unoccupied octagonal helipad had been constructed. "Too bad there's nothing on it, though," Logan said, nodding in its direction.

"You mean like a fake news chopper with a shot-out windshield and sign that says, 'Bad guy getaway vehicle. Fly the friendly skies'?" John retorted.

"There's no way they would've come back here. They're not that stupid. Not even close."

"Yeah. We never get the dumb ones, only the fucking mega-lomaniac masterminds hell-bent on global destruction. Our luck *sucks*," John finished.

"Let's see what happens when we get to the house," Logan said.

As scenic as the property and driveway were, it was the home that truly captured their attention. While neither one was well versed in modern architecture, they could both appreciate the inge-nuity and modern marvel before them.

The home was constructed of stark white stone that glistened in the rain, reflecting light off all five sections, which formed a subtle U shape. The center of the mansion in front of which they'd parked was three stories tall, with the top section built almost as a watchtower, with wall-to-wall windows through which both could see the sky over the bay behind the property. *I'll bet that's some kind of master suite,* Logan thought. On each side of the home was an-other two-story section, and on each end, a single-story completed the descending profile. The rooflines were narrow and sleek, with only a slight peak in the middle of the center. The shorter sections' roofs had the same pitch as the ones above it, creating a perfectly symmetrical modern masterpiece.

"It's gorgeous," John said. "It makes my A-frame back in Mon-tana seem like a shack, even with the enormous picture window. This has to be at least fifteen thousand square feet."

"It's something, for sure," Logan said, wondering how many millions the shipping tycoon's compound had cost to build.

Logan pulled the Explorer around the oval and stopped in front of the enormous black doors set in stark contrast to the white stone. Two security gates were propped open, one on each side against the walls.

As he placed the SUV in park, he looked up to the entrance just in time to see the left panel of the doors swing inward and the im-posing figure of Retired Marine Corps Commandant General Jack

Longstreet step outside into the rain, strong arms on display and crossed in front of him.

"Well," John said, "I guess that mystery's solved. He still looks like a brazen badass, even at his age."

"Yes. He does," Logan said, studying the figure of his former mentor. "You have your nineteen-eleven loaded, right?"

"Always," John said. "Otherwise, what's the point of carrying a gun?"

"Good. Don't hesitate to use it if this goes south. Now let's go reacquaint ourselves with one of the Marine Corps' beloved commandants."

CHAPTER 22

Logan and John stepped out of the vehicle and into the rain, walking cautiously up the multitiered stone staircase until they stopped one step below the man they'd fought alongside in Ramadi.

"Sir, I'd say it's good to see you, but I'm not sure it is," Logan started. "I guess I should thank you for the phone call yesterday, as it saved my life."

Jack Longstreet nodded and looked beyond the parked Explorer toward the entrance, as if expecting additional company. Then he looked Logan directly in the eyes, stuck out his hand, which Logan shook, and said, "It's the least I could do. I still owe you for Iraq. Now let's get out of this mess. We all spent enough time in the rain in the Marine Corps. No need to do it now."

The three men hurried through the open door, which Jack closed with a loud *clang*, shutting out the sounds of the raging weather.

Two men in black polos and dark-gray trousers stood off to the right inside an office that was obviously the home's security command center. They were both in their midthirties, clean-shaven, with short, neat haircuts, muscular physiques, and intelligent eyes. Both men wore CZ 75 SP-01 Tactical 9mm pistols in leather holsters on their right hips. The men nodded at the newcomers, *not in a hostile, challenging way, but rather, assessing us. These guys are pros, and I'll bet there are more of them around,* Logan thought. Both Logan and John caught a glimpse of stacks of monitors four levels high.

The inside of the home was even more impressive than the exterior, offering several multistory views of the Chesapeake Bay. While the front of the home was mostly solid white stone, the back was almost all glass, partitioned by steel girders that intersected at various V angles for stability. There was even a steel-and-glass suspended walkway halfway up the back of the room, which ran the full length of the center section of the home. Logan realized the ceiling of the main space was actually the floor of the third level. *I'll bet the view is even better from up there.* Every aspect of the design was intended to maximize the sweeping seascape of the bay, which was the essence of the home.

Through the panorama of glass and steel, Logan saw a patio, pool, and a multitiered deck that wound its way to the property's drop-off at the water. Below the drop-off, an enormous super-yacht was berthed along a long wooden pier. The ship's upper levels jutted into the sky above the elevation of the property. *She's got to be at least thirty to forty feet tall,* Logan thought.

"This way," Jack said, and walked through the viewing area, across the hardwood floor, to an oversized, arched entrance set in the left wall. As Logan stepped under the arch, he realized he'd been ushered into the office of Constantine Kallas, one of the richest—and apparently most powerful—men in the world.

Jack, Logan, and John stopped just inside the entrance, and two sets of glass doors slid closed automatically behind them, sealing them inside the spacious and luxurious office with a sound that reminded Logan of the vacuum tubes still used by banks. Two guards posted themselves outside the office, one on each side.

An enormous dark wooden desk sat at one side of the office, whose exterior wall was built of several panes of connected glass that stretched from the hardwood floor to the ceiling. The rain lashed against the windows in bursts, increasing and decreasing in intensity with a rhythm only Mother Nature understood.

The billionaire stared into the rain, as if searching for something only he could see. Finally, the tall, thin, elderly man with a slight, tired slump to his shoulders turned around to greet them, and Logan realized how deceiving appearances really were.

"Mr. West, Mr. Quick, I am truly thankful you could make it here today. We have a lot to discuss," Constantine Kallas said. While his physical form hinted at defeat, his brown eyes burned with life, forcefully meeting Logan's gaze and assessing him with a disquieting shrewdness and intelligence.

This must be how I make people feel, Logan thought, recalling the number of times both Sarah and John had told him how truly fierce and intimidating he could look with his green eyes and scar down the left side of his face.

"You sound like you knew we were coming," John said. "But that's only because the general here called Logan to warn him of the ambush yesterday, saying something that gave him away. Otherwise, we'd have no clue who you were."

Constantine smiled. "Do you really think Jack would be that careless? Of course he did—*because I asked him to.*"

The wheels turned in Logan's mind, and he realized instantly that this was the true puppet master, a modern Machiavelli who had been orchestrating events to serve his end. And somehow, Logan and John had just become pawns on the global chessboard.

Logan's hand slid to his right hip, where his Kimber was holstered in an outside-the-waistband Mitch Rosen leather holster that he wore when on official business.

John sensed the movement and began to react as well.

"Logan," Jack said calmly but in a commanding voice that Logan knew well and responded to, "it's not like that. In fact, it's not like that at all."

Logan looked at Jack, a hardness in his eyes fueled by the rising tide of anger he felt at being manipulated. "Then what's it like? What exactly is this?"

"This," Constantine said matter-of-factly, "is an invitation."

"For what? To join your yachting club?" John asked sarcastically.

"No, Mr. Quick. To help put a stop to the mess that I started decades ago and can no longer control," Constantine said.

John shook his head in frustration. "Wait a second. You want us to help you? Let me guess. You played Pandora and let the monsters out of the box, and now they're running wild. It's always the same with you guys. You're all a bunch of fucking megalomaniacs." His voice grew louder by the moment. "Personally, you can go fuck yourself. In fact, I think I'd love nothing more than to see you go out on that nice little rowboat out back and send yourself to the bottom of the bay."

Constantine Kallas stared impassively at John, but rather than defend himself against the verbal onslaught, he said, "Point taken, Mr. Quick. You're right on all fronts. I also appreciate the reference to Greek mythology, given my background."

"It was intentional. Why do you think I said it, jackass?" John replied sharply.

Logan had listened as John verbally lashed Constantine. Finally, he said, "John, I have a feeling we need to hear what this man has to say." He paused, allowing the beast within to run free, a brief respite from the pen inside Logan's psyche, its intensity dominating and without equal. "But I tell you this, Mr. Kallas—and this goes for you as well, Jack, history or not—if for one second I sense a betrayal of *any kind, I will shoot you both in the face* without remorse and without hesitation."

A silence followed his threat, which all in the room knew was not hollow.

"I'd expect nothing less from you, Logan," Jack replied quietly. "Now let's get started. We have a lot to discuss."

CHAPTER 23

By the time both Constantine Kallas and Jack Longstreet had finished describing the origin, accomplishments, and scope of the Organization, both Logan and John were numb from both the gravity of the situation and the significance of the past few years' events. The fact that it was all interconnected was the hardest part for Logan to process.

Without the Organization, Cain Frost may never have had the resources to build his army of private contractors, sucking Logan and John back into the thick of the global morass. What was worse was the possibility that had Constantine dealt with the problem quickly, the Council might not have turned on him, initiating the events in Sudan and Las Vegas that had ultimately led to Mike Benson's death.

He's gone now, and there's nothing you can do about it, Logan thought. He shut his eyes for a moment and inhaled deeply, trying to keep the anger at bay. The other part of the whole mess that pained him was the fact that he understood why Constantine had created his network. He was a practical man, and the Organization had achieved significant success, even if the world was unaware of it.

"I get it," Logan finally said. The conversation with Cain Frost after he'd run him literally into the dirt two and a half years earlier was still fresh in his mind. "Cain said something similar. He was driven by revenge for the death of his brother, and had he struck that blow in Tehran, there are a lot of Iraqi war veterans who would've cheered him on for it, knowing what Iran did to American men and women with their endless supply of IEDs to the insurgency. And that's not to mention what they're doing in Afghanistan. But I'm going to tell you the same thing I told him: it was never your call to make, no matter how you justify it. This is a republic, not a shadow dictatorship. *You are not the president,*" Logan said forcefully.

"No kidding," John said. "We know because we actually work for him, and I'm pretty sure you weren't on the personnel roster."

Constantine considered this for a moment, choosing his words carefully. "That may be true, but each administration has been aware of our existence, in one form or another, and we've never been at cross-purposes with the US government . . . at least until now."

"What the hell does that mean?" John asked sharply.

"It means that there are some very high-ranking members of the US government on the Council who are involved in this rebellion against this man here and the Organization, and we're trying to stop it before it becomes either a national or a global calamity," Jack said.

"We started yesterday," Constantine said calmly.

A flash of anger raced across his face, and Logan said quietly, "That was you on the parkway." He looked at Jack. "You pulled the trigger on General Taylor, didn't you?"

"I did," Jack said slowly. "He left us no choice. He was one of the members that turned. More importantly, he was starting to use his position as director of the NSA and the chief of Cyber Command *against* the national security interests of the United States."

It was the directness with which he spoke that unsettled Logan the most. There was no remorse, no hesitation. He spoke like a man of conviction, which hammered home one hard truth: *Whatever war we're now in the middle of is for keeps.*

"Does the fact that he was a Marine, a fellow combat veteran—like yourself—even bother you a little bit?" John asked accusatorily.

"Absolutely," Jack replied instantly, "but if we hadn't removed him from the board, the amount of damage he was prepared to do would've been catastrophic. If there had been any other way—any way at all—we would have taken it. But he was a believer and convinced that what he was doing was right. There was no talking him out of it."

"And what exactly was he doing?" Logan asked pointedly.

"Creating global instability, abroad and at home, all with one singular goal," Constantine said.

"What's that?" John asked.

"High treason," Constantine said. "He and the other Council members that have turned want to create enough global chaos to cause a constitutional crisis and ultimately lead to the resignation or impeachment of the president."

"That's impossible," Logan said. "The people won't stand for it."

"And who do you think is going to propel the president out of office? If you create enough chaos and sow enough fear, the people will do it for them."

"But how?" John asked. "You're talking about manipulating global events on such a massive scale that it could literally topple the most powerful government on the planet. That would take almost limitless resources."

"What do you think has been happening over the past few years, especially since you two have been right in the middle of it, aware or not?" Jack said.

"While I wouldn't describe it as limitless, what I've built is vast *and powerful.* It's also highly compartmented, meaning some elements of the Organization are not fully aware of the others' existence," Constantine said.

The genius of it struck Logan. "You've basically created the world's most powerful terrorist network, with one cell compartmented from another to avoid discovery. Jesus . . . "

"While I wouldn't characterize it that way, I understand the analogy," Jack said.

"But you still haven't answered the question. If the network is compartmented and secure, why kill General Taylor? There's something else, isn't there?" Logan asked.

"There is—a list," Constantine said. "General Taylor used resources at NSA to hack our servers, discover the full scope of the network, and create a list of all divisions and members of the Organization. With it and the appropriate authority, the kind that some of the Council members have, he and the other traitors could've activated it and used it to further their agenda."

The implications were staggering. It truly was Pandora's box. *In the wrong hands, it would wreak havoc,* Logan thought. His strategic mind took it one step further: it will never end. There is always going to be another Cain Frost, another Organization, another Constantine. For as long as humanity exists, the struggles of power among those who have it would endure. It was almost too much to bear.

Logan closed his eyes, resting his head against the headrest of the high-back leather chair. *What do you do now, Logan? There are no good choices.*

No one spoke. The rain sprayed across the window, soothing the voice that screamed for blood, the one that demanded that these two men—one of whom he had fought alongside—pay for their sins. But it was the logical part of his brain that gave him pause, that showed him the reality of the situation and the choice he had to make.

"So what exactly do you propose?" Logan asked.

"You're not seriously going to consider this?" John said.

"There is no better option," Logan said, trying to assuage his friend's outrage at the thought of working with them.

"But it still fucking sucks, brother," John said. "There has to be another way."

"John—" Jack began, but was cut off.

"Don't," John spat out viciously. He faced Jack and said, "Don't say a fucking thing. If it weren't for Logan, I'd be tempted to put you down myself . . . both of you, for that matter. You've *created a maelstrom of madness*, and now we're all going to pay for it, you sonofabitch." He looked back at Logan. After all they'd been through together, he trusted his friend's judgment. "But it's your call, and I'll execute whatever play you set."

A sudden commotion erupted outside the glass doors, and one of the guards spoke into a small handheld radio in his left hand. His CZ 75 SP-01 was out of its holster in his right hand, and he tapped the glass with the butt of the weapon. The second guard started sprinting across the floor back toward the main entrance to the mansion, his weapon drawn.

"Well, in my experience, that's not a good thing," John said, watching the running guard. "But I should've expected nothing less from a fucking James Bond–villain wannabe. I guess this is where the crying and dying starts."

"I really wish you wouldn't jinx us like that," Logan said, rising from the leather chair.

The glass doors slid open, and the guard with the radio said, "Gentlemen, we have a problem. We need to get back to the vault."

"It's what they call the security operations center you saw off to the right when you walked in. Let's go," Jack said.

Twenty seconds later, all six men were staring at the bank of monitors.

"Goddamnit. I told you not to open your mouth. You just had to go and spoil the party, didn't you?" Logan said.

"I think those guys are going to do it for me," John said, looking at the monitor on the bottom right. The camera providing the live feed was mounted on the roofline of one of the garages they'd passed on their way up the driveway. It had a panoramic view of the front of the home and the yard, including the eight armed men in tactical gear, assault rifles, and backpacks stalking their way across the open ground through the pouring rain. Black barrels were up and ready, piercing the sheets of rain as they closed in on the front of the home.

You're almost out of time, Logan. You have to act.

CHAPTER 24

"Any idea who they are?" Logan asked.

"Honestly, it could be anyone, even a legitimate military or law enforcement unit that's operating unofficially and outside the law. Right there," Longstreet said, pointing at the screen, "that's the kind of power and resources members on the Council have."

"Wonderful," Logan replied, leery of a gunfight with forces that might be legitimate friendlies. *This just gets worse by the second.*

"Please tell me your little private army here has an arsenal," John said bluntly.

"Get the QRF gear. Commandos and vests for everyone," Longstreet said to one of the guards, who was already at the back of the security room, entering a combination into an electronic keypad installed on the handle of a very heavy-looking steel door.

The door beeped, and the guard turned the handle and pulled, providing a glimpse into a much larger space lined with weapons, tactical black backpacks, and ammunition. Logan thought he even spied an automatic grenade launcher in the back next to two open bags of cash.

It reminded him of a story he'd once heard from another Force Recon platoon commander, one whose platoon was the first US unit in Afghanistan after 9/11. The platoon had linked up with a SEAL team at some airfield the CIA had taken control of with the Northern Alliance. Logan's friend, Todd Wexler, said, "We walked into the control tower, and there was this CIA guy handing out guns, cash—they had at least twenty million in black leather bags, swear to God—and ammo. He told us to take what we wanted and not sign for any of it. We were like kids in a candy store."

"Glad to see you haven't let your guard down," Logan said, as the guard started handing out guns and Kevlar vests like birthday party favors.

"Not now, not ever," Jack said. "By the way, my two boys here are former JSOC by way of the Unit," he said, using the name Delta Force operators preferred. "Delta Force" was for Chuck Norris and the movies. "Stan and Evan were with Squadron B. They're good to go."

"Good to know," Logan said, donning the Kevlar vest, which had four extra magazine pouches on the front and a medical kit on the back. He grabbed an M4 Commando, looped the three-point tactical sling around and under his left arm, pulled the charging handle back, and chambered the first round, ensuring the safety was still flipped on. *No need to shoot anyone yet. That will come soon enough.*

"Stan, get Boone and Hamilton on the radio. See if they can flank these guys. Let 'em know they're on their own, but we'll try to link up once the fighting starts," Jack ordered.

"Roger, sir," Stan said, then spoke quickly into his radio and gave Jack a thumbs-up, indicating he'd reached the other two men providing security on the compound.

"Is this all you have? Four men for this entire place?" John asked.

"You forgot me," Jack said, smirking.

"My bad," John replied. "You make five. May the odds be ever in your favor."

"Cute. I'd forgotten what a sarcastic bastard you are," Jack said. "We actually have an entire team, but they're up the road in Annapolis."

"After what you pulled yesterday, you didn't think that someone might come looking to end this little turf war before it really got started?" Logan asked.

"Actually, we considered it, which is why we were planning on leaving this afternoon," Constantine interjected. "I didn't think it'd be this soon."

"Unless this was part of the whole plan from the get-go," Logan said. "Doesn't matter. We're all in it now."

"Any thoughts, Logan? You always had a mind for this," Jack said.

"As a matter of fact, I do," said the former Force Reconnaissance commanding officer, front and center. "I don't like it, but it maximizes the chances of the most important thing right now."

"Which is?" John asked.

"Keeping this sonofabitch alive for as long as possible," Logan said, looking directly at the concerned face of Constantine Kallas.

———

Anne Arundel County Aviation Unit
Tipton Airport

Corporal Corey Taggert hung up the phone and screamed, "Wheels up in two minutes! We need to go right now!"

At least I don't have to finish the stupid inspection, he thought, grateful for any reason to ignore the tedious CALEA—Commission on Accreditation for Law Enforcement Agencies—safety certification he was engaged in at the moment. The safety checklist was necessary but an administrative burden.

The Anne Arundel County police helicopter pilot shouted across the hangar as he approached the dark- and light-blue police Bell 407 helicopter. "You better be moving, Williams!"

He heard sharp footsteps coming across the concrete floor of the hangar. "What's going on?" Private First Class Jeff Williams said as he zipped up his flight suit, his aviator's helmet with its built-in HUD display in his right hand. "What's the hurry?" he asked.

"FBI agents on the Chesapeake Bay in need of immediate air support. Sounds like it's about to be a gunfight. Go get the M4s and vests while I pull her out onto the tarmac."

PFC Williams didn't need to be told twice. A former enlisted Marine aviation crewmember on a CH-46 with two tours in Iraq, he understood the true meaning of urgency. He sprinted back to the office to get the weapons. *I guess today might not be a boring day after all.*

Front Yard of the Kallas Compound

The fact that there was no reaction to their presence was disconcerting to Terry Deavers, a tall, forty-two-year-old muscular man with a short haircut but full black, tailored beard. It told the former Hard Resolutions Incorporated mercenary and once-upon-a-time-in-a-different-life Special Forces Army Green Beret that the men inside—including the target—were either preparing defenses or had no clue their world was about to be blown upside down. It didn't matter which to him.

After Cain Frost had been killed and his private contractor empire had been liquidated—not in the literal sense—Terry Deavers had looked elsewhere for a new source of income. Never burdened by the moral compass most military men possessed, he'd been recruited by a Virginia drug cartel to help establish a base of heroin distribution in the rural spot conveniently named Spotsylvania. While the money had been excellent, the quality of his coworkers was lacking, their common backgrounds ranging from random street thuggery to armed robbery to murder. *Any fool with a gun can kill, but not everyone can be an operator.*

His delusional sense of self-worth had him believing he was a warrior, and warriors needed a mission. *Otherwise, what's the point?* That question had been answered when he'd been recruited once again by a former associate of Cain Frost. The man, who asked Terry to actually call him the Recruiter, had shown up at his Bethesda, Maryland, town home, with an offer of work—the kind he'd done at HRI—and a stack of former military résumés from which to screen prospective team members. Over the past year and a half, he'd done exactly that—built an efficient, proficient team of mercenaries and men looking for a purpose. They'd all been handsomely compensated, and their focus had been on one thing—train for the day when the Recruiter would call with an actual mission.

Fortunately, that call had come last night, and the mission was finally upon them. *Only one way to go, and that's hard and fast,* Terry thought, and smiled, thinking of a former team member who had had that motto on a bumper sticker on his pickup truck.

"Spartan Two," Terry said into a microphone attached to a loop on the shoulder of his Kevlar vest, "I don't like this quiet, even in the rain. Something's up. Call in the boats."

Now there's nowhere to go, boys. We've got you surrounded. The mission was simple—infiltrate and kill everyone inside. Period. For Terry Deavers, a man with no conscience but a lot of motivation, it was an easy assignment with no guilt or strings attached. It was the best kind of first date, just the way he liked it.

CHAPTER 25

BOOM!

The SIMON M100 Grenade Rifle Entry Munition fired by Terry Deavers blew both front doors inward and off the hinges, creating a gaping hole in the mansion.

Inside, Logan West waited patiently in the far-left corner of the enormous living room, the six minutes-of-angle red dot of the Vortex Razor Red reflex sight lined up on the front door. He'd chosen a position behind an enormous, thick dining room table that would at least provide a semblance of cover once the assaulting force breached the doorway. The Colt Commando rested on top of the table, and he had a full view of the entire living room, kitchen, front hallway, and front door. He knew with all of the furniture between the entrance and himself, it would take any attacker at least a second or two to acquire his location. *And that's all I need.*

Jack Longstreet was positioned in the far-right corner, behind a bookcase he'd moved away from the wall. The former Delta operator named Stanley had assumed the best and most dangerous vantage point—prone on the elevated walkway that ran parallel with the panoramic view. Due to his exposure, he'd donned a Kevlar helmet, although he knew if he took a round in the face, it likely wouldn't matter.

The entrance was covered by triangulated fire. *Good luck, guys. No matter what, whoever came through the door first would die. Welcome to the slaughter,* Logan thought. The FBI agent facade was gone, replaced by the predatory Marine and warrior.

A black canister sailed through the doorway, and with a soft *pop,* a cloud of thick white smoke enveloped the entire foyer.

Additional gunfire erupted from the front of the mansion. *The other two members of the security detail must have engaged. Hope they take a few down and even the playing field just a little,* Logan thought.

The sound of boots echoed through the smoke from the front steps. *Here they come. Time to work,* Logan thought, and pulled the trigger, unleashing a controlled burst of 5.56mm fire at the same time that Jack and Stanley opened fire.

An incessant *tink-tink-tink-tink-tink* sounded through the smoke as they fired into it.

What the hell? Logan thought, a moment later realizing what the sound was, turning his blood cold. *Oh no.*

The swirls of smoke suddenly dissipated, disintegrated by two assaulters entering the foyer in a crouch, carrying ballistic shields held closely together to ensure protection from the withering fire. The shields had enlarged triangular ballistic viewports, and Logan saw the two operators scanning the room, heads covered by black ballistic helmets rotating from left to right. *It's like a goddamned SWAT team.*

Logan shifted the sights to the floor, hoping to take their feet or legs out. His efforts were in vain, and the rounds harmlessly pinged off the shields, shattering a glass cabinet and punching holes in the walls.

"Shooter, twelve o'clock, on the catwalk!" Logan heard one of the attackers scream.

A moment later, a barrage of gunfire from several operators in the back of the assault formation struck the elevated catwalk, and just as Stan had foreseen, the Kevlar helmet did nothing to protect him. Logan saw Stan reach behind him, straining for something Logan couldn't see. Unfortunately, several well-placed rounds caught him in the face and throat, ending the shortest gunfight in which he'd participated during his life.

A large object fell off the back of the walkway, and Logan recognized the Mk 14 Mod 0 six-shot revolver-style 40mm grenade launcher. *Good man, Stan,* Logan thought. *You may have given us a fighting chance. Now I just have to get to the damn thing.*

Jack had the same thought and looked at Logan, who pointed and nodded toward the door, himself, and the fallen grenade launcher. Jack acknowledged the unspoken order and opened fire, initiating the diversion.

Forgive me, Sarah, Logan thought, and ran in a crouch toward the discarded weapon thirty feet away as Jack sustained the gunfire. Both attackers returned fire toward the retired general until someone spotted Logan dashing toward the Mk 14.

"Runner!" someone screamed. "Light him up!"

Thanks, asshole, Logan thought, and kept running.

Fortunately for him, the only two who had a direct line of sight on him were the front two assaulters, and the shields hindered the accuracy of the Bruger & Thomet MP9 submachine gun each wielded in one hand. Rounds ricocheted off the table, shattered enormous panes of glass that crashed to the hardwood floor inside and stone patio outside, and punctured holes in the furniture.

Logan dove to the floor, sliding across the hardwood surface, glass shards puncturing his vest and tearing at his khaki cargo pants. He reached the Mk 14 as the gunfire ceased, and he heard, "Reloading!"

His hand grasped the pistol grip of the grenade launcher, he turned on his side, found a clear line of sight under another table near the enormous bar in the back of the room, and extended his right arm at the two operators with the ballistic shields. *I hope you loaded it, Stan,* Logan thought, and pulled the trigger.

———

John, Evan, and Constantine were halfway across the patio, on the other side of the edgeless pool that ended where the patio stopped and the multitier deck started, when the breaching charge blew the front door to pieces and the battle began. Their objective was simple—get to the Sunseeker 131 superyacht and head out into the middle of the bay until the battle was over or help arrived.

In addition to being an expert marksman and former Delta sniper, Evan was also the yacht's captain. *These guys have a lot of collateral duties,* John thought, remembering the various hats he wore as a Force Reconnaissance platoon sergeant.

The three men hustled down the stone steps to a sloping wooden ramp as the sounds of gunfire intensified. To John's trained ear, the gunfight sounded like it was a give-and-take on both sides. *Hope to hell you're dishing it out better than you're getting, Logan,* John willed to his friend.

The ramp sloped downward to the right and back to the left multiple times, a dazzling view of the Chesapeake Bay at each switchback, reminding John of the old video game *Donkey Kong,* minus the giant gorilla. *And it sounds like these guys are throwing much worse things than barrels.*

A new sound appeared on the audible horizon, distinct and clear, even through the rain outside and gunfire inside.

"How fast can you get her started and away from the dock?" John asked as they sprinted down the final incline to the pier below. The yacht was docked sixty feet out into the bay, connected to a single pier that jutted out from the rocky beach.

"In less than a minute, once we untie her," Evan responded. "Why?"

"Because of those," John said as they hit the pier running. John pointed a half mile north to the point of Shady Nook, where two rigid-hull inflatable boats were maneuvering the rough waters of the bay toward them. Four dark figures hugged the top of the sponsons on each boat, two on each side, fighting the weather and the rain. John had run RHIB operations in much worse conditions, but he knew the additional attackers had to be professionals. *No doubt they're having a rough ride, but these guys came prepared.*

John turned around to check on Constantine Kallas, who moved at a much slower pace due to his age. He was still halfway down the second decline walkway when John shouted to him, "You better move faster unless you want to die on your pier! We have more company coming from the water!"

"Untie the three dock lines," Evan said crisply, as he and John moved toward the luxury boat. "And then I'm heading to the wheelhouse on the upper deck. I'll get her started and idling. Once you and the Founder get on the boat, shout as loud as you can. I'll hear you and get us out into open water."

"Got it," John said. "Hey, is there an arsenal on the yacht? All we have are these M4s against eight attackers and two boats."

"There is, but it's on the lower deck. There's a combination lock, like the one in the house. There are more M4s, ammo, flare guns, and vests, but all the good stuff was in the house. The combo is five-eight-four-five," Evan said.

Something about the numbers struck John as familiar, and Evan caught the reaction. "It's the date of V-E Day from World War Two. Founder's choice."

"Of course," John replied. "I guess today I get to find out how much damage I can do with one assault rifle against two boats full of amphibious raiders. Go me." With the last comment still on his lips, he dashed down the pier to untie the line closest to the bow, leaving Evan to scramble onto the platform at the stern of the boat.

I really am tired of boats, John thought, hoping for once they wouldn't have to sink one. *The North Korean cargo ship off the coast of Spain last year was more than enough for one lifetime,* he thought as he reached the thick black line and began to unwind it.

———

Thwunk!

The first 40mm grenade flew under the table between the hard, wooden legs. It struck the triangular port of the ballistic shield of the attacker on the right, detonating upon impact and propelling the shield backward, end over end like an out-of-control rocket. The edge of the shield crashed against the side of the head of the man who'd been holding it a second before, and it bounced crazily up and away, lodging itself horizontally in the windows that were still intact above the ruined doorway. The attacker fell to the floor, unconscious, *although not for long,* Logan thought, intent on exploiting the gap he'd just exposed in the enemy's defense.

With his mind only focused on one thing—*death for all of them*—he pulled the trigger of the semiautomatic grenade launcher as quickly as possible and sent the five remaining 40mm grenades directly into the middle of the group of attackers, with devastating results.

Four of the five grenades were direct hits on personnel, and one unfortunate soul was struck twice, the second grenade hitting him in the head and removing it in a puff of blood and bone. The fifth grenade sailed high and struck what was left of the doorframe on top. It disintegrated the wall and windows, and the ballistic shield that had been suspended for only a few seconds was released from the house's grasp. It dropped to the tile floor, already slick with fresh blood from the dismembered bodies, and bounced up and down, a shiny red buoy on a sea of carnage.

Logan gazed at the destruction he'd wrought, satisfied that he and Jack were the only living souls in the home. The shield fell over and lay still, breaking Logan's reverie. "You okay, Jack?" Logan asked as he stood up, the grenade launcher held in his left hand.

Jack, who had sought cover behind the bookcase, emerged unscathed. "I am now," he replied, and walked over to Logan, surveying the wreckage of bodies, glass, and shattered furniture around them. "Wow. I guess it's a good thing I bought that grenade launcher."

"You think?" Logan asked in a deadpan tone. "I mean, who doesn't have a semiautomatic grenade launcher? It's got to be great at parties. 'Come on kids. Fuck the clowns. Let's blow some shit up.'"

He unslung the M4 Commando and shouldered the launcher.

"Point taken," Jack replied. "But it did come in handy."

"I'll give you that," Logan said. "We need to get to John and your men, but I'm going to grab some more grenades. You never know. And Jack," Logan said in a voice suddenly sincere, "I'm sorry about Stan. At least he saved us and went out on his shield."

"He was an excellent soldier who thought the Organization was critical enough to join, even if it meant he was a criminal and a traitor in the eyes of the hypocrites who run this country," Jack said.

There's a part of me that sympathizes—more than that, that supports what they're doing. God help me. I get it, Logan thought.

Logan nodded, looking out the shattered wall of glass at the yacht below, and said, "We need to get out—"

"*Move!*" Jack suddenly screamed, and Logan reacted to the tone of his voice like a Marine to a drill instructor halfway through boot camp. He dove to the left as gunfire erupted from the front of the house.

Jack returned fired but stopped as Logan heard a grunt of pain. Jack fell to the floor. *Oh no.* Logan spun on his knees, drew a bead on the gaping hole in the front of the house, but only saw death and destruction. *Where'd he go?*

Logan crouched and moved over to Jack, who tried to sit up, his M4 useless in his right hand.

"He went back outside," Jack said through gritted teeth. "My shoulder's fucked, but I'm not out of it yet." he added, seething with a battle rage and focus that emanated from him like the sweat that had been triggered by the bullet wound.

"Let's get you up," Logan said, wondering why the shooter had retreated to the front yard. The silence from outside—other than the constant rain—was troubling, and he wondered what had happened to the other two members of the security team. *Well, if nothing else, it gives us time to get the hell out of the house.*

Unfortunately, the thought was as far his plan proceeded, for a moment later, a single man stormed through the doorway, a ballistic shield held in front of him. Logan saw the barrel of the MP9 near the right edge of the shield and reacted instantly.

"The office," Logan said forcefully, and pulled Jack with him as he dashed across broken glass toward the spacious office of Constantine Kallas.

———

The Sunseeker superyacht pulled away from the pier and into the rough waters of the Chesapeake Bay. The bay was usually somewhat choppy, but with the storm, rain, and wind, it was blowing five- to seven-foot waves, which was like relative calm to the luxury vessel. *But I hope it's beating the hell out of our friends on the RHIBs,* John thought.

From his perch nearly thirty feet above the water on the sky deck—the uppermost level of the yacht, which he knew gave him the greatest tactical advantage—he watched the two small boats bob up and down. They were still more than a few hundred yards away, although closing the distance. *Just need to hold out until reinforcements get here. Jake had better been able to call in air support, or we're dead in the water, no pun intended.*

The last thing Logan had done before John, Evan, and Constantine had fled out the back of the mansion was to place a call to Jake Benson, requesting immediate tactical and air support. While most local law enforcement might not be much help against the type of firepower they faced, a police helicopter could, as long as the team came prepared. *If not, at least they'll get some nice overhead shots of us all getting killed,* John thought ironically.

He looked through the reflex sight, trying to acquire a clear sight picture of the closest boat. The handguard of the Commando rested on the railing on the port side of the yacht, secured up against a vertical column that led to a small roof, on which were mounted the numerous antennae and radomes for the ship's communications and navigation systems. His left hand held the forward pistol grip. He adjusted the rifle. He planned to unload on the boats in order to create as much standoff distance as possible. *Might even get lucky and hit a few of the bastards.* He knew this type of gunfight wasn't like the movies. It wasn't as ridiculously hard as shooting out the tires of a moving car and watching it flip end over end, but it wasn't going to be easy.

The speed of the yacht increased, and he steadied himself, pressing his left knee against the glass railing for stability. The boats were less than one hundred and fifty yards away. He looked through the scope and managed to keep the red dot on the boat in front. Although the movement of the yacht shifted the sight slightly, it never dropped off the target.

More gunfire erupted from the mansion, although it sounded much more faint with the combined noise of the yacht, wind, and rain. *I'll take that as a sign,* he thought, and pulled the trigger, the fire selector set on semi to afford him the most accuracy.

Crack . . . crack . . . crack!

John paused after the third shot. At least one of the rounds struck home, as the front figure on the left sponson slid over the side, as if he'd decided to go for a casual swim. *Hopefully, all the way to the bottom, asshole.*

The boats suddenly split apart, the front boat veering left, the rear one to the right, as if their captains realized that a straight line at the yacht might not be the best avenue of approach.

John kept his focus on the front boat less than a hundred yards away, figuring if he could completely remove one of the boats from play, it would greatly increase their chances of survival. He opened fire again, concentrating on the driver of the boat, who stood at the center console.

Six shots and three seconds later, the driver of the boat jolted, as if surprised. He looked down at his chest and then slumped forward over the steering wheel and console. The driverless boat violently turned left, away from the yacht, and the driver was flung off the console and into the rough waters.

Two down. Not too shabby so far, John thought. With the first boat no longer a threat, John shifted the sight to the second boat, and a cold flush of panic gripped him. *At least these fuckers came prepared. I'll give them that.*

"Get down now!" John screamed, praying that Evan and Constantine in the wheelhouse directly below heard him.

He flung himself to the deck as the M134 minigun he hadn't seen until the last second opened fire, unleashing a barrage of 7.62mm lead that tore into the yacht.

————

As Logan and Jack passed through the glass doors and gunfire followed them into the office, Jack shouted, "Hit the button on the right and slide the switch below it to the right!"

The doors slid shut and closed with the vacuum-tube sound just as more bullets impacted the glass doors and created small craters in rapid-fire fashion on all four panes.

Jack grinned at Logan. "Constantine wanted ballistic glass in here for this very reason. This office is a sort of panic room, although we didn't reinforce the walls."

"Great. Now that you've confirmed your master plan works, how the hell do we get out of here?" Logan asked.

The gunfire stopped, and both former Marines turned to look through the distorted and spiderweb-filled glass. A large solitary figure with a long black beard, outfitted in the same tactical gear as the rest of the assault force, stood motionless, the ballistic shield no longer in his hand. The MP9 was held down at his right side. He cocked his head to the left, as if studying a painting in the National Gallery of Art. Something about the movement chilled Logan, reminding him of the unstoppable serial killer from the *Friday the 13th* movies from the 1980s. *Instead of a hockey mask and a machete, he's got a black Kevlar helmet and a submachine gun.*

"What's he doing?" Jack asked, his voice unconsciously lowered, as if speaking loudly would provoke their silent stalker into action.

As if reading their minds, the figure suddenly slid an assault pack off his large frame, placed it on the floor, and knelt beside it.

"I don't know, but whatever it is, it's not good for us," Logan said. "We need to get out of here now and figure out how to stop this psycho. What are our options?"

"Work our way through the rest of the house, but who knows if there are any more of these guys in either wing? Or flee out the back down to the water, which would expose us to whatever other tricks this joker has up his sleeve."

"I don't like either of those," Logan said. "I want to put this guy down, but we need an edge."

"Then there's only one way to go," Jack said. "Up."

————

The barrage of 7.62mm lead had temporarily stopped, providing John the opportunity to glance up from his prone position near the stairwell leading from the sky deck down to the upper deck. Bullet holes were everywhere, and the glass-and-steel railing he'd used for cover earlier was gone, a mangled skeleton of steel. The deck was covered with shattered glass of all sizes and other debris.

The boat with the minigun had turned back toward the first RHIB, which had come to a stop after veering off when John had shot the driver. Even accounting for the rough waters, it seemed to be tilting slightly to the right. *Maybe I got lucky and hit one of the sponsons. Might buy us some more time.*

The absence of gunfire hit John with another sensory revelation—the yacht's engines had stopped. *Fuckers managed to take out the engines. Great. Now we're sitting ducks . . . in water. Even better.*

He scrambled to his feet and started down the short flight of stairs, reloading the M4 as he descended. "Guys, we have a big problem!"

His call was answered by silence. He turned right, glancing at the similar destruction that had been wrought on the upper deck. The long wooden table and ten chairs had been decimated, leaving a pile of leather and timber. Surprisingly, one leg had survived the fusillade, leaving that end still standing, a solitary piece of wood still unscathed.

We don't have much time before they regroup and decide to come aboard.

John dashed past the wreckage and into a short passageway that led to the yacht's wheelhouse. The door was open, providing a glimpse into the interior. A pair of legs in gray trousers that ended in dark-brown Italian chukka boots stuck out from behind the door. *Oh no.*

He hurried through the door and immediately realized that while the destruction had been severe on the sky deck, the upper deck had sustained catastrophic damage. Holes had been punched into the slanted, cockpit-style tinted glass that surrounded the wheelhouse on three sides. The two plush, oversized leather chairs had been torn in several places, and white polyester stuffing stuck out of the holes and lay on the deck. The command stations in front of the chairs had been destroyed, and both three-monitor displays were shattered. As bad as the damage was to the wheelhouse, it had been worse to Constantine Kallas.

The elderly man who'd built a global empire and commanded one of the most secret organizations in the world lay on the floor, outlined in a pool of blood. Several holes had been punched through the Kevlar vest, and his legs had sustained multiple impacts, shattering the bones underneath. His eyes stared vacantly at the ceiling.

Evan, the former Delta operator, who'd been hit in the left arm, knelt next to the man, reached up, and closed his eyes.

A moment of empathy and sorrow filled John. It wasn't for the man who lay dead at his feet; it was for the little boy who'd had his life torn apart by the Third Reich, propelling him on a course that would change the world but still end his. *You can never leave it behind. The violence always stays with you. A life full of violence will end the same.* It was the ominous implication for him, Logan, and their friends that gave him pause. *At some point, it has to stop. But not right now. Now, you need to move.*

"I'm sorry about your boss, but we need to do something, or we're going to join him," John said. "The boat with the minigun turned and was heading to the one I disabled. It's only a matter of minutes before they decide to board and finish us. This isn't a capture mission for these guys: they were here to kill Constantine, which likely goes for us now, too. This is your show. Please tell me you have some kind of contingency for this. If not, we're fucked."

Evan looked up at John, stood, and nodded.

"He told me to give you this. It's the list we took from General Taylor. He said it has everything you need," Evan held out his left hand, in which was gripped a small, rectangular black flash drive.

John grabbed the flash drive and inserted it into a small zippered pocket on the side of his cargo pants, hoping that whatever he was about to do next wouldn't damage or destroy it. His mission had just changed—*survive, link up with Logan, and get this flash drive to Jake and the president.*

"Come on," Evan said, and hurried around his employer's body and out the wheelhouse door.

Through the windows on the upper deck, John watched as the last man of the disabled RHIB leapt over to the remaining boat with the minigun. The boat turned back toward the yacht, and John heard the increase in rpms from the outboard motor.

Both men hit the main stairwell in the center of the yacht, and John said, "We have less than thirty seconds."

"Just follow me down to the lower deck," Evan replied, already three steps down the curved stairwell. "We'll have time. Trust me."

In John's experience, anytime anyone used the *T* word, chaos and confusion often followed. *Then again, this guy is an operator. So just shut your mouth and see where the Delta boy takes you.*

Ten seconds later, the two men were on the lower deck, which was full of thin smoke that still allowed them to breathe and see.

"This way," Evan said, and the two men pushed toward the stern of the yacht, through a food preparation area, past the crew-members' quarters, and through another door.

"Wow," John said as he followed past the yacht's two enormous engines that powered the dual inboard propellers under the stern of the ship. Before they'd been struck by multiple rounds—the holes the attack had created in the hull ran the length of the engine compartment—they'd been in immaculate condition.

"We kept her pristine," Evan said with pride. "But wait until you see this," he added, a sly smirk on his face as he pulled a lever up on a metal door in the back of the compartment.

Evan disappeared into the space beyond, and John followed, estimating that this final compartment was at the very rear of the yacht. Evan moved aside, revealing to John their last line of defense—a bright-yellow three-person Triton 1650 submersible that looked like a blocky spaceship.

The minisub sat on top of an elevated platform but was also connected to an overhead pulley system attached at numerous points. The center of the minisub was a glass sphere, inside which John could see a large seat near the curved glass on each side and another seat a step up behind them. A center console with multiple joysticks was placed between the seats. The sphere was connected to a sloping rectangular compartment that housed all the various systems that powered the vehicle. Both the sphere and body were seamlessly connected to two ballast tanks, one on each side. Multiple black encased propellers were placed in numerous nooks designed into the body, providing a level of maneuverability at which John could only guess. Finally, two shiny, articulated manipulator arms were connected to a round steel shaft that spanned the gap between the ballast tanks. From the front, the machine looked like a big, yellow, bulbous bug, waiting to attack.

"Start disconnecting those cables. We need to hurry," Evan said. "I'm getting in and starting her. Once you're done, push us as far back on the rails as you can and get in. I'll seal us up and open up the rear door, which will flood the compartment and allow us to launch backward."

This is crazy, even for me, John thought. *But I guess it's better than nothing.* He leapt up to the platform and started unclipping the industrial carabiners from the attach points.

———

Terry Deavers was calm and methodical. While he respected the enemy's decision to stand and fight, it would only delay the inevitable.

In the wake of the elimination of his entire assault team, he'd been forced to take matters into his own hands. Once he'd entered the mansion and chased the two targets into the spacious office, his options had once again dwindled to one. His bullets had ricocheted off the glass doors. He would have to breach the office and keep hunting the two survivors, who had disappeared out of sight.

Fortunately, Terry and his team had come prepared, and he'd placed an M112 explosive charge with more than a pound of C-4 at the seam of the sliding doors. No matter what happened, he was eager to see what kind of additional damage he could do to the home. From a meager upbringing, he resented the opulence of this house. He didn't care that the man who'd built it was a Holocaust survivor and had earned every bit of his fortune through sheer will and survival. All Terry saw was arrogance, and he relished the opportunity to deliver as much humility as he could, *before I end their lives, of course,* Terry thought as he stood in the foyer around the corner from the office and pushed the small button on his hand-held detonator.

Boom!

Not designed to withstand direct explosives, the two sets of doors disintegrated into thousands of tiny fragments that were sent whizzing through the air at high velocity, peppering the walls.

Terry emerged from the foyer into the living room, pleasantly surprised at the huge chunks of wall that had been torn off, in addition to the glass doors. The thin steel frames of the doors were bent inward and twisted, but he'd succeeded: there was nothing stopping his progress.

He stepped through the bent metal and followed the blood trail to the right, recalling from the blueprints he'd been provided what this part of the office held—a private elevator that ran directly to the third floor and master suite of the home.

Okay, then. I'll take the bait. He knew the two men were likely trying to lure him into a trap. He didn't care. He relished the challenge, his twisted mind believing the harder the targets fought, the greater the honor it was for him to kill them. He stepped into the elevator—the side facing the bay a complete picture window from floor to ceiling—and pressed the top button.

Outside, the rain and wind raged on, *as does the battle for the luxury yacht,* he thought. From his rising vantage point, he saw that one RHIB remained and had pulled alongside the yacht to board her. Surprisingly, the rear compartment door was raised, but he saw no other boats in sight. *What the hell are they doing out there?* His focus turned back to his own predicament, as the elevator let out a quiet beep, and the doors began to slide open.

The vaulted-ceiling master suite was breathtaking. To the left was another wall of crystal clear glass, through which he noted a white stone-wall balcony and the luxury yacht beyond on the bay. An enormous four-post king bed on a raised cherry oak platform lay up against the middle of the opposite wall, on which an assortment of black-and-white photos were hung, displaying images of people he didn't recognize or care about. The master bathroom was to the right of the bed, but he couldn't see the rest of the space from inside the elevator. To the left of the bed, he recognized the legs of General Longstreet sticking out toward the balcony, the rest of his body leaning up against the side of the bed as he appeared to stare out into the bay.

He realized he had a choice to make—*left or right. No way around it. It's a trap. The old man is bait. The other one is waiting, either to the left . . . or right. Fifty-fifty. You get it right or likely die. Glory or death.*

He made his choice and slowly turned to the right, the MP9 up in both hands as he arced around the corner, ignoring the left side, thinking that was where his target wanted him to look. He chose wrong as he spotted a mirror mounted on the wall directly in front of him, and worse, the reflection of a ferocious-looking man holding a black pistol aimed at the back of his head. *Damn,* he thought as the man pulled the trigger.

———

Evan slammed the pressurized hatch shut, twisted the wheel as tightly as possible, and pulled the locking lever down. The interior was relatively soundproof, shutting out the sounds of the storm and the surviving RHIB, which had seemed precariously close seconds ago. Inside the minisub, everything seemed distant and muffled, although both men knew they were in direct and immediate danger.

"Okay, then. Here we go," Evan said, and pressed a button on the computerized display in front of him. The rear bulkhead of the yacht suddenly lifted up, slowly revealing the dreary daylight beyond. Simultaneously, the platform the minisub rested on began to lower into the water, and the minisub began to slide backward.

"You ever been on one of these before?" Evan asked.

"No, but I did see something similar get dropped on someone once, right before my partner shot and killed him," John said, recalling the research submersible Logan had used as a diversion in Alaska, unintentionally crushing a Russian gunman's legs.

"Actually, I saw that too," Evan said, and grinned. "That was wild stuff, man."

"How'd you see it?" John asked, wondering what kind of access this operator had.

"YouTube, brother," Evan said, and laughed. "Everything's on YouTube these days."

No kidding. How times have changed, John thought, as the minisub accelerated and crashed into the choppy Chesapeake Bay.

"Well, since this is your virgin voyage, buckle up and enjoy the ride!" Evan shouted like a crazed cowboy and pulled the joystick backward. The minisub shot off the rails and dropped off the bottom of the platform. The next moment, John had a vertiginous sensation as he stared upward at the bottom of the yacht, which stretched out endlessly before him from his new perspective, disappearing into the murky water of the bay.

"Thanks for the heads up, Jacques Cousteau. A little sooner would've been nicer," John said, his mind trying to regain his bearings as Evan brought the minisub level.

"And ruin the fun? No way, man," Evan said, and changed topics. "Now that we're here, let's do some real damage. You ever play video games, like those flight simulators?"

"I wasn't much of a gamer, but I do remember the days when that crazy game *Doom* was popular. We actually had a bunch of them linked together at Force Recon to do some tactical training— if you can believe it—and we used joysticks for that. Because nothing says 'tactical' like Marines killing space demons," John added for good measure.

"Good," Evan said. "Now grab those joysticks and get ready to hunt a different kind of enemy. We're going to ruin these fuckers' outing right now," he said with deadly intent.

"A man after my own heart," John said, and reached for his new weapon.

———

Logan pulled the trigger when he saw the attacker's eyes meet his in the mirror that hung over a dresser between windows on the front wall.

Bang!

While his enemy realized he'd been ambushed, he'd chosen to act rather than stand and die in place. Instead of turning toward Logan the way most men would have, ensuring their demise, he did the one thing that spared his life—he dropped to the ground.

The .45-caliber round struck the top of the black Kevlar helmet, flinging the protective headgear up and off the man's head but not stopping his momentum.

The man was fast, and before Logan could pull the trigger again, his opponent had turned and raised the MP9 up in an arc, knocking the Kimber Tactical II off to the side.

Logan dropped the Kimber and placed both hands on the strong wrists that held the MP9, realizing his only chance was to disarm his enemy. He found himself staring inches away and slightly upward into a face fixed equally in determination and hostile aggression. And then the brown eyes blinked in recognition, surprising Logan.

"I know who you are," the man said in a low growl. "You're not on my list, but you *are* in my way."

The man lashed out with a low roundhouse kick to Logan's left knee, but Logan turned to his right and lowered his body, taking the brunt of the blow with the outside of his upper thigh. He countered by driving forward with his left shoulder into the man's Kevlar vest, his hands still firmly locked on the wrists that held the submachine gun. Continuing his momentum, he propelled himself upward and slammed his left forearm into the bearded man's jaw, pressing his head against the wall. Logan turned into his opponent and delivered a strong knee that caught the man just below the vest. He repeated the attack, sensing the blows softening the man's midsection. Maintaining his aggression, he pushed and dragged his opponent along the wall, toward the sliding glass doors and stone balcony, his forearm grinding against the man's bearded jaw.

The man grimaced in pain, trying to yank his wrists out of Logan's grasp, to no avail.

"Let me put him down," Jack said from behind him.

"No!" Logan shouted in defiance. "This bastard's mine." He leaned in closer, his eyes boring into the man's face. He could feel him flinch, as if realizing for the first time the fight might be more than he could handle. "I don't know how you know me," Logan snarled, "and I don't care, but this ends now."

Logan slammed the man's head against the wall one more time, dropped his right hand to his hip, and withdrew the black Mark II knife from its sheath. Before his enemy could react, he plunged the blade into the man's unprotected left armpit above the vest. The man howled in agony, reflexively releasing his grip on the MP9 and jolting upright in pain.

Logan kept the blade in place with his right hand and grabbed the pistol grip of the MP9 with his left, crossing his left arm over the hand that held the knife, aiming toward the balcony. He found the trigger and pulled, and a burst of gunfire shattered the sliding doors and window. He flung the MP9 away and pulled his wounded prey backward toward the balcony, his right hand never leaving the handle of the black blade.

Logan felt his foot strike the casing of the windows, and he said, "You should never have come here."

The man's brown eyes had turned glossy, and his breathing was labored. *Might have nicked a lung. Good.*

Without another word, Logan yanked the blade out of the man's flesh, warm blood rushing over his right hand. He pivoted to his right, his left hand gripping the weaving of the Kevlar vest, and flung the man at the balcony, pushing off his back leg to add momentum.

Had Terry Deavers not been so tall, his death might have lasted longer, as he would have collapsed and bled out on the white stone balcony. Unfortunately, due to his height, the shock from the knife wound, and the loss of blood, he struck the wall waist-high. The impact stopped his lower body, but his upper torso kept moving from the force of Logan's throw. His upper half disappeared below the railing, and his legs followed, as if he'd chosen to dive to the stone patio below.

The distinctive *thud* of the body hitting the ground reached their ears, and Jack looked at Logan, whose final position after hurling his attacker made him look like a rock star, left arm extended, back leg straight, and right arm curled up.

"Nice move, Elvis," Jack said sincerely, a black pistol held in his right hand. "Let's get down to the pier and see if there's anything we can do to help our friends."

As the two men moved to the private elevator, a new sound joined the battle. Logan ran over to the balcony and stepped outside. *About damn time.* The rain had turned to a hard drizzle, and the view afforded him a clear picture of the events unfolding on the water. *No fucking way.* "Hold on a second. I need to make a call."

John fought a sensation of claustrophobia as he looked up and around. The Chesapeake Bay was notorious for its continuously opaque condition, muddied by miles of beach and shoreline erosion, as well as the storms that drove pollutants into its waters.

Evan pressed a virtual button on the touch-screen control panel, and a holographic underwater image in several shades of sharp blue appeared on the middle-left section of the glass bubble. The luxury yacht was clearly defined in front and above them, even though its hull was only partially visible. The screen also pinpointed the remaining RHIB, which had pulled alongside the yacht and was dwarfed in size by comparison.

"It's high-resolution three-D scanning and imaging," Evan said.

"That's pretty cool, and I've seen some pretty cool things," John said.

"Sometimes it's just the small technological advances that make the most impact," Evan replied. "Get ready. We're going to hit her hard, and then latch on with the mechanical arm to whatever you can."

Evan tilted the minisub at an angle, and the vehicle shot upward toward the surface, the environment gaining clarity as they climbed. The RHIB was completely visible as the underwater vehicle closed in on its prey.

This must be what Jaws felt like . . . if a shark had feelings, John thought, as the front of the right and left ballast tanks slammed into the underside of the RHIB with crumpling results.

The viewing bubble was filled with swirling water as the RHIB was lifted up and against the side of the luxury yacht. John manipulated the joysticks as he glanced from the water to the holographic image. A figure suddenly appeared in the water in front of them, weighted down with military gear. The right mechanical arm lashed out, and John closed the clamps down on the figure's right ankle. *Gotcha.*

A second struggling figure appeared in the chaos, upside down. *Must have fallen backward off the boat.*

John pushed up on the second joystick, the vise grip opening as it drew closer to the flailing figure. With nothing more than lethal luck, the steel claw closed on the figure's neck.

"Dive backward now," John said. "We'll drown 'em."

A moment later, the minisub disengaged from the RHIB, and John watched as they dragged their two captives deeper into the bay. The men realized what was happening, and they struggled wildly, kicking the mechanical arms that held them. A black combat boot bounced off the glass windshield with a dull squeak, and the Kevlar helmet fell off the man held at the neck, plummeting into the dark below.

"This is not how I would want to go," John said, empathy washing over him like the dark waters of the bay as the two men's struggles began to subside.

"I know, but they brought this on themselves," Evan said. "It'll be over soon."

"Shooting a man is one thing—and I've shot plenty—but this is something else entirely," John said, and exhaled, as if trying to clear his conscience.

Moments later, it was over, and John released both bodies, which slowly began to sink into the depths below.

"Okay. Now for the final blow," Evan said, and aimed the minisub back toward the surface.

———

"Are you sure about this?" PFC Williams shouted into his headset over the din of the rotors and the weather outside. He sat in the passenger compartment of the Bell 407 police helicopter, looking down through the open door, which he'd slid aside as soon as they'd arrived on station. Secured to the ceiling of the bird with a harness, he surveyed the surreal scene below him.

An enormous luxury yacht was dead in the water, a small RHIB rocked in the water next to its stern, and to top it off, *something from out of an old black-and-white monster movie from beneath the surface was attacking the smaller boat, pushing it repeatedly against the hull of the yacht. And I thought Iraq was a nightmare.* Four armed gunmen in black tactical gear stood on the lowest level of the yacht, firing into the churning water. Completing the picture of utter chaos were the two figures on the interconnected system of walkways, weapons aimed at the back of the yacht.

"Do it, Williams. That's an order," Corporal Taggert stated.

"From who?" PFC Williams asked. "We have no idea who's who in the zoo down there."

"Goddamnit, Williams. From the FBI director himself, the one who just called me directly and said, 'All armed subjects on the yacht are hostile. Eliminate them at all costs.' Is that good enough for you?" the helicopter's pilot asked sarcastically as he brought the bird around to provide his copilot—and only shooter—the clearest line of sight.

PFC Williams, a combat veteran and former Marine, understood orders. He'd taken his fair share of them in Iraq, often questioning them—as junior Marines were trained to do—until the commander's intent was made clear. Occasionally, there wasn't time for discussion, and the burden of command rested with his superior officers. He realized this was one of those times, and without hesitation, he opened fire on the four gunmen, praying he was doing the right thing, but doing it nonetheless.

Apparently the two men onshore had the same orders, for as PFC Williams fired at the unknown enemy, so did the two men on the walkways. *Is that a freaking grenade launcher?* he thought in surprise, but kept firing at his targets.

As soon as Logan had hung up the phone with Jake, having explained the situation in twenty seconds as he and Jack had worked their way down a staircase on the other side of the master suite opposite the elevator, he'd raided the security office, reloaded the grenade launcher, and hustled outside, praying he was in time to help John and his new friends, leaving Jack to catch up.

Shockingly, air support had actually arrived in time, and as Logan lined up the scope of the grenade launcher on the back of the yacht, gunfire erupted from the side of the police helicopter. *Good job, Jake.*

Logan pulled the trigger, and the first grenade arced through the air, sizzling through the drizzle at the back of the yacht. *Too low.* The 40mm projectile slid into the open launch compartment at water level and detonated inside, shaking the rear of the boat.

Jack had joined the gunfight, opening fire from the walkway above Logan with an M4 he'd picked up in the mansion.

Logan elevated the launcher and pulled the trigger a second time.

Thwump!

This time, he instinctively knew his aim was true, and he smoothly pulled the trigger four more times.

I think that should do it, Logan thought, and stood up to watch as the barrage of grenades struck the back of the yacht in quick succession.

Boom-ba-ba-ba-boom!

The remaining four attackers never had a chance. Two of the men were blown in half, splashing the wooden deck and white rails with buckets of blood. The other two amphibious raiders were propelled forward over the back of the railing—two grenades had landed right behind them—and landed in big splashes, disappearing moments later into the rough water.

The echoes of the explosions reverberated across the bay, disappearing into the sheets of rain and wind, leaving only the sounds of the helicopter in the aftermath of the battle.

Logan looked up and waved at the pilot, who held up his left hand in acknowledgment. Logan pointed from the helicopter to the house and then to the ground, hoping his charade skills conveyed his meaning—*land at the helipad behind the house.*

Moments later the helicopter rotated toward the mansion and the pilot pushed the cyclic lever forward, moving the bird toward the mansion's property. *Message received.*

"Jack, you still alive?" Logan asked as the retired general worked his way down the walkways.

"So far. Thanks for your concern," Jack responded drily.

"Uh-huh," Logan said, and ran toward the end of the pier to get a closer look at the carnage. The first wail of sirens reached his ears, which he knew would be followed by a cavalcade of police and emergency vehicles.

Christ. The parkway and museum yesterday; this today. The Founder and his enemies had turned DC and suburban Maryland into a war zone, and Logan had a sinking feeling the war wasn't close to ending. *The press is going to have a field day with this mess.*

———

Logan stood at the end of the pier, rain washing the blood from his right hand and arm. He'd slung the grenade launcher across his back; the M4 Commando lay across his chest. His Kimber Tactical II and Mark II fighting knife were back in their assigned positions, and he hoped there'd be no more bloodshed for the day.

The minisub had surfaced on the starboard side of the yacht, and Logan watched as the two encapsulated figures moved closer to the pier like a glass-encased water monster. He suddenly had a flashback to the crocodile in the Nile River—larger than the minisub; he shuddered at the recollection—that had killed and eaten the director of Sudan's internal security. *I'll never, ever forget the sound when it closed its enormous jaws on his head. Thank God I didn't have to watch.* He'd been swimming for his life at the time.

The minisub pulled alongside the pier, adjacent to a ladder that rose from the water to the walkway. Logan nodded at John through the glass, and Evan half crouched behind the pilot's chair, unlocking the pressurized hatch. Seconds later, the hatch was pushed outward, and the face of the former Delta operator appeared in the opening like a real-life whack-a-mole.

"Everything good in there?" Logan asked.

"Yup," Evan responded nonchalantly. "It was a little intense for a bit, but your friend can tell you all about it. I'm going to offload him, get this bad boy back to the yacht, grab one of the small rubber rafts, and meet you guys ashore. It will be a lot easier than trying to bring this thing to the beach. See you in a few."

Evan disappeared out of sight, and John Quick emerged, raising himself from the confines of the minisub.

"You have a nice dinner cruise?" Logan asked deadpan.

"Actually, no," John said, surprisingly serious. Even in the face of death and destruction, his irreverent sense of humor was usually present. "We used this thing to take two of the shooters at least thirty feet down and drown them. Wasn't fun watching them squirm, suffering with the knowledge they had taken their last breaths. Shooting a man's one thing. This . . . well, this was something else."

Logan looked around at the aftermath and back to the mansion, knowing what lay inside. *All this death is starting to take its toll on all of us. This can't go on forever.*

"I hear you, brother, but I'm still glad it was them and not us, and I always will be." Logan grabbed John by the forearm, helping him from the top of the minisub as he stepped onto the dock. "Come on. Let's get out of this mess and inside, where there might be some cover from the rain."

"Might be?" John asked.

"Yeah," Logan said. "We had a bit of a grenade problem inside."

"Jesus Christ, man. I leave you and the general alone for a few minutes, and it's like the streets of Ramadi all over again. Fucking Marines. Can't take 'em anywhere. This is why we don't have nice things."

CHAPTER 26

By twelve o'clock, the Shady Nook compound was swarming with both federal and local law enforcement. Jake Benson had arrived within ninety minutes of the end of the battle, choosing to establish an incident command center in the larger of the multicar garages. The first of several forensics teams had arrived and begun to methodically process the carnage for evidence. Multiple vehicles from DC's Office of the Chief Medical Examiner had arrived to transport the dead once the FBI finished examining the bodies. Shady Nook was in Maryland, but the DC medical examiner's office was more equipped than Anne Arundel County to handle the number of bodies on scene.

The Anne Arundel County police helicopter that had provided air support had transported Jack Longstreet to Anne Arundel County Medical Center, accompanied by a paramedic and an FBI agent. The bullet was lodged in his shoulder, and he required surgery.

The last thing he'd said to Logan, Jake, and John as he was loaded onto the helicopter was "Whatever you do, don't open that flash drive in front of anyone. And I mean *anyone*. You're not going to like what's on it."

"We got it, Jack," Logan said, acknowledging the threat the list on the flash drive posed.

"Good, because others will come, but I honestly don't know from where. You're holding the keys to the castle, albeit a very, very dark one," Jack said. "Be careful."

And with that final warning, the retired general—once a mentor who'd fought alongside Logan and John and Jake's nephew—had left, leaving the three of them to chart the next course of action.

"The media has already gathered outside the front gate. I don't know how long we'll be able to contain this. Fortunately, we're the only ones who actually know what's going on," Jake said, as the three of them now sat around a table in a private kitchen in the first part of the right wing of the house, which had remained unscathed from the battle.

"And what do you plan to do about it?" Logan asked. "You've got to brief the president. He has to know it's all connected."

"He's in a series of meetings this afternoon, and then he heads to Atlantic City tomorrow, but I've already had my execs arrange a meeting with him this evening. I'm going to be here all afternoon," Jake said.

"And what do we do about this?" John asked, holding up the black flash drive. He turned it in his fingers, as if puzzled that something so small could be so powerful and dangerous.

"Hold on to it. I don't trust anyone else with it, not even me, right now. Do *not* open it until you hear from me," Jake said. "You heard what Jack said about it. I shudder to think who and what's on it."

"Speaking of the good general, what's going to happen to him?" Logan asked. The former Marine officer had engaged in dozens—*if not hundreds*—of illegal operations, capping it off with the execution of the head of one of the most powerful intelligence agencies in the world, even if that Marine general had been a traitor himself.

The moral ramifications made him nauseous. Logan West was accustomed to a much bolder line between black and white, good and evil. It was that line that was supposed to guide his moral compass, especially when it was tested in the darkest of hours. But the line had become translucent, and he felt as though his actions and the events that had occurred were carrying him back and forth along a new spectrum of morality. And he didn't like it, *not for a moment.*

"Honestly, I don't know. His crimes are such that I don't know if it does more damage to prosecute him or recruit him. It's one of the things I need to talk to the president about," Jake said. "But until then, he's under guard. Hell, he's probably under the knife by now, as well. He's not going anywhere."

"Agreed," Logan said. "Which brings me to my next point: I want to get out of here and back to our HQ. I think we need to press our guest on what happened here," Logan added, referring to the treasonous former national security advisor, Jonathan Sommers, who had been captured and held in a cell in Ares' home base for the past six months. "I find it hard to believe he didn't know anything about Constantine Kallas' global operations or the enemies he'd acquired."

Jake nodded in agreement. "Sounds good to me. You might not hear from me until after I brief the president. If that's the case, get some rest after you talk to him. You're going to need it. This isn't over yet."

"It feels like it never is," John responded. "I feel like I could use a vacation."

"Well, if you and Amira do decide to take one, you can cross one thing off that list," Logan added.

"What's that?" John asked hesitantly.

"Underwater adventures," Logan said, and smiled.

"You're a child," John said, but laughed anyhow, some of the emotional tension he felt easing away.

"Negative, my friend. I've just been hanging around one for far too long. It's wearing off on me," Logan said, a full grin on his face. "Now let's get out of here. I'm sure traffic on the Beltway will be a nightmare, just to add to the day's fun."

"It's DC, brother," John said. "It's never fun."

"You have no idea," Jake said, reflecting on the cesspool of corrupt politicians and bureaucrats he'd spent his career navigating around. "Get out of my sight, boys. I've got work to do."

Logan and John looked at each other, stood up from the table, and saluted smartly. "Yes, sir." They turned about-face and marched toward the door, leaving the director of the FBI to stare after them. *They're going to need that sense of humor to get through what's coming. God help us all.*

CHAPTER 27

Logan sat across the table from Jonathan Sommers in the basement cell, which was in reality a spacious studio apartment, complete with DIRECTV, a bathroom with a shower, a kitchen area, and several bookshelves lined with hardcover and paperback books. *It's nicer than my place in college,* Logan thought, which was true, except for the prison bars and door that had been erected across the width of the underground facility. An HD surveillance camera was mounted in each corner of the basement, providing 24-hour coverage of the sole prisoner. The walls had been soundproofed so that even if someone were standing outside in back of the two-story building and Sommers screamed for help, the person wouldn't hear a thing.

While it wasn't ideal, Jonathan Sommers had realized what the alternative was—death and permanent disappearance.

In fact and unbeknownst to him, there actually had been a discussion with the president about executing him as a result of his traitorous service and dumping his body in the Potomac. The core members of Ares—Logan, John, Amira, and Cole—had voted

223

for the death penalty, especially in the wake of Mike's death, but the president had ultimately overruled them. As President Scott had stated, "He deserves death for what he's done. I won't deny you that, but there's something pulling at my conscience to keep him alive for now. Maybe we'll need him down the line; maybe we won't. I can always change my mind. I *am* the commander in chief, after all," he'd added.

Logan had to give it to the president. From the moment they'd first met, the leader of the free world—although he wasn't sure that ideal still existed with everything the task force had uncovered—had been a man of his word, a rarity in the political swamp of Washington DC.

Even though Sommers didn't understand how precarious his position was after he'd been spared, he'd adapted to the situation, willingly answering any and all questions about the Recruiter and what he knew about the Organization.

But regardless of the prisoner's level of cooperation, Logan and the team knew that a tipping point was at hand with Sommers. The setup at Quantico had been created to be temporary, and Jake Benson was in discussion with the president about how to handle their captive on a permanent basis. Multiple options had been proposed, including a supermax facility. At this point, Logan didn't care what the resolution was, but one needed to be found, and soon. Between Logan, the rest of his small task force, and several cleared HRT operators, someone was always on duty at HQ to ensure nothing happened to Sommers. *It's like being a second lieutenant in the Marine Corps all over again. The only bright side was I didn't have Sommers duty on my birthday, but if this keeps up, I'm sure that will change.*

In light of the day's revelations, something nagged at Logan, which was why he sat alone in the basement with Jonathan, studying the man who'd betrayed his country and Constitution.

"What is it? What's happened? Something has," the Harvard-educated traitor said. "Otherwise, you wouldn't be here." The boyish charm he'd once possessed had eroded away to a beaten state of acceptance.

"Tell me about the Founder," Logan asked bluntly, and sat back, waiting for a reply.

Oh no. Jonathan's mind rebelled. He wanted to scream in denial, but instead he focused on his breathing. *Inhale . . . exhale . . . inhale . . . exhale. The question means it's all over. Endgame scenario. No more choices left.*

The existence of the Founder was the one piece of information he'd kept to himself, a last-ditch bargaining chip he'd hoped to play at some point. The hope that somehow, in some desperate way, he'd be able to leverage the identity of one of the most powerful persons on the planet for salvation had been what kept him going. He'd known his captors could only keep him for so long in this ad hoc prison. A solution would ultimately have to be found. And that meant more people would learn he was still alive. The more who knew, the greater the likelihood that word of his survival would travel back to the Founder, who did have the strings to pull, no matter what the task force that held him thought.

Jonathan shut his eyes, signaling the end of any future he'd deluded himself into thinking he had. *The gig is up, as they say. Can't hold back anymore, not if he knows.*

"How did you find him?" Jonathan asked. "He's dead, isn't he?"

"Why do you say that?" Logan asked.

"Because I only met him once, but after that meeting, I knew there was only one thing that he valued on this earth—his secrecy," Jonathan said. "And if you now know who he is, he has to be dead."

There was no point in lying. "He was ambushed at his house, while John and I were there this morning. It got a little out of hand, but the good news is that the bad guys are all dead now, too.

And I'm willing to bet that the assholes who sent the little army this morning are the same ones who sent your beloved Recruiter to manipulate you into betraying not just the Organization but also your country."

Jonathan raised his eyebrows but kept quiet.

"Constantine told us about the rebellion he was having. Not exactly something he could go to HR with, from the sound of it," Logan said. "And that's what this has all been about—one big power struggle." He paused. "You realize it's madness, don't you? I know you're used to being the smartest guy in the room, but you do realize *for all that's good in this country,* that it's lunacy?"

"The world is a violent and dangerous place, Logan. It always has been, *and it always will be, no matter what we do.* It's the human condition to be biologically predisposed toward conflict. It's as if our minds are hardwired to rebel against the prospect of peace. Just look at history. Any time of prosperity and peace was usually followed by war and conflict. It's just a never-ending cycle, an endless merry-go-round of madness that has to be managed. And that's what the Organization did, as I'm sure the Founder told you. And quite well, I might add."

"While that all sounds rational, in a disturbed and megalomaniacal way, then riddle me this," Logan said, and leaned across the table, his intensity on full display. "If you supported the Organization for all those years, what made you suddenly betray it?"

God help whoever gets in the way of this man, Jonathan thought, but answered truthfully. "Because the pendulum had swung the other way, and there's nothing you or your friends or even the president can do. Chaos is coming, like it or not."

Logan's head hurt, and he felt the visceral impulse to make Jonathan Sommers share his pain. But in a twisted kind of way, he understood the pathological reasoning. It reminded him of the conversation he'd had with Cain Frost in the soccer stadium in Haditha. Cain had been a believer, a zealot in the pursuit of revenge for his brother's torture and murder. Iran had become his target, and there was nothing Logan could say to dissuade him from the evil course of action he'd chosen. It was the same logic with Sommers. He was a believer in his own cause, no matter what the facts indicated.

"You may or may not believe this, but I understand why you believe what you do. It's hard not to with everything that's going on in the world. Regardless of what your perceptions of me are, it's like I told Cain Frost, right before I captured him—I get it. Trust me. I've seen way more of the world than I'd wished, and the horrors that come along with it. If you let it, it can literally *suck* the life out of your soul," Logan said, an emotional gravitas underpinning each sentence. "But here's the difference between us, also what I told Cain: it's not your decision to make, *and it never was*," Logan said with such conviction that Jonathan recoiled. "This is a republic, where the real power resides with the people, *not* just their elected leaders. Your little Star Chamber is over, and I'm going to bring it all down, once and for all."

Silence engulfed the room, and Jonathan looked at the table, fearful of his captor's gaze.

Finally he looked up, and Logan was surprised to see him smiling. *What does he know that I don't?*

"You see the hypocrisy, don't you?" Jonathan asked, his voice growing stronger as he spoke. "We're the same, you and I. I know what I did was legally treason, punishable by death. But the end justified the means, objectively, in lives saved by what we did. I'll grant you that it's become rather messy—"

"That's a fucking understatement, smart guy," Logan interrupted.

"—but it had to be done. There was no way around it. The Founder wanted to shut the whole thing down. The problem is that the Organization has become a living, breathing entity, with a global network that can't be shut off. Here's the true reality, Logan," Jonathan said, leaning across the table. "We both operate in the shadows, just for different masters. Your actions are just as illegal as ours. The only difference is you have a president who is willing to excuse and pardon them. You wear your hypocrisy like a cape, but you're not always the good guys. I've seen what you do. So don't lecture me about right and wrong. You're as much in the gray space as I am. You just refuse to accept it." He finished and sat back, waiting for a response.

Logan West, a man convinced of his own righteousness, a man who never doubted that he was *always* on the right side of history, paused. Composed externally, he was a raging storm inside. He felt an irrational urge to grab Jonathan Sommers by the back of the head and smash his face repeatedly into the wooden table, stopping only when his last breath had been expelled from his toxic lungs. *But you know there's truth to what he says. Maybe, but it's not the whole truth. It's like everything else, half lies and deceptions.* He considered responding, but he realized there was no counterargument, no talking point that would negate the fact that Task Force Ares had jumped into the moral quagmire feet first. *The manipulative bastard has a point. But even if he does, you still answer to the president of the United States, and he's the legal guardian of the Constitution, not this guy.*

He suddenly felt tired, and he realized the conversation had reached an impasse. With the grace of a fighter, Logan slid off the chair, exited the cell, and slammed the door behind him, pausing as the electronic keypad engaged.

"The truth stings, doesn't it?" Jonathan said quietly.

Logan West turned quickly, facing his prisoner. "Careful. You keep talking like that, and I'll drag you from that gray space into the deep dark, and you won't come back."

His point made, he walked up the stairs, wondering how soon he'd hear from Jake. *This part is just like the Marine Corps. Waiting. Stand by to stand by.*

PART V

FULL CIRCLE

CHAPTER 28

Logan sat in the Sensitive Compartmented Information Facility—colloquially referred to as a SCIF—combing through classified FBI reports Jake's office had forwarded to his SIPRNET account.

The SCIF occupied the main area in the back of the headquarters, through the front entrance and behind a second steel door that had a cipher lock combination on it. It was an enormous space, sixty feet long and thirty feet deep. Several workstations that contained Unclassified, Secret, and Top Secret networks were arranged around the perimeter of the room, screens facing inward. The few windows in the room were barred and had blackout screens drawn down. The back wall contained multiple HD TVs, as well as several Smart Boards connected to the numerous networks.

In the back right corner was another cipher-locked door that emptied out into a hallway next to a stairwell, across which was what the team referred to as the "hurt locker." It contained an armory, several cages—one for each member of the task force—of various personal gear, and a communications area for the equipment they utilized on operations.

A door in the far left corner of the SCIF led to another hallway, stairwell, the gym, and the combatives room beyond, complete with the latest and best physical fitness equipment black budget government tax dollars could buy.

The second deck of the headquarters was not as deep as the first level. It contained several rooms that had been converted into sleeping quarters for whoever was on Sommers duty, as well as a larger recreation area that led to a second-floor patio on the roof of the rear part of the SCIF. There were also two large head areas that contained multiple showers, benches, and sinks, and Amira had commandeered one all to herself, posting a note to remind others, "Stay out. I have knives."

The door beeped, and Logan turned around as John Quick walked through the doorway, a propane tank in hand.

"What now? You going into the IED-building business? I figured you'd avoid that line of work, what with all the times you've been blown up," Logan said.

"Cute," John replied. "No. In fact, I'm trying to class the place up, tough guy. It's for the grill above your head. Figure with all the time we spend here, we might as well be able to cook out, you know, enjoy the great Quantico outdoors."

"Sure. Why not see if you can arrange a mixer with a sorority from Georgetown while you're at it," Logan suggested drily.

"I'm spoken for, remember? But I'll pass along the recommendation to Cole. I hear those sorority girls like rugged men with beards."

John walked toward the back of the room, setting the propane tank near the back workstation, at which Logan sat. "Any news from Jake?"

"Negative," Logan responded. "Just a bunch of background reports on the Kallas shipping empire. The accountants at the FBI are in the process of getting multiple warrants from DOJ to start going through his US assets. They're also going to have to loop Treasury in to investigate his foreign holdings."

"That sounds like fun, if you're into that sort of thing," John said.

Logan's cell phone began to chirp, and he held it up for John to see. "Well, look who it is."

Even though cell phones were banned in almost every SCIF the US operated in the world due to technical security risks, Task Force Ares was of such a nature that it made no practical sense to abide by that regulation. Instead, their personal cell phones were encrypted and scanned every day at a special terminal when they entered the facility to ensure an adversary had not remotely installed malicious software on their devices.

"Morning, Jake," Logan said, answering the phone.

"You still haven't opened the flash drive yet, correct?" Jake said, getting right down to business.

"I'm fine. Thanks. How are you?" Logan replied.

"Sorry, Logan. There's no time," Jake said. "In about ten minutes, you're going to have guests."

Logan looked at John, and asked, "Who?"

"The president's Secret Service detail," Jake replied. "I briefed the president last night, telling him everything we know, including the existence of the flash drive and the contents on it. When I left the White House, he said he needed to think on it, and he'd let me know this morning. I didn't speak to him, but I just got a phone call from the Secret Service stating that the president dispatched part of his detail to retrieve a critical piece of evidence down in Quantico."

"Well, it's his country, but I'm not sure how I feel about giving it to anyone but him," Logan said, mouthing to John, *Where's the flash drive?*

John pointed to the government two-drawer safe next to Logan's workstation.

"I tried to reach the president, but he's on Air Force One on the way to Atlantic City to deliver a speech on the economy," Jake said. "If that's how he wants to handle this, I'm sure he has his reasons. There's also no way anyone on his detail would know about the flash drive unless he told them. So I have to assume it's legitimate."

Something about the request nagged at Logan, though he couldn't place his finger on it. "What do you want me to do?"

"Give them what they want, and call me as soon as it's over," Jake said.

"Roger. Will do," Logan replied.

"Logan, there's one more thing," Jake said, and his tone sent shivers down Logan's spine, as if a skeletal ghost were caressing him with a solitary finger of bone. *It's how he sounded right before he told me that Mike was dead.*

"What is it?" Logan asked.

"It's General Longstreet," Jake replied, and for a moment, Logan was sure the general had died in surgery. *Who the hell dies from a gunshot wound to the shoulder?*

"He's gone," Jake said. "As in he disappeared from the hospital after the two Anne Arundel County police officers assigned to his recovery room were incapacitated."

"No way," Logan said.

"Looks like the team of operators he had staged in Annapolis realized what had happened at their employer's residence. They must have talked to that other operator, Evan, and realized they could do something about it," Jake said. "No one saw a thing, and the cameras were disabled electronically while whoever was there grabbed him."

"Those guys are good, which means the general is in the wind. Goddamnit," Logan said in frustration. *They just couldn't catch and keep a break. The Secret Service on their way here unannounced? General Longstreet missing? This is going south fast.*

"I know, but first things first. Give the president's detail what they want. I've been told they're bringing it back to the White House," Jake finished. "I'm going to check in with the special agent in charge of the Kallas scene and see if they've ID'd any of the bodies from the assault team. Keep you posted."

"Sounds good, and I'll text you after they leave," Logan said.

Another beep at the left door, and Cole and Amira walked in from the hallway, having been in the gym.

On the bank of security monitors that covered every square inch of the perimeter of the building and the grounds of the compound, a black Suburban appeared in the middle screen, stopping at the security gate at the entrance to the facility. Time was up—the president's detail had arrived.

"What's going on, boys?" Amira said.

"We have guests," Logan replied. "Gear up."

And with that, Logan explained what Jake had told him, as well as what Logan planned to do about it.

CHAPTER 29

The main door to the SCIF beeped, swung inward, and John watched from the main workstation as Logan entered, followed by a presidential detail of four Secret Service agents.

All four men wore dark-gray or black suits, complete with dark ties. Three of the special agents wore Oakley wire sunglasses on their heads, as if blinding sunshine might suddenly illuminate the room. Their suit coats were unbuttoned, and John made a mental note of the FN Five-seveN 5.57x28mm semiautomatic pistols that were holstered at the two o'clock position on their black conceal-carry belts. *These guys don't mess around. Those things are designed to go through body armor.*

Produced as a result of a NATO requirement, the FN Five-seveN fired several types of high-velocity ammunition. Even though the cartridge was longer than a standard 9x19mm round, the projectile itself was smaller, designed for maximum penetration and increased accuracy. Based on the characteristics, it was the handheld version of an assault rifle, specifically, the companion FN P90 personal defense weapon, which John knew the Secret Service used as well. *Serious hardware for serious men.*

Cole and Amira had assumed positions near the front left corner of the SCIF.

"If it isn't the Men in Black," John said, standing up to greet the visitors.

The lead special agent, a midfortyish man with a head of close-cropped gray hair, stepped past Logan and held out his hand. "As if we haven't heard that before," he said, gripping John's hand and shaking it firmly. "Special Agent Ben Harkens. You must be John Quick. The president told us about you. You're the funny one," he finished, adding a slight smile.

Or is that a condescending smirk? I can't tell. One cool customer, John thought.

"And good-looking," John added.

"Oh, good Lord," Amira muttered from the corner.

"I don't want to add to any self-esteem issues you might have, so I'm going to dodge that one and get down to business. I believe you have something for us?" Special Agent Harkens said.

The three agents stood behind him quietly, approximately five feet of spacing between each of them.

"As a matter of fact, we do," Logan said, and held out his hand, which contained the black thumb drive John had obtained at Constantine Kallas' mansion. "Here you go."

"Thank you," Harkens said. "I'll pass it along directly to the president once he returns. It will be at the White House until then. Unless there's something else, we'll leave you to whatever it is you do here, not that it's any of my business."

He turned around and nodded at the three agents lining the middle of the room. They turned and began to move in unison toward the main door to the SCIF, a synchronized line of black and white.

It's the fucking march of the penguins, John thought.

"Do you know what's on that thumb drive?" Logan asked quietly.

Special Agent Harkens stopped midstride but didn't turn around. "I do not. I was only asked to retrieve it. That's above my pay grade."

"It's an interesting who's who of sorts. A list, actually, as well as the intimate details of a global network of *very* bad actors," Logan said.

Harkens turned back to face Logan, who now stood in the back, legs naturally in a shooter's stance. "So you saw what's on it?"

Logan ignored the question, staring at the Secret Service agent. "Something about this whole visit seemed off to me, but I couldn't place my finger on it. But John here can tell you that when I start to fixate on something, I can't let it go. Isn't that right?" Logan said, staring at Harkens as he spoke to John several feet away.

"He's not lying, Harkens," John replied matter-of-factly. "He gets all Tonya Harding on it, minus the clubbing, of course. It's kind of scary."

The mood in the room had undergone a massive shift, as if a tension dial had been cranked from zero to insanity in the blink of an eye. The three Secret Service agents who had almost reached the front of the room were now facing inward, hands at their waists.

John, Cole, and Amira instinctively reacted, repositioning themselves to face the visitors.

"I can't help you with your feelings. All I know is that the president asked me to obtain a thumb drive, and since he is the president, I usually follow orders," Special Agent Harkens asked, a hard flatness now in his eyes.

"That may be true, but here's the thing—I've *never seen or heard your name before.* After you pulled up to our little clubhouse and introduced yourself over the speaker, I thought I'd phone a friend and ask about you," Logan said. His voice had taken on an aggressive quality his friends knew well. "Would you like to know what he said, secret agent man?" he asked with blatant derision in his voice.

There was no response from Harkens. The visit from the Secret

Service had abruptly turned into a confrontation, a modern-day Mexican standoff.

"You know, you don't have to do this. In fact, I'd advise you to not say another word," Special Agent Harkens said warningly. "All we have to do is walk out that door, and *poof*, we're gone," he said, suddenly bringing his hands in front of him like a magician.

Damn. He's fast. Worse, I'll bet they're all fast. The Secret Service trains some of the best shooters in the world, not just in accuracy but in speed. Be careful, Logan thought. He pressed on, holding up his cell phone, a text message on the screen. "My friend's response was quick. It said, 'Head of the vice president's detail,' which I found curious, even when that friend has some serious street cred as the director of the FBI."

"Do you have any idea how good my guys are, Mr. West?" Harkens asked, changing topics, a coldness in his voice. "I have some of the best gunmen in the service. It's unreal. Trust me. You can't win this."

"Do you know why the identity of your real boss matters at this very moment?" Logan finally asked, speaking past Special Agent Harkens' overt threat.

"This is the last time I'll say this: you can still walk away," Special Agent Harkens said.

"Because his name *is on the list*," Logan said in a low voice thick with fury.

Harkens sighed. "I really thought you might just keep your mouth shut and let us leave. Just remember one thing—you brought this on yourself. I just don't understand why. Do you always make things this difficult, especially when they don't have to be? Confrontation isn't the only way to get things done," he said, the veiled threat hanging in the air.

"Not always, but I'm making an exception in your case, you arrogant prick," Logan said.

He had realized moments earlier that as good as they were, Special Agent Harkens was right—they'd never win a straight-up gunfight with elite Secret Service shooters. As a result, Logan did the only thing he could. He rapidly drew his Kimber Tactical II and fired into the propane tank John had placed on the floor, turning the operational center of Task Force Ares into the most classified kill box at Marine Corps Base Quantico.

CHAPTER 30

Unlike in the movies or on television, propane tanks don't fracture into a thousand pieces of flying shrapnel. In reality, the aftermath lasts much longer than an explosion. The immediate *BOOM* was followed by a violent swishing sound as the propane tank spun crazily in the middle of the SCIF, flames shooting out several feet in all directions, setting chairs, tables, and even the tiled ceiling aflame. Smoke immediately billowed across the room and began to obscure visibility. The intense heat triggered the government-installed halon suppression system, adding an additional layer of noise to the cacophony.

The heat from the miniature fire tornado washed over Logan as he lunged to the left, away from the scorching conflagration. As he dove to the floor, he opened fire toward the last position he'd seen Harkens.

He heard additional gunfire from multiple sources, realizing the SCIF had turned into a full-on shooting gallery. *Eight guns and plenty of bullets—no way we get out of this unscathed.*

Smoke filled his lungs, and he involuntarily coughed. *This is a death trap,* he thought, as two of the mounted HD screens in the back of the SCIF exploded in a shower of sparks.

He glanced past the swirling flames and saw Cole and Amira, weapons aimed at the intruders, unleashing a dual volley of bullets. Amira glanced over, and Logan pointed to the door near them. The message was clear: *Get the hell out of here.* Then Logan nodded, turned on his heels, and moved toward the right rear entrance.

As Logan reached John, who'd been standing between him and the door, he said, "Let's move!"

Logan reached the door first and pushed down on the metal handle, which disengaged the external cipher lock, and shoved the door open. Smoke billowed out through the opening into the passageway, creating a dark tunnel.

John stepped out into breathable air a moment later and slammed the door shut behind him. "What now?"

The two warriors stood at the end of the right passageway, near the stairwell. "Three choices," Logan said, aiming his weapon down the hall toward the front of the building where it intersected with the main hallway. He'd already calculated the odds, and he didn't like any of them, especially since his team had been split up. As good as Logan and John were, two against a foursome of world-class marksmen trained by the best shooting instructors in the United States was not a winning proposition. "One—stand and fight. Not a good choice. These guys are pros, as you know. Two—head upstairs and try to work our way across the building to link up with Amira and Cole, but we have no idea where they are. For now, they're on their own. And three—get to the armory, gear up, and go to war with these fuckers. We need to get to the basement too. We can't leave Sommers down there, no matter what he's done."

"I'm all for war," John said, but before he could finish, a Secret Service agent appeared at the end of the hallway and opened fire. The bullets ricocheted off the wall and struck the stairwell behind them.

"New plan—downstairs. Now!" Logan shouted, and returned fire as the Secret Service agent ducked back down the main hallway fifty feet away.

John hit the stairs two at a time as Logan emptied the first magazine down the passageway, buying enough time to cover their movement. He reloaded as he followed John into the basement, wondering how the hell they were going to get Sommers and *come back up* past their waiting executioners. *Stupid government building. Should've had an emergency exit in the basement. Noted for the next headquarters we build, if we make it out of this one.*

———

Cole Matthews couldn't believe that four Secret Service agents, including the best the protective agency had to offer, had gone off the reservation and were trying to kill them.

Logan had suspected something was amiss, and he'd confirmed it by skimming the list before heading outside to greet the Secret Service detail. He'd only had two to three minutes, but it had been enough. They'd all glimpsed the list and had obtained a sense of the breadth of the network the Founder had built through decades of clandestine operations and organizations. It was staggering.

As for the former head of the CIA's Special Operations Group— which had been reorganized into and renamed the Special Activities Division; *SAD? Really? Some dumbass bureaucrats just don't think things through, especially at the senior executive level. Watch out! Here come those SAD guys*—Cole had seen everything every agency had to offer. The reality was that the Secret Service was one of the most straitlaced agencies in the federal government, comprising men and women who took their oath to protect the president with deadly gravitas. But then it had hit him, right before events had exploded, literally. *These guys were following orders, which meant Logan's hunch had been right.* Fortunately—or unfortunately, depending on your perspective—Jake Benson had confirmed it, *at the last possible moment,* Cole thought as he looked at Amira, who'd been trapped on this side of the flames with him.

The noise and confusion were a physical element that threatened to suffocate them like the smoke. He'd seen it before. *The fog of war. Too bad Von Clausewitz isn't here to see this shit.*

"We'll try to link up with them on the other side. We can use the exit in the gym," Cole said.

Amira answered by firing her SIG SAUER P250 into the back of the room. She turned, looked at Cole, and said, "Let's go. They're going to pay."

"No doubt about that," Cole said, and pushed the handle down. The two newest Ares operators fled the room, crossed the passageway, and entered the gym and combatives area.

Cole started to work his way in a beeline to the emergency exit in the far corner of the room, but Amira grabbed his left arm forcefully from behind. "Wait. I have a better idea."

Cole stopped and looked at her, his weapon instinctively rising to the door of the room in case they were interrupted by one of the attackers. "The last time you had a good idea, I watched you drop two stories on the outside of a building."

"I'm touched you remember," Amira said. "But if I'm right, we might get to even the odds a little."

———

Special Agent Harkens had a decision to make—escape from the compound while they could, or stay and finish the gunfight. As the head of Vice President Baker's detail, his decisions were usually more reactive than proactive, especially during the actual conduct of a presidential or vice presidential event. An identifiable threat usually meant only one thing—get the vice president to safety at all costs. Everything else was secondary. But this situation was different and escalating by the minute. More importantly, the vice president's instructions had been clear: "Whatever you do, get the flash drive and *make sure* that no one saw what's on it, no matter what. If they did, terminate them with extreme prejudice. It's that important."

He thought the fake call placed by one of his agents—not the president's—to the FBI director would buy them time; he'd been wrong.

Special Agent Harkens had been with the vice president for eight years, since Baker had been a Democratic senator for the great state of Virginia. While it wasn't normal for the Secret Service to protect senators, Senator Baker had received so many death threats that the president had issued a special executive order providing 24/7 protection. The fact that Senator Baker was the ranking Democrat on the Senate Select Committee on Intelligence had helped his cause.

The man had wielded power with the tactical prowess of Erwin Rommel. Special Agent Harkens had seen the vice president escape more political pitfalls in eight years than would be normal in ten political lifetimes. Like a suicidal cat repeating the same jump time and time again, he always landed on his feet.

Late in the senator's last term, Special Agent Harkens, a brilliantly perceptive man, had begun to suspect the senator was part of something bigger than just the Senate, bigger, in fact, than even the US government. It was after Baker had taken him to meet with a shipping tycoon named Constantine Kallas—by himself, at night, on a slow Tuesday—at the man's estate in Maryland that Harkens had confronted him, professionally and with respect.

The senator had been quiet for more than a minute, and Special Agent Harkens had grown concerned that he'd offended the man he was charged with protecting, wondering if he'd overstepped his boundaries. But then the senator had asked him a question, a question that had changed the course of his life and his core beliefs about the existing global power structure.

"Your brother was a DEA agent who died in a Colombian raid against the Cali cartel after Pablo Escobar was killed, correct?" then Senator Baker had asked.

"Yes, sir. He was," Special Agent Harkens had responded.

"What if I told you that there was an unofficial organization that existed to help manage the chaos in countries like Colombia, Mexico, and Iraq? An organization with unlimited resources, international backing from *dozens* of countries, and designed for one purpose and one purpose only—to bring stability and order to the chaos. What would you say to that?" Senator Baker had asked.

Special Agent Harkens had thought carefully, considering his response. He'd often wondered why the US didn't aggressively pursue its enemies, often abandoning its allies or leaving even its own military vulnerable for political reasons. It was infuriating, especially after what had happened to his brother, but it also wasn't his job to question those appointed over him. It was only his job to protect them.

"I'd say that sounds like a very good thing, if it were actually practical to do," Special Agent Harkens had finally responded.

"But what if some of its activities were in violation of the particular set of laws of one of the countries? What then?" the senator had pressed.

"Well, if dozens of countries with different interests could come together on one *agreed-upon* objective, I'd say that the collective good outweighs the interests and laws of any single nation."

Special Agent Harkens remembered watching the senator stare out the window as they drove through suburban Maryland back to northern Virginia. Finally, he'd said, "When we get back, let's talk in my office."

Since that night, Special Agent Harkens' eyes had been opened to an underbelly of the republic, a place where real decisions were made, even if the world didn't know it existed. There were enough conspiracy theories, from 9/11 Truthers to sightings of aliens in Nevada, to keep the real secrets hidden. He'd made a choice that night, and he'd voluntarily accepted the consequences.

And now here he was, forced to do something he didn't want to do but knew was necessary. Vice President Baker's words echoed in his head: "It's always bigger than any one of us, even me."

The four Secret Service agents gathered outside the main entrance to the SCIF. Miraculously, no one had been hit by ricocheting rounds or flaming debris. "Olson, you and I are going right. Jenkins, Lotz, you take the other two. We have the flash drive they gave us, but we need to know it's the only one, and they need to be put down. We have to contain this. Understand?"

Subtle nods acknowledged his order in silence.

All three had been personally vetted by Special Agent Harkens and indoctrinated into the shadow world of the Organization. Like him, they were believers in the cause.

"Then let's do this and be quick about it."

———

"What the hell is going on up there?" Jonathan Sommers asked, borderline panic in his voice.

"Just a little party with our friends in the Secret Service. You know how wild those guys can be. Don't you watch the news?" John replied sarcastically.

"Logan, what is your sidekick talking about?" Jonathan said.

"Stand back and shut the fuck up, or I'm going to let my sidekick kick your ass, understand?" Logan snapped.

As if recognizing the seriousness of the situation, especially at the smell of smoke as it wafted down the stairwell, Jonathan shut his mouth and stepped back and away from the barred door.

Logan punched in the code, and the door sprung outward, swinging on its hinges. "Let's go."

Sommers had stepped toward the doorway when he looked up and saw a black-suited arm with a pistol held in front of it come around the bend in the stairwell.

"Gun!" he screamed, and tried to point, as three things happened simultaneously. The Secret Service agent appeared at the top of the landing, exposing only the right side of his body. John shoved Logan forward and spun on his heels, the M1911 tracking the new target only thirty feet away. And both men opened fire.

Crack-blam! The two shots blended into a singular sharp and deep report, with similar results.

John's bullet struck the Secret Service agent's extended arm, tearing a furrow across the bottom of his forearm. The bullet dug deeper until it shattered against the pointed end of the man's ulna, forcing a tremendous roar of pain from the wounded shooter. The FN Five-seveN dropped to the stairs and tumbled end over end into the basement. The Secret Service agent disappeared back upstairs.

The bullet that had struck John in the lower left center of his chest was much smaller than the .45-caliber slug he'd fired at his attacker. He didn't feel the initial impact and only realized he'd been shot when he turned back to Logan, at which point an explosion of pain hit him on the front left side of his torso. He wobbled and gritted his teeth as he felt the blood begin to slowly leak through his shirt from below his rib cage.

"Fuck," John said, and steadied himself against the iron bars. "I'm pretty sure his shooting days are over, though."

"How bad? Can you keep moving?" Logan asked. "We have to get up and out of here, or we'll burn to death."

"You know they're going to be waiting, likely at the end of the hall, right? No way they miss us again," John said.

"I know we need some concealment." Logan looked around the room for anything they could use. *Where was MacGyver when you needed him?* "Sommers, grab that," Logan said, pointing to an object up against the underside of the stairwell.

Jonathan didn't hesitate but ran over and grabbed the object, which felt heavy. "It's full," he said.

"Good," Logan said. "Now let's go. We need to get out of here as quickly as possible."

The three men climbed up the stairwell, crouching when they got to the midlevel landing that double-backed up to the first floor. Logan and Jonathan crept up to the highest possible point where their heads were still below the floor of the first level and out of the line of fire. John was right behind Logan on the left, his M1911 still in his right hand.

"On three, you throw that thing as high and far as you can. You understand? As soon as it's out of your hand, you start running up those goddamned stairs as fast as possible. I'll get you concealment, but you better run for your life, or I'll shoot you myself and step over your corpse. We need to get upstairs." Logan turned and looked at John. "As soon as he moves, you move. Can you do this?"

"Absolutely," John said through gritted teeth. "I can't let you have all the fun."

"Good. Fight through it," Logan said, and looked at Jonathan. "One. Two. Three."

Jonathan Sommers, terrified for his life, from both the Secret Service upstairs and the men who held him, did his first good thing in the past six months of his existence. He swung the midsize fire extinguisher back with both arms and hurled it up the stairwell. His aim and strength were true, and it sailed up and over the landing, arcing toward the ceiling. He was already two steps up when Logan pulled the trigger on the Kimber Tactical II.

Bam!

The fire extinguisher was punctured, and like the propane tank, released its contents in a swirling, whooshing cloud of noise and fury. Instantly, the hallway was filled with the acrid smell of potassium bicarbonate, propelled by the compressed carbon dioxide.

"Go! Go! Go!" Logan urged, even as the two former Marines led by one of the world's worst traitors dashed up the steps. Sommers and John were already halfway up the stairwell to the second deck when the first shots from the concealed Secret Service agents rang out.

Please God. Two more seconds, Logan thought as he heard a round strike the railing two feet below him. Three or four more shots impacted the stairs, and he felt the step on which he stood tremor as a round tore a piece of concrete from it. *Move. Move. Move.*

He reached the midlevel landing to the second deck and lunged forward as more rounds began to impact higher in the stairwell, hitting the back wall. He forced his heart rate to slow and took a deep breath as he reached the top of the stairs, where John and Jonathan waited. Blood had formed a dark splotch on the blue polo, and John held a piece of cloth he'd torn off a cargo pocket over the wound.

"Jesus, that was close," John said. "What now?"

"You parked around back like always, right?" Logan said. "Please tell me you have your keys on you."

A smile formed on his paling face, and John said, "Of course. Didn't have time to take them out of my pocket."

"Good. Then follow me. We're going through the rec area to the patio and from there to the ground. Sommers, you're up front. Let's go," Logan said, knowing every moment lost was another drop of blood gone for John. *I don't know if he's going to make it. Shut that shit down and concentrate. Control what you can, and allow the rest to happen. Now move!*

———

Cole lay prone next to a weight rack in the rear right corner of the gym, the sights of his SIG SAUER P229 lined up on the doorway. He'd kept the lights off, and the only illumination was the natural gloom from outside through the windows. There were multiple pieces of gym equipment in the right half of the gym, while the left side had an assortment of BOB martial arts dummies, suspended heavy bags, and other close-quarter weapons and gear. He waited patiently, knowing he had the tactical advantage. *Anyone comes through that door, he's a ghost,* Cole thought. He just needed to distract—*or better yet, kill*—them long enough for Amira to execute her plan.

A minute passed, and another thirty seconds later, Cole grew uneasy. *Did I miss something?* A sudden flurry of gunshots reverberated through the ceiling from somewhere upstairs. *What the hell is going on up there?*

A slight squeak startled Cole from his right, and the realization of what it was sent him scrambling forward even before he looked. Had he hesitated for even a second, he'd have been dead.

Due to the lack of efficient ventilation, the members of the task force always kept the back door slightly propped open for fresh air. The door was old, like the building, and the hinges squeaked every time the door moved. He'd been meaning to WD-40 the noisy hinges, but he kept forgetting, getting distracted by something else every time he intended to act. Later, he'd thank the gods for his momentary memory lapses.

When the two Secret Service agents pushed through the door,

Cole realized his nearly fatal mistake—the two suits had known they'd be lying in wait, ready to ambush them if they came in through the main door, and they'd flanked them, going outside and around.

As he lunged forward, he shot his arm out to his side and pulled the trigger several times, the reports magnified inside the enclosed space. The sound never ceased to amaze—and deafen—him. Most people had no idea how loud a gunshot actually was without hearing protection.

Crack! Crack! Crack! Crack!

He heard glass shatter, as well as a large metallic clang as one of his bullets struck a piece of equipment. He slid on his belly back toward the door, finding refuge behind another weight rack, as the two shooters spread out and opened fire.

Bullets impacted the equipment around him, but the iron weights, especially the 45-lb. plates, took the brunt of it.

Where the hell is she? Any longer and they'll be taking résumés for my replacement.

A second later, he felt the impulse to move, though he knew movement meant death. *It's better than dying in place,* he thought, looking at the door to the hallway still twenty feet away, which may as well have been on the far side of the moon. *If I can make it to the door, at least I have a chance. Need to suppress them, first. Here goes nothing.*

Cole Matthews rolled to his left, still in the prone position, looking for the first black-and-white figure he could find. *Bingo. Black-and-white behind the dual-pulley functional trainer.* He opened fire, rounds ricocheting off the cable machine.

The two Secret Service agents zeroed in on Cole's position and returned fire. Ironically, it was their proficiency that doomed them. Focused on the threat they could see, they forgot about the one they couldn't.

From the farthest corner of the gym, left of the door, dashed the running figure of Amira Cerone, her compact SIG SAUER P250 blazing away at the two agents. She moved quickly and across the span of the room, her weapon barking every few feet, the muzzle flashes highlighting her path.

The first shooter never had a chance. Multiple rounds struck him in the chest, and one round tore into the right side of his face. He fell backward, striking his head on the top of one of the functional trainer's weight stacks and lay still.

Cole seized the moment and scrambled to the right toward his original ambush position. He assumed a crouch and moved quickly across the back of the gym.

The second shooter, distracted by the assaulting figure who'd entered the gunfight, never saw Cole leave his prone position. As a result, he also never saw the former Unit and CIA man squeeze the trigger on the SIG SAUER pistol, and he certainly didn't see the 9mm hollow point as it entered the side of his head right above the left ear, tearing away the top of his ear lobe on its way to ending his life. He fell to the floor, motionless and dead.

"Took you long enough," Cole said.

Amira had opened her mouth to reply when she heard the start of an engine out back, followed by the sound of tires chewing up the gravel lot. *That's John's truck,* she thought.

"You're welcome," Amira said quickly. "You have your keys on you? Mine are in my locker upstairs."

"As a matter of fact, I do, but I'm parked out front," Cole said.

"Then let's get to your SUV and kill anyone on our way," Amira said fiercely, and stormed out the door, leaving Cole to follow. *God, this woman's scary.*

———

Sommers reached the corner as Logan said, "Stop. Don't go any farther."

John leaned up against the wall, and Logan studied his friend for a minute. "You still good to go?" The pressure appeared to be working, staunching the blood flow. The entry wound was small, which was the only good thing about the gunshot wound. The fact that it was still lodged inside him was the bad thing.

John nodded. "Until the end."

"Roger, but that's not yet. Wait here for a second," Logan said, and stepped past Jonathan, extending out into a prone position. The upper hallway was relatively dark, a corridor of shadows and uncertainties. He figured the lower he was, the lesser the chances that he'd get his head blown off.

Logan low-crawled forward, holding both his breath and his Kimber, and peered around the corner. Still certain he was alive and hadn't been sucker-shot, he stared down the long corridor, as if by doing so he could illuminate the space. Certain pockets of darkness loomed alarmingly along the walls, tempting him to move forward. *Bad guys downstairs and the unknown ahead. I'll take the lesser of two evils. Forward it is.*

He pushed himself backward with his forearms, stood up, and looked at Jonathan. "Here's the deal. It looks clear, but for all I know, Harkens has a fucking fire team waiting for us. The first door on the right is one of the entrances to the rec room. It's got a levered handle on it and pushes inward. Once you open it, step inside and to the right, and I'll come in right behind you. Got it?" Logan said.

Jonathan nodded in understanding.

"Good. Be quiet, and we'll be fine," Logan said. "Now let's get out of here."

Sommers moved forward, inching quietly down the hall. As he cautiously and deliberately placed one foot in front of the other, he thought, *How did it come to this? I never thought I was on the wrong side of history. But you are,* his subconscious shot back. *And part of you knows it, deep down. You got yourself into this mess, and only you can get yourself out, with their help, if you're lucky.*

He reached the levered handle and heard Logan and John stop behind him. He paused for a moment, listening. *Nothing.* Light from the multiple windows added visibility inside the room, but the French door had a thin curtain on it, distorting the view. A moment later, he exhaled, pushed the lever down, and swung the door inward. He was greeted with silence from within.

Thank God, he thought, and stepped inside and immediately to the right, stopping directly in front of a Secret Service agent who stood with his black pistol aimed squarely at his chest.

Jonathan Sommers, a traitor responsible for death and destruction across the globe, realized that his prayers had fallen on deaf celestial ears. *My luck just ran out,* he thought as the Secret Service agent pulled the trigger multiple times, striking him squarely in the chest with three bullets in a tight group that shredded his heart.

Behind him, Logan was halfway through the door when he heard the shots and realized what had happened—an agent had waited up here to ambush them in the event they decided to escape from the second floor, which they had. Logan also knew that Jonathan Sommers was dead. The shots were at point-blank range, and there was no way the shooter would miss.

Logan wasn't filled with remorse, even as Sommers' body still stood, the shock and destruction less than a missing heartbeat away. There'd been a time when he'd wanted to kill the man himself. If there was a silver lining, it was that his death would not be on his conscience. He took advantage of the moment and did the only thing he could—rushed forward, slamming into the back of Jonathan's dying body.

The impact drove Sommers forward, and Logan pushed harder until he felt the body he'd used for a battering ram slam into the Secret Service agent. Driving his legs forward, he pressed against Sommers' back and shot his right arm alongside his waist and into the Secret Service agent's stomach. He didn't hesitate as he pulled the trigger three times, the roar of the .45 filling the room.

Unlike the agent's bullets, Logan's didn't strike the man in the heart, and somehow, the wounded shooter retained the strength to try to raise his right hand with the FN Five-seveN in it.

Logan wrapped his left arm around the waist of Sommers' corpse and grabbed the rising wrist, pressing down to keep the barrel lowered. The gun fired, and Logan felt the impact strike Sommers somewhere in the lower body, although he was fairly certain that the traitor hadn't felt the bullet.

Applying more pressure with his left wrist, he simultaneously angled his Kimber upward, and in a full Jonathan Sommers death hug, he pulled he trigger.

Bam!

The round struck the agent under the chin, splattering the back wall with skull and brain fragments, ending the struggle. The dead man fell to the floor, and Logan stepped backward, withdrawing his arms from under Sommers' armpits. Jonathan's corpse followed suit and crumpled, coming to rest near the dead agent as blood from both bodies began to pool together. *Two traitors' blood commingling in death. Fitting.*

"Jesus, I almost feel bad for him," John said from behind Logan.

Logan turned around, and said, "I don't. Not for one second. He got what he deserved, maybe better. More importantly, let's get you out of here before more of these bastards arrive."

Logan walked over to John, slung John's right arm around his shoulders, and walked toward the patio doors. The fire alarms were still going off throughout the building, adding to the surreal quality of the rec area.

They reached the doors, opened them, and stepped out into the morning. Fresh air thick with summer dew cleared their senses for the first time since the battle had started.

Logan reached the edge of the waist-high patio wall and turned around. "I'm going over. As soon as you hear me call you, you need to do the same. Drop down, and I swear I'll catch you, although it's probably going to hurt like hell," Logan said.

"Thanks for the pep talk," John shot back. "Can't wait."

"Don't be a wuss," Logan said. "You're not dead yet."

"So tender and caring. Jump over the wall before I throw you over," John said, even as Logan smiled, swung up onto the wall, and placed his hands in a firm grip on top of the bricks. A moment later he stepped backward and managed to walk his way down until he was fully extended. His hands suddenly disappeared, and John heard him hit the ground below.

This is going to suck, John thought, and limped over to the wall, the pain increasing in intensity. He looked over, and saw Logan looking up expectantly. *No point in delaying the inevitable.*

John lay down on top of the wall, and rather than walk down the way Logan had, he began to turn his body until his legs and then torso dropped straight down, pulled by gravity. His body suddenly screamed in agony, and at the moment of full extension, pain exploded in his torso. He reflexively let go and plummeted to the ground . . .

. . . into the waiting arms of Logan West. Both men hit the ground, hard, and John let out a low growl of pain.

"Okay," John said through gritted teeth, "let's never do that again."

Before Logan could reply, gunshots from the left side of the building indoors reached their ears.

"We need to help them," John said.

"No," Logan said definitively. "We need to get you medical

attention, or you will be dead. And then, well, then you won't be good to her or anyone. I can see the wound, brother. It's not good. You don't have all day, or even morning."

John realized his friend's mind was set. *No way I'm changing it.* "She's more deadly than I am, and Cole's not half bad."

"You're right on both counts. Let's get in the truck and get out of here. We can have FBI and Marine PMO here in six minutes, if not less," Logan said, referring to the Marine Provost Marshall Office, responsible for law enforcement at Marine Corps Base Quantico. "They'll be fine."

The gunfire continued as the two men got in the pickup truck. *Time to get the hell out of Dodge,* Logan thought as he floored the accelerator, kicked up loose gravel with the F-150's tires, and navigated the pickup around the side of the building through the grass. As the truck reached the front of the building, tearing up the lawn before the tires finally hit the gravel road, he didn't see the two Secret Service agents, including Special Agent Harkens, running toward the black Suburban.

PART VI

A BAD WAY
TO START A DAY

CHAPTER 31

"Are you ready, brother?" Logan said, his voice steady, his hands tightening his grip on the steering wheel, the roiling rage he'd been fighting for six months ready to be fully unleashed.

"Fucking A," John replied. "And congratulations on becoming a dad. I love you, brother."

"Ditto." There was no time left to talk. The two warriors had reached the end of the proverbial and literal road.

Logan reached forward and pushed the power button on the stereo, twisting the dial to the right. Fuck it. Might as well go out with a little music just for the occasion.

"Here we go," Logan said, and gripped the steering wheel tighter. "Buckle up and enjoy the ride. It's going to be a rough one."

––––––––

Quantico, Virginia
Thursday, 0745 EST

"Here we go," Logan said, and gripped the steering wheel tighter. "Buckle up and enjoy the ride, brother. It's going to be a rough one."

Logan slammed the accelerator to the floor, and the pickup shot forward, a missile on four wheels with only one target—the open compartment of the Suburban.

John pointed the Kimber through one of the holes in the front windshield and opened fire, trying to minimize the rise and sway of the barrel as the vehicle rumbled across the end of the gravel road.

The Secret Service agent holding the RPG flinched and seemed to nonchalantly relax, and the front of the rocket lowered, pointing at the road.

Did I hit him? John wondered. It was a question he'd never get to answer. The agent pulled the trigger, obscuring the Suburban in a huge flash and puff of smoke. The rocket shot downward into the ground, striking the spot where the pavement met the gravel road. Incredibly, it failed to detonate and ricocheted upward at an angle.

Both Logan and John had seen RPGs defy physics and do nearly impossible things—career off cars when they should've detonated, tear into the side of a Humvee and fail to detonate, and even impale a Marine after failing to explode. For a moment, both warriors thought the same thing—*It's going to hit us.*

But then the rocket shot over the pickup's roof so close that Logan momentarily smelled the exhaust and felt the heat. *Thank you, God,* was all he had time to think as the pickup accelerated and closed the remaining distance to the Suburban.

With a deafening crunch, the front of John Quick's F-150 smashed into the side of the specialized Suburban, rocking the vehicle onto its two right wheels. The impact crushed the RPG-wielding agent, slamming the empty launcher into the bottom of his chin, shattering it and slamming his head backward. The blow knocked him unconscious, which spared him the pain as his body was flung across the compartment inside the Suburban and into the edge of the opposite open door, breaking his back.

A loud *boom* reverberated across the ground and shook the

pickup as the RPG detonated behind them over the second Suburban.

Both airbags in the pickup deployed, and the smell of gun smoke and burnt plastic was added to the mix of noxious fumes inside the cab. Logan's head snapped forward, but he was far enough away from the steering wheel that only his forehead struck the inflatable safety device.

The pickup shoved the Suburban sideways, but its size wasn't enough to flip the heavily armored SUV. Both vehicles ground to a halt, and the weight of the Suburban shifted back to the left, pushing the F-150 backward as its left two wheels touched back onto the ground, the nose of the pickup embedded partially in the open compartment.

Logan sat slumped against the door, his neck sore from the impact. He opened his eyes, and all he saw was the white of the air-bag slowly deflating. He heard a moan from his right, and John muttered, "You really are trying to kill me."

His friend's voice spurred Logan into action. *We're not out of this yet. Not even close.* "Stay here. We'll get you help soon, brother. Just hang in there."

John coughed. "I'm not going anywhere. Just don't stop for coffee in your quest for help. You know what I'm saying?"

"I got this," Logan said, confidence and concern in his voice.

John recognized his friend's tone and knew what he said was true. *These guys are about to get both barrels from Logan West. I just hope I don't die before I see it.*

Logan heard a movement from the front seat of the Suburban. *No way they get away with this. No way.*

Unbuckling his seat belt, the shock from the impact wearing off and the adrenaline from his rage surging, he withdrew the Mark II fighting knife from its home on his belt. He needed to move fast.

He pushed the deflated airbag aside, revealing several holes where most of the center part of the windshield had been shattered and was missing several large pieces. Aware he only had seconds before the agents from the second Suburban reacted, Logan crawled over the dashboard and through one of the large holes, his pants catching on the jagged edges. He heard a tearing noise and felt the laceration, but he didn't care. It was fight or die.

He spilled out onto the crumpled hood of the F-150 and low-crawled to the edge of the nose. Not stopping, he rolled onto his right shoulder and brought his legs up slightly and around. His momentum carried him off the front of the F-150, and he landed on his feet inside the Suburban.

Directly in front of him was the driver of the Suburban, half out of his seat, trying to climb over the bank of radios and communications equipment that was mounted between the seats in a rack on the floor. The Secret Service agent heard Logan approaching, and his head whipped around over his right shoulder. He managed to climb on top of the radios, but that was as far as he made it, even as he attempted to draw his Five-seveN from a holster on his belt inside his suit coat.

With a burst of speed and power, Logan rushed forward, his arms outstretched in front of him, the knife held in his right hand, but angled back. In two short strides, he reached the agent and struck him as if he were an offensive lineman hitting a practice dummy. The Secret Service agent was thrown backward and crashed into the mounted Panasonic Toughbook laptop computer.

He grunted with pain, but even off balance, his training demanded he fight back, and he tried to reach for his weapon once again.

"No!" Logan screamed, plunging the Mark II knife directly into the agent's chest, just below the sternum. *No vest. Good.* He felt the agent recoil in shock, but he didn't care. All Logan West could see was clouded over with a black veil of rage. "You're done. I killed

your friends, I'm going to kill that motherfucker in charge of your detail, and now I've killed *you*," he snarled as he withdrew the blade and quickly stabbed him two more times, shredding the bottom of the agent's heart. "So just fucking die already." There was no mercy to be found inside the Secret Service SUV. *You brought this ruin upon yourself.*

Blood flowed from the wounds and onto Logan's hands, and when the agent's body stopped trembling and his eyes turned vacant, Logan pulled the knife out and let the dead man fall backward against the computer.

Logan bent over, withdrew the FN Five-seveN, resheathed the knife after wiping the blood on the agent's suit pants, and risked a glance out the window. The Suburban that had chased them had stopped forty feet behind the F-150, its windshield pockmarked with small spiderwebs and holes where shrapnel from the RPG ricochet had peppered it. The driver's side door was open, and Special Agent Harkens had one foot on the gravel road.

Logan pulled his phone from his front pocket and checked the home screen. *Damn. Still no bars.* He looked back out the window, realizing his only move was to exit the Suburban on the passenger side and try to flank Harkens. But then he saw past the parked Suburban and smiled. *This will all be over soon.*

CHAPTER 32

Cole aimed the Ford Explorer at the side of the stopped Suburban thirty yards in front of him, preparing himself for the impact. Amira did the same in the passenger seat, bracing herself with one hand on the handle over the window and another on the middle armrest, her muscles taut to absorb the energy. Cole smiled. *Whatever idiot spread the lie that you should relax your muscles before an accident should be shot.*

Once they'd fled Ares headquarters, they'd only been less than a minute behind Logan and John. As they'd sped toward the entrance, they'd caught up enough to witness Logan's Last Stand and the ensuing RPG ricochet.

But now, with the last sounds of battle fading, Special Agent Harkens heard the Ford Explorer behind him, and he turned to face the newest threat.

With quickness that Cole respected from a professional standpoint, the head of the vice president's detail drew his Five-seveN, leaned against the parked SUV for stability, and started firing at the speeding Explorer.

"He's fast. I'll give him that," Cole said, his hands clenching the steering wheel as the armor-piercing rounds hit the windshield with limited results. Several pockmarks appeared on the level eight bullet-resistant glass, but none of the high-velocity rounds passed through.

"Fuck him," Amira said.

"Absolutely," Cole replied, and pressed the accelerator. "Hold on."

Realizing he had no direct approach at Harkens since his body was pressed against the Suburban, Cole quickly swerved to the left and then back to the right, giving himself a better angle of attack.

Ten yards . . .

Special Agent Harkens realized he had nowhere to run, and he did the only thing he could—he leapt back into the open door of the Suburban.

The front right corner of the Explorer crashed into the back left door of the Suburban and shot forward, grinding up the side of the vehicle. The Explorer tore along the black metal and smashed through the open door, bending it backward until the metal hinges snapped, pinning the door against the left front quarter panel.

Amira looked out her window and into the Suburban, spotting the prone figure of Harkens lying across the front seat, his hands on his head. *Don't worry. We're not done with you yet.*

The damage done, the Explorer disengaged from the Suburban as it roared past, leaving the destroyed door to drop to the gravel road.

Cole slammed on the brakes, and the Explorer slid across the loose rock and onto the pavement of MCB-1. The hard surface gripped the tires, and the vehicle jerked to a stop between the Suburban and John's pickup.

Cole looked in the rearview mirror but saw no movement. He looked over at Amira, who was already unbuckling her seat belt.

"I take it you're fine?" Cole asked.

"Of course," Amira replied calmly. "Let's get this bastard."

"Unless he gets him first," Cole responded calmly, pointing to the bloody and purposeful figure of Logan West striding across the pavement toward the Suburban and its human trophy inside. His face was a mask of merciless determination, an expression Cole had only witnessed a select number of times. *Uh-oh. This isn't going to end well.*

———

The door inside Logan's mind was wide open, and the beast that was his suppressed rage and frustration was running wild throughout the synapses in his brain. All that was wrong with the world, all the death and violence that he and his team had endured, the Organization that was responsible for the global mayhem, and most painfully, Mike Benson's death—Special Agent Harkens represented all of it. It was an insidious cancer, and Logan intended to fight it until his last breath and cut out every tumor possible, beginning with the one stumbling out of the Suburban in front of him.

Special Agent Harkens fell to the gravel, tottering from the aftereffects of the blow he'd sustained inside the SUV. He rose to his knees and stood up, using the exposed frame where the Explorer had sheared off the door. He looked forward and saw Logan West, and for the first time that day, he thought, *What did I get myself into?*

Stalking methodically toward him was a man of purpose and intent, his front soaked in blood. He held a Secret Service–issued FN Five-seveN in his right hand and a cell phone in his left. He didn't speak, and Special Agent Harkens realized a half second too late that there was no conversation to be had. *He's going to kill me,* he thought, even as his body responded to the threat and impending doom pitilessly staring him in the face.

Logan waited, knowing the moment had arrived. The battle rage had returned in full force, yearning for its master to bear witness to its power. *Not yet. Not yet,* he thought again, step after step.

Harkens then did exactly what Logan had hoped for—he reached for the FN Five-seveN on his hip. *Thank you,* Logan thought, and raised his right arm in such a fluid and fast motion that one moment his arm was down and the next it was pointing directly at the Secret Service agent, fifteen feet away. He squeezed the trigger.

Crack!

The 5.57x28mm SS190 projectile punctured the Kevlar vest Special Agent Harkens wore under his suit—precisely as the ammunition had been designed to do—stunning the agent. He looked at his right hand, which had cleared his holster by only a few inches and now held his own Five-seveN. He looked back at Logan as his consciousness started to fade owing to the catastrophic damage to his heart from the armor-piercing bullet. Logan's eyes bored into his, dancing with a ferocious intensity. *He's death incarnate,* was his last thought as the black edges of his vision closed together in front of him.

Logan pulled the trigger again, placing two more rounds in the center of Harkens' chest. He elevated the Five-seveN and fired one last round from less than eight feet into the unconscious man's forehead, definitively ending his life. Harkens fell to the gravel next to the Suburban and lay still.

Logan kept walking toward the corpse, and without uttering a word, he stepped over the dead agent, an Oakley boot unintentionally kicking his side. *Fuck him,* his mind registered as he looked at his cell phone—which still had no bars—and then inside the SUV.

The round antenna on top of the Suburban was still intact, and the electronic countermeasures controlled by the computer equipment built into the SUV were still activated. "Enough with this shit," Logan said in frustration, and emptied the fifteen-round magazine into every piece of equipment in the front seat.

The armor-piercing rounds tore through steel cases and computer terminals, resulting in several pops as sparks showered the interior, which was filled with electrical smoke moments later.

Finished, Logan looked at his phone. *Bingo.* He pulled up his contact list, hit the sixth name on the list, and waited.

Looking back toward the F-150, he saw Cole and Amira had exited Cole's Explorer, and Logan shouted to them, "John's in the front seat. He's been hit. Go check on him."

Amira's expression turned to one of concern, and she whirled on her black tactical hiking boots and dashed toward the remains of John's pickup.

Cole walked toward Logan, and said, "Are you okay?"

Logan only nodded as Lance Foster, the head of the FBI's HRT, answered his phone.

"What's up, brother-man?" Lance said in his typical nonchalant voice.

"Lance, listen closely. There's been an attack on the compound. John's been shot. Sommers is dead. How fast can you get a medic over here at the entrance to MCB-One? You'll see the wreckage. You still have the helo on standby, right? John needs to get to a hospital," Logan said.

"Jesus," Lance said, obvious anger and concern all wrapped into one word. "Wait one," he said. Logan heard shouting in the background as Lance issued orders to whomever he was talking to. It continued for twenty seconds until he came back on the line. "We'll be there in less than five minutes, and then we'll get him to Inova Fairfax Hospital. They've got a level one trauma center, which is his best chance. Just keep him alive until we get there. We'll take it the rest of the way."

"Roger, brother," Logan said, a slight tinge of relief in his voice now that he knew the best medical help was minutes away. "One more thing. After you drop John off, I need you to come back and get us at the compound. We have a trip to make to see Jake at FBI Headquarters in DC, and then we're going hunting."

"You got it," Lance said. "And myself and a few of my guys will be coming with you. What level of threat are we dealing with so I can get my guys kitted up?"

Logan paused. *It's not going to sound any less crazy, no matter how long you wait.* "The highest, Lance. We're going to take down the vice president of the United States." He smiled for the first time that morning at the expected silence. "Almost forgot, I just found out Sarah's pregnant, too. I need to call her right now. See you soon."

Rather than wait for Lance's response, Logan hung up and ran over to the F-150 to check on his wounded brother-in-arms. He never heard Lance Foster utter, "Just when I thought I'd heard it all . . ."

PART VII

EXECUTIVE
ORDERS

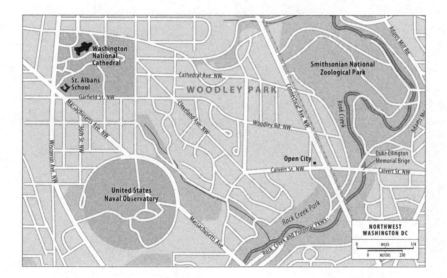

CHAPTER 33

J. Edgar Hoover Building
Northwest Washington DC

The roar of the rotors echoed across the concrete canyons of down-town DC as the helicopter descended. The side doors of the FBI HRT Black Hawk helicopter slid open as soon as the skids touched down on the helipad on the roof of the eight-story building that comprised half of FBI Headquarters on Pennsylvania Avenue.

Logan West, Cole Matthews—both now in fresh khaki cargo pants and dark-blue polos—Lance Foster, and eight HRT members in full tactical gear and OD green Nomex assault suits piled out both sides of the black bird. They wore black backpacks and carried black gun bags filled with weapons, ammunition, communications equipment, and body armor. After what Logan had told him, Special Agent Foster had decided to pack heavy, loaded for bear . . . and rogue Secret Service agents.

Logan walked over to the solitary figure waiting on the roof, as the pilot immediately began shutdown procedures on the Black Hawk. Logan squinted in the high-noon sunlight and heat. *Christ, it's hot up here,* he thought. *Not Africa hot—or even worse, Kuwait hot—but hot enough.*

"How's John?" Jake Benson asked as soon as Logan was within earshot.

"He's in surgery, but he was conscious when they dropped him off at Inova Fairfax. Amira's with him and will update us as soon as she knows something. He's as tough as they come. He'll pull through," Logan said, shaking his head. "It went south as soon as you sent me the text confirming Harkens wasn't actually part of the president's detail. Have you been able to reach him?"

"Negative," Jake replied. "He's in the middle of delivering his speech right now. I've got the director of the Secret Service in contact with the head of his detail. Director Mullins told me he'd have the president call me as soon as he's finished, but there's no way in hell I'm having that conversation with the president on my cell phone, even if it's supposedly encrypted and unbreakable, not these days. I also have no idea who called me and pretended to be from the president's detail, but I'm guessing it was someone that you killed this morning."

"I'd take that bet for a dollar. What's the plan, then?" Logan asked, as Cole and Special Agent Foster waited patiently behind him.

"Tell your pilot to stand by," Jake said to the extremely fit Foster, an African American with a goatee and head of the FBI's HRT. "He can wait in my office or up here: it's his choice. And if you need him, he can be anywhere inside the DC diamond within two to three minutes."

"You got it, sir," Special Agent Foster said to his friend and ultimate boss. "But that leads me to my next question—where are we going?"

The director of the FBI, a tall man with the air of an elder statesman that belied the cunning agent he truly was, smiled. "To the White House, so we can have a little privacy when we talk to our commander in chief."

"Roger, but what about all this gear and all these guns?" Special Agent Foster asked, aware of the strict Secret Service White House policy on firearms for anyone other than uniformed law enforcement on official business. *Pretty sure that going after the vice president isn't covered under the definition of "official business,"* he thought.

"Leave the gear and the guns in the SUVs. If we need them inside the White House, then we definitely have much larger problems than a treasonous vice president," Jake replied.

"What SUVs?" Logan asked, suddenly smirking. "I'm pretty sure you don't have any up here, unless you have cars that can fly now."

"Keep it up, and I'll ask your friends to see how well *you* can fly," Jake shot back. "My detail is getting three Suburbans ready in the garage as we speak. Come on. Let's go."

"Well, then," Logan said, suddenly serious. "I guess it's time."

"Time for what?" Jake asked, as the large group of men walked toward a door in the side of a small building that jutted up from the roof.

"Time to direct the hate and rage at the motherfuckers who deserve it and make them pay for what they've done to this country, to your nephew, and to John," Logan said. "And there's not a goddamned thing anyone can do—including me—to stop it."

"It's like the president said when we started this counteroffensive after Sudan—we do whatever it takes," Jake said soberly, and put his hand on Logan's shoulder as they walked. Logan was family to Jake, and the two men had grown closer since the loss of Mike Benson. *Lord, please protect this man and his friends,* Jake thought. *They're going to need it.*

CHAPTER 34

The White House Situation Room was actually a complex in the basement of the West Wing. It was composed of three principal conference rooms, a watch floor that provided 24/7 classified intelligence and unclassified situational awareness, and several smaller breakout rooms. Renovated in 2007, it contained all next-generation technology that provided the White House with the ability to ingest information and intelligence from the Intelligence Community, as well as communicate to every leader in the free world. It also connected directly to the president of the United States, no matter where he was, be it flying on Air Force One or traveling in a ground convoy in the Beast, his armored limousine. It was this last capability the assembled men in the main principal conference room were utilizing at the moment.

CIA Director Sheldon Tooney, FBI Director Jake Benson, Logan West, Cole Matthews, and National Security Advisor Christopher Moran—who'd been promoted from deputy NSA after Jonathan Sommers' treachery had been discovered—stood around the dark cherrywood table that was polished daily. The plush black leather chairs had been pushed against the walls so that the five men could stand when the president appeared on the large HD video teleconference monitor at the end of the room.

A chirping suddenly came through the large speakers under the monitor, and a monotone male voice announced, "Stand by for the president." A second later, the face of President Preston Scott filled the screen. Flashing lights and shadows streamed behind the good-looking president, giving the appearance of motion.

"Gentlemen, please sit down," the president commanded.

Even as the chairs were pulled to the table by two of the world's most powerful men, two of the world's most lethal, and one courageous national security advisor, the president said, "What is so urgent that you had to have the director of the Secret Service reach out to my detail and get me? We just walked out of the Borgata, and I'm in the Beast. There's no one else in back with me. We're on the way to the airport, and I'll be back in DC in less than ninety minutes."

"Sir, I asked that the communications officer stop recording this VTC the second you appeared," Jake said of the classified video teleconference, pausing before he continued. "Do you remember when you found out that Sommers had betrayed our country? When Sheldon and I told you he was a traitor?"

"Of course," the president responded. "I was furious. I could have killed that sonofabitch myself. He betrayed everything we stand for as a nation. Part of me still agrees with you all that he deserves to die for his crimes."

"Sir, that won't be necessary anymore," Logan said respectfully.

"What do you mean?" the president asked, suddenly attentive.

"Because he died this morning in an attack on Ares headquarters at our compound in Quantico," Logan responded.

A man accustomed to receiving not just bad but globally catastrophic news on a regular basis as a result of his position, the president kept his expression unchanged. "How? Do you know who's responsible?"

"Yes, sir, we do," Jake replied. "It's why I asked you about how you felt after Sommers. Because this is way worse, sir."

"How can that be?" the president asked, concern finally showing through the VTC.

"Because it's the vice president who had his personal detail try to kill us," Logan said as quickly as he could.

A silence engulfed the room as the assembled men and patriots waited for a response.

"I knew this day would come," the president said disgustedly. "Tell me everything."

CHAPTER 35

After listening to the recitation of information discovered over the past three days, the president sat silent, the only sound the background noise as the Beast rolled toward Atlantic City International Airport.

"Where is he right now?" President Scott finally asked.

"Sir, he's at his residence. He leaves in an hour for the National Cathedral for a special practice by his son's choir at St. Albans," Jake said, referring to the elite Episcopalian boys' school on the grounds of the National Cathedral. "It's a last-minute visit, according to Director Mullins, who's kept informed of any changes to the vice president's schedule."

"Sir, we have two choices: we can try to take him at the vice president's residence at the observatory, or we can intercept him at the National Cathedral," Logan said. "Both offer significant challenges."

"How so?" the president asked.

"Sir, we don't know how many other agents on his detail are with him and know about his role in the Organization," Logan said. "It could be just a few, or it could be every damn one of them. We could call ahead of time, but if everyone's in on it, he gets tipped off, and he can get out of Dodge before we track him down. If we show up, it could turn into a firefight fast, especially at the sight of us."

"What's the other option?" the president asked.

"We intercept him at the National Cathedral. We show up unannounced, explain that there's an imminent threat to him, and that we need to take him back to the White House, where you're expecting him," Logan said.

"Jesus Christ, Logan," the president said. "There's going to be a full choir of kids and who knows how many other civilians present. I won't risk that kind of collateral damage."

"Sir, I understand your concerns. Believe me, I do. But even if the vice president is a Council member in the Organization, he's not a sociopath. These guys are ideological and believe they're making the world a better place."

"So did Hitler, and look how that turned out," President Scott said.

"Sir, he's not Hitler. I don't think he'll risk a confrontation. Remember, his *son* will be there. There's no way a father would put his own son in danger. He's a traitor, but he's not that kind of monster," Logan finished.

"Sir, I agree," Sheldon Tooney said. "I've known Vice President Baker a long time. He'll come quietly if we get to him before he realizes what's happening."

The president shook his head, considering his options. "What a goddamn mess . . . Gentlemen, I appreciate your input, but this call is on me." His voice suddenly grew stronger. "I won't risk the potential loss of innocent life. I can't. Too many people have died because of the Organization, and *I am not going to add to that body count.*" He sat back against the leather seat of the vehicle. "I can't. I'm sorry."

Jake Benson had spent a lifetime negotiating and arguing with presidents, senators, congressmen, and other senior leaders in the US government. A master of political nuance, he understood the point in a discussion when a decision had been reached from which there was no turning back, and he'd trained himself not to push past it. There was no changing the president's mind. It would have to be the vice president's residence at the Naval Observatory.

"I understand, sir," Jake said.

Logan suddenly interjected. "Sir, we can still show up unannounced and use the national security threat angle. I don't want to tip him off that we're coming. After this morning, I guarantee he's on edge since he hasn't heard back from Harkens or anyone else on the detail. He knows by now that something went way wrong, and he'll have his guard up. But if we can separate him from his detail somehow, we can get him without firing a shot."

"Very well, Logan," the president said. "Make it happen, and notify me as soon as you have him in custody. I'll either be on Air Force One or on the way back to the White House."

"We will, sir," Jake said. "In fact, I'm going to stay down here and hijack one of these conference rooms and run this operation from it. I'll be able to get to you immediately, sir."

"Roger, Jake," the president said, falling back into the military lingo from his Air Force pilot days. "Gentlemen, good luck, be safe, and Godspeed. See you soon. Out here."

The screen suddenly turned blue once the call was disconnected, although "White House Situation Room" remained on the HD monitor in white letters.

"All right, gang," Logan said. "You heard the man. Let's get back up to the vehicle, fill in the rest of the team, and get to work. Jake, Director, set up shop and call me on my cell once you're up and running."

"I'm going to get the director of the Secret Service down here as well," Jake said. "He needs to know what's about to happen."

"He's going to love that," Logan said. "We've already killed enough of his guys for one day."

"I doubt Director Mullins will be broken up about it once he finds out what those agents really were. I've known him for a long time. He's an honorable man," Jake said.

"Sir, it seems like all of these guys we've been chasing have been honorable men," Cole said, breaking his silence. "Yet we still end up having to kill them."

Realizing Cole had a point, Jake said, "Noted, and you're right, but I trust him. And if he turns out to be something other than what I believe him to be, I'll put a bullet in him myself," he finished, opening his suit coat to reveal a Glock 17 9mm pistol in a tightly worn shoulder rig. "I *am* law enforcement, after all, and this sure as hell is official business."

"Very nice, sir," Cole said.

"No kidding," Logan added. "I hope it doesn't come to that, but if it does, aim for the head and make it count."

"Mike taught me how to *really* shoot, not just the marksmanship I learned in my early years with the FBI," Jake said, suddenly serious after speaking his dead nephew's name aloud. "Trust me. I won't miss."

"Good to go," Logan said. "Neither will we. Come on, Cole, let's get upstairs and get the show on the road. We've got a traitor to trap."

CHAPTER 36

Vice President Josh Baker was exhausted from the stress and relent-less pace of the past three days. Truth be told, he was relieved that the charade would soon be over, at least the pretending-to-be-a-vice-president-who-cared-about-the-country part. Once the Council had revolted against the Founder, he knew it was only a matter of time before a full-blown war broke out. And he'd been right, just as he'd been right that Constantine Kallas wouldn't go gently into that good night. Once he'd realized that his network had been compromised, he'd fought back, executing the director of the NSA in broad daylight.

That bold move had accelerated Josh's plans, forcing him to make the fateful choice to send the head of his detail and several special agents loyal to the Organization to the secret compound that housed the president's special task force. He'd hoped to have that flash drive with its list of the Organization's most secret and powerful members, but when he hadn't heard back from Special Agent Harkens, he knew the mission had failed. The only good thing about it was that Harkens and the men he'd taken with him had had the day off, which meant the vice president had at least until tomorrow morning to vanish from the face of the political earth—no small feat for the second most powerful man in the United States, at least on paper. He'd planned to disappear no matter what, but now there was a deadline.

Fortunately, two Council members opposing the Founder had coordinated his escape, which would be perceived publicly as a homegrown terrorist attack and kidnapping for ransom. Somehow—and he hadn't asked for details—the Council had two teams in place, as well as digital and physical evidence that would implicate a well-organized and well-funded militia from Montana that opposed the federal government and—this was the smart touch—the vice president's staunch opposition to a new pipeline laterally across the heart of Montana, through the top of Idaho, and across Washington State to the Pacific Ocean.

The North American Oil Company was furious, but Josh didn't care. The ironic part—something North American Oil would never know—was that he hadn't opposed the pipeline because of some democratic or conservational ideal. No. It was much simpler than that. He just didn't like the CEO, who'd been a classmate of his at Yale. The satisfaction he derived from making Taylor Albritton's life miserable far outweighed the thousands of jobs the pipeline would create. No matter what else transpired, Vice President Joshua Baker was a man who made his enemies pay a price, either justifiably or unjustifiably so. *And I'm good with that. Politics is war, and the victors are the ones who fought dirty and played by no rules but their own. And I'm the reigning king of them all.*

By the end of the day, Josh would be on a one-way trip to South America, while the rest of the federal government focused its investigation and herculean resources out west.

The only person he would truly miss was his son, Jacob, who was an innocent pawn in his father's alternate existence. That paternal bond was why he'd ordered his detail to arrange an un-announced visit to the National Cathedral to see his son's choir practice. His wife he could do without; all she did was revel in the DC elitist circles.

Instead of the normal full presidential motorcade—in that respect, both the president and vice president were treated the same, complete with a route car, pilot car, staff car, CAT team, ambulance, electronic countermeasures vehicle, and communications relay vehicle—he'd pressured the detail of the day into limiting his footprint to the vice presidential limousine—smaller than the president's Beast—along with one SUV for his detail, one CAT team, the ambulance, and the communications relay SUV. The only ones inside the cathedral would be his detail, as they were also the only ones who knew the real intent of the unannounced visit—to provide the Council's team the opportunity to snatch him away from the grounds of the Naval Observatory, which were guarded by both the Secret Service and the Department of the Navy.

He glanced at his watch, then looked around the master bedroom. The wedding photograph on the dark dresser stared accusingly at him. He tried to dismiss the twinge of guilt he felt. *You made your choice long ago. The Organization always came first, no matter what.*

He exhaled, allowing his normal—some might argue cold and calculating—nature to resettle over him. *Time to go. No point in delaying the inevitable.*

Vice President Joshua Baker strode purposefully for the closed doors and never looked back.

Chapter 37

Standing atop St. Albans Hill on Wisconsin Avenue, the Washington National Cathedral was a marvel of Gothic architecture. Built of Indiana limestone over an eighty-three-year period, the enormous Episcopalian house of worship was shaped in a giant cross—apparent from any passing aircraft—with a five-hundred-foot nave and two smaller transepts.

Flying buttresses soared into the sky and supported the walls and rooftops along the outside of the nave on both sides. Two twelve-story towers stood like sentinels at the west end of the nave. In between and below the two towers, an observation deck accessible to all visitors provided a breathtaking view of the entire cathedral, including the main bell tower, which rose three hundred feet above the ground. The hill itself had an elevation of three hundred feet, making the top of the bell tower the highest point in all of DC.

The interior of the cross-shaped cathedral was an awe-inspiring, reflective cavern of hundred-foot ribbed, curved, vaulted ceilings, window scenes in stained glass along both sides of the main nave at both ground level and near the ceiling, an enormous high altar at the east end of the main nave, and balconies in the north and south transepts, as well as the west end of the nave. Above each of the balconies was a magnificent rose window, each depicting a major theme: Creation, the Last Judgment, and the Church Triumphant. As a result of the geographical layout, on a clear day, sun spilled through the stained glass and the rose window on the south side of the cathedral, creating a multicolored collage that glowed and shifted across the limestone.

In addition to the enormous cathedral, the sprawling hilltop contained multiple buildings, a library, its own special police force, and three different elementary schools due east of the cathedral. Several sports fields were built at different heights like multitiered enormous plateaus of recreation that descended down the east side of the hill into the urban Northwest sprawl below.

Former Spanish Army 19th Special Operations Group Capitán Sebastian Bautista glanced out the diagonal-paned window of the south overcroft—what a normal person would call an attic—directly under the roof of the south transept. The brown pools of his eyes and his angular, dark complexion gazed back at him from his reflection.

A veteran of Spain's foray into western Afghanistan in 2005 as one of the nation members of the International Security Assistance Force, a chance encounter with a US paramilitary team had changed Sebastian's career. While he and his platoon were enjoying the relative safety of Qala i Naw Airport in Badghis Province as part of reconstruction efforts, a CIA hunter-killer team had swarmed into the area on the trail of a Taliban shadow governor.

The CIA had zeroed in on his bed-down location—they never told Sebastian how—and executed a raid in the middle of the night on the outskirts of the village. The operation had bagged the high-value target, and then Capitán Bautista's team had provided perimeter security.

For some reason still unknown to Sebastian, a Taliban teenager had thought it would be a good idea to surprise the exfiltrating force on the way to the helicopter extraction point. Sebastian, who'd been providing rear-area security during the movement, had spotted the jihadi as he'd opened fire with an AK-47, the Taliban weapon of choice. Fortunately, Sebastian's response with his H&K G36 assault rifle was more accurate than the wild rounds that had kicked up dust around the CIA team leader, and he'd mortally wounded the boy, leaving him to die alone on the trail, cursing the Americans and praying to Allah.

Once the assault force had returned to the base, the CIA team leader had made him an offer: if Sebastian ever left the Spanish military, he should contact him before choosing a new career.

Sebastian had thought it a noble gesture between two warriors who'd fought alongside each other, but three years later, the CIA agent—whose real name was Matthew Riggins—had fulfilled that initial promise, indoctrinating him into a clandestine and covert world that Sebastian had never suspected even existed. But once his eyes had been opened to the realities of the global struggle for power, he'd embraced the Organization and never looked back.

The past few years of training had developed his skills to such a level of proficiency that the Organization called on him and his team for especially sensitive missions. But even for him, what he was about to attempt was something else entirely, especially after his three-man team had been ordered not to interfere in the battle at the Udvar-Hazy Center.

Sebastian studied the scaffolding—a permanent fixture following the earthquake that had struck the area—that wrapped around the south apse, as well as the bell tower. It provided a background and legitimized their presence. *Who looked twice at a work crew on scaffolding? No one,* Sebastian thought. The fact that his entire team also looked like Mexican immigrants helped them blend in with the culturally diverse DC population.

He spoke in English—on the incredibly long chance that some-one was listening—into an encrypted Motorola handset. "Five more minutes, and he should be here. Final status check. Go."

Several voices replied "go" confidently, as he knew they would.

If this goes our way, this will be one for the books . . . books that are never read by anyone, ever, he reminded himself, and smiled. *But we'll be talking about it for years to come.*

———

Vice President Joshua Baker sat in silence in the back of St. John's Chapel, which was separated from the main altar by a partition and columns that rose to the vaulted ceiling. The back of the chapel was open and ended at a short set of stairs that descended to the floor of the south transept only a few feet below. Josh looked down at the chair in front of him, noting the red cushion with the large upper-case letters that spelled JOHN F. KENNEDY. Each chair in the chapel had a cushion with a different name of a noted American, as well as symbols embroidered to represent his or her accomplishments.

His ego noted that he'd never have his name on one of these, but he didn't care. What he did care about was the last "Alleluia" that the St. Albans School fifth-grade boys' choir sang as one beautiful, singular, harmonious voice. Knowing that it would likely be the last time he heard the magical sound, a tear formed in his eye, reflecting the pain of a father about to lose his son.

The notes echoed off the limestone walls and ceiling, fading into the dusty sun. Finished, the boys stood and began to shuffle toward the rear of the chapel, which emptied down into the south transept.

The boys walked past, a moving mass of sport coats, collared shirts, and ties, and several of the fifth graders nodded politely or acknowledged him with a humble "sir." While all the boys knew who Jacob's father was and had seen him several times before, he wasn't the only powerful parent with a boy at St. Albans. For them, the real treat was his Secret Service detail. *All* the boys tried to steal a glimpse of the holstered pistols hidden beneath buttoned suit coats. *Boys will be boys,* Josh thought, as his fresh-faced son stopped in front of him, looking up with awe, love, and admiration.

"What did you think, Dad?" Jacob asked him, his brown hair cascading across his forehead.

Josh knelt down and hugged his son, holding him a second longer than usual. "I thought you were fantastic. You always are." He released him and stood back up, keeping his hands on his shoulders as he memorized the face he knew he would not see for quite some time, if ever. *God forgive me. This is hard.*

"I don't care what those eighth graders say. I think choir is cool," Jacob said. "*And* I play soccer and baseball. So if I want to sing, I will."

At that moment, an emotional rift opened up inside Josh, and an overwhelming sense of pride and love for his son poured forth, threatening to sabotage everything. He looked at his son, seeing the man he would become, and said, "That's right, Jacob. You do what you want to, and as long as it's for the right reasons—and I mean the *really right* reasons—then don't let anyone dissuade you from what *you* want to do. You're the one that has to live with who you are, and as long as you're happy with it, that's all that matters." He paused to let the gravity of the words sink in. "You understand?"

His son looked up at him, as if sensing something amiss. Any other father imparting mature words of wisdom to a fifth grader might have raised eyebrows, but Jacob Baker was no normal eleven-year-old, and his father was the second most powerful man in the country. "I understand, Dad. Thanks for getting it."

"I always do, son," Josh said. He suddenly knelt back down. "Come here. One more hug for your old man. It's been a long day."

"You bet," his son said, and wrapped his arms around his father's neck, pressing his head against his shoulders. "You're the best, Dad."

No matter what happens, this is the moment I'll remember, Josh thought, feeling the suffocating love but dreading the next moment, trying to stretch it out. *One more second, please.*

His son unlocked his arms and stepped back from his father. "You sure you're okay?"

"Of course I am," Josh said, smiling. "I got to see you. Now go catch up to your friends, and don't forget what I said."

His son grinned, a normal fifth-grade boy once again. "I won't. See you tonight, Dad." He suddenly turned and moved quickly down the short stack of steps from the elevated chapel. "Love you," he said, as he moved away, not realizing it would be the last time he'd utter those words to his father.

"Love you too, son," Josh said quietly. "Always and forever."

Silence.

Josh watched his son disappear around a column, moving toward the rear of the cathedral with the throng of boys. He shut his eyes and breathed deeply, trying to calm the raging storm inside. Sounds of the cathedral assaulted him, as if mocking his emotional vulnerability. The knock of a chair. Footsteps on the floor. A door closing. He heard all of it and none of it. *I just said good-bye to my son.*

"Sir, it's time," a soft-spoken voice said from behind him.

Josh—once again Vice President Baker—turned, eyes glistening. Special Agent Thomas Brennan and the other three Secret Service members who were part of the Organization stood quietly, providing him with a moment to gather himself. *The hardest part is over,* he thought. *Shut it all down. You need to be sharp for what's coming next.*

He took a deep breath, exhaled, back in control. "It is. Let's do this, Tom," Vice President Baker said.

"This way, sir," Special Agent Brennan replied, guiding the vice president to the left corner near the back of the south transept, where an alcove entrance was secured by a medieval-period iron gate. A small passageway lay beyond, and Special Agent Brennan pulled the gate open and stepped through. "The elevator is just around the corner, sir."

Vice President Baker, followed by the remaining three men of his conspiratorial detail, walked behind Special Agent Brennan. "Wow. It's cramped around here."

"You should see some of the spiral staircases. There's only room for one," Special Agent Brennan replied.

He rounded a corner, stopped in front of what was a solid-gray elevator door, and pressed a gray round button. He looked at the vice president, hesitated, but finally asked, "Are you absolutely sure you want to do this, sir?"

For a surreal and crazy moment, Josh considered walking away, uncharacteristically throwing all caution to the wind. It was the thought of Jacob that triggered the doubt. But then the hard thought of prison pushed it aside, and his determination to stay the course won the internal struggle.

"I'm sure, Tom. Thanks for asking," Vice President Baker said. "Now make the call."

"Roger, sir," Special Agent Brennan said, and lifted his left sleeve to his mouth.

CHAPTER 38

Rule one in any engagement was simple: things never, *ever* went according to plan.

When the first of the three black FBI Suburbans pulled up to the north entrance to the Naval Observatory, the uniformed division Secret Service officer manning the gate approached the driver's window. He nearly made it to the window when he realized the driver, a serious-looking African American with a goatee, was outfitted completely in tactical gear. The only thing that stopped the thirty-two-year-old officer from unholstering his weapon and drawing down on the driver was the set of FBI credentials the man held out the window.

"I'm Special Agent Lance Foster, head of the FBI's HRT, and we're here directly on behalf of the president. There's been a threat to the vice president, and for reasons I can't explain, he dispatched us to locate and secure him. In fact, I strongly recommend you contact the Joint Operations Center, who can patch you through to the White House Situation Room, where Director Mullins—your boss—is right at this moment," Lance finished.

"Sir, I have no idea—" was all the officer uttered before he was cut off.

"Listen to me very carefully, Sergeant," Lance said forcefully but quietly. "I have an eight-man HRT team in the two Suburbans behind us, as well as two very dangerous men in this one. Trust me. You want to make that call, and you want to do it right now. This is national security, and we're not here on a picnic. So please, just make the call, or we'll have to make it for you, and you don't want us to get out of these SUVs to do it."

The young officer never hesitated. He'd seen and heard enough to know the man in front of him was not only telling the truth but was as dangerous as he appeared to be. "Wait one," he said, and returned to the guardhouse.

"I guarantee you his head his spinning," Logan said from the passenger seat as he watched the uniformed division officer nodding his head subconsciously on the phone.

Less than twenty seconds later, he sprinted back to the vehicle. Breathless, he said, "Sir, Director Mullins confirmed who you are. I still can't believe I just spoke to him; however, there's a problem. The vice president left early twenty minutes ago for the National Cathedral. As far I know, he's there right now."

"Of course he did," Logan said in frustration, a sense of foreboding growing that this would be no easy afternoon.

"Roger that," Lance said. "You'll have to excuse us, but we're going to tear like hell out of here. Thanks for the help."

Lance yanked the wheel to the left and accelerated, conducting a very sharp turn in the confines of the entrance lanes. Seconds later, the SUV was roaring up Massachusetts Avenue.

"I'm calling Jake. He needs to get Mullins to let the CAT team and other guys out front of the cathedral know that we're coming in fast. I don't feel like getting shot at again today by the Secret Service, even if it's by the good ones," Logan said.

"Right now, we're the only guaranteed good guys in this fight," Cole said from the backseat.

"You got that right, brother," Logan said as he hit the call button on his cell to connect to Jake. *And until we know otherwise, everyone else is hostile. No chances get taken today, not after this morning.*

———

National Cathedral
Overcroft above the South Transept

The gray door slid open, and the five men in dark suits—four of them holding their FN Five-seveN pistols—exited the cramped elevator. The four Secret Service agents with the vice president in the middle of their group worked their way around a corner, stepping into the gloom of the vaulted-ceiling, attic-like space.

Directly in front of them stood a Hispanic man in a bright-yellow Pepco polo and khaki cargo pants, his arms lowered with his hands crossed in front of him. A large-paned window to his right was cranked open, and Vice President Baker felt the warm air rushing into the musty room. The rest of the space, long and rectangular, which extended toward the center of the cathedral, held an assortment of objects and relics, including a table-sized replica of the cathedral that dated back to the 1920s and once stood on display near the main entrance.

The left side of the room was an enclosed office with CONSTRUCTION ARCHIVES printed on a blue placard. Beyond the office, though, were dark shadows that shifted with the sun-reflected clouds of dust.

Directly opposite the way they'd entered in the other corner of the room was a narrow, circular stairwell inside a limestone tube that disappeared below.

"Mr. Vice President," the man said, "I'm Sebastian, and it's my job to make sure we get you out of here safely and quietly. Are you ready for what you have to do next, sir?"

The vice president walked over to the man, nodded his head, and said, "I am, as hard as it's going to be."

"Very well, sir. Then let's get started," Sebastian said.

Vice President Baker nodded and turned to face his detail, all of whom knew about the Organization and had been with him for the last three years. He wasn't fond of farewells, especially like this and especially after the loyalty these men had shown him. The four agents faced him as he spoke.

"Tom, there's no easy way to say it, and you've been more than a loyal agent. You've been a friend, and I'm sorry I have to go, but there's no other way. It has to be like this."

Vice President Baker reached out to shake Special Agent Tom Brennan's hand, initiating the sequence of events he would not be able to undo.

From the shifting shadows behind the detail, three figures silently appeared—one from behind the archive office, one from near the cathedral replica, and one from behind a large statue of Jesus that had once stood in the cathedral below. The men wore bright-yellow Pepco tee shirts and khakis, but more critically, they held black pistols with cylindrical suppressors attached. In one synchronized move, they raised the weapons.

"I'm really sorry about this, Tom. Good-bye," Vice President Baker said softly, gripping the agent's hand firmly as three triggers were pulled simultaneously.

Thwack-k-k!

The three shots formed one extended sound, the suppressors minimizing the reports to audible *smacks*. The three Secret Service agents were each struck in the back of the head, their blood sent spraying in a fine mist in multiple directions, droplets splattering across the facade of the white replica cathedral.

Special Agent Tom Brennan recognized a moment too late that they'd been led into an ambush by the man they were charged with protecting. It was the ultimate act of betrayal. His eyes widened, blue irises flaring in anger, and he yanked his hand out of the vice president's grasp. He managed to raise the weapon in his left hand slightly and turn halfway around before a round struck him in his left temple, snapping his head to the right. He fell to the ground at his master's feet, unseeing eyes staring accusingly up at him.

Vice President Baker sighed. *So much death. The turncoats on the Council—including you, Josh, don't forget—should never have let it get this far.*

The three shooters holstered their weapons under their yellow shirts and vests and moved toward the open window.

"Now, sir, are you really ready?" Sebastian asked, studying the vice president's expression in the wake of the sudden violence.

"I am," Joshua— who no longer thought of himself as the vice president the moment his detail had been murdered—said. "Saying good-bye to my son and leading my men to their slaughter was the hard part. Let's get on with it."

"Very well," Sebastian said. "Then please step over to the window and get ready for a ride."

CHAPTER 39

If it hadn't been for Director Mullins of the Secret Service, the four
CAT members in black BDUs armed with Kings Armament Company SR-16 E3 CQB Mod 2 5.56mm assault rifles would have rid-
dled with bullets the black Suburbans that screeched up the curved
driveway to the front of the National Cathedral. They wouldn't
have damaged the armored SUVs, but it would have turned the
front of the house of worship into a temporary war zone, which
was not what the Episcopalian founders had intended.

The four men—all prior enlisted operators from various Special
Operations units—stood behind their black SUV, weapons at the
ready and tracking the vehicles. Normally, CAT remained out of
sight, but the call from the Joint Operations Center to the communications vehicle had forced them into a defensive posture. Even
though they'd been told that three Suburbans with the head of the
FBI's HRT, two other unknown task force members, *and* an eight-
man HRT were en route on orders of the president, they took no
chances.

The other Secret Service agents who manned the ambulance
and communications vehicles had also assumed defensive positions

behind their vehicles, which formed a line in front of the main entrance.

The first Suburban slammed to a halt next to the CAT vehicle, and Special Agent Lance Foster opened the door, his FBI credentials in his hand. "Who's in charge here?"

"That would be me, sir," the CAT leader, a thirty-eight-year-old former SEAL Team 5 member, said. "Are you Special Agent Foster?"

"The one and only," Special Agent Foster said, walking toward the CAT member, his FBI credentials held out in his left hand. He reached the back end of the black Suburban, noticing the weapons of the other CAT members trailing him, although not pointed directly at him. "Here you go," he said, and handed the credentials over.

The CAT member looked them over, glanced up at Special Agent Foster, nodded, and handed the badge back to its owner. "Good to go, sir. What can we do?"

Special Agent Foster turned back to his vehicles, raised his right arm to shoulder height, and made a small circling gesture, as if calling the forces of nature to him.

All the doors on the vehicles opened simultaneously, and out stepped one of the most lethal units in US law enforcement, Kevlar helmets on and modified M4 assault rifles in hand.

Logan and Cole joined the CAT leader and Special Agent Foster. Logan carried his personal M4—a holdover from his Marine Force Reconnaissance days—and Cole wielded a modified HK416 with a red-dot reflex scope and pistol foregrip.

"Where is the vice president at this moment?" Logan asked. There was no doubt to the CAT leader that the fearsome man with the unnerving green eyes, blue polo, khaki cargo pants, and physical presence was in charge.

"He's inside. This is the only way in or out. All other exits are secured. His son's choir practice should have just ended," the CAT leader said.

"Can you please radio his detail, tell them there's a situation and that they need to get out here as soon as possible?" Logan asked urgently.

The CAT leader pressed a button on a wire that dangled from the headset and boom microphone he wore over a plain black baseball cap with a dark-red Punisher emblem. "Trailblazer Actual," the CAT leader said, referring to the vice president's code name, "this is Reaper Actual. What's your position?"

Silence.

"I say again, Trailblazer Actual. This is Reaper Actual. What's your position?"

More silence.

"Goddamnit, it's already started," Logan said. "We're going inside. Lance, you and Cole are with me. Have one of your teams secure the entrance from inside and the other spread out and search the main cathedral. I haven't been here in years, but if I recall correctly, there are two or three chapels in the basement, as well as several levels above and tons of places to hide."

Logan looked at the CAT leader, and said, "Secure this entrance. Weapons hot. If anyone comes out other than us, you either light them up or figure out who the hell they are. If the vice president comes out, treat him and his detail as hostile. I say again—*hostile.*"

The CAT leader stared at the man, stunned. A warrior and operator who had seen and done more than most, he was rarely nonplussed, but the man's words had nearly stopped him midthought. "Are you serious, sir?"

"Absolutely. I can guarantee you one thing: if the vice president and his detail come out this entrance, it's going to be guns blazing, and they will put you down if you try to stop them. So *don't fucking let them.*"

"One more thing," Logan said. "Please give us one of your men so he can communicate with you out here."

Without hesitation, the CAT leader looked at a thin, lean team member with short black hair. "Krazinski's my best shooter," the CAT leader said. The man's mouth turned up slightly in recognition. "Keep me posted."

"Roger that, boss," Special Agent Krazinski said.

"Thanks. Talk to you as soon as we have something," Logan said, and turned away, not waiting for a response. There was no need; he'd made his point. "Let's get in there and hope that God is on our side," he said, and dashed up the stairs, leaving the CAT leader to issue orders to the rest of the agents who remained outside with him.

CHAPTER 40

Logan crept up the limestone stairwell, placing each padded Oakley boot softly on the step above it. He breathed deeply as he focused on the narrow passageway upward. *If they hear you, you're all dead men,* he thought, with Cole, Lance, and the CAT team member named Krazinski right behind him. The two four-man HRT teams had remained in the main cathedral. *Just us four amigos against God knows what.*

A docent in the south transept had informed them that the vice president had decided to see the rooftop accessible from the south overcroft. They'd only gone up two to three minutes before Logan and his assault force had entered the building.

Counting each step, Logan proceeded with the utmost caution once he hit step two hundred and ten, knowing the stairwell contained two hundred and twenty steps, as the docent had informed them when he'd asked.

He thought he heard movement above, and he paused, raising his right hand. The four men stopped, modern knights in a medieval castle, and waited. Logan listened. A small *bang*, as if a door closing, carried to them in muffled echoes. A whizzing sound followed. *What the hell? Keep going. There's no time.*

The four apex predators, led by the most dangerous one of all, continued on. Logan realized he was near the top of the stairwell when he was struck by a wash of light. Steadying himself, he thought, *You can't die in glory if you don't try,* and rushed quickly up the remaining steps, the red dot of his reflex scope tracking in line with his right eye.

He rounded the last curve, reached the floor of the overcroft, and processed instantly the scene before him. The vice president's detail was dead, the vice president was gone, and a member of the Organization team responsible was disappearing through the open window, khaki cargo pants still visible inside.

Had he appeared a few seconds earlier, the disappearing man would have seen them and likely opened fire. Logan realized his good fortune and timing, and rushed forward, releasing the M4, which fell across his chest and Kevlar vest, the assault rifle dangling across his upper body.

He reached the window as the man's tan boots disappeared outside. Acting rather than thinking, he shot his hands out into the sun and grabbed both of the man's ankles. In addition to catching his prey, he was rewarded with enlightenment, although not the kind he would have liked. *The vice president is gone. They zip-lined him down to the street. Smart motherfuckers.*

A taut wire connected the skeletal scaffolding around the cathedral to the statue of George Washington on horseback several hundred feet below at the base of a long staircase that led from the street next to the cathedral farther down to a side road for St. Albans School. A metal pulley with handles hung from the wire, and a nylon harness was connected to the bottom of the entire mechanism.

Logan heard the man speaking quickly, but his words were lost in the wind and external noise. Even as Logan wrestled with the man, who was sprawled out on a wooden plank, he saw three Pepco trucks below and a man in a dark suit being pushed into the middle one. *Bingo.*

"The VP's gone!" Logan screamed, hoping Cole and Lance heard him as he was yanked halfway out the window. Warm air and wind assaulted him as he was dragged along the wooden plank that had been laid across the skeletal scaffolding to create a platform. "They're using Pepco vehicles to disguise their getaway. Get CAT down to the south side of the cathedral on the street below! And get the Black Hawk in the air! We need to track those vehicles!"

As if sensing his intent, the three vehicles pulled away from the base of the statue, accelerating down the winding road toward the multiple soccer fields and park.

As Logan finished his ad-hoc SITREP, the Pepco impersonator reached the zip line, grabbed the handles, and disengaged the brake. The trolley shot down the wire, sending its operator and the dangling figure of Logan West into open air more than one hundred and twenty feet above the concrete pavement below.

———

Cole and Lance watched as the two men shot down the sharp incline toward the statue more than two hundred and fifty feet away. *Hang on, Logan, whatever you do.*

Cole turned to Special Agent Krazinski—as Lance was issuing orders over his own HF radio net for the Black Hawk to launch—and said, "Get the vehicles back here as fast as you can. Let's go."

The three men raced back into the dark stairwell, leaving the dead Secret Service agents alone in the dimly lit space.

———

This wasn't the smartest plan, Logan thought as the trolley screamed down the wire toward the George Washington statue on Pilgrim. Between the weight of the Kevlar vest and the M4 still slung across his chest, he held himself up awkwardly, his arms wrapped around the man's ankles, which left his head exposed and adjacent to the man's knees.

He looked up and saw the man staring at him—*almost too casually,* Logan thought—even as the pulley reached the halfway point and gained speed and momentum. The only good thing was that he knew the man would not release his grip with one hand to draw a weapon and shoot Logan off of him. If he did that, he wouldn't be able to hold both himself and Logan up, and they'd both plummet to their deaths.

Logan glanced down as the three Pepco trucks sped away around a curve in the direction of the sports complex, which held a soccer field—that also was measured for football—a baseball diamond, and seven tennis courts. He prayed the CAT vehicles would be here soon. If they lost those trucks, the likelihood of the vice president escaping increased exponentially in the urban maze of northwest DC.

The statue loomed closer, and Logan braced himself for impact, praying his head didn't hit stone. The pulley reached maximum velocity with only forty feet to go. *This is going to hurt . . . a lot.*

Screeeeeeech!

The pulley dramatically and violently slowed, and Logan realized his rider's intent—to cut the speed quickly and fling his freeloader off into the statue. Unfortunately for Logan, it was a sound tactic.

As the brake bit into the taut wire, the pulley's speed decreased and suddenly stopped. A moment later, Logan found himself perpendicular even as he fought to hold on, but to no avail. He was flung forward and found himself holding thin air, face down. The ground rushed by below him and suddenly lurched up as gravity propelled him downward. *Here it comes.* He curled his head and neck forward, trying to protect them both.

He landed at an angle on his left forearm, side, and leg, but then momentum flipped him backward as the ground gripped his body. He rolled several times to his right, attempting to keep himself rigid and minimize the chance of injury. His boots slammed into concrete, and he realized he'd hit the statue. He turned once more and stopped, eyes staring into the patch of dirt and grass at the base of the statue.

Thump.

Oh no, Logan thought, as he realized the Pepco man had dropped to the cobblestone walkway. One thought roared in his mind. *Move!*

He scrambled forward, his Oakley boots gaining traction on the dirt and grass, the M4 swinging wildly on his chest. On all fours, he lunged toward the only sanctuary he had—the backside of George Washington.

Small explosions of rock sent stone shrapnel in his direction, and he heard more suppressed gunshots. He dove forward and out of the line of fire, landing on his stomach and the M4, the impact softened by the Kevlar vest. Within seconds, he had unslung the M4 and had his back to the statue. *Jesus, that was close.*

At least out of the frying pan, he'd bought himself a few precious moments to make the most basic and critical of decisions—left or right. It was a no-kidding coin toss—his pursuer might choose to wait, but more than likely, he'd come for him in order to end the confrontation and hasten his escape.

But then another thought occurred, and a malevolent smile spread across his face as he recognized his third option. *Come and get it, Pepco man.*

———

Sebastian held the Glock 17 in front of him, contemplating his choice the way Logan West had—*right or left.* It seemed such a mundane decision on which his life now rested, but he knew he had to make it, and he had to do it quickly.

Having ordered the Pepco trucks to leave him behind—the mission came first, even at the cost of his own life—he intended to escape on foot and blend into the urban environment. But in order to do that, he had to deal with the threat that now lay just beyond the figure of George Washington. He didn't know who the man was, and he didn't care. The only thing that mattered was that in order for him to escape, this man had to die. *Some things in life are just that simple. Right or left.*

The fact that the statue stood in a clearing that was carved out of a wall of woods complicated his tactical decision. Had it been in the open, he'd have backed off and slowly moved around the statue, maintaining a clear line of sight on every square foot that revealed itself. Unfortunately, he was bound by the woods on both sides, which closed in less than fifteen feet from the statue.

For no other reason than that he was left-handed—even though he shot right-handed, a contradiction not even he could explain but which came naturally to him—Sebastian Bautista chose left.

Let's get this over with. I need to get the hell out of here.

He started to circle the statue to the left, quietly shuffling his feet sideways, his eyes looking beyond the sights on his Glock, searching for a target. He maintained his focus as close to the statue as possible, knowing his prey had to be using it for cover. The only thing that mattered was which direction the target was facing— away from him, and Sebastian had him dead to rights; toward him, and Sebastian was just dead.

He exhaled as he realized the moment was at hand. *It's now or never.*

He quickly took three steps to the left, lunging into the space behind the statue, his finger on the trigger, waiting to either shoot or get shot.

What the hell? The space behind the statue was empty. *Where did he go?* And then he heard a small *crack* from the woods on his left, and he realized his fatal mistake. *Damnit, Sebastian, you weren't thinking outside the box.*

Knowing these were his last moments on earth, he said a prayer and turned to face his fate.

———

Logan waited quietly on his belly just inside the woods. Realizing the only vantage point that gave him a tactical advantage was one *as far away from the statue as possible,* he'd moved carefully backward to the edge of the woods and then slid into a prone position, careful not to rustle the underbrush. He knew from this angle that he'd spot the Pepco man before he was seen, and he had no doubt that he'd have time to adjust the M4 and engage.

He'd guessed his attacker would come from the right, and he'd been correct. As soon as his opponent rounded the corner of the statue, Logan placed the red dot of the reflex sight directly in the middle of his head, tracking him with the scope.

He saw the man's surprise that Logan had vanished. *That's right, motherfucker. No one's home.*

Logan exhaled in preparation, and his chest compressed a small twig underneath him, splitting it in half.

Snap.

The man stiffened at the sound, paused, and then straightened, realizing he'd been outmaneuvered.

Time to face the music, Logan thought, his finger on the trigger of the M4.

Even though he knew it was pointless, Sebastian Bautista spun to the left one last time, searching for his executioner.

Logan West slowly squeezed the trigger.

Crack!

The sound of the shot bounced off the George Washington statue, echoed up the wide staircase to the cathedral, and reverberated across the campus as if signifying to the holy site that another soul was up for the taking. The bullet itself tore into the Pepco man's left cheek at an upward angle and ripped into his brain, killing him instantly. He crumpled to the ground, and blood leaking out of the wound onto the grass.

Logan stood and emerged from the wood line, looking at the dead man. *Should've stayed on the other side of George.*

The sound of roaring engines grew louder, and Logan left the dead man in the quiet shade, stepping to the curb of Pilgrim Road as the three FBI Suburbans screeched to a halt.

Logan looked up the stairs to the cathedral and saw Lance, Cole, and Special Agent Krazinski bounding down the steps.

"It's about time. Took you all long enough," Logan said, even as he opened the front passenger seat door. "Lance, you're up here with me. Cole, you and CAT K there—no offense, I don't want to jack up your name—hop in the second Suburban."

Special Agent Krazinski smiled and nodded. "None taken. You can call me Krazy. The rest of the team does."

"Great," Logan said. "Another lunatic operator—you'll fit right in. They're in three Pepco bucket trucks and have a good minute and a half head start. Maintain comms at all times. It's a goddamn shell game. Three vehicles, one vice president. Let's go."

As soon as they'd loaded the vehicles, the convoy accelerated down and around the curve, gaining speed toward the sports complex.

Logan turned in the seat and faced Lance, who was reaching for the black handheld encrypted multiband Motorola radio the driver held out to him. "Please tell me the Black Hawk is up, and we have eyes on."

Lance grabbed the radio, shook it slightly at Logan in emphasis, and spoke into the handset. "Raptor One, this is Raptor Actual, how copy? What's your position?"

The sound of roaring engines in the background came through the speakers, followed by a clear voice. "Loud and clear, sir. We're a quarter mile southeast of the cathedral. Be there in less than ten seconds. What's the situation?"

"There are three Pepco bucket trucks that just left the premises southeast toward your location. We need eyes on all three. I say again. We need eyes on all three. The vice president is in one of them," Lance said.

"Roger that, sir. Wait one," the HRT pilot said.

The Suburbans passed the athletic fields on their left, approaching the intersection of Pilgrim and Garfield. The convoy stopped at the intersection, waiting for guidance from its eyes in the sky.

After an interminable silence, the radio erupted. "Sir, I've got them, but there's a problem."

"Here it comes," Logan said under his breath, looking at Lance. "It's never easy for us."

"The trucks split up and are heading in different directions."

"Awesome," Logan said. What was already difficult—tracking three utility trucks through the claustrophobic and congested streets of northwest DC—had just become nearly impossible.

CHAPTER 41

"One truck is heading north on Thirty-Fourth," the pilot reported. "Another is still on Garfield and traveling east, and the third is traveling in the opposite direction, west on Garfield. I can maneuver into a position and elevation where I can maintain visual contact, at least until one of them gets too far away on the horizon."

"Roger. Do that. Keep reporting back, and stand by for further instructions," Logan said.

Logan spoke again, this time to the trailing two Suburbans, even as he urged the HRT driver to turn left. "We've got the truck heading east. Cole, you and Krazy take the one heading north on Thirty-Fourth. Brock, you and your guys take the one heading west on Garfield," Logan said to the senior HRT member in the third Suburban. "I think the package is in ours, but we won't know for sure until we take down all three trucks. Try to gain on them without being spotted, but no matter what, do not lose your target vehicle."

Logan heard two "Rogers," put the radio back in its mount between the seats on the dashboard, and pulled his cell phone out of a nylon pocket that was Velcroed to the side of his Kevlar vest. "I'm calling Jake and asking him to put a BOLO out on *all* Pepco trucks. We need to stop those vehicles, no matter who does it."

"Understood," Lance said from the backseat. "We'll get these guys. All they know is their leader—if that's what he was—is gone, but they don't know we're in pursuit."

Jake answered on the first ring, and Logan cut him off politely and provided the first SITREP to the FBI director since the team had arrived at the cathedral.

A moment later, Jake said, "Consider it done. In a couple of minutes, I'll have every cop inside the district stopping every Pepco truck they see."

What a goddamned mess, Logan thought, even though he knew this was their best—and only—option. "Let me know if anything happens. I'll keep you posted. Back to the slow-speed pursuit. Out here."

"Be safe, and try not to destroy too much of the capitol," Jake said, and disconnected the call.

Logan smirked at the last comment. Jake had a point. When it came to the Organization, nothing went as planned, as the events of the last two and a half years—*and days*—had proven.

Logan watched the streets and rows of homes flash by. The local shops, restaurants, and even the sidewalks were packed with people eager to be outside in the warm summer sun. The high risk of collateral damage concerned him. *The more violent and aggressive we are, the quicker we can end this, though,* which he knew lessened the threat to innocent lives.

The HRT operator drove aggressively, but even as he weaved in and out of the slow traffic, Logan knew he blended in with the free-for-all that was DC driving. "What a nightmare. DC midafternoon in the summer—the only good thing is there won't be school traffic."

He grabbed the radio once more. "How far are we?" Logan asked the pilot.

"You're about a quarter mile away and gaining. He just passed

Washington Marriott Wardman Park. Also, it's now Woodley Road you're on. Garfield turns into it."

"Roger. Stand by," Logan said, looking at the bend to the right in the road. "He's got to be just past the bend. Speed up."

"On it," the HRT driver said, and slowly depressed the accelerator, increasing the speed of the Suburban. Seconds later, the SUV shot through the curve and into the straightaway of Woodley Road. Logan squinted through the two lanes of traffic. *Bingo.* "He's dead ahead, two hundred yards. Catch up. We need to end this."

The driver responded, and the Suburban accelerated, maneuvering recklessly between vehicles. The Suburban swerved behind a pickup back into the left lane. *What the hell? Where'd he go?*

"The target just turned south on Connecticut," the pilot said.

"Floor it!" Logan shouted. "Use the other lanes. Just get to Connecticut!"

The Suburban roared through the traffic, swerving in front of oncoming vehicles as necessary and working its way east.

"Great. You're going to get us killed before we even get into a gunfight," Lance said.

"I've got this, sir," the driver, HRT operator Special Agent Simmons, said.

"I know you do, Simmons. Just keep your eyes on the road. It's not you. It's Logan. He has a tendency to make things go *boom*."

"Hey, that's not completely accurate," Logan said in his defense.

"When have we ever been together when something didn't explode or someone didn't die?" Lance asked.

Logan considered for a moment, just as the Suburban finally reached Connecticut Avenue, and said, "Good point."

The Suburban slowed down dramatically and cut across the front of the right two lanes of traffic, turning south. Logan looked at the driver of a white Lexus SUV and waved, receiving the middle finger in return. *DC . . . what did you expect?*

"Nice job, Simmons," Logan said. The Pepco truck was less than fifty yards ahead and moving slowly. "Get as close to him as you can."

Once again moving at an acceptable speed—by DC standards—the Suburban closed in on the Pepco truck, which had its left blinker on to turn onto Calvert Street. *Perfect. We'll have him blocked off at both ends.*

Logan grabbed the Motorola. "Raptor One, as soon as he's on the bridge, I need you to descend and block him. We're going to trap the sonofabitch on the bridge," Logan finished, referring to the Duke Ellington Memorial Bridge that crossed over Rock Creek more than one hundred and fifty feet below.

"Roger. Descending into position now," the pilot said.

The light turned green, and the line of vehicles began to move forward. The Pepco truck turned left, and two vehicles behind it, the Suburban followed. Seconds later, the Pepco truck drove across the beginning of the bridge.

The Suburban passed an Afghan restaurant on the left, accelerating to move around the maroon Toyota sedan between it and the truck.

"Do it now—" was all Logan had spoken into the Motorola when an enormous garbage truck shot out of a side street next to an apartment building that overlooked Rock Creek Park.

Logan's last thought was, *It was a trap,* and nothing else, as the dark-blue garbage truck slammed into both doors on the driver's side, lifting the Suburban up onto its right two wheels.

There was a horrendous screech as the Suburban was pushed violently across the pavement, sparks flickering from the junction of concrete and steel. The blue monster's engine screamed with the effort, and the Suburban was shoved over the sidewalk and against the limestone railing and column that marked the beginning of the bridge.

The garbage truck lurched in reverse, the damage done, and began to back away from the vehicle it had destroyed. Free from its grasp, the Suburban suddenly fell back onto all four wheels, its dazed occupants struggling to react. Several bystanders, unaware of the confrontation, slowly approached the wreckage . . . at least until the two men in dark coveralls and black neoprene balaclavas stepped out of the garbage truck and opened fire with their fully automatic SIG516s, SIG SAUER's version of the AR-15.

The gunfire energized Logan West in the front passenger seat as pockmarks appeared on the bulletproof side windows. "We need to move. *Now!*"

While gunfire was a common occurrence in certain parts of Washington DC, full combat was not, and the panic-stricken pedestrians and joggers fled in all directions as the first volleys of fire were exchanged.

CHAPTER 42

"Our tango is traveling northwest on Massachusetts Avenue," Cole said into the multiband Motorola.

No response.

"I say again, our truck is heading northwest on Massachusetts Avenue."

Silence. *That's not good.*

"This is Raptor One. Raptor Actual is out of the chase. I say again, Raptor Actual has been hit by a garbage truck, and two hostiles are engaging their vehicle with automatic weapons fire. I'm moving into position to support. My guess is the VP is in this truck, based on their countermeasures." Now speaking to both Cole and the third Suburban HRT team, the pilot continued. "Recommend both Reapers Two and Three take down your target vehicles. This is where the party is. Raptor One, out."

"Jesus Christ. It never fails with this team. Just one of these goddamn times I'd like the bad guys to just come out with their hands up and say, 'Okay. You got us. You win.' But no, it turns into a fucking shootout *every single motherfucking* time." Normally calm and collected in the thick of conflict, Cole felt his blood pressure rising, and for a moment he experienced the outrage that Logan felt on a daily basis directed toward the enemies of civilization. *And it feels good.*

Cole looked at Krazy and said, "I'm done playing with these bastards. We're going hot." To the driver, he said, "Pit maneuver his ass off the road. I don't care what you have to do. Understand?"

"Absolutely," the driver responded with enthusiasm, and floored the accelerator, shooting down the middle of Massachusetts Avenue.

In the backseat, Krazy pulled the charging handle back one last time on the SR-16 E3 CQB Mod 2 to ensure a round was chambered and flipped the selector switch upward to semiautomatic. *And I thought we were bad motherfuckers,* the CAT shooter thought. *These guys are something else. Game time.*

———

Special Agent Kyle Hood turned in the pilot seat and spoke to his copilot through his headset. "Get the minigun up and running. We're putting a stop to this right now."

"On it," Special Agent Steven Brewer responded, unbuckling his harness and stepping into the middle compartment of the Black Hawk, even as the bird lowered itself gradually into the chaos below.

"Just don't shoot any innocent bystanders," Special Agent Hood said semiseriously.

"Come on, Kyle. You know me better than that. I'm just like Jesse the Body in *Predator.* I *got* this," Special Agent Brewer said.

"Jesse actually died right before they leveled the jungle. Get your damn movie facts straight," Special Agent Hood said.

"Damn," Special Agent Brewer said. "You might be right. But either way, I'm still a goddamned sexual Tyrannosaurus," he added, referencing another famous *Predator* line.

"You're a goddamned idiot. Now get to work," Special Agent Hood said, grinning as he turned the Black Hawk broadside. *Here we go.*

―――――

Special Agent Terry O'Bannon revved the engine, having maneuvered the Suburban directly behind the Pepco truck, whose driver had finally realized they were being pursued.

The bucket truck sped away, the International DuraStar maneuvering aggressively. Cole watched as the bucket truck slammed into the left side of a black Honda Pilot, sending it over the curb and into a large grassy area in front of several tall condominium buildings.

Cole realized the chase had taken them into the area of American University. *Great. Students out and about, even in the summertime.* But then he saw the traffic circle forty yards ahead and recognized the tactical opportunity that had presented itself.

"Do it now," Cole said.

"Hold on," Special Agent O'Bannon replied.

The two vehicles raced onward, leaving vehicular havoc in their wake. Cole heard several crashes to his right and behind them, but he didn't have time to concern himself with the bystanders.

The Suburban had pulled alongside the left rear quarter panel of the truck. Cole stuck his HK416 out the window that he'd already lowered and opened fire. Rounds struck the body of the truck, punching small holes in the sheet metal. More importantly, several 5.56mm bullets tore into the left rear tire, which was not designed for combat, unlike the Suburban's run-flat tires. The tire exploded into large chunks of rubber.

"Hit it now!" Cole screamed, and Special Agent O'Bannon responded immediately.

The front right of the Suburban slammed into the left rear wheel well as the two vehicles crossed into the traffic circle. The back of the Pepco truck was pushed sideways, even as the Suburban accelerated, propelling the vehicle through the traffic lanes.

The truck's driver tried to adjust, turning into the skid, but he panicked as a large UPS truck approached him head-on from the left. The driver turned the wheel back to the right, and like a wounded animal dragging a damaged leg, it shot into the middle of the circle, the exposed left wheel leaving a deep furrow in the grass.

Special Agent O'Bannon slammed on his brakes as he realized what was about to happen, and the Suburban disengaged from the careening and out-of-control Pepco truck.

The Suburban slid to a halt, and Special Agent O'Bannon and Cole stared in amusement as the Pepco truck slammed into the base of the enormous statue of General Artemas Ward, for whom Ward Circle Park was named.

The truck's rear lifted up into the air from the impact, but the damage to the statue was catastrophic, and the towering bronze figure—which had turned a pale green from age—fell forward, smashing down on top of the right half of the cab of the Pepco truck. Glass from the shattered windows exploded outward, and the roof crumpled inward from the pressure, dropping the height of the cab by several feet.

"Absolutely awesome," Krazy said from the back of the Suburban.

"Let's go. O'Bannon, update Raptor One. Krazy, with me," Cole said, opening the door and emerging with his HK416 raised and locked on the right passenger door of the truck.

Krazy emerged from the rear driver's side, his SR-16 steady as he combat-walked toward the demolished Pepco truck.

Ignoring the shouts of surprise at the appearance of armed gunmen by gawkers who had stopped to witness the aftermath of the accident, Cole and Krazy moved methodically forward.

Creeeeaaak!

The driver's door swung outward, and a figure tumbled out of the elevated cab onto the grass.

"*Stay on the ground, hands where I can see them!*" Krazy shouted in the commanding and authoritative voice all law enforcement officers were trained to use. The sudden verbal assault was usually shocking enough to intimidate and subdue the average criminal. Unfortunately, the Pepco impersonator hadn't received those crime statistics.

He moved to his knees, his right hand slowly raising the black pistol as if he were performing a slow-motion parody.

"*Drop it now!*" Krazy screamed one last time, less than ten feet away from the suspect.

Either disoriented from the accident or suicidal—Krazy didn't care which—the man raised his gun past the forty-five-degree angle mark, and Krazy fired.

The CAT shooter's marksmanship was as excellent and lethal as advertised by his team leader. Both shots struck the man in the forehead, squarely between the eyes, in the same spot. The second round did the most structural damage, punching a hole through the back of his head and lodging in the pedestal of Major General Artemas Ward.

Screams from stopped drivers echoed across the traffic circle, and Cole heard the faintest of sirens. *I'll bet American University doesn't have that on its curriculum. There's some real-world education for you,* Cole thought as he glimpsed a few college students to the left of the traffic circle, mouths open in shock and horror at the violence.

Krazy closed the distance on the dead driver and kicked the

Glock away. *What is it with bad guys and Glocks? They are pretty damn reliable, though.* He looked into the cab, his weapon trained on the interior. "There's no movement."

"Roger," Cole said from the other side of the truck. He heard no sounds from inside. "Opening the door on three, two, one. Now." *Please let this asshole be unconscious.*

Cole yanked the door open with his left hand, his right hand never leaving the pistol grip of the HK416, his finger on the trigger.

Fortunately, there was no more need for gunplay. The tricorne hat that General Ward clutched in his left hand had done the job for them. The top of the hat that protruded from an angle out of the general's bent arm had pierced the cab of the truck and crushed the top of the passenger's head. Blood dripped from the pale-green statue, as if it had been dipped in dark-red ink. The body lay across the bench seat of the truck.

Cole reached in and felt the side of the man's neck, just to be certain, avoiding the matted black hair glistening with blood. There was no pulse. *Not coming back from that one.*

Other than the dead passenger, the cab was empty. *Dry hole. We took down one of the diversions. At least these bastards are off the streets.*

"It's empty. No VP. Let's update the rest of the team and stand by for the DC PD," Cole said. "Sounds like they're almost here."

The two men walked back to the Suburban, where Special Agent O'Bannon, who stood next to the driver's seat, was ready to jump back in at a moment's notice.

"Nice shooting, Krazy. Any double-tap in the exact spot is noteworthy," Cole said. "If you ever get bored with CAT, let me know. I might have something for you someday."

"I'm pretty happy where I am, sir," Krazy said. "But I do appreciate the offer, and *I will* remember it. You never know when that rainy day might happen."

"You are absolutely right," Cole said. "But today is definitely not that day."

"I'll second that, sir," Krazy said, and put his weapon back on safe.

CHAPTER 43

The bullets bounced off the armored vehicle, and the echo of gunshots roared across the bridge and canyon of Rock Creek Park below. The only good thing about their position was that even though they were pinned down with literally nowhere to go, the Suburban was armored and could sustain the damage it was taking from the two automatic assault rifles. *If we time it right, we can all exit the vehicle at the same time. They can't keep us pinned down with only two of them,* Logan thought.

"Fuck these guys," Logan said. "On my count, we all open the doors. Lance, you think you can toss a few flashbangs at these assholes? Simmons and I can use the diversion, exit, and drop 'em."

"Absolutely, brother," Lance said, reaching for the rear door handle with his left hand, his right hand on an M84 stun grenade on his chest rig.

"Three. Two. One. Go!" Logan said, and three doors on the disabled Suburban opened in unison.

A sudden tidal wave of sound and disintegrating pavement raced toward them like a man-made force of nature. Logan glanced right and saw the barrage of minigun fire from the FBI Black Hawk moving like a screeching, solid finger yearning to destructively touch something with its fiery lead. A second later, it did.

The 7.62mm rounds reached the two garbage truck gunmen and turned them from gun-toting attackers into bullet-riddled corpses in an instant. Both men appeared to collapse inward, bone structure and flesh disintegrating under the withering fire. Logan couldn't help but stare with awe at the pure power and terror of the minigun. Split seconds later, the minigun stopped its screeching death cry, breaking Logan's daze.

The three men leapt out of the Suburban, looking away from the piles of human debris toward the Black Hawk.

"The truck!" Special Agent Simmons said, reflexively pointing at the escaping Pepco bucket truck as it started to accelerate across the bridge.

"On it," Logan said, and started sprinting toward the fleeing vehicle.

What the hell is he doing? Lance thought, and then he realized what Logan had already discerned: the Pepco truck wasn't going to make it, thanks to the brazen FBI pilot of the Black Hawk.

The HRT helicopter descended directly into the path of the hybrid bucket truck, and another tongue of gunfire lanced out from the middle of the helicopter, strafing from left to right the pavement directly in front of the accelerating truck. Chunks of roadway exploded in the path of the truck, puncturing the radiator grill and peppering the windshield.

Logan watched the confrontation in fascination, even as he tried to keep his breathing steady and heart rate under control. The M4 rattled in his right hand as he sprinted, the sling slapping against the underside of the pistol foregrip and magazine. He was still fifty yards away. The lethal game of chicken, helicopter versus truck, would be over by the time he reached it, but he ran anyway.

The truck barreled forward, cutting the distance to the hovering Black Hawk in half.

This is going to be bad, Logan thought.

A third barrage of gunfire, expertly directed by the brash operator, ripped across the top of the hood, pulverizing the engine compartment.

The driver panicked with less than fifteen feet of space between the Pepco truck and the Black Hawk, and he yanked the wheel to the left. The vehicle shot into the oncoming lane—traffic had blessedly stopped at the sight of the descending helicopter—jumped the curb, and slammed into an iron lamppost, which crashed down on top of the forty-two-foot bucket and bounced off, rolling across the bridge. The vehicle fishtailed across the wide sidewalk as the driver fought the momentum.

A loud *pop* highlighted the exploding right front tire, and the vehicle lurched to the right. The driver, in full panic mode, overcompensated, yanking the steering wheel hard and to the left. The remaining tire gripped the surface of the bridge and pulled the truck sideways, allowing speed and friction to complete the destruction.

The truck flipped onto its right side, facing northwest, and slid across the sidewalk. The top of the cab and ruined engine compartment punched a hole through the pale-green iron fence. Chunks of fence fell away to the road and woods below. The truck stopped, its cab dangling over the edge of the bridge.

Jesus Christ, Logan thought. All he could see was the ruined undercarriage of the truck as he approached at a flat-out sprint. *You'd better not be dead, Mr. Vice President, because I'm going to kill you myself.*

CHAPTER 44

Logan approached the Pepco truck, his M4 out in front of him once again, moving to his left to get a better vantage point of the cab of the truck, which lay next to the edge of the bridge.

The Black Hawk hovered over the bridge with nowhere to land owing to the stopped traffic, and its rotors drowned out all other sounds. Logan glanced up at the bird, catching a glimpse of the pilot, who was beckoning down below the truck.

What the hell is he pointing at? Logan raised his left arm in the universal "What?" gesture, his right hand holding the pistol grip of the M4. The pilot put his left hand back on the collective pitch control, and the hovering helicopter slid sideways in the air and away from the bridge. The pilot once again pointed down, and Logan realized in frustration what the pilot was signaling.

You sonofabitch. Oh no you don't. Logan placed the M4 on safe and slung the weapon over his back. He drew the Kimber Tactical II from his thigh rig and dashed around the rear of the vehicle, approaching the cab from behind.

What the pilot had been beckoning toward had been blocked by the angle of the cab. The bucket truck's aerial device in the middle of the back of the truck was extended and dropped down out of sight over the edge of the bridge. *You've got to be kidding me,* Logan thought, hoping for just one break.

He reached the extended arm, the Kimber held down and in front of him. Taking a breath to steady his pounding heart after the sprint across the bridge, he exhaled and popped his head out over the edge.

The arm dangled down more than forty feet toward a sloping hill that dipped into Rock Creek Park and connected to the road that ran under the middle of the bridge. At the end of the arm and attached to the bucket, a white rope had been tied, dropping another sixty feet to the grassy slope mostly covered by trees. One figure in a Pepco uniform was still on the hydraulic arm, shimmying toward the bucket, but the other two occupants of the truck, including a man with grayish-black hair wearing a dark suit, were already rappelling down the rope.

Realizing the three men had a head start, Logan pulled out a pair of black Oakley SI assault gloves from his left cargo pants pocket. He'd never adapted to shooting with gloves the way many other operators had—he preferred the feel to the protection—but he always had them with him. He slid them on, secured them at the wrist with the Velcro strap, and holstered the Kimber pistol. *Semper paratus,* Logan thought. *The Boy Scouts would be proud.*

He stepped out over the edge of the bridge and broken railing and mounted the hydraulic arm with his textured gloves and tactical boots firmly gripping the metal. He glanced down, found his target, and eased the tension in his hands and feet, loosening his grip.

As he'd predicted, gravity accelerated his slide, and he rocketed down the first half of the hydraulic arm in less than two seconds. He risked another look down and smiled inwardly. *I wish I could watch this rather than be doing it.*

His momentum increased, and the beam suddenly narrowed as he passed the joint where the hydraulic arm bent. He squeezed his feet together, soles threatening to lift away from the steel beam. *Another second. Don't lose your grip, or you lose your life.*

He bent his head forward and looked down between his chest and the rushing beam. *Bingo.*

His boots crashed into the shoulder blades of the Pepco gunman who was still on the beam, working his way to the bucket only a few feet away. The hovering helicopter had masked Logan's precipitous descent, and the man never had a chance.

Logan felt the man's grip on the beam let go, even as Logan's own momentum was dramatically decreased by the human obstruction in his path. He heard a scream as he gripped the beam with all of his strength.

The man fell the remaining distance, and his back slammed into the large metal bucket. He bounced forward off the bucket and tumbled into thin air as Logan's feet slammed into the metal with a jarring impact that sent pain up his legs and back.

He looked down in time to see the man disappear headfirst into the top of a tree. Logan thought he heard—or at least imagined—a faint *crack* of a large branch over the rotors, but he didn't have time to contemplate it.

He scrambled onto the bucket, exhaled, and looked over the side. *Thank God.*

The remaining Pepco impersonator and the vice president hadn't reached the ground. *There's still time.*

Logan scampered across the bucket and reached the white rope. He let his legs dangle over the edge, remembering the last time he'd fast-roped, out of a Spanish helicopter in the Alboran Sea to the deck of a North Korean cargo ship. He prayed this time went better.

He secured the rope in a J-hook between his feet, wrapped his left arm around the rope, and unholstered the Kimber .45. He'd need the weapon for the next phase of his reckless assault.

Once again turning his gaze earthward, he loosened his grip and separated his boots, allowing the rope to slide between his feet as he descended.

Damnit. Logan felt the rope sway, and he saw the vice president sprinting toward the road that passed under the center of the bridge. *Moves fast for an old politician. At least he's out of the way.*

Logan aimed the Kimber at the remaining Pepco gunman, who had nearly reached the ground. He looked back up the rope, and Logan realized his target had the same idea when a pistol appeared in the man's right hand.

Logan didn't hesitate, opening fire under the Duke Ellington Bridge.

Bam! Bam! Bam! Bam! Bam!

At least two of the rounds struck the man in the upper chest, and he lost his grip on the rope. The man fell to the earth, looking up at the looming figure of Logan West descending toward him like a mythological god of death and destruction.

Logan saw the man crash to the ground on his back, the pistol still in his hand, but he didn't move.

Logan increased his speed, racing the last twenty feet to the ground. His legs slammed into the grass, he bent his knees, and he executed a combat roll across his right shoulder, keeping the Kimber aimed away from his face as he tumbled. The slope carried him forward into a second somersault, and he transitioned onto his feet.

He looked toward the road and saw the vice president fifty yards away, moving quickly. *Great. I get to chase the fittest politician in DC. Go figure.*

A grunt startled him, and he looked back up the hill ten feet away at the man he'd shot. *Not dead yet. Too bad. No second chances today.* The man still had the pistol in his right hand, and he struggled to sit up, two gunshot wounds to the chest or not.

Logan aimed back up the hill and fired one shot into the top of his head, killing him instantly and ending his futile sit-up.

Logan turned back toward the fleeing figure of the vice president, noting the second broken body, that of the man he'd knocked off the hydraulic arm, and began to run. *I'm getting tired of all this running,* he thought, and sprinted after the vice president.

Vice President Baker had already reached the upward slope on the other side of the road, but Logan ran hard, concentrating on his breath as he'd done many times before.

He reached the bottom of the hill at a full-out sprint, calculating his path across the two lanes of moving traffic, which hadn't stopped at the sight of the battle up the hill. He dashed into the southbound lane behind a dark-green SUV, crossed into the northbound lane as a white Mercedes sedan sped past, and reached the other side without losing a step.

No way you're getting away. No . . . fucking . . . way. Logan closed the distance to twenty yards, gaining ground quickly.

Intellectually, he understood he shouldn't kill the vice president of the United States, but emotionally, the beast from his primordial psyche was in full control, and there was no putting it back in its cage until its thirst for vengeance had been quenched. But before he could exact justice, he had to catch the man.

He worked his legs harder, increasing the tempo as he sprinted up the hill covered in trees. *Gotcha, asshole.*

Logan West, a man of singular purpose and intent, reached his target and leapt off his feet, slamming his right shoulder into the vice president's lower back with a tremendous thud. The two men sprawled into the grass face-first.

Logan reached his feet as the vice president tried to get to his hands and knees. Allowing the fury that coursed through his body—thoughts of Mike Benson, *dead*; John Quick, possibly dying or already dead; and all the countless victims of this conspirator's evil actions—he grabbed the vice president by the back of his suit coat collar and his belt and flung him forward.

There was an exhalation of air as his chest hit the ground, but he managed to roll over, looking up at Logan West with a smile.

For the first time that day, Logan West froze, the fury that he wielded like a physical weapon abated, and he stared at the man below him. *No. It can't be.*

CHAPTER 45

Georgetown, Washington DC

The silver Ford Explorer with Virginia plates and tinted windows crossed the Francis Scott Key Bridge, leaving the bustling college enclave of Georgetown. The SUV blended in with the exodus of vehicles, obeying all traffic signals and maintaining a speed five miles per hour above the limit. The driver knew that to drive the actual speed limit in northern Virginia would draw more attention than slightly breaking the law.

"I'm sorry about Sebastian," Joshua Baker said to the other three passengers in the SUV.

"As am I," the serious-looking Hispanic man in casual clothes in the front seat said. "But he understood the risks involved in this operation, and he accepted them willingly. The most dangerous part is over. Believe it or not, you can breathe easy, Mr. Vice President."

"What about the other trucks?" Josh asked. The diversion had been brilliant. After riding down the zip line—which he'd actually enjoyed, even under the stressful circumstances—he'd entered the Pepco truck, which had sped away from the George Washington statue once Sebastian had given the order. He didn't know what

347

had happened, but the driver had obeyed, and the three-truck convoy had left their leader behind.

Inside the vehicle, he'd been given a blue Under Armour hoodie, khaki trousers, gray running shoes, a gray-and-white Under Armour hat, and Oakley sunglasses. He'd known the change of clothes was coming, and he'd managed to transform in the truck into a normal citizen in less than thirty seconds.

As soon as the convoy of trucks was out of sight of the cathedral—still on St. Albans School property—and past the first curve, the truck had stopped momentarily, concealed on all sides by trees and the curve in the road. Josh and another man dressed in similar civilian attire had fled the vehicle directly into the woods, leaving two men in the truck, which had disappeared with the convoy less than two seconds later. The walk through the woods had been the most stressful part of the plan, but they'd emerged onto Garfield Street, walked west, and been picked up by the Ford Explorer on Massachusetts Avenue.

To Josh's surprise, no one had paid any attention to the two men walking along the street, nor looked twice as they'd disappeared into the SUV. It had almost been too easy. The pedestrians they'd passed had been staring at their smartphones, listening to music with over-the-ear headphones Josh still didn't understand, or talking rapidly on the phone. *It's DC, Josh. No one cares about two middle-aged men. They're all absorbed in their own lives. Most importantly, none of them will remember seeing you.*

"I have no idea. Their instructions were specific—no radio contact with each other, and they have no way of reaching us. It ensures there's no digital trail that connects them to us or you, Mr. Vice President," the man said.

"Please call me Josh. As of twenty minutes ago, I'm fairly certain I'm no longer the vice president of the United States," Josh said. "That life is gone."

"Maybe. Maybe not," the man said. "But as you wish. It makes more sense to use your first name anyhow, considering the trip we have ahead of us."

"How so?" Josh asked. "I was assured the Organization had a guaranteed way out of the country."

"We do," the man said. "But it's not like the movies. We're not going to whisk you away on some secret plane in the middle of nowhere. You can't get away with that these days. Too many State Department and Customs regulations for registering all flights out of the country. No. We're doing this the old-fashioned, easy way."

"What's that?" Josh asked, deeply interested as to how his personal safety was being handled.

"Several vehicle changes, several stops at places where we have all control and access, and then a diplomatic vehicle into Mexico that Customs won't be able to search. It may take a week to ten days, but by then, your entire government will assume you're out west or dead," the man said. "We'll be heading toward the Blue Ridge Mountains and working our way south from there. In case something happens, we have multiple alternate vehicles ahead and behind us we can switch to. We're covered, no matter what. For now, just sit back and enjoy the scenery."

"I think I will. It's been a hard day," Josh said, easing back into the seat. He watched the traffic pass by, knowing it would be the last time. He closed his eyes, hoping to lose some of the tremendous tension he felt from the day's events. Instead, visions of his son's face invaded his peace, and he fought back a sorrow he knew would haunt him for a lifetime to come.

CHAPTER 46

"From the look on your face, I believe you mistook me for someone else," the man dressed and disguised to look like Vice President Joshua Baker said. Up close, there was no resemblance whatsoever. The man was in his midthirties with a dark complexion of Hispanic or Spanish origin. Unlike the vice president, he was physically fit and lean, which explained why he'd been able to cover so much ground from the crash so quickly. *But from a distance and in the heat of battle? No way to know he wasn't the real McCoy. It was brilliant,* Logan thought, his sense of triumph replaced with disgust that they'd been duped so flawlessly.

"Where is he?" Logan asked.

"That's the best part—I have no idea," the man said with pure pleasure and contempt. "None of us know. You could capture all of us, but you won't get *a goddamn thing.*"

The furious buzzing in Logan's head went quiet. A cold, merciless silence replaced it. The man before him represented everything that had gone wrong in the past three days. While the puppet master himself may have escaped, the false flag Baker had not. *And he's about to pay the price for his failure. Should've run harder, tough guy.*

"Get up," Logan said quietly.

The man sensed something disconcerting about the way the words had been uttered. "You're not going to arrest me, are you?" He stood, brushing off his black suit trousers absentmindedly.

"No. You don't deserve to go to jail," Logan replied. "Pull whatever blade you have on you: you guys always carry one. I'm only going to give you to the count of three, and then I'm going to shoot you in the face."

"No need to get huffy and puffy," the man said, reaching under the suit coat. His smile had been replaced by a look of fierce determination. He understood the stakes: this was a fight to the death. He withdrew from a sheath on his belt a black Zero Tolerance blade that looked as sleek and lethal as it was beautiful. He held it in his right hand, the slim blade pointed upward at an angle. He pulled his right foot back slightly into a fighting stance.

"That's a nice knife," Logan said. "I'll add it to my collection when this is over."

"If you say so," the man said. "I'd add something like 'over my dead body,' but there's no point."

"Exactly," Logan replied. "And that's the plan, anyways." In one fluid motion, he holstered the Kimber in the thigh rig and pulled his Force Recon Mark II fighting knife from its sheath on the front of his Kevlar vest. A moment later, he unslung his M4, yanked the Velcro straps apart on the bulletproof vest, and slid out of the protective shell.

"You do know there's no such thing as fighting fair, right?" the man asked.

"You have no idea, asshole," Logan said. He placed his index finger on the spine of the blade.

Before the fake vice president could respond, Logan cocked his arm backward, registering with amusement the sudden look of concern on his target's face. He stepped forward as if throwing a baseball and brought his arm down toward the fake Baker, who had finally started to react, albeit too late. The knife began to slide out of his hand and gain momentum, his wrist slightly whipping forward to control the blade. He completed the throw, his finger pointed straight at his target, as the knife hurtled through the air and buried itself with a sickening *thwack* in the man's upper right chest.

Pain exploded across the man's chest, and he let out a grunt of agony. He looked down as blood spread across his white designer dress shirt. He pawed at the blade with his left hand like a wounded animal desperately trying to free itself from a trap.

"Huh," Logan said nonchalantly. "I wasn't sure if that was going to work." He stepped forward toward the mortally wounded man. "It's not as easy as it looks. *Lots* of practice, getting the blade to fall into the target," Logan said pitilessly. "In this case, that's *you.*"

The blood had covered most of the shirt, but the man still stood, as if in denial of his fading existence.

Logan stepped within reach of him, and said, "I'll take that, now, like I said I would." The calmness in his voice contradicted the rage he still felt. He grabbed the man's wrist, pulled up his arm, and pried the Zero Tolerance knife out of his hand.

Logan stared into the face of his victim, oblivious to the pain etched across his face.

The man smiled at him, coughing a rivulet of blood from his mouth. The sound was tinny and hollow. *Not long now,* Logan thought.

"It doesn't matter," the man gasped. "You still lose." His breath caught, but he added, "And you know it."

Which is the worst part, Logan thought. *He's right. But he doesn't have to get the satisfaction of being right.*

Without uttering a word, Logan yanked the Force Recon blade from the man's chest as he simultaneously slid the Zero Tolerance blade under his rib cage, piercing his heart.

The impostor let out a short shriek, as blood poured from both wounds.

Logan pulled out the Zero Tolerance blade, and the impostor collapsed to his knees, his eyes rolled up, and he fell sideways onto the grassy slope.

"No more vice presidential impersonations for you," Logan said, not realizing he'd spoken the words aloud, his body trembling from the effects of the adrenaline and rage.

He turned and looked around as he emerged from his battle haze, his ears registering once again the sounds of the Black Hawk helicopter. He'd left the underside of the Duke Ellington Memorial Bridge littered with bodies. *It's my goddamned MO,* he thought. *The curse of Logan West.*

But then a second voice interjected. *Only if you let it be, brother,* Mike Benson whispered from beyond the grave.

Thanks, brother. I'm trying, Logan thought. *But I'm not done yet.*

I know, but remember what I said: Don't lose who you are. You're going to be a father.

The reminder brought him back to reality. He sheathed his newly acquired Zero Tolerance blade and his Force Recon Mark II and hurried up the slope to rejoin his team.

PART VIII

AFTERMATH

CHAPTER 47

Inova Fairfax Hospital
Eleventh Floor
Three Days Later

Logan looked out the pristine corner room of the South Patient Tower, a recent addition to the sprawling Inova Fairfax Hospital Medical Campus. At the top of the tower, the large picture windows provided a panoramic view to the south and west. The hills and woods of northern Virginia rolled away endlessly in both directions, camouflaging the mass of humanity concealed within.

His gaze trailed south with the knowledge that the Marine Corps Museum, a modern creation of glass and steel that rose several hundred feet into the air, its shape recalling the iconic photograph of raising the flag on Iwo Jima, lay over the horizon. *You never really get out, no matter what,* he thought, knowing it was both a blessing and a curse. He also acknowledged that the former definitely outweighed the latter, regardless of the cost.

The scenic view of tranquility contradicted the chaos that had fallen across the country like a thick invisible blanket of fear. The truth that he knew and what the public had been told overlapped in spots and diverged in others, shifting as needed in pursuit of one undeniable fact—the vice president had vanished from the face of the earth.

And there wasn't a goddamned thing any of us could do about it, Logan thought. The outcome had been predetermined, even before he and his friends had jumped into the fray.

The entire federal government, including all law enforcement and Intelligence Community agencies, was focused on the theory that the Montana Freedom Movement had somehow orchestrated the kidnapping of the second most powerful man—at least on the organizational charts of DC—in America.

A single cell phone record from one of the dead former Spanish Special Forces mercenaries had rocketed the investigation into overdrive. A call to Montana had been placed the day before the vice president's escape. Once the federal government obtained warrants for the number the mercenary had dialed, cell phone records, bank transfers, emails, and grainy photographs had linked the leader of the movement, Jared Evans, to a known mercenary-military contractor organization operating in Europe on the black market. Evans' servers and computers were encrypted just enough to delay the FBI and NSA from obtaining actionable intelligence for forty-eight hours, but the hunt across North America was now into its third day.

Logan suspected it was all a smokescreen. The Montana Freedom Movement had to be a diversion intended to cover the Organization's tracks. He'd conveyed his concerns to the president, Jake, and CIA Director Tooney, who all agreed, but they still had to pursue the militia angle to its dead end. But in addition, the CIA director had activated its most sensitive network of operatives—a special access program called LEGION—to clandestinely pursue the location of the vice president. If he left the country, they hoped to reacquire his scent once he landed on foreign soil.

But as far as the public, the media, and the cable news networks relishing every moment of the hunt, the nexus was still Montana. The thought of blaming a right-wing militia for one of the worst crimes in recent history had sent the media into a frenzy. *At least until someone has some common sense to ask why an ultraconservative, nationalistic movement would contract with foreign nationals, whom it fundamentally opposed on principle,* Logan thought. Then again, the media wasn't always concerned with the facts, only with the narrative that served its own political agenda. Common sense and journalistic integrity had left the building with Elvis years ago. *What a fucking fiasco.*

"You daydreaming again, brother?" John said from his hospital bed behind Logan.

"Not exactly," Logan replied, and turned, looking at the only other person in the room. Amira had finally left John's side after the doctors had determined that there was no infection from the bullet wound. "More lamenting the fact that the sonofabitch is out there somewhere, breathing free air."

"Fuck him," John said. "He didn't win. If anything, we won this round. Don't you see that?"

Logan stared at John before responding. "You got shot. You could've—hell, probably should've—died."

The bullet had penetrated John's peritoneal cavity, lodging itself in the fluid-filled area between his internal organs and the abdominal wall. The only damage had been to the parietal peritoneum, which lined the inside of the abdominal wall.

Once the trauma surgeons had identified the extent of his wound, they'd decided to remove the bullet laparoscopically rather than cutting him open, minimizing the chance for infection and leaving a scar only where the bullet had entered. Out of an abundance of caution, the doctors had prescribed antibiotics and had transferred him to the patient tower to recover for one week and to ensure the antibiotics worked.

"Thanks for the moral support. Your bedside manner sucks," John added.

"You know what I mean," Logan said, still serious. "You're lucky, and you know it. It actually reminds me of something that happened at the Infantry Officer Course years ago," Logan added, referring to the legendary and challenging Marine Corps infantry training, which had continued to evolve based on lessons learned in Iraq and Afghanistan.

"What's that?" John asked. "Did you manage to destroy everything at that place too?"

"Ha," Logan replied. "Not quite. As part of our education, since we were learning the business of tactics, weapons, and war, we also had to learn about the types of horrific injuries sustained in combat. As a result, each of us spent one night in a local emergency room or trauma center, observing the doctors and nurses treat the wounded. About halfway through a surprisingly slow Saturday night, a thirty-year-old male was brought in, with *twelve*—and I mean no kidding, twelve; I counted—gunshot wounds to his chest. He was part of some southeast DC crew, got ambushed, and the guy who shot him stood over him and fired a burst from a Tec-9 submachine gun point-blank into him."

"Jesus," John replied.

"No kidding. The guy should have died. Hell, the entire staff expected him to, but once they got him up to the OR and opened him up, they discovered every single bullet had missed a vital organ. I think the only thing this guy lost was his spleen," Logan said. "It was a miracle."

"Who really needs a spleen, anyhow?" John quipped.

"Exactly. It was a small price to pay for something that changed his life. I heard months later that he'd been born again after his near-death experience, managed to escape his gang without too much more damage, and became a pastor, starting a church in southeast DC."

"That's actually an inspirational story, man," John said. "But no matter what, I assure you, I'm not becoming a preacher."

Logan laughed. "That's not the point. The point is that he got lucky, and like we've learned over the last few years, having luck is often better than being good." His tone changed, deepening. "But at some point, brother, *luck runs out.*"

John knew Logan spoke the truth, and he contemplated his response for a moment. "You're right, but you know what? And I mean this—fuck luck. We'll play this out until we can't play it anymore." His voice grew stronger. "Should I have died? Maybe. Maybe not. It doesn't matter. I didn't. But here's what I do know, and this is what really matters: the Organization is in shambles, its founder is dead, we've uncovered another traitor at the highest level of the United States government, and here's the best part—wait for it—we're all *still alive.* In my book, brother, that's a win. Hell, that's a *huge win,* and you need to realize it."

Logan sighed, and a grin broke out on his face. "Since when did you become such a ray of sunshine and silver linings?"

"Must be Amira's influence," John guessed.

"I'd bet on that," Logan responded. "You're not smart enough to have these thoughts on your own."

"That's right. You were the officer, after all. I was just a working man, doing what I was told."

"Brother, I don't think you ever just did what you were told," Logan said, his tone softening. "But that's what made you one of the best men I've ever had the honor of serving with."

"Thanks, man. You're not too bad, yourself," John responded in kind. "What's next? Are you going to go see him?"

Logan hesitated before answering. He knew he had no choice,

but he wasn't looking forward to the confrontation that was inevitable. "I am. I have to. You know that."

"I do, but I also know that with him, I guarantee there's an explanation. Give him, of all people, the benefit of the doubt," John said. "Besides, you can always kill him later, if you're so inclined, since you do have a penchant for sending men to meet their maker. Now if you'll excuse me, I'm going to see what they have on this new cable system. The picture on this HD TV is awesome. The nurse told me they even have pay-per-view, and since this is on Uncle Sam's dime, why not?"

"Wonderful," Logan said. "Try not to watch too much porn. That might look awkward on a government credit card. And I'm fairly certain Amira would kill you, and there's not a damn thing I can do to stop that woman."

"You and me both," John said.

Logan walked over to the side of his friend's bed. He reached out and put his hand on John's shoulder, bypassing the formality of a handshake. "Get some rest. I'll let you know how it goes." He squeezed gently and took a step to the door.

"Roger that. Now *that's* an order I can follow," John said, and turned on the TV.

CHAPTER 48

The only good thing about driving into Washington DC was that it was a Sunday, and Logan knew the traffic would be nonexistent compared to the bedlam of a weekday. After leaving John, he'd called Jake to confirm his appointment at the White House. What he was about to do was necessary, no matter what the personal risk to him.

He grabbed his cell phone and hit the line for Sarah. The Fox News commentator's voice discussing the latest reported Vice President Baker sighting disappeared, replaced by a ringing.

His wife picked up immediately. "Hey, hon, where are you? Did you already leave the hospital?" she asked, a slight edge to her voice.

After the initial phone call before the final battle at the compound and momentarily facing the possibility that her husband might not survive long enough to be the father to their firstborn child, Sarah had been understandably protective, as well as righteously angered.

Logan had called her to let her know he was alive the moment he'd hung up with Lance Foster after requesting HRT support and a medevac for John. That brief period between the time she'd told him to fight hard to the time he'd called her back to say he'd survived but that John had been shot was only a few minutes. But in those minutes, she'd envisioned a life without Logan, a baby without a father, and a lonely, tortuous existence without the man she loved. It was agonizing, and it had shaken her temporarily to her core. She knew she could do it—*would do it*—but Sarah West believed with all her heart that she was meant to do it with Logan, not as a single mother.

All wives, husbands, fathers, mothers, sons, and daughters intellectually understood the risk their loved ones faced each and every day in the military. But when the nightmare scenario had nearly materialized into reality, she found herself still struggling with it only a few days later.

"I did," Logan answered, acknowledging her concern. "He's fine. You know John—he's nearly impossible to kill, like yours truly," he added, hoping to assuage her fears with a little humor.

"That's not what you said the other day," Sarah shot back, instantly regretting the comment.

Realizing his failed attempt at levity had only upset his wife, justifiably so, Logan said, "I know. You're right. I'm sorry."

"So am I. I'm just still struggling with the fact that for once, it finally hit me that you might not make it, and the thought was *unbearable*," Sarah responded, her voice quiet with emotion. "I'm pregnant with our child. That changes *everything*."

"I know. Believe me, babe. I do," Logan said. For him, the reality that he was going to be a father still hadn't sunk in. There'd been no time to process the information, to contemplate the life-changing implications of it. "We'll sit down and talk—*really talk*—soon. I love you more than you'll ever know. You keep me from the brink. This is an ugly business we're in, babe. I'm self-aware enough to understand it. I'm not some superhero, immune to the effects of what we do." He paused. "But I also know that I'm one of the few people, along with John, Amira, and Cole, that can actually confront these kinds of threats facing our country." His voice grew stronger with each word. "If these bastards succeed, the fabric of our country would be changed, and *no one would even know how it had been done.* And the thought of our son or daughter growing up in a country like that? Well, that terrifies me more than the thought of dying. I can't help it. It's who and what I am," he finished, hoping his words didn't exacerbate the emotional and psychological stress she was experiencing.

Sarah never hesitated. "It's why I love you, Logan. I know *exactly* who and what you are." She was proud that her husband was one of the fiercest warriors she'd ever known. She felt her concern and hesitation slightly abate at his resolve and acknowledgment of her feelings, briefly in awe at how far they'd come in the two and a half years since she'd been attacked. *Parenthood? That might make the assault in Maryland seem like a walk in the park.* "And I wouldn't want any of it to change. The country has you, even if ninety-nine-point-nine-nine percent of the population will never know who you are. I just want your child to have you, too."

"I promise you both will. It might not be easy. I have no doubt I'll have to go away from time to time, but I'll always come back. No matter what," Logan emphasized.

Sarah laughed, her voice lighter. "Babe, I married a Marine. Don't make promises you can't keep. You and I both know there are no guarantees, but I appreciate the sentiment, and I know you'll do your goddamnedest to try. And that's all I can ask for."

The wave of emotion was swift, threatening to drown his words before he could speak them. *It's why I married you. You get it, more than anyone.* "Thanks, hon," Logan replied. "One more thing, though."

"What's that, babe?" Sarah asked.

"You can ask me *for anything,* no matter what the cost," he said sincerely.

"Ten million dollars and world peace?" Sarah said playfully.

"I am about to go see the president. I'll see what I can do."

"I'll settle for a coffee cup with the presidential seal on it, in that case."

"Understood, Mrs. West," Logan said in his best command voice.

"Uh-huh. Whatever," Sarah said with mock exasperation. "Go do your thing, babe. Text me when you're on your way home. I'll run a bath when you're ten minutes out."

The thought of his gorgeous wife in a bathtub distracted him from the task at hand, and he said, "Great. Now I'm going to have images of you in the tub while I'm in the Oval Office." He heard his wife laugh. "I'll try to make it quick."

"You do that, and I'll be waiting. I love you."

"I love you, too," Logan said, and hung up.

His world had changed in its entirety, but the fact that he had Sarah to face the unknown with was all he needed.

Thoughts and images of her settled his nerves for the meeting he was about to have with the most powerful man on the planet. He only had one objective for tonight's conversation—to ensure that the rest of the world had changed with him.

CHAPTER 49

The Oval Office

Logan West was ushered into the Oval Office by the president's secretary, a stern, attractive brunette in her midfifties. A Secret Service agent stood next to the door in the secretary's office, nodded at Logan, and closed the door behind him once he entered the inner sanctum of the White House.

A true oval nearly thirty-six feet long, twenty-nine feet wide, and nineteen feet tall, the room had four doors. He'd entered through the one in the northeast part of the room. Directly ahead of him at the south end of the office in front of three floor-to-ceiling windows, the *Resolute* desk stood, the key piece of furniture used by multiple presidents. A cursory glance around the office revealed multiple busts that he'd seen on the news; bookshelves neatly lined with heavy-looking leather-bound books; the president's flag, three American flags, and each service's flag near the four doors and windows; numerous paintings of former presidents; and a fireplace to his right, on top of which grew the Swedish ivy that had overlooked the room since 1961 and was once featured in *Time* magazine.

In the center of the room, two brocade couches in a neutral

earth tone faced each other on top of the Oval Office rug, which had the president's seal in the center. The media had reported that the rug was the sunburst rug that President Reagan had utilized. A slim coffee table sat between the couches within arm's length, and two end tables sat on the side of the couches near the fireplace. The final pieces of furniture were the two high-back chairs that were featured most often in pictures when foreign dignitaries visited.

In Logan's heightened state after the past few days of violence and chaos, the overall impression was overwhelming. The weight of the power and responsibility slipped over Logan as if it were a part of the room's atmosphere. It was impossible not to be affected by the historical tradition and significance of the seat of power of the world's most dominant democracy. *Remember why you're here. Stay on task.*

President Scott stood in the southwest corner of the room. He looked weary, the events of the past few days having taken their stressful effect on his youthful appearance. A normally striking man whose looks had garnered female votes by the millions, his black hair was more unkempt than the last time Logan had seen him. *He has the look of someone who's been in combat.*

The president was still, staring at the sculpture of a cowboy on a bucking bronco. The bronze statue stood on a console table in between the Marine Corps flag and the Army flag. *Not a bad space to be in,* Logan thought.

"It's called *The Bronco Buster*. It was made in 1895 by Frederick Remington and is supposed to represent the western frontier," President Scott said, and turned to face Logan. "To be honest, I love it because—for me—it epitomizes American toughness and resilience. I believe we'd all be better off from time to time if the American cowboy showed up occasionally."

The president laughed, and Logan sensed an emotional vulnerability—almost melancholy—emanating from him. *He knows I know. This could be easy, or this could be very hard.*

"Or maybe I'm just conflating how I think it should be with how I think it was. Hell, I wasn't there, and neither were you," President Scott said.

"No, Mr. President. We weren't, but I do agree this country could use a little toughness, especially right now," Logan replied from his position near the doorway.

The president was silent and stepped away from the statue. "Come on. Have a seat. Let's talk." He walked to the couch on the west side of the room and sat at the end closest to the fireplace.

Logan simultaneously moved to the couch closest to his entrance and sat down opposite President Scott. He looked the most powerful man on the planet squarely in the eyes and opened his mouth to speak.

"His name was on the list, wasn't it?" President Scott asked matter-of-factly, cutting Logan off. "I know it was, or else you wouldn't have requested this private meeting."

Logan had delivered the thumb drive to Jake once the dust had settled in Rock Creek Park. He'd instructed him to keep it safe until his meeting with the president had concluded.

He didn't even let me talk. Give him a chance, Logan. "It was, which means you also know why I'm here." There was no accusation in his tone, only an earnest desire for answers.

"To see if I followed in the footsteps of a man who was an original member of the Organization. A man that I adored as a boy, worshipped as an adolescent, revered as a member of the military, and respected as a man—my father," President Scott said with a tinge of sadness Logan had recognized earlier.

He's genuine. Your instincts about him the first time you met him were right. But you still have to be sure, especially now. "Sir, your father was General Harper Scott, the chairman of the Joint Chiefs of Staff. A career infantry officer, company commander, battalion commander, and Seventh Special Forces Group commanding officer, he was a legend," Logan said. "I did my research on him, at least what I could find. After his time with Special Forces, he was promoted to brigadier general, earning another star every few years until he found himself as the chairman of the Joint Chiefs." Logan paused. "But you know all this, sir. The thing that I need to know—*the thing that matters*—is when you found out, because it's obvious to me, now, that you've known all along. You said, 'I knew this day would come,' when we told you about the vice president. I didn't think about it at the time—I was too focused on catching Vice President Baker—but I realized afterward that you sounded like someone who had always known about the Organization, known *before* we told you about it. So I'm going to ask you, sir, with all due respect to the sacred office that you hold, that I *believe* you execute with the utmost of reverence, *when* did you learn about the Organization?"

Logan had said what he'd needed to say: he'd leveled an accusation that both knew was true at the president of the United States. *But there has to be a reason.*

"On his deathbed four years ago, when I was still a senator in Georgia," President Scott answered with no misdirection or guile.

There it is. Step one—admission, Logan thought, a mental image of a poster of the AA Twelve Steps racing across his mind. "Then why didn't you do something about it? Why did you let all of this happen, sir? If the FBI had known about the Organization, it might have been able to dismember it then, before Cain Frost, before six months ago. All of this bloodshed could have been avoided," Logan said quietly.

"No, Logan, it couldn't have," President Scott said.

"I don't understand, sir," Logan said. "How's that?"

"It's actually quite simple," President Scott said, resignation in his voice. "Because I never learned who they were."

"How could that be?" Logan asked, confused.

"My father was dying," President Scott said. "The man that I had known my entire life, who had raised me to become the man I am, was leaving this mortal coil for whatever awaits us all." President Scott's voice changed, regret injecting itself into his tone. "I never learned who they were because he died before I could get any answers. Soon after he confessed his participation in the Organization, he slipped in and out of consciousness and was gone before I knew it. It was as if he'd wanted to get that one last thing off his chest before moving on to the other side."

The president sighed and looked away. "Unfortunately, he took the names with him, allowing the chain of events over the past two and a half years to unfold, leaving me to watch, guiltily wondering if there was anything else I could have done."

CHAPTER 50

President Scott sat back against the couch, studying Logan, letting the warrior and Marine in front of him process the truth. "And now you know, but more importantly, I hope you *believe* what I just told you. It's the truth, and there's not a damn thing I can do to change it. It weighs on me every day, like a physical illness, the knowledge that had I not been overcome with grief for my dying father, had I only probed harder, rather than let him die peacefully, I might have been able to prevent the chaos and death that has unfolded around the world in the last two and a half years."

"There's nothing you could have done, sir," Logan said instinctively, realizing as soon as he'd spoken the words that he'd already judged the president to be truthful and sincere.

"Do you think that matters?" President Scott asked. "There's been a rogue republic operating inside our government and across the globe. It wasn't democratically elected. It doesn't have a Constitution that its members swore an oath to. It does what it wants when it wants. While Constantine Kallas may have intended it to be a force for good—and I'll even grant that it may have done good—its real nature, the sick underbelly of it, has finally revealed itself. You want the brutal, honest truth?" President Scott asked Logan.

"What's that, sir?" Logan answered.

"Unchecked power like that always corrupts, and the Organization has become corrupted," President Scott said. "But guess what? It's . . . going . . . to . . . stop." His voice hardened, reminding Logan of the first time he'd met the former A-10 pilot six months ago. "Because I'm the goddamned president of the United States of America, and with Ares, you, and your friends, I can make it stop."

The man that Logan West had respected and felt an affinity for upon first meeting him had returned to form. His honesty and admission had not changed Logan's perception of him. If anything, his display of vulnerability had only strengthened Logan's belief in him. Logan knew that men who lacked self-awareness and introspection had no business being leaders, but President Scott had both in spades. *This is the right man to take the fight to our enemies.*

"I'm fairly confident that I speak for all of us when I say that we're with you all the way, Mr. President," Logan said. "You're a good man, and this country needs you. I can't tell you how to deal with the guilt you feel, but I can tell you one thing: if we can stop them, we can restore the balance of power. And that should go a long way."

"Then you better get to work," President Scott said, the full stature of the presidency back in control. "And as I told you before, whatever you need."

"I'm happy to hear you say that, sir," Logan said, a merciless smile spreading across his face, green eyes blazing. "Because I'm going to need your approval on what I need—*and want,* if I'm being honest—to do next."

CHAPTER 51

Scotland, Maryland

Standing on the isolated pier, Adam Mathias stared out at the calm waters of the Chesapeake Bay. The former Norwegian businessman known as the Recruiter in the inner circles of the Organization wore a white polo, khaki shorts, Under Armour navy baseball hat—*like everyone else in Maryland,* he thought—and leather sandals. In other words, he looked like a typical bay resident in the summertime.

Scotland was the southernmost tip of rural Maryland, jutting out into the water and splitting the Chesapeake Bay to the east and the Potomac River to the southwest. He looked back at the five-thousand-square-foot colonial home built at the end of a dirt road that was an offshoot of State Route 5. The backside of the home featured enormous picture windows that reflected the mid-day sun back into his eyes. *Not nearly as spacious as the Founder's, but it will do.*

It had been the ideal location for him to wait out the storm that had fallen upon Washington DC in the wake of the "kidnapping" of the vice president and the killing of Constantine Kallas. The home was owned by a midwestern businessman who operated a railroad line from the Great Lakes to the East Coast. The Organization had used it to transport various items discreetly from time to time, and Adam had acquired the permission to use the home as he saw fit.

The numerous branches of the Organization had gone to ground, intent on preservation and survival. He'd been forced to make a critical choice—the Founder or those rebelling on the Council. His calculus had been simple: who had the better choice of surviving the internal war? As it now stood, the outcome was still uncertain, but the fact that he had a rendezvous in the Bahamas at the end of next week was encouraging.

He looked at the Sea Ray Sundancer 540 fifty-five-foot yacht—another possession of the railroad baron—and wondered if he should start his trip early. He planned to depart Maryland tomorrow morning, stop in Florida at one of the Key islands, and finish the trip the following day. He'd be in Nassau in four days with plenty of time to spare before his meeting.

Why not? There's nothing else keeping you here, he thought, and made his decision. *It's only three o'clock. I'm leaving now.* As he'd told the numerous members of the Organization over the years, there was no point in delaying the inevitable. He'd leave while he still could, not that he was concerned that his identity had been compromised. The only man who knew his multiple aliases was Constantine, and he was dead.

He glanced across the bay, spotting several hundred yards away a lone fishing boat with an outrigger jutting from both sides to maximize the number of rods and lines for trolling. *Good luck. The water's too hot to fish this time of day.*

———

"Are you sure you have it?" Cole asked Logan, who lay next to him across the nautical hide site they'd created just under the canopy of the fishing boat and cabin cruiser. Expertly crafted of leather cushions and several towels, it concealed both men from all passing boats.

Logan stared through the scope of the M40A5 Marine Corps sniper rifle. The Recruiter swayed slightly in the sights of the Schmidt & Bender Police Marksman II LP scope, the center of the mil dots slowly moving back and forth over his upper legs. At four hundred yards and no elevation, his only concern was the motion of the boat. They'd been fortunate that the waters of the lower Chesapeake Bay had been flat. Otherwise, they'd have been forced to improvise and consider a land approach, which would have risked their compromise by residents of the small peninsula.

"I have it," Logan said confidently, his cheek pressed against the integrated check piece that moved horizontally and vertically to accommodate each shooter's precise facial configuration.

"I'm going to ask you this one last time—and I know it's going to piss you off, but I don't have a history with him—are you sure you can trust him?" Cole asked, staring through an angled spotting scope at one of the most wanted men in the world, if only wanted by the handful of powerful people that knew he existed, one of those being the president.

———

The night before the meeting in the Oval Office, Jack Longstreet had phoned Logan from a cell phone that registered as "Unknown" and was untraceable. Logan hadn't even bothered to try; he knew better when dealing with the general.

The conversation had been abrupt and to the point. "Logan, I have the location for where the Recruiter is going to be in the next few days."

"Why are you telling me?" Logan interrupted. "You do understand the trust factor is rather low right now, right? You had your boys whisk you away. If you're even in this country right now, I'd be shocked."

"Everything I've told you has been the God's honest truth. I swear it on the Eagle, Globe, and Anchor," Jack said, invoking the symbol of the Marine Corps to emphasize his point. "I can't make you believe me, and honestly, I'm not going to try. You have your job to do, and I have mine. What's left of us who were loyal to the Founder are going after the traitors who are still in positions all over the globe and could easily wreak more havoc on the world. The Recruiter is one of them, and I thought you'd want to be the one to take him off the board, as he's the one responsible for coordinating the vice president's escape, as well as the ambush at the museum."

Logan knew every word the general spoke was absolute truth. He knew the commitment of the man, the depth of his character and principles. His onetime mentor and commanding officer was a warrior, pure and simple, who still lived by a moral code. But now that the Founder was gone, General Jack Longstreet had become a modern-day ronin, following his own path.

He took a deep breath, calculating his next words—*the president would freak at what I'm about to say*—and said, "You could always come work with us. I can talk to the president. I think I can get him to see the benefit of it."

Jack laughed, not disrespectfully. "Logan, I truly appreciate that—I do—but I'm going off the grid. I need to do this my way."

Logan understood completely. The two former Marines were cut from the same cloth. *You can take the man out of the Marine Corps but you can't take the Marine Corps out of the man.*

"I understand," Logan said.

"I know you do," Jack said sincerely. "Here's the deal. He's using a summer home in Scotland, Maryland, on the Chesapeake Bay as a staging area—I'll text you the address later from a burner phone—and then he's taking a small yacht down the coast and into the Bahamas for a meeting next week. I don't have the details on that, but I'm sure you can obtain them from him," Jack said, the implication clear.

"Roger all, sir," Logan said, reflexively slipping into his former persona as a Marine officer.

Jack laughed. "I appreciate the sentiment, son, but we're a long way from the Marine Corps on this one."

"Old habits, Jack," Logan responded, snapping back to his current self. "Good luck, and be safe."

"Semper Fi, Marine," Jack said.

"Semper Fi, General," Logan replied, and the line went dead. *For God, Country, and Corps*, he thought, *let's get them all.*

———

Exhaling as he watched the Recruiter turn around on the pier, Logan replied, "I *know* we can trust him. He's a man of honor," and slowly squeezed the trigger on the M40A5.

Thwut! the rifle spat, the suppressor preventing the sound from carrying across the water.

Logan and Cole tracked the vapor trail of the 7.62x51mm NATO round as it soared across the glassy water before striking the Recruiter in the back of the right knee. A huge puff of red mist exploded in front of him, and he fell face-first into the deck. His faint screams carried across the water to their boat.

"Glad he doesn't have neighbors," Cole said, standing up from his prone position next to Logan, and then added, "By the way, I thought you were going for his upper leg."

"I was," Logan said. "I must have been off a click on elevation." He turned to Cole, a slightly sadistic grin on his face, green eyes blazing. "Sucks for him, but it won't really matter in the long run, now, will it?"

CHAPTER 52

Bloody Point, Chesapeake Bay
2100 EST

Adam Mathias sat on the deck of the fishing boat, staring at the metal cuff on his left ankle. He'd lost hope hours ago. The Bahamas were a breezy dream he'd never see, and he'd known it the second his right knee had blown out, shattered into several pieces on the wooden pier.

He'd been lying there writhing in pain, screaming in agony for what seemed like an eternity. When he'd finally calmed down enough to try and crawl to the house, it was too late: Logan West and Cole Matthews had appeared on the pier. His pain had distracted him, and he hadn't heard the fishing boat dock in front of the yacht.

Without a word, the two men had picked him up, dragged him to their boat, and departed just as quickly as they'd arrived. He'd initially had hope—Cole Matthews had bandaged his knee and provided him with two 800 mg Motrin—but that hope had faded the second he'd seen the other supplies on the deck of the boat.

A 45-lb. Olympic-style circular weight plate, the kind with a hole that slid on to the end of an Olympic bar, lay in the corner, a chain threaded through the hole. At the other end of the chain, a gray metal cuff sat open, waiting to close and seal his fate. He'd looked from the rigged anchor to the face of Logan West, who'd only stared at him pitilessly. It was in that gaze, devoid of mercy, that he'd seen his demise. And now that end was finally at hand.

"We'll be visiting your friends next," Logan said to the Recruiter, shrouded in the darkness of the Chesapeake Bay. "I assure you, the remnants of the Organization that went rogue will be destroyed. You can take that to your grave."

The only sound was that of the waves gently lapping against the side of the boat. Lights from fishing vessels flickered in the distance. Closer, off the southern end of Kent Island, an old abandoned lighthouse rose out of the water. Infamously known to locals as Bloody Point thanks to a variety of historical anecdotes, including drowned slaves and hanged pirates, it was the deepest channel of the bay.

"There's nothing I can say or do to change this outcome, is there?" Adam asked.

Cole stood behind their captive, observing the exchange, his hands behind his back.

"No. There's not," Logan responded. "But unlike those that have died at your hand, directly or indirectly, I'm giving you a choice—the gun or the water. Don't make me choose for you. Have some backbone and face it like a man." There was no condescension in his tone, but there was no warmth either.

"Can I have a moment?" Adam asked.

"You have thirty seconds, and then I need an answer," Logan replied.

Adam Mathias, who'd spent a lifetime manipulating others, murdering out of necessity, and orchestrating chaos, hung his head and prayed. He didn't think God would listen—he'd committed too many atrocities to count—but he prayed that if there was a sliver of cosmic mercy, he'd get it. He looked back up into the darkened face of Logan West and said, "I'll take the gun."

The convicted man sat up straight in his final act of acceptance.

At least he didn't cry like a coward or beg for mercy, I'll give him that, Logan thought. "Very well," Logan said, and nodded at Cole, who stood still behind the kneeling man.

"Adam Mathias, on behalf of the president of the United States of America, I sentence you to death for numerous crimes against the United States and humanity. The sentence will now be carried out," Logan said.

"Wait!" Adam nearly shrieked. "The president?"

Logan smiled in the darkness. "Of course. We wouldn't do this if the commander in chief hadn't ordered it to be done. This might not be exactly official, but it's as legal as it's going to get. The president has declared war on you and the Organization. God have mercy on your soul."

Cole Matthews raised a Glock 19 with a suppressor he'd held behind his back, aimed, and pulled the trigger.

Thwack!

The 9mm bullet struck the back of Adam Mathias' head, and the dead man crumpled forward, his face coming to rest several inches above the deck, dripping blood between his outstretched legs. The Recruiter was no more.

Logan and Cole stared at the dead man in silence, respecting the fact that they'd taken a life, even if it was at the direction of the president. While neither man considered this a murder, this was different from shooting an armed combatant in the heat of a gunfight. This had been an execution, but both Logan and Cole had discussed it beforehand and had made their peace with their respective gods.

"Are you good?" Logan asked quietly.

"I am," Cole responded in kind. "This monster deserved much worse than this, but *this* needed to be done, and I'm good with it."

"Understood, brother," Logan said, grabbing several towels and a mesh bag that would contain Mathias' body. "In that case, let's send him to his final resting place."

"Definitely," Cole said.

The two men wrapped the towels around Mathias' ruined head in order to prevent further bleeding on the boat, and Cole held them in place as Logan slid the mesh bag under and around the dead man's body. Moments later, he zipped the bag down, from head to toe, leaving a small opening at the bottom for the heavy chain. Logan grabbed the weighted plate and stacked it on top of the body.

Logan and Cole moved the bag to the back of the boat, just to the right of the two outboard engines.

"You ready?"

"Yup. Let's do this and get out of here," Cole said, reaching down and grabbing the dead man's lower legs.

Logan slid his arms under the shoulders and grabbed fistfuls of the mesh bag to secure a grip.

"On three," Logan said. "One. Two. Three."

Logan and Cole stood up, using their legs to lift the dead man. "I always forget how heavy the dead are," Cole said.

"In more ways than one," Logan countered.

"Amen to that," Cole said.

Lifting higher, they raised the corpse, set it on top of the flat railing, and pushed it over without another word.

The bag hit the water with a splash, the weight still on top of the dead man's chest. It hung suspended for a moment, but then the bag rolled, and the weight slid off and into the deep dark. Seconds later, the bag was suddenly jerked under as the weight reached the end of the chain. The last thing Logan saw was a ripple of suction as Adam Mathias was dragged 160 feet to the bottom of the Chesapeake Bay.

Within weeks or months, there'd be nothing left of the man's body. Either the fish or the legendary Chesapeake Bay crab would devour him, leaving a chained skeleton in a watery grave.

Logan turned to Cole one last time. He put his hand on his shoulder in a brotherly and reassuring gesture. "You sure you're good?"

"Absolutely," Cole said, his face illuminated by the boat's controls. He smiled. "That is unless you hug me, in which case I'm going to kick your ass and send you in after our friend."

Logan laughed. "I wouldn't dare. I'm not that brave."

"Good. Now let's get the hell out of here. We have another trip to plan," Cole said.

"Agreed. I'm going to text John to let Amira know it's done," Logan said, stepping up to the elevated cabin where the dashboard and controls were. He turned the key in the ignition, and the two Yamaha motors roared to life and idled as Logan punched in the message. He hit send and put the phone back in his pocket. "I'll tell Jake later, and he can inform the president."

"Sounds like a plan," Cole said.

"In that case, hop in that copilot's chair," Logan said, nodding at the chair to his left as he pushed the throttle forward, "and as always, sit back and enjoy the ride."

ACKNOWLEDGMENTS

Writing a series is a unique experience. The trick is to make every story unique but with the same feel as the others. With *Field of Valor*, the intent was to start off with a bang and not let up until the ride was over. I hope you, the reader, are satisfied with the end product, as the only thing that matters is the experience you have while reading. I'm content that I've done my best to make *Field* another roller-coaster ride. (Then again, we all know what Sean Connery said about doing your best in *The Rock*.) Regardless, I hope you enjoyed this ride, and fear not, Logan will be back. He's a hard motherfucker to kill . . . for now.

And like Logan, I have a world-class team that works constantly to bring Logan West to life. First, major thanks to Will Roberts, my agent at The Gernert Company, who has to suffer my rants and raves about nearly everything. His patience is tested, I'm sure, but it all works out in the end. Thank you. Second, my editor, Emily Bestler, an icon in the business who has been behind this series 1,000 percent from Day One. Her insight, feedback, and constructive criticism are critical to who I am as a writer. Here's to many more. Thank you. Third, my publicist, David Brown, who probably listens to me rant even more than my agent. He knows where the bodies are buried. He is the man with the plan to get this series the visibility it needs. Go Yankees. (He's a Mets fan.) Thank you. Fourth, Lara Jones, Emily's assistant, who is Emily's first line of defense and handles day-to-day responsibilities. May you get an assistant yourself one day. Fifth, George Newbern, actor on ABC's *Scandal* and the narrator who brings Logan and friends to life in the audiobooks. You. Are. The. Man. Thank you. To Jen Long at Pocket Books, responsible for the mass market paperback versions of my books. You do an outstanding job expanding the readership by putting the books in as many markets as possible. I never tire of seeing my books in my local grocery and drug stores. My ego thanks you. To fellow authors Joshua Hood and Don Bentley, who both provided answers to a few key questions, here's to you both getting your next deals. Thank you for being fellow warriors who understand the military way of life. And for everyone else that I missed but who contributes in ways I may not see on a daily basis, thank you. Contrary to popular belief, publishing is a team sport.

> Until next time, Friendo.
> Semper Fidelis.
> *Matt*